# Salem

Neil White is a criminal lawyer and lives with his wife and three children in the north of England. Salem is first published work. His second book, *Creek Crossing*, is due to be published in the spring of 2005.

# *Salem*

## Neil White

*Thanks Callie*
*hope you enjoy*
*the book*
*Neil White*

## TSJ PUBLISHING

www.crimewriting.co.uk

# SALEM

First published in 2004 by TSJ Publishing, England.
www.crimewriting.co.uk

ISBN 0 9547530 0 3

A catalogue record for this book is available from the British
Library

Book cover design by Samantha Wall
© 2004 Samantha Wall

Printed in Great Britain for TSJ Publishing by
Antony Rowe Ltd, Chippenham, Wiltshire

# Salem

# One

My name is Joe Kinsella and I'm a private detective. I live in a quiet seaside town in England. I serve court papers and I spy on cheating spouses. I do small things in a small town, so when I was hired to go to Boston to find a missing girl, I should have sensed trouble.

It had started well, almost idyllic.

I came off the flight into a spring afternoon. A silent cab driver took the scenic route, the banks of the Charles River flanked by brownstones and zig-zagged by fire escapes, the smooth blue water bouncing starburst flashes as the signs of the city passed by: shining steel and dusty street life, leafy trees and rusty piping, commerce and cramped apartments.

I caught my reflection in the rear-view mirror. The wind ruffled my hair, flickering grey like an old movie, and the lines around my eyes deepened as I squinted. I looked away. Thirty-five shouldn't look like that. I watched the roller-bladers instead, and then saw the towers of downtown recede, high-rise became mid-rise, and my ride turned over the river into Cambridge. The scene changed from urban to collegiate as brownstone was replaced by clapboard, joggers by long shorts and tie-dye. Ahead of me, up a slight rise, I could see crowds and signs of life.

We drove past the jammed sidewalks of Harvard Square and found my hotel on Irving Street, pristine white clapboard and mascara-black windows, just off from the main din and close to Harvard Yard.

I settled in and went for a walk. I needed to look around.

I wandered through the campus grounds to reach Harvard Square. I bought a Boston Globe from the central newsstand and a coffee at a nearby coffee shop. I stayed for around two hours, watched the day surrender to dusk. The pastel yellow and blue houses that back onto Harvard Yard turned pink in the sunset, with skateboard clatter as a backing track. I watched the homeless haggle for change and listened to the impatient sound of car horns, a city's worth of activity crammed into a huddle of bars, restaurants and bookshops.

It should have made me feel good, a new city, a new country. It didn't. It made me edgy instead. It was different to home, a different buzz, a different sound, but I couldn't forget why I was there. I was in Boston to find Sarah Goode, an English girl missing for four weeks.

I had met Sarah's parents the previous day. They talked a little about Sarah and sobbed a lot. They showed me photographs, letters, told me all that they could to help me. They were decent people. Their daughter was in trouble and they needed my help. I wanted to help them.

But it wasn't as simple as that. Sarah Goode wasn't just a missing person. Sarah Goode was wanted for murder.

Sarah had been doing a sandwich year at Boston University. She had become involved with a Boston fireman, Brad Howarth. All had been going well, until Brad was stabbed to death in her bed and Sarah disappeared without a trace. He was found naked, on his back, with a knife sticking out of his chest. There was only one suspect: Sarah Goode. Boston Police were officially calling it a missing person investigation. The subtext was that she was a murderer on the run.

I had asked her parents about Brad, the dead fireman, but Sarah's father just shook his head. He hadn't been on the scene long. There had been phone calls at Christmas, things overheard that a father doesn't want to hear, but that was just sex. Nothing serious.

I wasn't convinced. Even if the fires burn softly, they can still burn.

But it was the credit card that was making me edgy, sat hot in my wallet.

Sarah's parents came to me because I used to be a lawyer, so I knew about evidence, about proof, might know what would be useful.

I had smiled but not told them the story. They didn't need to know. I had been a lawyer, but a bad night in a police station had brought me down.

I had a bag-head making noise at me after I'd had too many late nights and worked too many hours. He complained for too long and it made me burn. I burned hard, and I punched my career away to the sound of him screaming for the police. I was too angry to appreciate the irony. I spent the rest of the night in the next cell, my victim laughing at me through the grille in his door.

The police didn't take it any further, but the Law Society weren't so forgiving. They stripped me of everything I had. Struck off. Don't practise again. Thanks for your time. So I became a private detective.

The Goodes didn't just want the new private detective. They wanted the old lawyer. My job was to go to Boston and look for other suspects, create doubt and uncertainty, but that was only if the police got to her first. If I got there first, I had to give her a credit card, an additional card on her mother's account, and tell her to ring home. Sarah's parents were good people, I knew that, but their daughter was in trouble, and they were determined to beat whatever system stood in their way.

I wasn't just in America to find Sarah Goode. I was there to help her escape.

# Two

Sarah was sobbing.

She'd been in the room for a couple of weeks now. She had almost got used to the screaming, the noise, the light, the constant light, but she could feel herself weakening. It was relentless, and she had long given up trying to understand it. She just tried to deal with it. It was better than the box.

Sarah called it a room, but it was barely that. It was a large metal container, around fifteen feet by ten, like the back of a small delivery truck. She had walked around it, banged on the walls, but it was sound-proofed, the bangs bouncing back as dead thuds. There were no windows, no view out. Just one door at one end, and at the other, a toilet and a shower.

The light was constant. A collection of spotlights hidden behind Perspex, tough and unbreakable, shining halogen light into all of the corners, like bright car headlights.

The lights hadn't been turned off since she came into the room. Constant brightness, all day, all night, until day and night became the same, an endless ordeal of fatigue and terror. Even when she closed her eyes, it still shone vivid red.

Sarah had tried to break the Perspex, to try and break the lights, just leaps and punches, but they had no effect. All she did was hurt her hand and twist her ankle when she landed.

The light was bad, was always there, but it was the noise that made it impossible to sleep.

The only other thing in the room was a television screen, a large one, protected by more Perspex, with speakers set into the ceiling, booming the sound around the metal walls.

It was the noise of what was being played that turned it into torture.

The pictures on the screen were home movies, video footage edited together into a constant loop of captivity and torture. Even when she shut her eyes hard and clamped her hands tight over her ears, the metal walls bounced the screams and pleas around her defences and rippled terror into her head.

But what scared Sarah most was the setting on the film. The view on the screen was the same as the one around her, all shot in the same metal room she was in. Which meant it had happened before. Young woman, old women, children. They were all there. Hour upon hour of people in the same mess she was in. And Sarah couldn't watch what was happening to them. Women being raped, being throttled, being bound helpless and sliced open slowly. Burnings, blindings, amputations.

Sarah hadn't looked at the screen for a long time, but she was aware of the screams of agony, the pleas for mercy, the post-rape sobs of despair, all piped into the room at a volume too loud to ignore. It stopped her from sleeping, from thinking, from doing anything but concentrate on blotting it out. When would those horrors visit her?

The room had felt like relief at first.

Sarah had spent the first week of captivity in a box no bigger than she imagined her coffin would be. She had been placed in it blindfolded, tied by her wrists and ankles, straight from the rear of the car.

She remembered how she had been taken.

She'd answered the door, was grabbed and bound, and then had been taken out of her apartment backwards, naked feet banging on the steps. She had been bundled into the boot of a car, a handkerchief pushed so far into her mouth that she gagged. Then her wrists were bound behind her back, her ankles tied together, with a short rope connecting the two. She would never be able to stretch out her legs without breaking her back. When she had been taken to the car, she thought the night was full of the sounds of her panic, but when the lid closed, she found herself in stifling silence, the darkness filled only with the short rasping breaths against her gag.

The car doors had slammed shut, there was a low bass rumble of two talking voices, and then the car had pulled away.

The car journey had almost suffocated her. They drove for what seemed like all night, but it was only around an hour. She hadn't been able to stretch out. The car was old, so the suspension bottomed out of every bump, sending a kick to her back like a wild horse, and then it rode the spongy bounces as it recovered. She had rolled around at one point in an effort to get comfortable, to try and tease away the beginnings of cramp, but she had been seized by panic as she found herself wedged in, with her chest and face pressed against the lid of the boot, her hands and ankles trapped underneath. That was the point when she had almost screamed, but she remembered the gag, knew it would be pointless. Instead, she tried to fight back the panic and took some deep breaths before squeezing herself back onto her side.

When the car eventually came to a stop, she was pulled out by the rope, limbs strained to breaking point, and thrown onto the floor in a heap. She was dragged along a woodland path, and then across concrete, and then into the metal room.

But it wasn't the room that was her first place of captivity. That came later. The box had been first, and it had been hell.

The box was just that, lying long on the floor like a rifle chest, but entry was at one of the ends. Sarah had slid in on her back, with her arms by her side. The box was only just wide enough to fit, so that her arms were wedged against the sides, impossible to move. Her head pushed against the other end, and when the open end of the box was slammed shut, Sarah had cried out with pain as the lid banged against her feet. The sides or front had no give to them. No hinges to strain at, no cracks in the lid to allow a view of the world outside the box. Sarah had been slotted in like a corpse in a mortuary drawer until she had been consumed by darkness, her breaths against the box making the air warm around her face.

The first couple of hours had been consumed by raw terror. The darkness filled every part of her body, so that she became lost in time, in location, in reason. As time went on she became aware of her sobbing, and when she did, she tried to stop herself. She didn't want to lose control of her mind, because if she did, there would be nothing left to defend her. She thought hard instead on how to stay calm, how to think and how to rationalise.

But then they had returned and turned the box over.

Sarah had spent the next two days face down, unable to move her arms, not knowing when she'd ever be able to move again. Her captivity pressed hard against her head, her feet, her back, her front. No water, no food. It was worse than being buried alive, because she knew it would take longer to die.

Sarah had been tipped out of the box on the third day and allowed some water. The light from the room was blinding, and she spent a few precious moments of movement trying to get used to the glare.

This went on for another three days. No talk, no reasons given. Just captivity and silence.

Except sometimes they would play games.

One game they played was turning the box on it end, so that Sarah was upside-down, her body sliding down onto her head, unable to get her arms free to provide support. The only things that kept her in place were the tight dimensions of the box. Sarah stayed like that for a few hours, and she thought she was going to suffocate on the weight of her own body pressing down on her.

Another game was banging the box with hammers. Just noise, the only break in the silence, but the hammers banged around her wooden jail, jolting her crazy.

Sarah's ordeal in the box came to an end after seven days. She was pulled out of the box, and she spent the first few hours of release lying on the floor in tears, a picture of broken misery. When she had worn herself out by crying, she tried to get her legs working again by walking around the room. It was hard. Her legs had cramped up because of the lack of movement, and the desire to just curl up and drift away was strong.

But the lights and the noise had made her snap, had made her angry.

She had been seen leaping at the lights and so she had been burnt. One of her captors had rushed in, a heat-tipped soldering iron hissing into the cold air of the metal box room. He had grabbed her arm, forced it to the floor, and pressed the iron to her arm, the sound of him snarling competing with the sound of Sarah's feet scuffling against the floor, desperate, in agony.

He had left the room straight after, leaving Sarah on the floor, prostrate, sobbing, holding her arm. She crawled over to the shower and turned it on, set for cold.

She screamed as the torrent hit her fresh blister, and then she passed out.

At last, oblivion.

# Three

I woke for the fourth time at seven-thirty. My body was in Eastern Time but its clock was still somewhere along the Greenwich Meridian.

I eased myself out of bed, my limbs leaden, my mouth dry. I needed coffee or beer. My watch told me coffee.

Harvard perked me up again, the rustling trees in Harvard Yard caressing me awake, but I only stayed for breakfast. I wondered about Sarah, where she was, what she was doing, so I stocked up on homefries and sunny-side up and caught the red line into Boston.

I didn't know what to expect from the city. The guidebooks I'd read only showed off the tourist traps, and I wasn't expecting to find Sarah walking the Freedom Trail. If I was going to find Sarah Goode, I was going to have to find the real Boston, away from the camera glossies. I needed someone to help me. Sarah had shared an apartment with another student, Katie Gray, so she was my first call. From a map I'd bought the previous evening, Sarah's address wasn't far from downtown, just across the Common and on the other side of Columbus Avenue.

The first view of Boston was the one I'd had the previous day, from a distance, the blue of the Charles River and small boats winding themselves around a backdrop that was half big city, half old town. The brownstones of the Back Bay I'd gazed at the day before were now peeping over bank-side trees and dwarfed by the phallic glass and steel of downtown.

My first closeup view of Boston was a surprise. I'd been expecting a cityscape, some kind of high-rise geometric shadow. But instead I was greeted with the white wooden steeple of the Park Street Church and twisty city streets that seemed to disappear in a cloud of underground steam and traffic fumes. It felt good, like how cities should be.

I wandered over Boston Common, over cracked old tarmac and under shadowy old elms, a patchwork of history and monument that seemed to sum up the city. I looked around and saw how the city seemed inescapable. Buildings surround it, all facing it down, so that the Common's escapism seemed almost a trap. A group of black homeless hung around a derelict fountain, making white tourists nervous, while business men and women streamed towards the city going on over my shoulder.

Once off the Common, I kept on walking, away from the tourists and the rush hour, and then I crossed Columbus Avenue. I felt the scene change. I was the only person heading into the area. Everyone was heading out, making their way into the city. I was in a neighbourhood, a real neighbourhood. The sidewalks were made of old bricks, uneven and slick, and the street lamps seemed bent double with age. The walk was green-lined by the sidewalk trees and leaves brushed my face as I walked. I felt the pace slow down.

I found Sarah's street, a dead-end of four-storey brownstones just behind Tremont Street. The place looked deserted. But it would have been hard to detect signs of life anyway. The windows looked dusty, and the light hid behind a window mesh so that every window looked lifeless. I rang the bell and waited a while. No response. But then I saw the outline of a face looking out of a window.

I waited a minute and then the door opened. I flashed a smile. I was looking at a tall blonde-haired woman with eyes like jewels. She was mid-twenties, Gap khakis, a loose t-shirt. Her hair bounced long, and she stood slender in the doorway.

"Yes?"

She was curt. She brushed away a few hairs that weren't really in the way and put one foot behind the other. She would have seemed coy if she hadn't been so hostile.

"Katie Gray?" I asked.

"Who wants to know?" came the response, her voice cautious, suspicious.

I shrugged, tried to disarm her. "My name is Joe Kinsella, and I'm a private detective from England. I've been hired by Mr and Mrs Goode to try and find their daughter, Sarah." I smiled, looking for a way in.

The woman facing me seemed taken aback. She brought her back foot forward again and her hand came away from her hair. Her mouth formed an '0' shape and I could see she was thinking about her response.

"I understand she used to have a room here?" I ventured, trying to pull her into conversation before the door shut in my face.

"She still does." The response was loaded, but I sensed curiosity.

"Her parents told me that she was a good friend of Katie Gray." I noticed a twitch of the eyes. "It would be helpful if I spoke to Katie first, to get the proper picture, if you know what I mean."

I watched as she toyed with her response, unsure of what to say.

"Her parents just want to find Sarah, to help her, to make sure she's alright." My voice was soft and low. I could see that the door was still open, doubts and questions keeping her there.

"Have you ID?" she asked, and I saw her resolve melt into the sunshine.

I shuffled in my pockets and found a business card. I passed it over and waited. As soon as she asked for ID, I knew I was as good as in. Once ID was produced, how could she refuse?

She looked at the card, then at me, and then at the card again.

I was right.

"You had better come in," she said, and stepped aside.

As I went in I smiled. She gave a quick smile back, as if she was too polite not to respond but wasn't sure if she should.

I walked into a small apartment, the building obviously divided many times over. The walls were painted New England cream and a deep blue rug covered a smooth wood-panelled floor. The old Boston look was ruined by glossy pictures of a young film star I vaguely recognised but couldn't name, and a dart-board hung on the back of a battered old door. I sat myself down on a bumpy old couch and felt myself sink on sagging springs. I gazed up at my host. She looked as if she didn't know what to do next. I let her lead.

After a few awkward seconds she glanced over to the kitchen. "Do you want coffee?"

I said yes. Coffee meant I would be there for at least twenty minutes.

I noticed a twang in her accent. Coffee wasn't pronounced with the same nasal burr that I'd noticed elsewhere in Boston, as if it was spelt 'cahffee'. Instead, she sounded warm, homely. I needed to distract her.

"Where are you from?" I asked.

"I thought you were here to talk about Sarah," she shouted from the kitchen.

"I am. I just noticed an accent. It was different."

She returned with two coffees. "Kansas," she said, putting the coffees down. "Cream, sugar?"

"Just milk please. Where in Kansas?"

"Would you know it if I told you?"

"Probably not," I replied, watching her stir, trying to work her out.

"Wichita," she said.

I stared back blankly.

"Do you know it?"

I shook my head.

"Largest city in Kansas," she said, by way of explanation. "A big nothing in the middle of nothing."

"What about Kansas City?" I asked.

"That's in Missouri. Well, mostly anyway."

I nodded and smiled, sensed that her mental trip back home had relaxed her. Her body language was no longer defensive and her voice had lost the cautiousness that had put me on edge. "I presume I'm talking to Katie Gray," I said, and I was pleased to see her smile. It lit her eyes for the first time and gave her face warmth.

"Tell me again who you are," she said, blowing into her coffee, cradled in both hands. She looked cute now. Her eyes did tiny dances, and as she talked her head gave small flicks to tease away stray hairs.

I took a drink. I knew I had to put her at ease, gain her trust. This was the person in Boston closest to Sarah.

"My name is Joe Kinsella," I said, smiling again, sitting back and trying to look comfortable. "I'm a private investigator from Morsby, Sarah's home town back in England."

Katie nodded as she listened.

I leant forward and put my coffee on the table.

"Sarah's parents are paying me a lot of money to find her, and so here I am. I know about the build up to her disappearance, and I have an idea what the police think. I just need to know more."

"Where have you been so far?" asked Katie.

I gave a rueful smile. "You're the first. I only got in yesterday."

"Where else are you going to look?"

I felt my nerves go keen. Katie seemed interested in my movements and I wondered about her motive.

"Wherever it takes me," I replied.

17

We fell silent again. I looked at Katie, saw the steam from the coffee make her cheeks glow misty red, and then looked around the room again. I noticed this time that the walls were sparkling clean. There were no cobwebs around the light fittings and the tabletops gleamed their scuffs and scratches. I looked back at Katie and saw that she appeared a little distant, and I wondered what she had been through in the last few weeks. I suspected that the apartment had been thoroughly cleaned to try and wipe out the memories of what had happened. Katie still had to live here, and I tried to remember that Katie had seen herself the scene that had started this whole thing, Brad half in and half out of the sheets, a knife sticking out of his chest.

I must have subconsciously glanced towards the corridor leading away from the living room, because Katie interrupted my train of thought.

"Would it help you if you looked at Sarah's room?" she said.

I looked at her, did badly in hiding my surprise. "Yes," I said, "I suppose it would."

We put our coffees down and went to a room just off a small corridor leading away from the living room. Katie groped around the corner for the light switch, and then she pushed the door open to let me in. I noticed she didn't follow me.

The room seemed strangely normal, as if I'd expected some kind of blood-soaked den. Instead, colour-washed walls seemed bright and clean, and in the corner of the room there was a dresser covered in photograph frames. There were no carpets, and the bed was long since gone.

I went to look at the photographs. There was a picture of Mr and Mrs Goode relaxing in a suburban garden. Elsewhere, there were pictures of groups of friends, of family pets, one of Morsby harbour. It was the dresser of a happy young woman a long way from home.

I opened a drawer. T-shirts were stacked in two piles, one or two pulled about as if she'd gone for one at the bottom. That was a good sign. Sometimes people can be too tidy. The next drawer was better, panties and socks just thrown in as if it had been done in a rush.

I had a quick rummage, but I didn't go too far in. A box of Trojan condoms sat in the corner of the drawer, but only three of the twelve were missing.

I quickly checked the other drawers. Again, a collection of clothes, but nothing else.

I sighed to myself. The police would have removed anything useful.

I turned to look into the room. I looked towards where the bed must have been, and I tried to imagine the scene. I couldn't.

I went to stand where the head of the bed would have been. I looked around the room again, from the viewpoint of Brad's final look at the world. I could see a window looking out to the street, the same view as from the living room. I looked towards the door. I could see into the kitchen at an angle, the line of sight cutting across the corner of the living room. The kitchen went off the living room as an alcove filled with equipment, and opposite Sarah's room there was a door was either the bathroom or Katie's room.

I leant against the wall and tried to imagine Sarah walking slowly towards the bedroom. Brad would be able to see her. He'd be lying in bed, on his back, hands behind his head, while Sarah walked slowly back to the bedroom. Her hands are behind her back and she is naked. She has got all the way to the bedroom before he realises something is wrong. He is trying to get out of bed when she produces the knife.

I looked closely at the wall. I thought I could see slight knocks and nicks where the bed had banged against the wall from time to time. It wasn't a high bed. Brad would have been low down. Sarah will have used all her downward pressure to fend off any attempt at defence and to plunge the knife in deep. It would have to be deep: she would only get one attempt. One knife wound, one death, one English suspect.

I scratched my head and rubbed my eyes. The time zones were playing with me, dragging me down.

I returned to the living room.

Katie was sat on a chair by the window, looking out. The television played a daytime soap but Katie wasn't paying attention. She looked back round. "Was that any use?" she asked.

"No alarm bells rang, but I don't know what I expected."

"What, you mean it doesn't look like the room of a crazed killer?"

I sensed the barb. Thought first, speech second, I reminded myself.

I smiled apologetically. "Yeah, something like that." I sat back. "I'm sorry about that. It's just hard not to think about these things."

"You forget about the presumption of innocence?" Katie said. "Do they have that in England?"

"Oh yeah," I replied. "In droves. But human nature always gets in the way."

Katie smiled. She stood up and rested her arm against the window. She sighed. "I'd be lying if I said I haven't thought about it."

I watched Katie as she looked out onto the street. She seemed distant again, and I wondered what this had cost her. The longer I was there, the more I noticed lapses of concentration, long blinks, a listlessness. Katie was now just leaning against the window, staring outwards. I looked myself. There was nothing to see. The street was deserted.

"Do you think I might know where she is?" she asked.

The question surprised me. It came from nowhere. Katie stayed looking outside for a moment longer, and then turned to me and raised her eyebrows as if to repeat the question.

I thought for a moment. "No, I don't think so," I answered. "If you did, you would have told the police."

"But you don't know me. I might have her hiding in the cellar, protecting her from the police."

"Do you think Sarah has anything to fear from the police?" I stared at her intently, but all I saw was sudden sadness.

"I don't know," she said quietly. "Anyway, we don't have a cellar."

I laughed and sat back down.

"Why don't you just tell me about her," I asked.

Katie relaxed back into her chair and took another sip of coffee. "How are Sarah's folks?" she asked. She looked away as she spoke.

"Somewhere between frantic and sad, I think. It's hard to tell," I replied. "That English reserve isn't always a good thing. This is not a happy time for them."

Katie shook her head. "Not for any of us," she said, and then asked, "what do you need to know?"

I shrugged. "Just tell me about Sarah."

Katie looked back towards the window, and then began to speak.

"We became friends not long after Sarah arrived in Boston," she said. "She was staying at some expensive lodgings near downtown. We'd seen each other at college and talked over coffee. I was renting this place and I needed a roommate. I asked her to move in, and she did. And we just kind of got on. We went out together, double-dated together, and studied together, when we could. It was a bit harder for me. I had to do well, because I would be living in this country after I graduated. Sarah just wanted the experience, so she wanted to do things when I didn't. That's when she met Brad. She'd gone for a quick beer at a bar on Boylston, a bar I work at, and she got talking to a couple of guys. Anyhow, this one guy asked her for a date, she went on it, and the rest you probably know."

"Who was Brad?" I asked.

"He was a fireman. The fire station is just a block from the bar, and he'd gone for a beer when his shift ended. I used to see him in there if our shifts collided. He seemed to hit it off with Sarah." She paused for a moment. "I suppose she was different to his normal dates. Sarah was your usual English rose, you know, all prim and proper and reserved. I think he liked it."

"What did Sarah think of him?"

"Oh, she thought he was cute. He was a handsome guy. Six foot, muscular. But they didn't live in each others' pockets."

"What do you mean?"

"Sarah thought she should enjoy her time in Boston, and not spend all her time with just one person."

"What, you mean Sarah was sleeping around?"

"No, no, no. We would double date, meet men, you know, but Sarah never let it go anywhere. It was just a social thing."

"Did Brad know?"

"I don't know. I guess he knew she would go back to England in the summer, so what the hell. And anyway, I used to hear them in the night." Katie blushed. "She wasn't always reserved."

I smiled, and then asked, "do you know if he was seeing other people?"

She smiled. "Don't men like Brad always see other people?"

I said nothing, but I guessed it was true.

"But did she mind, if she thought he was seeing other people?" I asked.

21

"Enough to go crazy, get a knife, and stab the wandering bastard?" She raised her eyebrows and then shook her head sadly. "I doubt it. It wasn't an exclusive thing. You know, they both knew what was going on, but didn't mind as long as they didn't know the details." She looked sad for a moment. "They would have been a sweet couple if they'd met at a different time in their lives, but I think they were just going to turn out to be a nice experience. You know, he'd grow old thinking about the sweet English girl he once knew, and she'd go home and tell her friends about the hunky fireman."

"So what do you think happened?"

She rubbed her face with her hand. I thought she was going to cry, as if thinking about everything had opened it all up again.

"I'm sorry," I said. "I didn't mean to upset you."

She waved a hand at me. "It's alright." She gave a little laugh. "If I knew the answer to that question, perhaps I wouldn't be going through what I am right now."

I smiled. "If it helps you, you have helped me."

Katie looked at me. "How?"

I shrugged. "You've made me think perhaps she didn't do it. That must be a help."

I was lying of course. Sarah's parents thought that she might have killed Brad. Perhaps they've seen flashes of rage that Katie hasn't? Perhaps Brad saw one, and maybe that was the last thing he ever saw? A small number of murders occur from straight sadism, some more from pure criminality, but the rest, and most, come from extremes of emotion, the raw nerves of the human existence laid bare and acted upon.

Katie smiled. "Thank you, Joe Kinsella. It does help."

I could tell the conversation was coming to an end. It would appear better if I ended it, rather than being asked to leave. I stood up and held my hand out.

"Thank you Miss Gray, you've been most helpful."

She shook my hand and smiled. Her shake was firm and warm.

"Can I call on you again if I think of anything else?" I asked.

Katie shrugged and nodded. "Sure. If it helps, fine. And call me Katie."

I smiled. "Just one more thing"

"Go on?"

"Who is in charge of the investigation?"

Katie flicked her eyebrows upwards. "Lieutenant John Cornwell," she replied, a trace of dislike showing. "The station's only a few blocks that way," and she jerked her thumb backward over her shoulder.

"What's he like?" I asked.

She made a mock whistling sound. "A mean bastard."

I winced. Great!

"Well thanks again," I said. "I've taken up too much of your time"

I made my way to the door, making small talk about the weather. As I got to the threshold, Katie asked, "where are you going next?"

"I really don't know," I said. "I might take in the city for a couple of hours, see what there is to see, look for inspiration. Maybe chase up some names."

"Yeah, you should. It's a beautiful city, and it might help you find Sarah if you get a feel for the place first."

I nodded. It sounded like a good idea. My plan hadn't been formulated beyond where I was stood at that moment, so some time out might clear the head and get some focus.

Katie smiled. She looked thoughtful for a moment, and then said, "say, what are you doing tonight, at around seven?"

"Nothing."

"Meet me in the Pour House, on Boylston, at six-thirty. We'll talk more then. I'll think more about Sarah, and I'll try and find something useful in here," and she tapped her head with her finger.

I smiled. "That sounds good. Thank you."

I returned to the Boston streets and felt like I knew Sarah better.

Sarah guessed it was morning. It was the warmth that gave it away. She had shivered so cold during the night that every minute had turned into hours, her own tight hugs the only way to mark time. The walls kept the heat in during the day, but at night, it left the room like steam through an open window.

For the first time in what seemed like a long time, Sarah wondered what was happening outside.

She'd lost any sense of how long she had been gone. The room was always the same: damp darkness illuminated by a constant spotlight. Days became nights and nights became days. It was only the cold that gave it away. The early hours were like torture. The cold crept up and she didn't notice it until it was too late. And then it had you, making every moment into a lifetime, a constant yearn for some way of shutting out the cold. But there never was. Time was the only cure, and as sure as day somewhere follows night, the air becomes warmer, and then she waits for the sounds of movement.

Sarah had no bed, no bedding, so all she'd been able to do was pace around the room to generate heat. She could do twelve paces in an oval pattern before she was back where she started, so she did twelve more, and then twelve more after that.

The view never changed. Just a steel wall, and then another after that. The grey view was broken every fourth wall by the flickering horror of the television screen, but that just made her walk faster to the next grey wall, the sound from the footage chasing her as she paced, faster and faster, more heat, more noise.

The spotlight had been left on all night, as it always was, so Sarah had tried to sleep with her head turned into a corner. The sheer weight of her tiredness had given her a couple of hours, her sleeping head somehow blotting out the noise of the screams, but then the cold had woken her.

But it was the cold that kept her mind in place. It made her focus, gave her something real to think about it. It became about survival, about coping, and less about the horror of it all. And Sarah knew that if she was ever going to get out of there, she had to have a clear mind.

She had taken to chanting a mantra. As she paced, and then as she jumped on the spot, Sarah would say, "keep strong, keep strong," like saying it would make it come true.

But it's easier to be strong when you are on your own. There is no-one to hurt her, just her darkening thoughts as the weight of her captivity bore down on her. So when the door opened, the strength disappeared.

\*　　　　　　\*　　　　　　\*　　　　　　\*

I went next to the fire station on Boylston. I'd had a grounding on Sarah. It was Brad's turn now.

It's a small station, just a couple of arches over the Turnpike filled with red firetrucks. But as I strolled to it, I saw down the streets of the Back Bay, purple buildings and trees dipping into the distance, cars shooting across intersections, and realised how it fitted the neighbourhood. Kind of a hustle and bustle squeezed into nothing.

I walked in and saw that there wasn't much going on. There was water around the engine as if it had just been washed, but otherwise, there were no signs of life.

I ventured further in, and then a huge black guy came through a door at the back of the station, laughing at something going on in the back.

He saw me and the laughing stopped. He came over to me. "How you doing? You need something?"

"Good morning," I said cautiously, eyeing his size. I reached into my pocket and then handed him a business card. "My name is Joe Kinsella, and I'm a private investigator." He looked at the card and said nothing. "I've been hired to try and find Sarah Goode."

His eyes flashed deep with anger, but he still held my card.

He looked at the card some more and then at me. "I spotted the accent, but I can't believe the police would hire some limey to come over and do their job. What's the crack, mack?"

I tried to smile apologetically. "I just need to speak to anyone who knew Brad and Sarah."

"Don't mind me being rude, mister, but we have had plenty of people round here speaking to us about Brad, and we're getting kinda tired."

"I'm sorry," I said, holding my hands up defensively, "but I've come a long way. I won't take long."

"And we have all the answers?"

I shrugged. "I doubt that, but I have to start somewhere."

He started to look a little less uncertain. "So, you're not a journalist?"

I shook my head. "Absolutely not."

"Brad was a good man."

I nodded. "So I understand."

He weighed me up once more, and then put his head back into the doorway he'd just come from. "Hey, Paul, get your ugly ass out here, there's someone to see you."

While I waited, the other guy hung around, watching me. I smiled, but it wasn't returned.

Eventually, the door opened again and a small guy with a shaved head emerged. He looked fit and lean, his body bulging through a blue t-shirt and blue trousers, fire service issue. He marched purposefully, making me edgy, but I relaxed when he held out his hand to shake. "How are you doing, I'm Paul Blincoe. How can I help?"

I wondered why it had to be him, not the other guy, but maybe he was just closest to Brad.

"Thanks for seeing me at short notice." I paused and wondered how to phrase it. I decided on simplicity. "I'm looking for Sarah."

He held up his hands. "Whoa, whoa. What's going on? You mean, Sarah? Brad's Sarah?"

I nodded. He looked me up and down and glared suspiciously at me. "Who the hell are you, for a start?" he said.

I introduced myself to him, and he looked at me thoughtfully.

"Why are you looking for Sarah?" he asked eventually.

"Sarah's parents are paying me," I replied. I knew I had to give a bit more to open him up. "They're worried she might do something stupid."

I wasn't lying. It's just that Sarah's parents regarded something stupid as giving herself up to the police. The only thing Sarah's parents were worried about was Sarah getting caught.

"They know Sarah's in a lot of trouble, but they want the courts to deal with her. It's better than leaving Sarah to deal with herself."

I was lying now.

I saw Paul Blincoe soften slightly, become less cautious. "I just need a short talk," I continued, pleading, "that's all, to try and find out a bit more. Have you the time?"

"Why me?" he asked. He sounded frustrated, as if he'd spent the last few weeks trying to provide answers to people and thought he'd said all there was to say. "Why not Sarah's college friends, or her room-mate, or even Brad's family?"

The other fireman dropped something metal, as if to remind me he was there.

"I've spoken with Katie, her room-mate," I said. "I've only been here a couple of days, so I haven't got round to her college friends, but I will do. I'm just looking for people who knew them both."

Paul glanced towards a clock on the wall and gave a look of resignation. "I can't tell you where she is, if that's what you want." He was starting dismissively, reluctant.

I smiled. "I would be suspicious if you could. No, I just want to build up a picture of Sarah and Brad's life. It might lead somewhere."

"Well, you'll need to build up two pictures," he said. "They didn't have that much of a life together. They saw each other, had some fun together, were maybe even hot for each other, but they weren't getting serious."

"How would you describe their relationship?" I asked. "You say they weren't serious, but I get the impression that they were 'Brad and Sarah', you know, a couple."

He snorted. "That's because she killed him. I think of Brad and then I think of Sarah. But I didn't a couple of months ago. Back then, Brad was my friend, and Sarah was just one in a line of girls he'd dated."

"So it was casual?"

"Casual? Yes, very casual," he answered. He sighed and then leant back against a fire engine. "Yeah sure, they liked each other. He respected her, was fond of her, but they both knew it wasn't going anywhere. She was all English, you know, kinda restrained, but he was full of Boston, brash and confident. It seemed like they'd just decided to enjoy each other while they were together, and not worry when they weren't." He shrugged his shoulders. "It was no big deal."

I thought about the transatlantic phone calls. "What if I said Sarah was getting in a bit deeper, that perhaps she was in deeper than Brad?"

Paul shook his head. "If she did, Brad didn't mention it. He was cool about it all," and then by way of afterthought, "right to the end." Paul went thoughtful for a moment, and then he smiled. "You've been in a few relationships, I guess?"

I nodded and shrugged.

"Well, they were at the 'let's fuck all the time' stage. You know what I mean by that? I mean, it doesn't mean they were serious, or

27

that they were even faithful to each other, but he enjoyed her company. She's a sweet girl, or at least I used to think so."

"If Sarah had been staying in Boston longer than a year," I asked, "do you think Brad would have been more serious about her?"

He shrugged. "I don't know, I don't think so. I think he was just enjoying her. She seemed very sweet, was bright, clever, fun to be around. I know Brad got off on her mannerisms, the Englishness, and I know that's why he liked sleeping with her. You know, outside of the bedroom, cool as ice, reserved, coy, but inside, whoa, man." Paul smiled. "Brad said she was hot. He said it was like peeling off a mask, you know, like the angel was really the devil in wings and a white dress."

I understood what Paul and Katie meant. It was all about passion, about sex. It had never been about love. But that would make Sarah less likely to kill him in a moment of rage.

"Was there anyone else?" I asked.

Paul gave a light smile. "There was always someone else. He was a good-looking guy in a fire-fighter uniform. He was never lonely."

"Names?"

Paul shook his head. "He didn't tell me that much. I don't think there'd been anyone special for a while, just the occasional date or meeting in a bar. He was a man who didn't always say no, so Sarah may have become jealous, but I'll say again that I didn't think they were much of a permanent fixture. He liked her, sure, but he wasn't in love with her."

"She with him?"

"You'll have to ask her that if you catch up with her. I could never tell what she thought really. She had that shield, but I don't know what was behind it."

"Okay, okay." I paused, and then, "was there anyone before Sarah, you know, someone special who hadn't been off the scene for long?"

"Ah, ha," he replied, raising his eyebrows, "the jealous ex-lover." He smiled. "No, not for a while anyway. The last serious one was Carla. Brad dated her for about eighteen months. It ended about a year ago."

"And how was Carla about the split?"

Paul laughed. "Oh hell, she was just fine about it. They would probably be together now if Brad hadn't found her in bed with a lawyer from Marblehead."

I tutted in disapproval. Damn lawyers.

"So not so jealous?"

Paul shook his head. "No, not at all. She was last seen carrying his files to court and arranging his diary."

I watched the other fireman cleaning some equipment. Why didn't he want to join in? Did Brad have enemies?

"What about the day he died?" I asked, turning back to Paul. "Did you see him?"

"Oh sure," he answered, memories softening his voice. "Brad was working until ten o'clock."

"At night?"

"Yep. It had been a quiet night, nothing much going on. We finished at ten, went for a beer in the Sam Adams bar down the road, then he said he was going to say hi to Sarah." Paul smiled and said, "I knew what 'say hi' meant," and then looked sadder when he continued, "and that was the last I saw of him, heading off to get laid." He looked morose, but said, "perhaps a fitting end. Isn't that how all men would like to go?"

I smiled, because it seemed the right thing to do. Then I sensed him getting restless, as if I was on the point of being there too long.

"Is there anything else you can think of, any reason why Sarah might have killed him?"

Paul shook his head slowly. He looked sad, his head full of memories again.

"Thanks for your time," I said. "If you think of anything, will you call me at my hotel," and I scrawled a name onto the card.

He nodded an okay, but as I turned to leave he said, "if you find her, just tell her she's hurt a lot of people."

I smiled. I was getting that message.

# Four

I was in the Pour House for six-thirty. Katie was sat at the bar, a beer in her hand.

"Hi, I hope I'm not late." I was out of breath and hot.

Katie waved my apology away. "Don't worry. I only finished my shift a half-hour ago and I wanted a drink. Coors okay?"

I nodded and agreement and then looked around the bar. It was dark, with booths of tables along one wall. Swirled paintings decorated the tabletops and young couples in baggies sipped beers. The bar was long and stretched away into the darkness, towards a television showing a baseball game. The place seemed to attract a young crowd, but more student than trendy. I could see work going on in the kitchen, just the other side of the bar.

A young Spanish-looking barmaid must have seen me looking. "Do you want something to eat?"

Katie overheard her. She glanced at her watch. "We should have time," she said, and then to the other barmaid, "get the guy a cup of chilli. I'll pay."

The Spanish girl gave me a sly look and raised her eyebrows at Katie, who answered with a playful slap. "This is the English guy I was telling you about."

The other barmaid smiled and said 'hi', while a fat guy at the other end of the bar shouted down, "hey, if you girls are gonna wrestle, get yourself some bikinis and a pool o' mud."

Katie gave him the finger while he laughed at his own joke.

I looked down the bar and said, "I guess that's my undercover work gone."

"People won't come to you if they don't know you're there."

I took a swig of my beer, smiling. It was a cold one. I sat down on the stool. It was a nice bar. Not plush or fancy, but it had a good feel, relaxed and friendly. The chilli arrived quickly. I took a spoonful, and then took a bigger swig of the cold beer. It was good chilli, but it was hot.

"How's your day been?" she asked.

I fanned my mouth to take away some of the heat, and said, "tiring."

"Did you see much?"

"Yeah, I caught most things. I walked the Freedom Trail, drank a couple of beers." I watched her. "I went to see one of Brad's friends at the fire station."

She paused and then asked, "which one?"

"A guy called Paul."

Katie nodded recognition, and then asked, "what did he say?"

I shrugged. "Same as you, pretty much."

I took a drink of beer and then we were joined at the bar by a young man in his early twenties. He had short blond hair and dimples sucked his cheeks in. He was about Katie's age, and I could see her turn towards him when he came in.

"Hey, Katie, how are you doing? Get me a beer, will you."

She smiled. "Hi Danny. I'm off duty now, so no can do." She turned towards me. "This is Joe, he's from England."

He looked at me. There was a pause. He eyed me up and down, and then held out his hand. I shook it. "Hey fella, what are you doing around here?"

I smiled and shrugged nonchalantly. "You know, this and that."

"He's here to find Sarah," Katie said seriously. "He's a private investigator."

Danny let go off my hand. "You've got yourself a tough job there."

I smiled. I didn't want too many people to know why I was there, but Katie seemed to trust him, so why shouldn't I? "I think you're probably right."

"I mean," he said, by way of explanation, "half of Boston Police are looking for her. I'm not a gambler, but given a choice between a Brit hack and Boston's finest, I know where I'd put my money." He smiled and patted me on the shoulder. "No offence, fella."

I smiled back. He had a good point. "None taken."

Katie smiled at me and nodded towards Danny. "Ignore him, he drinks too much."

"Only when you're on duty, sweetheart."

Katie smiled but said nothing else. I got the message: she was off-duty now, so let her enjoy herself.

Danny peeled away from us, nodding at me. I smiled back. "See you around."

He nodded a smile. "Yeah, maybe. Enjoy yourself."

I watched him walk away and then turned back to Katie. She had watched my beer go down quickly and got two more sent over. I relaxed into my seat and let the sounds of the bar wash over me. I let Katie talk, and I joined when I could, but it felt good, like a beer after a long day.

I nodded again at Danny, who was still looking over, and then took another drink. It might turn into a long night.

The television went black, the sound stopped, the door opened, and Sarah's captor came into the room. The silence chilled her.

He didn't wear a mask, and that frightened Sarah more than if he had. It meant he wasn't frightened to let her see his face. Which meant that he didn't expect her to have to recall it to anyone. This room would be the last thing she ever saw.

He smiled. "Pleasant sleep?"

Sarah didn't respond.

His smile disappeared.

Sarah noticed he was carrying a towel. He caught her looking at it.

"It's time for your shower." It was said matter-of-factly, as if it was part of their routine, like a mother to a child.

"Shower?"

His smile returned.

Sarah grabbed the open neck of her shirt and pulled it tight, a subconscious reaction to a sexual threat. She didn't want to get naked in front of him, she didn't know what would happen if she did.

"Is the camera on?" she asked nervously. She knew that there must be one somewhere, but she didn't know where. Things were changing, she sensed it, and she knew that what she had seen on the screen had happened in there. She could feel herself start to shake.

His smile widened but he never showed his teeth, like stretching latex over metal bars.

"No," he whispered, his tongue just running along the edge of his top lip. "This is just you and me." He said it like a hiss, a low menace, his eyes bright, a determined stare.

He took one step forward. Sarah felt herself take one back. She started to moan.

He shook his head slowly. "No. It's showertime."

Sarah stepped back again, but she felt the cold of the wall as she came up against it. His smile broadened.

He reached forward and flicked undone the top button on her shirt, and then the next one. The shirt was too big for her so it fell open. He could make out where her breasts began to rise away from her breastbone.

His smile stopped. He shut his eyes slowly and took a deep breath, exhaling at length through his nose.

He flicked the next button down. He could see her cleavage, flecked with beads of sweat despite the cold. He ran his finger down between her breasts and then gently placed his hand inside the shirt. She was warm.

He removed his hand and cupped her face. He noticed a tear trickle from one eye. He leant forward and kissed it away as it fell from her eyelash. He kissed her again, softly on the lips. He brought her face down and kissed her on the forehead, saying softly, "if you don't, I'll hurt you."

Sarah gasped and then choked on a sob. She closed her eyes and steeled herself, tried to ignore what she was doing.

Sarah stepped out of her clothes and into the shower.

The water was warm, and despite her captivity, she felt better for feeling the warm water wash over her and cleanse her. But she was aware of the eyes watching her, so she turned her back to him, let the water run down her face, hiding the tears.

She wet her hair and let it fall down her back. She stayed like that for a few moments and then stepped out, back onto the metal floor.

He stepped forward with the towel and wrapped her in it, breathing heavy, and buried his face in her hair. Sarah went rigid against him, a sickness taking the place of hunger. She could feel what he was thinking and it made her gag.

He sank to his knees and buried his face in her stomach, his arms clasped tightly against her waist. Sarah stared at the ceiling, blinking back tears, moaning with fear.

Eventually he got to his feet. He stood up, grabbed the towel and left the room.

He'd left no food. When he'd gone, Sarah noticed that he had taken her clothes. She was naked. No blankets. No bed.

Then she saw the television flicker back to life and the sounds of screaming filled the room once more.

Sarah sank back against the wall and felt herself slide, her cries mixing with the sounds from the television, the old horrors mixing with the new.

Three hours later, Katie seemed drunk. I could feel my cheeks flush and the jet lag started to creep up on me.

Katie had talked and laughed for most of the evening, and I had enjoyed it. She had seemed bright, alive, and it felt like we knew each other better than during that first awkward meeting.

She paused and smiled. "I like the way you English drink."

I raised my eyebrows.

"You know, like someone is about to take it off you."

I laughed. "Drinking is what we do best. It's our heritage. Do they do it different in Wichita? Something to do in the big nothing in the middle of nothing?"

She looked puzzled.

"It's what you called Wichita," I explained. "This morning, when I called at the apartment."

Katie smiled. "It's a Kansas thing. We all love it, but we never talk it up."

"So why Boston?" I asked.

She shrugged. "It's a good university, a good city," and then she tilted her head backwards. " And they've got Fenway Park."

I looked puzzled.

"Baseball," she said. "The Red Sox. The greatest team in baseball."

"Did Sarah ever go the baseball?" I asked. It seemed like a reasonable link, all things considered.

"Everyone who comes to Boston should go to Fenway Park."

"Did she enjoy it?"

34

Katie looked at me. She had seemed animated, fun, earlier in the evening, but now she looked a little bit more direct, focused. She'd become serious again.

"No, not really," she replied. "It was just another stop on the list of things to see, but baseball is a game for the heart and mind, not the eyes, and I'm not sure that Sarah ever really got it." She shrugged. "Perhaps she came at the wrong time. She wasn't here for long before the season ended, and then this Brad thing happened when the season had only just started." She turned to look at me. "She was a victim of bad timing."

"You've lapsed into past tense," I said. "You pulled me up for that."

Katie didn't respond. She knew I'd guessed what she secretly thought, that Sarah was dead or gone, never to return.

I had got her back onto Sarah again, and I wondered whether she would tip out more detail now that she was past a few bottles of beer.

"What was her temperament like?"

Katie looked thoughtful. "Fairly even," she said. "Like I said, reserved and polite, the English thing, you know, less is sometimes more."

I smiled. I knew what she meant. "Did she ever argue with Brad?"

She looked less serious, as if I'd just asked a ridiculous question. "No," she replied, "I said before, it wasn't that kind of thing. If they had argued, they would have ended it."

I nodded. I understood.

"How had Sarah been on the days leading up to Brad's death?" I asked.

"I don't know," Katie replied, not looking at me. "I'd been away for a couple of days, back in Wichita. I didn't get back to Boston until the day after. Things were normal when I left, chaos when I returned."

"So what happened when you got back here?"

Katie looked at me now. She held up her hand in a stop sign. "Not tonight," she said. She looked into my eyes and took hold of my hands. "Thank you for the good time tonight, and I want to help you, I really do, but you coming has just brought it all back when I thought everything was returning to normal. I'll help you as much as I can, but just take it slowly. Is that okay?"

I looked at her back. I saw vulnerability, hurt, pain, anguish, sadness. I gave her hands the slightest squeeze. "Of course it's okay. And I'm sorry."

Katie smiled and she dropped my hands. "Don't apologise. You've a job to do, I understand that."

We lapsed into silence for a while, but we broke it with small-talk. Katie got her laugh back, but when I thought it was time for another try, she told me she was going for a cab.

"I'll walk you back."

She smiled and shook her head. "Thanks Joe, but no."

I shrugged. "That's okay. There is one thing you could help me with though."

Katie looked wary. "What is it?"

"Just tell me," I said. "Was Brad's death big in the news?"

Katie looked surprised, as if it wasn't the question she had expected.

"It did for a couple of days, I guess. The Globe did a spread on it, but soon lost interest. The Herald went for the 'good old boy' angle, talked about Brad, but other things took over pretty quick. I guess it will all come back when she is caught."

"Don't you mean 'found'?"

Katie said nothing. She knew what she'd said.

I nodded thoughtfully, and we fell silent, but then I said, "I'm sorry, I'm holding you up. Will you be available tomorrow, if I need any more help?"

"Sure, sure. I have class tomorrow, but after that I'll either be here or working at the bar."

I smiled a thank you. Katie nodded, gave me a warm look, and then she got up to leave the bar.

I watched her go, smiled to myself, and then ordered another beer. There was time for one more. I felt like I had got under Sarah's skin. Where that would take me could wait until the morning.

# Five

Sarah woke up screaming.

The cold made her hug herself hard, trying to clamp some warmth into her naked body. She had spent the previous evening walking around, clapping her body, making it warm. She'd jumped, she'd stomped, she'd shouted, her arms wrapped around her chest for some vain attempt at privacy. At one point she'd worked up a sweat, like a film of heat, but as the evening wore on, that flew off into the night like a last broken promise.

Sleep had come more by way of fatigue than comfort, as lack of food weakened her, and instead Sarah let her body warm a small piece of floor. For a few hours, the noise from the screen faded away.

But the dreams had been fitful and frightening, coming at her without mercy.

Sarah had seen herself running down corridors, no chance of escape, no other way out except forward. Something was behind her, she didn't know what, but she knew she had to keep running, her rising breaths echoing through darkness, the corridor becoming a tunnel, the walls narrowing, fear pushing her forward. There was no door, only a patch of shadow, with mist at the edges like dry ice, curling into the light and drawing the air back in. She hurtled for the shadows, breathless and frightened, the sound of her tormentor getting close. As she slammed into the darkness, she sat bolt upright and screamed, then returned to the floor, sobbing lightly, chest heaving.

She propped herself on her knees, her hands on the floor, head down, hair hanging.

"Fuck," she said, and banged the floor with her fist.

She stood up and walked over to the shower. She twisted the tap that had brought warm water the day before and was surprised to see steam again. She had tried the shower through the night, hoping some steam might warm the room, but each time there was just cold water. Now there was warmth.

For the briefest of moments, Sarah was pleased. There was some way of getting warm, something to do to fill the minutes, even if only for a short time. But then Sarah realised that if the water was on, he must be watching.

The water soon heated itself and Sarah stepped in.

Despite her situation, the water felt good. Water filled her ears, and for a few seconds, the only sound she could hear was the noise of her thoughts racing around her head. Her skin prickled as the goosebumps felt heat and for a few precious moments Sarah lost herself in the cascading water, felt her hair go wet down her back, the grime of old tears washed away.

Sarah sat down and let the water run over like a summer rainstorm. She looked through the steam, the mist blocking out the room so that it seemed distant. She covered her eyes, sought solace in the darkness.

She thought back to her life in Morsby and how it seemed so far away. She felt the tears well again as she thought about her parents. She wanted them with her, wanted to hear her father say that he would look after her, make everything alright. She wondered if they knew what had happened, thought about what Brad would have told them. Brad would have called the police when she didn't return to the bedroom, but how do you explain someone disappearing into the night like that?

Then she thought about Brad. Had something happened to him? Why hadn't he come out to find out what was going on?

Sarah sat back against the metal wall and let her head hang down, the water running off her nose and onto her bare legs.

She wondered whether he was watching her now. Was he taping her like he had taped the others? Tears came again. Was this the end? Did she only get to so few years, so much not done, allowed to die in a metal box somewhere so far from home? And what was to come before the end?

Sarah stood up and stepped out of the shower. There was nothing to dry herself on so she walked around and shook her limbs, throwing spare water onto the floor. The shower was still running, filling the room with steam, making her warm.

She walked around the room and she felt as good as she had at any point during her captivity. The dawning reality of her certain death had given her a sense of finality, that anything that needs to be done should be done, and that she had nothing to lose by trying.

Sarah found herself gazing upwards, looking at the joins around the ceiling. There was no way out there. The room looked just like the back of a truck, so everything that made up the room was as solid as that. The only way out would be through the door, and that hardly ever opened, just briefly to pass in the occasional meal. So the only way out was with the connivance of her captors.

Sarah knew there were two. There was the one that she knew, the one she had spent time with in the days before Brad, and she hated him now. The other one was older, and he was the one who had kept her captive, brought her meals. He had been the one who had made her take her shower and who had stolen her clothes.

Just then, the screams from the screen died away. Sarah heard someone outside the door. She froze, her stomach turning sideways. What was coming now? Was it her turn to scream in agony?

The door opened and in walked her captor.

Sarah almost laughed. He looked like a valet, with a blanket slung over one arm and her clothes from the previous day in a bag in his hand. She folded her arms across her chest and felt herself cross her legs as she stood.

He smiled and put the bag on the floor, and then went back out of the room. He returned almost straight away with a plate of food, warm soup and bread, with coffee, and something else.

Sarah glanced from the food to her clothes to the blanket and then back to the food. Then she looked at what else she had in his hand. It was a clear plastic bag, and in it, she could see a pen and some paper. She noticed then that he was wearing surgical gloves and was holding the bag away from himself. She knew what she had to do. It was time to write letters again.

He put the food on the floor, away from her. He walked over to her and passed her the pen and paper. He then reached into his pocket and passed her some pre-prepared scrawl of his own.

"You know the drill. Copy that and you can have the food. Do it first time and you can have your clothes."

Sarah looked at him and felt anger. How can he be allowed to do this? It was time for a little victory of her own.

"Give me my clothes first and I'll do it."

He smiled warmly, like he was pleased to have a game to play. "They're my rules, not yours." He nodded towards the clothes. "Do it now and you'll get your clothes. If you don't, I walk out and you won't see me for days."

He bent down to pick up the bag of clothes.

"Okay, okay," Sarah screamed, panic racing, "I'll do it." Tears began again. "Don't go. Please."

Sarah's skin crawled when she saw the delight on his face. He was enjoying it too much.

He held the bag open and she took out the pen and paper. Sarah looked at what she had to write. It made her shiver. She looked up and he smiled back at her, nodding. She knew she had no choice, so she wrote, her mind numb.

She put the pen and paper back in the bag, which he was holding open, and she covered herself again as he checked it. Once satisfied, he walked out of the door, holding the bag in front of him like it might explode.

Sarah felt heavy, weighed down with despair. She looked over at the food and realised how hungry she was. She drained her soup, drank her coffee, and then put her clothes on in a rush. It felt good to be warm again.

Sarah lay on her back, looking at the metallic swirls in the polished walls. She looked at nothing for around twenty minutes, but then she realised that she could see them clearer than she could before. The grooves were sharper, showing shade in the scrapes. The light bounced around them, making them move, like a slow pulse, rainbows flashing around each bend and swirl. Then she could sense them moving. She became transfixed, wanted to see where the lines went. They spun and danced as she looked, came towards her as if the walls were collapsing. She felt herself scuttle backwards, suddenly scared, feet kicking against the floor as she sought refuge from the wall. Sarah ended up on all fours, but as she flashed a look around, she saw all the walls were moving, beating in time with her heart, faster as her fear grew, the swirls blurring together.

Sarah screamed and wrapped her head in her arms, and then she felt a door close in her mind. It came to her quickly, a dead certainty. Something had been in that food. She didn't feel right. Her thoughts felt like they were being pulled backwards through a small hole, reality imploding, the unreal taking shape.

She felt herself panic. She knew what was happening but knew she couldn't stop it. She slithered to the floor, unable to move, flat on her back, her legs turned too heavy.

Sarah snapped her eyes shut, but the lights were still there. First red, lighting her eyes, then purple, then blue. They went to green, then to yellow, then back to red. Then it started again, only this time faster, the rhythmic change becoming a streak, becoming a blur, the noise of the colours screaming in her head like pressurised air.

She opened her eyes in fright. The ceiling rushed at her. She covered her face, but when she moved her arms away, the ceiling flew away, the swirls becoming a scream. Sarah began to scream with them. Reality was hell. This was worse.

# Six

The next day didn't bring inspiration, just another morning, so I started at the library. I figured that the newspapers might contain some leads.

I wasted an hour taking in more of the morning chaos in Harvard Square before eventually getting the train, so it was ten o'clock before I passed through the doors of the Public Library, near an already bustling Copley Square. Skateboarders were taking over the pavements, and tourists and strollers were loitering on the fringes of the Square. It was more peaceful in the library, like an off switch for the clamour.

I found the newspaper room and so I made for the day after the discovery of the body. I found copies of both the Globe and the Herald. The Herald went for the basics of the story, giving the facts bluntly but clearly. The Globe did much the same, but with more restraint. It was clear from both that Sarah was the main suspect.

The Herald did award the story the front page:

### Fireman Brutally Killed, Girlfriend missing
*A twenty-seven year old fireman was found stabbed to death in his lover's bed. Bradley Howarth was found by his girlfriend's roommate yesterday afternoon, in an apartment in the South End, after she returned from a trip out of town. The dead fireman's girlfriend, Sarah Goode, has not been seen since.*

*Sarah Goode is an English student spending a sandwich year at Boston University. Friends and neighbors are shocked at the incident.*

*"I can't believe this," said neighbor Bob Westland. "I never thought anything like this would happen. I just can't understand it."*

*Police were called to the apartment last night and found the body of Bradley Howarth lying on a bed, with a long-handled knife sticking out of a chest wound, said Lieutenant John Cornwell.*

*"The man was lying on a bed," said Cornwell. "He was naked. There was a knife protruding from his chest."*

*There was no sign of a struggle, although it seemed as if the man was trying to get out of the bed, said Cornwell. The occupant of that room, Sarah Goode, was not present at the scene, and hasn't been since the estimated time of death, some eighteen hours earlier.*

*The neighbors said the dead man had been seen with the missing girl on a few occasions but had not been aware of any problems. No one has reported any unusual activity at around the time of the killing.*

*"Sarah seemed such a sweet girl," said one neighbor. "We'd only passed in the hall, but she always said 'hi', and seemed so very, very nice. It has hit me hard."*

*Bradley Howarth had been a fireman for four years and worked at the station on Boylston Street. He earned an award for bravery two years earlier when he rescued a young child from a blazing apartment block in Dorchester.*

*The dead man's colleagues spoke of him in the highest terms.*

*"He was a good fireman and a fine friend," said Paul Blincoe. "Boston Fire Department is poorer for the loss of a good officer, and I am poorer for the loss of a good friend and a good man."*

*The police appealed for help in locating Sarah Goode.*

*"If anyone can help me to find Sarah Goode, they should contact me at Boston police Headquarters straight away," said Lieutenant John Cornwell.*

*This is a savage and senseless killing of a servant of the people of Boston, and the sooner the killer is brought to justice, the better it will be for the people of Boston, Lieutenant Cornwell went on to say.*

I put the paper down. The inference was clear: find Sarah Goode before she finds you.

I picked up the Globe. The article contained the same basic facts, but put it differently, and this time on page five:

### Fireman Killing Leaves Suspect On Loose
*Police investigating the South End murder of fireman Bradley Howarth appeal for girlfriend to come forward.*

*Police were called to an apartment in the South End last night after receiving a hysterical phone call from an occupant of the apartment, Katie Gray. Miss Gray had been visiting relatives in*

*Kansas, and when she arrived back at her apartment, she found*
*Bradley Howarth dead.*

*"Miss Gray is shaken and shocked," said Lieutenant John*
*Cornwell. "She returned from a happy family trip to find a dead*
*man in her apartment. The body had been there for around*
*eighteen hours."*

*Police say the fireman died from a single stab wound to the*
*chest. He was naked.*

*The other occupant of the apartment, Sarah Goode, is missing.*
*Miss Goode was involved in a relationship with Bradley Howarth,*
*but this wasn't described as volatile or serious, and many of the*
*neighbors commented on Miss Goode's polite and friendly manner.*

*When asked if they were looking for anyone else, other than*
*Miss Goode, in connection with the murder, Lieutenant Cornwell*
*said that they were keeping an open mind at the moment, but urged*
*Miss Goode to come forward.*

*A spokesman for the Boston Fire Service spoke of Bradley*
*Howarth in the highest terms.*

*"He had an excellent service record, and in his short time with*
*the Service he has been credit to himself, his uniform, and to all the*
*people of Boston who have entrusted their personal safety with him*
*and many others like him. It is a sad, sad day indeed for the Boston*
*Fire Service, and an even sadder one for the people of Boston."*

I put the paper down.

I didn't need to read anymore. The police were after Sarah.
They would try their hardest to find her and they would have the
resources. What did I have? So far, contact with Katie and a couple
full of expectation back in England.

I wiped my eyes. I felt like putting all the newspapers back and
disappearing into a bar, but I willed myself on. I leant back in my
chair and examined the pile of newspapers in front of me. I'd found
every Globe and Herald since the date of the killing. It seemed like
a long and laborious task.

I spent the next hour going through paper after paper after
paper. The stories started to die down fairly quickly. News has to
be new, and there is no story in nothing happening. The police
made a few more appeals for information, the funeral got a mention
and some tributes, but as a newsworthy incident, it ceased to exist
after about five days.

Until I noticed a piece from the previous week.

I'd gone onto auto-read, the pages turning in front of me without registering, when I came across an article in the Globe:

### Letter to Friend Adds Little But Confusion

*The police investigating the murder of a Boston fireman, Bradley Howarth, killed in his lover's bed, were saying little about a letter apparently sent to the main suspect's former room-mate.*

*Katie Gray, who still lives in the South End apartment where the murder took place, is reported to have received a letter from the main suspect in the killing, Sarah Goode, expressing some responsibility.*

*"A letter was received yesterday which appears to be from Miss Goode," said Lieutenant Cornwell, "although it would not be right at this stage to disclose its contents."*

*The letter is thought to be from Sarah Goode, Cornwell confirmed, and she does indicate some responsibility for the crime, but no indication has been made whether Miss Goode's whereabouts have become known.*

And that was it. There was nothing in the Herald, and as I scoured the remaining papers with more purpose, I realised there had been no mention of the letter since then.

I closed the newspapers and sat back. No-one was talking about a letter. Katie hadn't mentioned it. Why was that?

I left the library and sat in Copley Square, watching the crowds. There was movement all around me, the insistent blaring of horns, the rumble of rollerblades, the chatter of pedestrians, but all I could hear was the hush of the library. I'd bought an orange juice, and as I sipped I thought about the letter.

Did Sarah's parents know about it? The paper only gave it a passing mention. But if it wasn't worth a mention, it wouldn't have been mentioned. Is that why I was hired?

I realised I needed to know what it said, where had it come from, and why no-one was talking about it. It was the silence about it that said most to me.

I picked myself up and walked away from the square. If I kept on talking to people, someone might say something they shouldn't.

\*        \*        \*        \*

Sarah was curled up in a corner of the room, her knees to her chest, her eyes staring forward.

She was screaming. Long, hollow, frightened screams, tearing at her hair, feet scrabbling at the floor.

The colours had stopped, but now it was the door. It was opening and closing, glimpses of hope, and when it opened, it went for her. The edges had teeth, and when it yawned open, they snapped with giant jaws, just clipping her feet, pushing her back into the wall.

She scrambled backwards each time, and when the teeth receded, when the door began to close, she saw into the opening. She saw light. It was sunlight. It was bright, it was clean, it was warm. It glowed yellow and soft and drew her in. Sarah could see into it and could see the shape of all her dreams, moulded from clouds, willing her forwards. She pulled away from the wall, tried for the light, but the door banged shut, the noise echoing off each wall, making her clamp her head tight. And when the door was shut, it became thick and heavy, shutting out all hope.

Then the door opened again, the light rushed in, the teeth bared, and she was back in the corner, crying with fear, the noise of her cries being sucked from her and out of the room.

Hell.

I marched towards the University, the mention of the letter bringing me a new direction, some drive. I decided to talk to Katie later, but there other people I needed to speak to first.

As I walked, I thought about what I had learnt so far.

There was nothing to indicate why Sarah would kill Brad, but that wasn't the only problem. My job was to get Sarah out, if I could find her, but I knew that Sarah had disappeared without a trace. Her credit cards and keys were still at her apartment, so there was nothing to track. She wasn't expected back, but she hadn't packed anything. It was if she had walked out of her apartment and just kept on walking. Sarah would be difficult to find, I knew that much. That's why I wanted to see that letter. It might contain some hint as to where she is, something only a friend or parent would spot. If I can get the letter, I might get closer to finding her.

But the police were also looking hard, and I had a second role to play. I was supposed to be finding other suspects, setting up the doubt before the case started. But there weren't any others. Brad died. Sarah left. It's like May follows April.

My mind was racing by the time I reached the university. The apartment blocks and traffic had given way to the Green Line tram and a low-rise collection of shops and college blocks.

Boston University spreads itself along the banks of the Charles River, taking over terraced streets and broken up by modern college buildings. I got directions to the history department from a student in long shorts and a goatee and found myself looking at black doors at the top of a short set of steps in front of an old grey building, the end one in a long kinking terrace, the sound of cars screaming along Storrow Drive as a backdrop. I climbed the steps and found myself in an old corridor, mock marble on the floor, staring down a line of closed black doors. I wandered aimlessly, until I was challenged by a stern middle-aged woman.

"Can I help you sir?"

I smiled my most disarming smile and rummaged in my pocket for a business card. "Hi, I'm a private detective from England. I'm looking for Sarah Goode's tutor, hopefully her personal tutor. I understand she's a student in this department."

"What's she studying?" She had her arms folded loosely across her chest but her eyes were tough and business-like.

"American history of the 18th Century. I paused. I guessed she was bluffing, playing dumb, so I came straight out with it. "She's the girl who disappeared," I said.

"The girl who killed the fireman?"

I smiled. "So they say, although ask her family, and they'll say she is innocent."

"Yes sir," she scoffed, "they say the same thing about Lee Harvey Oswald."

"His brother doesn't."

She stalled at that, but then asked tersely, "why do you need to speak to one of our professors?"

I smiled. I had said tutors, not professors. I was right. She was playing dumb.

"Background," I replied. "If I find her, I'm going try and talk her into coming back and clearing her name." It was a lie, but she had started the game.

She looked at me with disdain, but then walked off down the corridor.

I guessed I was supposed to follow, so I trailed behind her until we came to a door marked 'Professor Lowenski'. She looked at me in a way that told me to wait, and when she re-emerged, there was a man stood behind her. He stood around six feet five, with a mop of wild white hair that raised his height a further five inches. He was wearing a red silk bow tie around a dirty shirt collar, and the look in his eyes made me fear for his sanity. His clothes creased themselves around a lanky body, which was shrinking to a stoop with age.

"A-ha, a visitor from afar. Come in, come in."

I nodded at the woman, who flashed back a cold smile before walking off, and then followed the professor into the room.

It was a small room, maybe only ten feet by ten, but made much smaller by piles of dusty books and old coffee cups. Black and white photographs were stuck on the walls. I looked at them. Small groups of people in seventies fashions, huge collars and wide ties, the women in thin white dresses that reached towards the ankles. In all of them a younger version of the man in front of me beamed out.

He brushed aside a magazine from an old green chair in the corner and waved at me to sit down. I sat down with a crump and a thin cloud of dust drifted into the air.

I thanked him for seeing me at short notice and started to treat him to my usual spiel. "I know who you are," he interrupted. "You've come a long way. How can I help you?"

I noted his impatience, wondered whether it hid anything else.

"I just want background on Sarah," I said as a start, giving a helpless smile and a slight shrug of the shoulders. "Anything really. What kind of student was she, who did she associate with, who were her enemies, her admirers?" I paused for a moment. "You do know who I mean, don't you?"

He scowled and waved my suggestion away. "Of course, of course." Then he softened and smiled for the first time. "I'm sorry, young man, but this business has been very hard for me."

"Why is that?"

I must have sounded like I was making an accusation of some kind, because he bent forward and peered at me over non-existent spectacles. "Young man, I was, am I guess, her personal tutor. I see it as my duty to this university to look after any overseas students studying in my faculty, as pompous as that may sound. I would see her once or twice a week, much more than my own students, and we would talk, just to check she was alright. Nothing more than that."

"But she is an attractive young woman."

He smiled at that. "Yes, she is, but I'm an old man, and I'm her tutor."

I held up my hands. "I'm sorry, professor. I didn't mean to imply anything." He nodded acceptance of my apology, so I asked, "were there any admirers in particular?"

He exhaled loudly and ruffled his hair. I saw why his hair was so untidy. He had a habit of ruffling and tugging his hair, so that now his hair had trained itself into a mess.

"I guess so, but it's hard to be specific," he said, and then, after some thought, "I'm not sure she would have told me anyway. Our relationship was, I guess, professional." He smiled. "Anyhow, don't young woman like Sarah always have admirers?"

I smiled back and then asked, "who were her friends?"

"Well," he said, stroking a beard he hadn't grown and glancing at the ceiling, swinging round on his chair so that his musings came in waves, "there is that girl on the course she lived with, Katie I think, and a couple of other girls and boys from that group. I remember a young guy from a bar started to appear on campus, but I didn't think anything of it."

"From a bar? Could that have been the fireman who died?"

Professor Lowenski laughed. "If he's a fireman, I'm a lumberjack. Scrawny, glasses, humourless. Scruffy little guy." He gave little waves away as if he was trying to swat him.

"So, did Sarah ever mention this guy from the bar?" I asked.

"Not really. I once asked who he was, and she just said he was some guy she'd met." He paused for a moment, before continuing, "although thinking about it, I don't think I've seen him since Sarah went." He cocked his head to his left and answered his own suspicion. "I suppose I wouldn't though, no reason to come here, if Sarah isn't going to be here."

"Did you ever know a name? Or from which bar?"

He stroked his chin some more and shook his head slowly. "I can't remember a name, I don't know if he was ever introduced to me. I saw him a couple of times just waiting for Sarah, to walk her home. Creepy guy. As for the bar, it was probably the Pour House. That's where Sarah went mainly, although she tried to see a few." The professor smiled. "Cheap beer, friendly company. That's all a bar needs if you're a student."

I laughed. "I remember it well, professor. Tell me, did Sarah ever mention having somewhere else to go, somewhere where she could get away from it all?"

He shook his head. "Get away from what? She was having a good time, meeting new people, seeing new things. There was no need to escape, and if there was, she didn't mention it to me."

That made sense. I scratched my chin absent-mindedly. I looked out of his window. I could make out a sliver of blue from the river, between the trees and over the road. I caught the professor snatch a glance at the clock. "Did she ever hint that she might want to stay in Boston after her year had ended, because she'd met someone? Did Sarah ever mention Brad?"

"You ask many questions, young man. You should have been a lawyer."

I twitched. "That doesn't answer the question though."

He smiled. "You're right it doesn't. And no, she didn't."

I was surprised. "She never mentioned Brad? Not once?"

Professor Lowenski shook his head. "No, not once. But why should she? I was Sarah's tutor, although," and here he looked suddenly bashful, "I hope I was a bit more than that. But even as friends, we were casual friends, as tutor and pupils can only be. So she would only disclose the casual things to me. The close things would be saved for the close friends." He looked at me for a moment and then asked, "have you managed to speak to anyone else?"

I nodded. "Yeah, sure. A guy called Paul Blincoe from the fire station, and Katie, Sarah's roommate."

Professor Lowenski just nodded, tugging at his lip.

"Can you think of anything that might help me?" I asked. "Has anything been puzzling you about this since it happened? Anything at all?"

He stayed silent. I thought about the letter.

50

"Have you heard anything about a letter Sarah sent to her room-mate?"

He shook his head slowly and said, "no, not at all." He looked thoughtful, and then he asked, "what are your intentions if you find her?"

I smiled. "Just tell her parents that she is safe and well, and then leave it up to her. Get her a good lawyer maybe." I wasn't too far from the truth.

"Shouldn't you tell the police? The police are after her, and you may have committed a crime if you don't tell them."

"I don't recall reading that she was wanted by the police. I got the impression she was, but nothing specific was said."

He went red. "Y-yes, yes," he stumbled, "that's what I meant. I didn't mean to imply anything. I'm sorry."

I shrugged. It didn't really matter, but there had been one or two slips since I had arrived at the University.

I decided to end it there. I wanted some time out to think about the Professor. I had the impression that he had been expecting me and he seemed in tune with the investigation. I didn't know what it was, but some time alone may bring it to the surface.

I smiled and stood up. "Thank you very much Professor Lowenski. You have been very helpful, maybe more than you think. If you can help me more, here's my number," and I wrote the hotel telephone and room number on my business card.

He looked at the card, and then just seemed to forget about my presence as I moved out of the room. I waited for some signal, some acknowledgement of my departure, but there was none. I started to walk out of the door when I felt a light hand on my arm.

"Just before you go, young man," he said, looking sad, "if you find Sarah, just tell her that if things have gone wrong for her, she'll have made an old man very sad."

I smiled. "I've got a quite a few messages for her now," I said. I nodded my goodbye and made my way out of his room and back out to the streets of Boston.

I spent the next few hours wandering the streets, thinking about a direction, trying to get a feel of the city, hoping that it might get me a feel of what Sarah might be thinking. I called in at the fire station, and Paul Blincoe said he nothing about the letter, if there was one.

I returned to the hotel to report back to her parents and make some notes, and when I opened my door, I found a ticket for the Boston Red Sox pushed underneath it.

It seemed like I had to go to a baseball game.




Sarah lay in the middle of the floor, laughing out loud.

The images had passed, the nightmare was fading. The room was beginning to sink back into itself, becoming the shape it had been before her meal. The light returned to normal, and once more she was sat in her cell, with only her fears to keep her company.

But she had the urge to laugh, as if she was relieved to come out of it intact. It had gone on too long. Sarah thought she had lost the battle, but she had come out of it.

She rolled around laughing, pointing at the walls, at the door, then holding her stomach as it ached. Too much laughing.

The walls had stopped moving, the door stayed closed.

Sarah carried on laughing as the day turned to cold.

# Seven

I was panting by the time I reached Fenway Park. People were streaming through the gates as I worked out where I was supposed to be, signs and numbers pointing everywhere. America can get a man to the moon, but it couldn't get me to a numbered seat in a small ballpark. I realised I was going to be late.

I found my seat eventually, and I felt a lift when I saw Katie sat in the one next to it. "Sorry I'm late."

"Hey, don't worry," she said, smiling. "This is baseball. We're just here for the show. Have you ever been to a ballgame before?"

I shook my head.

She smiled. "Good. Enjoy it. This is a grand old ballpark, and a grand old game."

I looked around, saw how it was all corners, cute and cranky, and how it all seemed so green, so full of summer. There was movement everywhere, and chatter, as if people were there to enjoy themselves, not endure the pain of a weekly ritual that seemed such a part of English sport.

She let me take it in for a while, and then asked, "how did you get on today?"

"I went to see Professor Lowenski."

"You did what!" She looked aghast. She had been watching the Red Sox pitcher, but she'd turned her face to me now.

"I was getting nowhere, so I went to see Sarah's personal tutor. Why what's wrong?"

"That man isn't just Sarah's personal tutor," she said, her eyes wide. "Professor Lowenski is one of America's most prominent historians, and you march in there and see him because you've run out of ideas." Katie shook her head and whistled. "Man, you're crazy."

I shrugged my shoulders and gave a look of innocence. "He seemed the crazy one to me," I said.

"Oh, he is. He's as mad as a hornet, but the guy knows his subject." Katie shook her head some more and laughed. "Wow, man, Professor Lowenski," and she slapped her leg a couple of times.

"He seemed to spend some time with Sarah, seemed to know about her."

"Of course he does, everyone knows about her now. She was headline news around the campus for a week, and the newspapers went to him so they could get the foreign student angle. One of his jobs is to look after the foreign history students, and one of them is labelled a killer and disappears off the face of the earth. Oh, he'll make sure he knows about her, all about her."

I was intrigued. I turned to look at Katie, but she'd turned back to the game.

I looked at her face. I saw a sparkle in her eyes, the beginnings of a smile as she watched the game.

Then I wondered about what else she might know, what else lay behind the sparkle, and I wondered about the letter mentioned by the newspaper.

"What's this talk about a letter sent by Sarah?" I asked innocently.

Katie turned slowly towards me. Her smile had gone and I could see shock in her eyes. "Who told you about that?" she said, carefully.

My eyes grew keen. The newspaper had been correct. "I read it, in one of the newspapers, at the library. It was mentioned briefly."

Katie was silent.

"Is there a letter?" I asked, persisting. "It could be important."

"Can't we talk about that later, this guy's getting through the order," she replied, pointing at the pitchers mound. Her mood was quieter now, suddenly withdrawn. I vowed to pursue it. Her eyes had lost their sheen and now she looked distracted.

I looked towards home plate and saw the last vain swing of a bat. The Red Sox players jogged back to the dugout, while the hitter trudged back to his own, swinging his bat at the ground.

I left it for a while. We just watched and talked the game for five innings, with just the occasional break for beer, and Katie got her sparkle back. The Boston pitcher had just been retired and replaced by a relief. The new guy was busy warming up on the mound so I turned the conversation back to the letter.

"What does the letter say?" I asked.

"What letter?" She was still distracted by the game.

"The letter Sarah sent. What does it say?"

Katie turned to look at me, some of her edges knocked off again. "I'm not supposed to say. I've been told not to say anything."

"So there is a letter?"

Katie nodded.

"And who told you to say nothing? Sarah?"

Katie shook her head. "No, not Sarah, the police. I haven't seen Sarah since before Brad died."

I paused and wondered what it must say for the police to warn her to be quiet.

"I realise you made a promise, but I just want to find Sarah," I talked softly, trying to win her over. "Don't you want that?"

"Of course I do," she said quietly, "but trust me, this letter won't help you do that."

"Can't I be the judge of that?" I looked at her, and I could see a softening, a desire to help. "Tell me, for Sarah's sake."

Katie stayed quiet, and then turned her attention back to the game. I let her change the subject. I could sense that she was almost there, but I didn't want to push it.

"Do you know how many people must have sat here and seen this same view?" she said quietly. "Just afternoons and evenings, watching men throw a ball around?" She looked at me. "Too many to count, from so many generations. So many games here have been part of peoples' lives, and one day someone may look back and say the same thing about this one, but we'll all be gone, and this conversation will mean nothing."

"A bit morbid," I said.

"But still true." And she sounded sad when she said it. "Having your life changed by what happened to Brad makes you morbid. That's why I like coming here. It doesn't seem so important, because so much has gone before." She turned to look at me. "And that's what keeps me going. However bad things may be now, in the great scheme of things, it doesn't really matter. Doesn't matter at all."

"But do you need this ballpark to tell you that?" I asked.

Katie shook her head. "Not really. It just reminds me, that's all. Maybe the ballpark's a bit ragged now, you know, like if that guy in front leans back he'll break my knees, and it's pot luck whether you end up behind a girder, but I loved this park before, and I still love it now." Katie shrugged. "Maybe you're right, I don't know.

Maybe it's just me that clings to these things. I think back to last season, the few games I went to with Sarah. She was just an eager tourist from England, and I was just a history student. The park hasn't changed, the team is almost the same, but now Sarah is a wanted killer on the run and I have to sleep with that picture of Brad burnt into my mind. I want to go back to how it was, but I can't. But for three hours, I do. Sat here, I could be at any time in my life, and I don't have to think of the things Sarah made me see."

"Why do you say Sarah made you see them?" I asked. "Do you believe Sarah killed Brad?"

She looked at me. Her eyes had lost their sparkle, and her face showed I'd taken her away from the game and back to that room in her apartment.

"That letter," she started to say, "that letter." She looked down and her fingers toyed with themselves nervously. "It's a confession, to Brad's murder, addressed to me," she said, before looking back to the game.

I was silent, stunned. A confession. That took it up a couple of steps. I wondered if Sarah's parents knew, and how they would take it if they did.

I thought back to my instructions from Sarah's mother, the message to call home and to pass on the credit card. Perhaps they did know.

"Where is it?" I asked. "The letter?"

Katie looked back round. "The police have it."

Oh great, I thought. "What did they make of it?" I asked instead.

"They were interested. But they haven't mentioned it since."

"What do you mean, 'since'? How often do you see them?"

She shrugged nonchalantly. "I see them around every few days. They come to see if I've heard from Sarah."

I was silent, and worried. Perhaps I shouldn't tell Katie too much.

"And no," she said, interrupting my thoughts, "I haven't told them about you." And she smiled. I was glad to see it; it had been a long time gone.

I felt relieved. "What did the confession say?" I asked.

Katie turned and gave a confused smile. "If you come back to the house, I'll show you." I looked mystified. "I've scanned it into my computer, for reference purposes" she said, and I saw mischief in her eyes.

My response was lost as the crowd roared a hit into centre field. The Red Sox hitter scampered around the first base until he came to a skidding halt at second.

I was lost in thought for a few minutes, thinking about the confession, what might flow from it, about going back to Katie's apartment. The next Red Sox hitter swung at a curve ball and it sailed harmlessly into the shortstop's glove.

"Boston have blown this one," Katie said, standing. "Do you want to go for a beer?"

"I'd rather go looking at confessions," I replied, and I smiled warmly at her as we collected our things and headed for the exit ramp.

Sarah barely looked up when the door opened.

Her laughing had ended hours ago, replaced only by a deep despair.

She didn't care when he brought the bed in, a camp bed, dragging it across the metal floor and putting it against the wall. He threw some blankets on it and walked out of the room.

Sarah curled up on the floor, expressionless, and wished for death.

The walk back to Katie's was good. The air was cooling, but the night had that feel of early spring, a mix of warm days and old rain. I started to think about Katie, tried to shake off a niggle in my stomach. It reminded me of years ago, when I cared about things, when I cared about people. I was getting sweet on her. I fought the urge to take her hand, but somehow it felt so natural that I should that I wondered what would happen if I did.

Back at Katie's we made small talk. For a while she disappeared into the kitchen to put on coffee, and when she came back she flicked on the television, for background noise.

I let Katie pour the coffee, watched her as she fell silent, and then asked, "where's this confession?"

"I told you, it's on my computer. I scanned it in." She paused and looked thoughtful. "I should warn you though, it's not a confession in the strict sense. In fact, I'm not really sure I understand it."

"What do you mean?"

"I don't know." She took her time, sipping her coffee. "It's the language used. I put it down to English dialect and a more formal way of speaking, but it just doesn't sound right. Something off-key, not right."

"Did you say this to the police?" I asked.

Katie looked into her coffee.

"I didn't think it was my job," she said. "They seem to know what they're doing, and I got the feeling they didn't want a lecture from me."

Katie went to the bedroom to boot up the computer, and then she beckoned me in.

I was surprised to see it untidy. Clothes were scattered over the floor as if she just discarded them en route to the bed, and a pile of books was stacked by one end of the bed, some open, some closed. There was a feminine smell, a mix of cosmetics and mild perfume, but the hum of the computer fans disturbed the karma. It was blinking away in the corner, chattering its way through grids and lines and text as it spluttered and ground its way into action. After what seemed like forever, we were both sat in front of the screen, Katie on a battered old stool, me on the edge of the bed.

"Hang on," Katie muttered. She glanced at me quickly. "I encrypted it so the police wouldn't know I still had it. It's one of those programs that make it invisible, so I'm trying to remember where I put it."

Katie navigated though files and folders, the screen changing and flickering like a quickly-turned book. Eventually she stopped clicking and leant back. "There you are. See what you think."

An image of hand-written text appeared onto the screen. It looked nice and neat, written on lined paper and smooth and clean.

I shuffled towards the screen, scratching my chin absent-mindedly. I leant forward and read.

*"They said Sarah Goode was of so turbulent a spirit, spiteful and so maliciously bent, that her detractors could not suffer her to live in their house any longer. Ever since these detractors turned her out of their house she has behaved herself so crossly and maliciously. She must kill somebody with a knife. If you take her life away, God will give you blood to drink."*

I stared at the screen, puzzled. I looked at Katie, who just shrugged, so I looked back at the screen. I read it and re-read it, but I struggled to make it make sense. I turned to Katie again. "What do you make of it?"

"Just about the same as you did. I just don't get it. It's in the third person, it uses strange language, it refers to her being thrown out of her house." She scratched her head and sighed. "I just don't get it."

I sat back and exhaled loudly. Things had gone weird. Nonsense letters from a suspected killer.

"Have you ever asked her to leave?" I asked.

"No, never. We were, sorry, are, friends."

I scratched my head.

"How do you know it's from Sarah?" I asked.

"The handwriting, I recognised it straight away. She has a controlled style, very restrained and deliberate. It's a bit like her, all repression and formality."

"Oh come on, repression is a good thing," I said, trying to lighten the tone. "Remember, I've seem the Jerry Springer Show. Sometimes it's better to leave the lid on, if you know what I mean."

"Yeah, and what you get is one dead fireman and a kooky letter talking in abstract. If she was keeping all of this in, that was one lid that was always gonna blow."

I fell silent and wondered about the message. It was if she was quoting something, had taken something old and inserted her name. It certainly wasn't modern text. I noted the phrase, *"maliciously bent."* That certainly wasn't a phrase I'd ever heard used in England.

"Was Sarah religious?" I asked. "Did she go to a church while she was here? Will there be a chaplain she might be confiding in?"

Katie gave a slight laugh. "That was one of the few things we didn't agree on. I go to church, I always have done, and I suspect I always will do. Sarah never went, and she used to say that she never would. She said that her family were Church of England but didn't really practise, and the bible was just something that washed over her at school."

"So her threat that," and I glanced back at the screen, " *'if you take her life away, God will give you blood to drink,'* is one Sarah would be unlikely to make?"

Katie nodded. "Sure, that would be unlikely. I don't know if she thought that I'd see it as a serious threat, but it doesn't sound like her, sure."

I ran my hands over my face, trying to pass the pressure into my hands. I didn't know what the hell it meant.

"Katie?"

"What?" She looked nervous. She went to brush away a fringe that was causing no trouble. She looked my way, and I could sense her backing away slightly, an almost undetectable shrink.

"Do you think she did it, do you think she killed Brad?" I asked. "What do you think, deep down?"

"What do I think, deep down?" she repeated. She let out a deep breath, as if the question was a relief from the one she thought I was going to ask. She brushed away her fringe once more and sought refuge in her computer screen. The flickering light from the computer bounced back as doubt in her eyes.

She answered eventually, a cagey, defensive response.

"What I think is that Brad is dead, that I will see his deadness in my mind for the rest of my life, and that the only person who could really tell me what happened has run away. The only contact we have with the only witness is this letter, and I can't make sense of it." She looked away from the screen and at me. I thought I glimpsed a film of tears, but they were blinked away. "That's what I think, for what it's worth."

"But Sarah gave you no sign that she might be losing it?"

"No, none at all," she replied. "But she was a bit like that." Katie sounded sad.

I looked once more at the screen. "Could I have a copy?"

Katie nodded, and after a few clicks, a printer by her feet whirred into action. Within five minutes of entering Katie's room, I had a copy of the so-called confession.

I wandered back into the living room and poured myself some more coffee, looking again at the letter. I wondered at what Sarah could see when she wrote this. Where was she? What was she thinking? Would she make contact again? Katie seemed sure that Sarah had written it, although in what state of mind we weren't sure.

Katie came back into the room, and I thought I could see a pale redness under her eyes.

"What is it?" I asked softly. "Sarah going, or what you saw before she went?"

She slumped down on a chair opposite. "I don't know," she replied. "I don't think it's Sarah anymore. We were close, or at least I thought we were, but going to college makes you used to moving on. I don't know, I just don't know."

I thought she was going to start crying, but she steeled herself and reached for the coffee instead. "I liked Brad, he was a nice man," she continued, "but I don't think it's Brad either." She smiled thinly, and then sniffed as a small tear appeared in the corner of her left eye and began to make its way down her cheek. "Oh, I'm just being selfish," she said tearfully. "You know, why did it have to happen in my apartment? Why did it have to mess up my college year? Why must I have to get over seeing what I saw? Why me?"

I stayed silent and waited.

After a few minutes of silence she looked at me. "You know, you English must all be alike. Sarah was just like that, no words of comfort, just sit out the storm until it passes."

I smiled. "As I said, Jerry Springer," and I was pleased to see her smile back.

"Look," I said, keeping an eye on her changes of mood, "it might help me if I can ask you some questions, more detailed questions, if you feel up to it. If you don't, fine, or if you want to leave it for another time, fine, but it might help me." I paused to let the questions sink in.

"Typically English again. You can't ask an awkward question without including a get-out clause for the other person. Be American: just ask."

"Okay," I said, smiling, "can I ask you some more questions?"

Katie smiled back. She wiped her face and took a deep breath, as if to start over. "Fire away, limey."

I settled back in my seat. "Tell me what you found, in detail."

She exhaled, a flick of the eyebrows, thought for a moment, and then began.

"I'd been away for a few days, back in Kansas, and I think Brad was planning to stay over while I was away. I didn't mind him staying over when I was here, but I reckon they just fancied having the run of the place. Anyway, I flew in early evening, about seven-thirty, and when I came in it was quiet. I thought nothing of it, and I'd been in the apartment a couple of hours before I thought about going into Sarah's room."

"What made you go in?" I asked.

Katie curled her mouth as she thought about it.

"With hindsight, I probably suspected something was wrong. I don't normally go into her room. I remember seeing her toothbrush in the bathroom, so I knew she hadn't gone away, and Brad's was there as well. But for all I knew, they could have just gone to a bar." She shrugged, wiping the hindsight clean. "Maybe I just wanted to say hello. I'd left my family again, been sat around airports for a few hours, so maybe I just felt like saying hi. I knocked on her door but there was no response. I waited a few moments, I went into her room, and..." She paused there, her voice breaking. A steely look and a sip of coffee restored order and she continued, trying to be matter of fact. "Brad was on the bed, there was blood on the floor and on the walls, and there was a knife sticking out of his chest."

At that her voice broke again, but this time the tears came. I went over to her and held her. I felt her warmth as she nestled into my shoulder, could feel her shaking softly with tears.

We stayed like that for about five minutes before she pulled herself away from me and sat upright. She wiped her face and I saw her steady herself again.

"I didn't know what to do," she said quietly. "I could tell he was dead. He was still, his face had kinda sunk, you know, like it had lost its life, and the blood on the floor was dry. The room was a mess. Even though he was in bed, it looked like he'd been in a struggle. There was blood on the walls, on the door, on the floor, it was everywhere. But he was just in bed, a sheet still covering his legs, his arms spread out as if he'd been laid on a cross."

"Was he naked?"

Katie just nodded.

"Was there blood anywhere else in the apartment?" I asked.

"I didn't notice, but the police said they found traces in the bathroom, around the sink and on the faucet. Only traces though."

"Was anything taken?"

"Not as far as I could tell. Her toothbrush was still there, her books, clothes, bags, letters, all still there."

"Purse?"

"I couldn't see it, but the police said they found it on the other side of the bed." She paused. "I didn't go that far into the room."

I thought for a moment. Things were looking bad for Sarah. It couldn't have been someone else breaking in for money, because her purse was still there. But if Sarah was running, she didn't have any money. No blood elsewhere in the apartment, so there couldn't have been a struggle with Sarah, unless it was a bloodless struggle. I thought for a moment of strangulation and disposal, but then I realised that she couldn't have written that letter if she had been killed in the apartment. What about the blood around the taps and plug? Washing away the evidence is calculated. But if it's Sarah, why not be calculating enough to take some money if her life was about to be on the run? Empty her account and hit the road? Cash is more invisible than plastic.

Something was bothering me. I knew it sounded like Sarah was the killer, but the facts didn't fit. No known motive. No known history of mental health problems. No means of support. Calculated cover-up after the event.

But Brad must have known the killer. His feet were still wrapped in the sheet, so he hadn't got out of bed to struggle with an intruder. He felt safe enough to stay in bed until the moment the knife went into his chest. The fact that only his feet were covered might be the result of trying to move out of the way, when he realised that he was in the last split-second of his life. But until then he was happy to lie in bed, naked, vulnerable.

"When I was speaking to Professor Lowenski," I said, "he told me about some guy Sarah had met in a bar who had sort of attached himself to her."

Katie looked up and nodded.

"Do you know who that might be?"

"What did he say he was like?"

"Blond, small, scrawny."

Katie looked grim, as if she was about to spit. "That'll be Jimmy, Jimmy Walsh. A creep."

"How did they meet?"

"No, what you mean is how did he leech onto her."

I sensed her contempt.

"We used to spend a lot of time in the Pour House," she said. "If I was working, Sarah would come to meet people, knowing she'd be safe. Anyway, this guy, Jimmy Walsh, just approached us and started talking to us. Well, to Sarah really. He was hitting on her."

"What was he like?" I asked.

"Just a regular weedy guy. Small, blonde, glasses. He seemed easy-going, you know, but he seemed quite persistent, somehow unnerving. He would stand too close, invade her space, try and impress her with tall stories. He wouldn't ask about Sarah, he would just talk about himself. It gets kinda dull eventually. I wanted to tell him to get lost, but Sarah was too polite. She listened to him, encouraged him to carry on, and then she just kinda got used to him. I mean, he was an inoffensive kinda guy, just a little dull, and he sure was nice to her. He'd take her out shopping sometimes when I was too busy, and I guess she just thought her time here was too short. America is too big a place to be lonely in, so why cause trouble?"

I understood. Sarah just did the polite thing; it was no big deal.

"Was Sarah seeing Brad then?"

Katie nodded. "It was in the early days, but Brad was around. He seemed a bit pissed about it, but he didn't say anything."

My mind wandered back to the scene of the crime. Would I see something I hadn't seen the previous night?

"Can I look at the room again?" I asked.

"Sure, why not," she replied, and she led me to Sarah's room and opened the door. "The police asked me to leave the room as it was until they found Sarah, but I couldn't deal with it."

I looked around the room again, but I saw nothing I hadn't seen the day before. It did strike me how clean and ordered it looked, with the fresh paint and varnished floors.

"My daddy came to see if I was alright, and he did all this while he was here," she said by way of explanation, reading my thoughts.

I pointed towards some boxes in the corner by the window. "Does all that belong to Sarah?"

"Yeah," Katie replied, "although the police took most of her things."

"Do you mind if I look? You never know, they might have missed something."

"Be my guest, although I won't stay to watch. Just don't take anything without telling me first."

I nodded agreement and sat in front of a collection of personal property. Clothes sat in bags nearby, and files and books showed their corners over the rims of boxes.

I went for the books first. There was a collection of novels, mainly crime fiction: John Grisham, Patricia Cornwell, James Patterson. There was nothing in her reading material that showed any sign of Sarah being anything other than a normal, mainstream young woman. I flicked the pages. Nothing fell out. No passages highlighted.

I went through her academic books next. History, exclusively history. It was weighted towards the American Revolution, although from an English perspective. I'd learnt that Boston was a good place to learn it. Again, a flick of the pages revealed nothing.

Her music tastes revealed nothing unusual. No obsession with the devil, no Marilyn Manson. Not even 'Helter Skelter'. I'd lost touch with popular music, but the names that sprang at me from the clear spines were names that were known to me. Mainstream pop and a smattering of film soundtracks. Sarah seemed to be nothing other than a well-balanced young woman enjoying a year in the States before settling back in her native England.

I found some personal papers, but they were just scraps of her former life, a collection of receipts and cash withdrawal slips. A couple of thrillers from "Buck-A-Book" on Tremont Street, some bagels from Quincy Market, nothing special.

I wandered back into the living room.

"Did you find anything that helped?" Katie asked, her eyes not moving from the flicker of the television screen.

I shook my head and answered no.

I sat down and let out a sigh. "None of this makes sense," I said, running my fingers through my hair as I rested my head on the back of the chair. Katie looked my way. "No sense at all." I sat forward. "Everywhere I look," I continued, giving a speech to talk the problems through for my own benefit, "I see an ordinary girl. But all the signs point to her doing an extraordinary thing: taking a knife to her semi-casual boyfriend and killing him with one blow."

"I know," Katie said softly. The tears welled up once again and she looked at me. "Have you worked out what that letter means?" She looked suddenly vulnerable.

"Fuck the letter," I said. "How are you? That's more important."

She shook her head, rubbed her eyes, and then sat upright. She'd brought herself back. I looked at her with concern, but she gave me a smile that said I should consider her to be okay. I looked apologetic.

"Not a thing," I said, getting back to the letter. "I can't work out what she means anymore than you can. Perhaps this whole thing is not as straightforward as we think." I shrugged. "Perhaps it's some kind of joke," I said.

"Yep, hilarious," Katie replied with disdain.

She looked angry for a moment, as if she suddenly hated Sarah for what she was putting her through, but then I caught her glance towards the corridor leading towards the bedrooms and she looked sad, as if she missed another person being in the apartment.

"What if she is in danger?" Katie stared at me with brown-eyed worry, and for a moment I doubted myself.

"That's just something I'll have to deal with." I thought it was a throwaway comment, nothing more.

Katie just shrugged and stayed silent. Then she looked at me. "Do you think you'll find her?" she asked, the question loaded with doubts.

I gave a thin smile. "I guess I'll have to."

Katie turned back to the television. I leant back in my chair, put my head back, and looked upwards. The television was painting blue and white flickers across the ceiling. I knew Katie wasn't watching it, I could see from the corner of my vision that she was sat in the armchair with her knees pulled on to the cushion, her head resting on the arm.

I thought more about the letter. Why send something like that? It didn't tell anyone anything, so it couldn't be a cry for help, but it implied guilt and hinted at some kind of a mental disturbance.

I let out a sigh. Perhaps there was no need to think why she had sent it or what it meant. In the end, there were only two possibilities: she had killed Brad and run off, or someone else had killed him and she was in danger. I remembered the remit of my job: to find Sarah. Did it matter why she had sent it or what it said? No, probably not. All I had to worry about was finding Sarah before the police did, and then give her a credit card.

The purse bothered me though. It implies she left in a hurry, in a rush. That would go with a theory that she had killed Brad in an extreme of emotion and then run off in a panic. I could forget about the letter for the moment. I just had to work out where she would be, go there, and give her the credit card and the message from her mother.

Something occurred to me.

"Katie?"

"Yep?"

"You are of similar age to Sarah, right?"

Katie nodded.

"Well, imagine yourself in a strange place where no-one really knows you. You're a nice girl in bad circumstances. You can't return to your own place because something awful happened there, and because the police will be waiting for you to arrive. You have no money, no clothes other than those you are wearing, and no credit cards. You can't use anything traceable. If you had plenty of time, you could set up a false identity in a new town, get some credit, use a dead persons details, but this all happened in a rush so you didn't have time. Your mind isn't right. You're in shock, scared, desperate."

Katie looked at me expectantly.

"How would you get by?" I asked simply.

The question was loaded, and the look on Katie's face told me she understood that.

She shook her head. "Sarah wouldn't do that, she isn't that kind of girl."

"Would you have believed she was a killer a few weeks ago?"

Katie shook her head slowly and sadly. She reached for the remote control and snapped the television off. Although it was quiet, there was no silence.

"Are you saying she is selling herself?" Katie said eventually. "Is that what you think she might be doing?"

I shrugged my shoulders. "I don't know, I'm just theorising. But you have to accept it as a possibility."

"Yeah, along with living off handouts in homeless shelters or petty theft. Why do you assume she has resorted straight away to selling herself?"

"That's what you thought I meant. It's the first thing that came into your head, isn't it? And a few weeks ago, you wouldn't have thought Sarah capable of murder, but now you aren't so sure." I leant forward and tried to look sincere. "I'm not saying anything about Sarah, but the unthinkable becomes the possible when you are in desperate circumstances."

"Yeah," she said, defending her friend, "but she might just be hiding out somewhere, waiting tables in Maine, something like that."

I nodded. That might be true. "How did you get the letter, the confession?"

Katie didn't say anything. She knew the answer and she knew what it meant. It was hand-delivered, so she was still in town.

"There's only one thing to do," she said, as she went looking for a coat and her car keys. "Let's go looking for her."

"Would you know where to look?"

Katie shook her head as she pulled her coat on. "No. But if we drive for long enough, I'm sure we'll end up in the right place.

I smiled. Progress. I stood up and followed her out of the apartment.

Progress didn't last long.

Katie and I toured some of the darker streets of Boston. We approached prostitutes, went into roughhouse bars, flashed Sarah's picture and looked for answers. All we got were blank or dirty looks, and none of the street girls had seen Sarah working. It had been a grim couple of hours. There had been no heroin chic. It had been all addiction and hollow eyes, rattling junkies and desperate drunks, and I realised that Katie's instincts had been right: Sarah was not the kind of woman who would sell herself.

When we arrived back at Katie's apartment, we opened some beers. We felt like we deserved them. We sat and drank, silent in our own thoughts, when Katie turned to look at me. "How long have you been doing this?" she asked. "This private eye thing?"

"Oh, not many years. You know, it pays the bills."

She smiled. "Is it exciting, you know, subterfuge and mystery, staking people out?"

I laughed. "I wouldn't say it was that glamorous. It has its moments, like baseball, but mostly its routine. You know, serving court papers, collecting evidence for divorces. Occasionally, I'll get a job tailing someone suspected of lying in civil court papers, saying they're confined to a wheelchair and I catch them on video jogging the dog round the local park."

Katie laughed. "I always thought you English played fair. It sounds as corrupt as this place."

I tipped my bottle towards her in salute and she tapped its neck with hers. Katie drained her beer, indicated I should finish mine, and then she went to get some more.

When she returned, she said, "so if Sarah scorned working the streets, how else could she get by?"

I shrugged. "I don't know. Working as a nanny or waitress, as an illegal? Or petty crime? Homeless shelters?"

"Well, if she's joined the invisible workforce, it's going to be hard to find her. But if she has turned to petty crime, she won't be very good at that either. And the same would go for an attempt at prostitution." She smiled. "And what happens to criminals who aren't very good at it?"

I returned the smile. "They get caught and they go to court."

Katie's smile broadened. "I'll make a private eye of you yet," she said laughing. "So what do we do?"

I wanted to grab her and land a big kiss on her forehead. But I didn't. I grinned, nodded, and then said, "we'll go to the local courthouses and see if she has been arrested."

Katie clapped her hands. "Well done, although we should just concentrate on the court bailiffs. The police will be looking out for Sarah Goode, so Sarah is unlikely to give her real name, so it is only Sarah's likeness they'll recognise."

I wanted to hug her. I couldn't tell if she wanted to hug me, but there was a moment where we were both silently grinning at each other, not sure what to say.

The moment passed, so I said, "I want to find out more about this dork who latched onto Sarah. What was he called again?"

69

"Jimmy, Jimmy Walsh. Why? Do you think he's involved?"

I shook my head. "Probably not, but you have to eliminate as many possibles until only one possibility is left."

"Am I a possible?"

I smiled warmly. "No," I said softly, "you never were." Katie looked pleased by the answer, although I don't know why; she had a watertight alibi. Perhaps it was just because somewhere, for some reason, she attached some blame to herself. "You can help though."

Her eyes widened and she looked pleased. "How?"

"Set up a meeting with Jimmy Walsh. I'll tail you, you find a reason to leave, and then I'll tail him."

"I can do that, sure," she said, "but I can tell you where he lives, if that's what you want to know."

"No, it's not just that. I want to know who he is, where he goes. He might have some connection, you never know, so if he has, he might lead us to Sarah." I looked at her and gave an apologetic look. "It may be a waste of time, but it is better to know it's a waste than later regretting not knowing."

Katie nodded. "That's okay. And afterwards I'll go round the local courts, see if Sarah has appeared."

I grinned. "How did you know I was going to ask that next?"

Katie grinned back playfully. "You're a man. Everything you do is predictable. You're probably hoping now I'll let you sleep here, rather than let you go back to your hotel at this time of the morning."

I went red with embarrassment and tried to cover it by checking my watch intently. It had been my thought as we came into the apartment, but I'd hoped it hadn't been obvious.

She sighed. "Don't worry," she said, "you can sleep over, but you're on there," and she pointed towards the couch.

I shrugged and smiled. Why not?

Once Katie was ensconced in her room, I let a Californian ballgame come to end in the background while I thought about the progress.

I pulled out the letter and read again:

*"They said Sarah Goode was of so turbulent a spirit, spiteful and so maliciously bent, that her detractors could not suffer her to live in their house any longer. Ever since these detractors turned her out of their house she has behaved herself so crossly and*

*maliciously. She must kill somebody with a knife. If you take her life away, God will give you blood to drink."*

I put it down again. I was baffled. I just didn't understand it. If that was a confession of some sort, written by a young woman, she had taken her historical studies too seriously. It wasn't a way of speaking I recognised. It sounded mired in a forgotten century; certainly not one I'd ever lived in.

I then thought about each sentence and wondered if it fitted the facts. I read again.

*"They said Sarah Goode was of so turbulent a spirit, spiteful and so maliciously bent, that her detractors could not suffer her to live in their house any longer."*

I knew that didn't make sense. I'd heard a few descriptions of Sarah now, but I hadn't heard anyone describe her as spiteful or malicious. Even-tempered, reserved and polite was how most people described her. And Katie was certain there had been no move to evict her. Certainly, on the night she disappeared she was still in residence because her boyfriend was in her bed. All her personal belongings were still there in the next room. Most of those were in plastic sacks, but as these had 'Boston Police' written on them, I thought it was safe to assume they had only been put in bags after Brad's death.

*"Ever since these detractors turned her out of their house she has behaved herself so crossly and maliciously."*

Again, this didn't make sense. This sentence was saying that she had behaved herself "crossly and maliciously" since being turned out of the house, but Brad's death came before Sarah left, if she is responsible for it, if that's the 'behaving herself so crossly and maliciously' she is referring to. The timing was out.

*"She must kill somebody with a knife."*

Well, if this was a confession, she did kill somebody with a knife. This letter was surely written after Brad's death to fit in with the references to being thrown out of the house, but if that was the case, why say "must" kill somebody with a knife. It should be past tense, not telling of a future intention. The act had already taken place.

*"If you take her life away, God will give you blood to drink."*

I couldn't work out what the hell that meant. It was clearly a threat not to inform on her, but according to Katie, there was no information to give. It was possible that Katie knew much more than she was letting on, but that didn't fit with Katie giving this to the police. If Katie was holding some secret on behalf of Sarah, some promise to help her out, why would Sarah have to turn it into a threat? And why put it in writing, in a form that could be used in court? And why would Katie hand it over to the police? It would only put her at risk. I wasn't that familiar with American laws, but I was fairly sure that helping out a fugitive murderer was a criminal offence of some kind.

I rubbed my eyes. The beer was wearing off and I was starting to droop into sleep. My final thought of the day was that it looked like a confession, but it just wasn't right.

But if it was Sarah's writing, why was it sent? Was it saying something else?

My mind gave in to sleep. Overloaded.

# Eight

Sarah lay awake for hours, enjoying the feel of the bed beneath her.

The depression had passed as the drugs subsided. She suspected LSD, but she had no experience of it, so it was only a guess. But she'd heard The Beatles, all those "marmalade skies," so she felt on solid ground.

She pulled the blanket up to her neck, the sensation of something wrapped around her bringing some comfort. Sarah wondered how long she had been held captive now. She had lost count of the days long ago.

Sarah tensed when she heard a noise outside the door. She'd been without the screams from the screen for a day now, and instead her ears strained for the slightest sound from outside. There was never anything. Just silence. So when she heard something, it had to mean a visit. She felt herself flinch when the door opened.

She could smell the food before she saw it, and it scared her. She remembered the last time she'd eaten. Hours of hell. She wasn't going through that again. But the food smelled good. It pulled her in, made her defences slip.

Her hands gripped the edge of the blanket, and she wondered for a moment whether she would be able to use it. Would she able to wrap it around the neck of her captor, pull on it with all her weight, do just enough to get her out of that door? She didn't care if she killed him. She wanted to kill him. She wanted to hear him beg for mercy, wanted to look into his eyes as surprise crossed to fear and then crossed to darkness as the last of the lights turned themselves off.

Sarah realised she would have to get used to the routines so she could work out when to strike. She felt a little piece of resolve store up a lot of hope. If there was food, then it couldn't be her time yet. Whatever that held for her, it wasn't coming yet.

Sarah lay still, listening to the sounds.

She heard the footsteps come into the room. One step, two steps, three steps, then pause. The tray then went onto the floor, then she heard him let out a breath as he straightened himself.

Then there was nothing. Sarah knew he was watching her. She lay still, all quiet, just the sounds of his breaths filling the room. What was he doing?

Then she heard him spin on his heels and shut the door behind him.

Sarah turned around. She smiled when she saw the tray of food against the wall. He would have turned his back on her to place it there.

Sarah got out of bed and walked to the door. From there, she walked to the tray. She did it in two paces. So he must have walked in two paces, one more pace to face the wall, and then paused as he put the tray on the floor. He would have turned his back on her.

Sarah was getting an idea.

But first, she needed strength.

Sarah looked at the food. Fresh bread, bacon, eggs, water.

The food looked good, it smelled good, and Sarah knew she had to eat, but she remembered the last time she had. She remembered the trip, the nightmares.

She shook her head. Be strong. Try and do without it.

It was hard. The bread looked edible, drug-free, and the eggs and bacon looked divine. An English breakfast. It must be harder to lace that. Perhaps if she ate that and avoided the water?

But she needed water.

She looked at the toilet. She could always drink that. It would be liquid, and it did flush. It should be clean water.

The thought of the food took over. She wanted it now, more than anything.

Sarah felt her stomach. It ached with hunger.

She broke a piece of bread off and examined it. It looked just like bread should. She nibbled it. It tasted fine. She took a bite, chewing slowly, carefully. Sarah groaned. It tasted good. And Sarah knew that if she was going to make it out of there, she had to be strong.

She sat down and devoured the food. When she had finished, she looked at the water. No, that was too risky. Sarah went over to the toilet bowl and peered inside. It looked like fresh water. She flushed it to make sure, and when it had finished flushing, she threw the water out of the cup and dipped the cup into the bowl. She got a cupful and held it up to the bright spotlights. It looked just like water. She smelled it. It smelled of nothing.

Sarah took a deep breath, put the cup to her lips, and drank the water quickly. She finished sighing. It felt good not to be thirsty. She put the cup back into the bowl for a refill and finished that.

She stood up and began to pace around the room, the room echoing now with the noise of her feet on metal, beating a time, walking off the days.

She felt strong again.

I was sat in the rotunda at Quincy Market, surrounded by tourists and shoppers, when I saw Jimmy Walsh with Katie. He'd just walked in and gone to where she was sat.

We'd planned it that morning. Katie called him to say she was enquiring after Sarah, to see if she'd been in touch. She was wary of this; there was nothing to suggest he had anything to do with Brad's death or Sarah's disappearance, but she accepted my reasoning that we had to look at everyone involved. She called him before I left, just to make sure that he was available for coffee. He was. She suggested breakfast at Quincy market, and that's where I was, waiting, when I saw Katie with him. The plan was that she'd keep him occupied long enough for him not to be suspicious, and then she would say she had to go to college. I would then be able to follow him by getting lost in the crowd, and Katie would do the rounds of the courthouses.

We'd debated whether I should just hang around outside his apartment, but I was worried about following the wrong man, and I would be too conspicuous just loitering in a residential neighbourhood. No, this was best, just another man in a big crowd. But just to be sure, she gave me his address on a slip of paper.

I'd been sat there for nearly an hour before I saw him. Katie had been there about twenty minutes when he walked in.

At first I just admired the surroundings. Quincy Market is the focal point of downtown, pulling in the tourists in droves. A five hundred and fifty-foot granite food hall, its columns and central dome bring a touch of Greek revivalism to the Faneuil Hall area. Faneuil Hall itself stands at one end, all pleasing red brick and white turret, the scene of many a revolutionary meeting during the run up to War of Independence. The granite market hall is flanked on either side by glass canopies housing stalls and restaurants, and what were once grand warehouses on adjoining streets are now a series of shoppers' enclaves. It's a place to relax and people-watch, a colourful stream of human movement, but we had agreed a strategy and I knew I had to stick to it. I had a camera with me, and I'd already taken pictures of the market, but the rest of the film was for Jimmy Walsh.

When he arrived I was halfway through a pizza slice and my second coffee, and I decided I didn't like him the moment I saw him. I spotted a leering look at Katie as she went to sit down, and his gaze travelled very slowly from her chest back to her face. He was scrawny, somehow insipid. He had a small blonde fringe trying to make its way to round-rimmed glasses and a loose blue jacket that didn't hide his skinny frame. He seemed very particular, cautious and self-conscious, as if his confidence wasn't high or he thought he was being watched, which of course he was. His gaze was deliberate, his smile nervous and twitchy. I only saw them together for a few minutes, but I didn't see any humour, any warmth. I winced when Katie gave me the slightest of glances, but his look that followed hers didn't seem to settle on me.

I was pleased they only had drinks. I'd been spinning my food out, and I was waiting to be told to move on, but no-one had bothered me. I was at the other side of the central rotunda, so there were a few tables and an aisle between us, but I didn't want to draw attention to myself by a noisy eviction.

I watched them. Katie made little attempt at being talkative. She spun her cup, watched the drink swirl and dip, and looked mainly at the table. He looked at Katie constantly. He kind of dipped as he sat, his forearms flat on the table and his shoulders hunched. It was as if he was used to people ignoring him, so he gets their attention by dipping his head low and getting back under their gaze. I felt suddenly bad for judging him just on his looks, I'd never spoken to him, but he seemed like a creep. Katie seemed to think that, and Katie was a woman I thought I could trust.

Jimmy had been there for about five minutes when Katie seemed to decide it was time to go. Her coffee wasn't finished, but I thought her enthusiasm for the plan had, which was that she would make as if to go off to college and leave Jimmy Walsh behind. I muttered, "shit" as he got up with her. They both left the

76

shade of the rotunda and set off through the sun-baked throng of tourists, becoming lost in a tangle of t-shirts and shopping bags.

I threw my wrappings and cup into a litterbin and ran into the crowd. All I could see were bobbing heads, hairstyles and sunglasses, but then I looked in the direction of Faneuil Hall and saw that Katie had stopped by a bench and was checking her shoelace. I felt relief. I sensed it was a ploy, but I seized the moment. I buried my face in a shop window and watched their reflection to see where they went next.

The pursuit began once more, but I was closer this time. As they walked away from the shade of Faneuil Hall and onto Congress Street, I was about thirty yards behind them. As we reached the traffic junction near the Old State House, the pedestrian light showing red, I drew up alongside them both. I was wearing sunglasses so he wouldn't be able to see that I was watching, and so I tried to tune into their conversation. I was about five feet from him at this stage but I got no sense that he knew who I was or why I was there. I was dressed like a tourist, had a souvenir bag with me, and I was gazing towards the Old State House in awe as I listened. I could hear Katie just telling him that she was doing okay, was trying to put it to the back of her mind until the end of semester. He was nodding and smiling but not saying much. He was a couple of inches shorter than Katie and all the while he gazed up at her. Katie always looked straight ahead.

I followed them past the Old State House and along the route of the Freedom Trail. Katie was walking quickly, and he had to skip past other pedestrians to keep up, all the time talking at her. Katie never looked back to see where he was or let up her pace, but from his efforts she must have been aware that he was always there. We marched past the Park Street Church and then we started a slower ramble across Boston Common together. Although he was starting the conversations, Katie was answering with smiles and the occasional two-way dialogue. I didn't see him look back at any point. He just talked and looked and seemed reluctant to break away.

I realised I would need some decent photographs, so I ducked off the path and headed over to the grass at the higher Beacon Street side. I reached the path on that side of the Common and was able to put on a spurt to get ahead.

I took some pictures from the path I was on, looking down the slope and into the busier part of the Common, framed by trees and the buildings of Tremont Street. Katie was nearest to me, so his face was turned towards the camera. I rushed onto the softball pitch, close to the entrance on Charles Street. I took a few pictures of the Common, pointed the lens up and down Charles Street so as not to be conspicuous, and then I turned the camera on them. I had them coming right at me. I looked just like another tourist snapper taking in the view, but I zoomed in close and ran off four good shots as they made their way towards wherever.

I was still taking pictures when they passed me. Katie looked nervous, and I'm sure she shot a quick look my way as she walked past. I didn't notice Jimmy look my way at all.

I had to rush to catch up, but as we got to Charles Street proper I was only about 10 yards behind them. I felt safe, cocooned behind sunglasses and an air of nonchalance, anonymous in a city fast becoming familiar. Why should Jimmy Walsh notice me? I'd been just another head lost in the crowd, and then even on the Common I was just a strolling, snapping tourist.

Then they stopped abruptly on the corner of Charles Street and Beacon Street.

I suddenly felt the openness become claustrophobic. I was trapped, nowhere to go. I was on Charles Street walking directly towards them. All I could see behind them was Beacon Hill disappearing into the distance and I didn't know where to go. They were both stood talking on an open junction, long views down straight streets in all four directions, with the shelter-less Common behind me. They were at a busy intersection, car horns sounding and a huddle of Japanese tourists making their way up from the Cheers bar further down Beacon Street, but I couldn't see anywhere to hide and bide my time.

I had no choice but to walk past them. As I went past I heard Katie ask, "so where are you going now?" and I was sure this was a signal for me, but all I caught was a slight shrug of the shoulders. I was sure I'd blown it as I scuttled across the intersection and into the Public Gardens.

I took a mental swipe at myself and debated what to do. What if I'd been seen? What would be the point in carrying on? He would be deliberate over his movements and I would learn nothing. But I'd had no clue that I had been spotted. He hadn't looked at me, he hadn't challenged me, he hadn't seemed concerned at all. I decided I would carry on.

Katie went her own way eventually, and as she left she was still talking but raising her hand to him, as if she had to tear herself away. I watched him watch her for a couple of minutes, as if he couldn't turn to go away until she was out of sight. Then he did an about turn and set off across the Common again.

I had a good view of him. His path was slightly elevated now, taking the path I had taken before, going across the top at the Beacon Hill side. I wandered out of the bushes and was able to cut across Charles Street further down and walk on a different path. He was in my sight all the time, glimpses caught through the trees, and I watched him head back towards downtown.

We started with a return to Quincy Market. He bought himself a coffee and read a magazine, oblivious to the crowds. I pulled out my camera out and ran off a few more shots. I found myself a table where I had a good view of the market hall and I used the tourist cover to take some more pictures.

Just as I was putting my camera away he stood up and walked slowly into one of the streets running between the market hall and the old warehouse buildings. He headed back the way he'd walked with Katie, past the Old State House and on the route of the Freedom Trail, following the painted red line, but when he got to School Street and the Old Globe Corner Bookstore he kept going. I found myself in a part of downtown that seemed much more what I expected. Department stores and boutiques lined the streets, hi-fi and bookshops, and I seemed to be wandering amongst Bostonians now.

It was easier to keep track. I was able to look in shop windows and follow his movements by reflection. He flitted from store to store, not usually going in. He did go into two bookshops, but each time I waited outside rather than risk finding myself staring at him over a book I was holding upside-down. He bought two compact discs and then spent some time looking at some track shoes in a sportswear store.

I'd begun to relax, doubts appearing about him, when he drifted into Saks. I knew I'd be alright in there; I could see the crowded displays and the throng of shoppers, so I knew I'd be able to duck and move around and keep an eye on where he went.

I watched him go through the doors and make his way past the perfume counters. I followed through the same doors and immediately I saw Jimmy Walsh in front of me. It was as if the needle had just spun off the record. He was about six feet in front of me, by a Gorgio display, staring. He was staring hard, and there was no doubt he was staring at me. His eyes bore into me like shards of glass and he looked angry.

I faltered. It was one of those moments when we both knew what had just happened. He'd spotted me, but I tried to pretend it hadn't happened. I walked into the store, tried to look nonplussed, but I didn't do it well. I didn't walk past Jimmy. Instead I turned left and made for the other side of the store. I didn't know what I was doing or where I was going. I picked my way through people, felt his gaze on me all the time, and found myself stepping onto the moving staircase that would take me to the upper floors. As I stepped on, I afforded myself a quick look, but when I did, Jimmy Walsh was still looking at me. I thought I saw his expression become a thin smile as I ascended, Jimmy and the rest of the floor receding below me, and just as the second floor began to obscure my view I saw Jimmy head towards the exit doors.

I stamped the moving step in frustration. The young mother with a child behind me on the escalator gasped while I punched the moving handrail. I was on an unstoppable ride to the upper floor and all I could do was watch my day's efforts come to nothing.

I stepped off the escalator and stood and thought. I felt a tight feeling in my chest, a mixture of panic and adrenaline. I felt a slight shove as the young mother came to the top of the moving staircase and directly into me. I remembered where I was and apologised. She grunted and marched off, dragging her young son with her. I skulked away and returned to the streets of Boston with a more obvious plan: try and rationalise the day's events, make it seem not so bad. I grabbed some orange juice from a pharmacy and found a bench opposite the Old South Meeting House.

What had really gone wrong? Jimmy Walsh wasn't a real suspect. None of them were. He was just some creep who didn't sit comfortably with Katie's social network, someone who had shown some possessiveness towards her, insofar as he'd monopolised her time when there was someone else who she would prefer to be with. No, the only real suspect was Sarah herself, the ever-present missing person. I was just trying to make Jimmy a suspect.

I decided eventually that I might as well go see where he lives, see what he does if I put him under some pressure. I pulled out the piece of paper Katie had given me earlier and went looking for a cab.

After a short taxi ride, I found myself stood outside a small row of dark-bricked housing, just behind a street of pizza restaurants and delicatessens in the heart of the North End. There was a light on in the upstairs window of the house on the end. It was the address Katie had given to me and I had taken a walk to the front door. The second doorbell had "J. Walsh" on, so I leant against a nearby streetlight and waited. And waited, and waited.

I made some notes. I took some pictures. There was no point in pretending. I had to make a record, these things may turn out to be important.

I waited some more, and I began to wonder whether I should stay here after dark. I didn't have much of a coat on for the cold, and I wondered about the safety of the neighbourhood. I was in the Italian sector and it didn't seem particularly seedy. Just busy. There always seemed to be something being shouted from the main street, always some car shooting past or groups of people walking around.

I was beginning to consider going back to Katie's when I saw the maroon Buick pull into the street. For some reason it made me nervous. My eyes were drawn to it. Other cars had pulled into the street while I'd been stood there, but I seemed hypnotised by it as I watched it crawl down the street. I felt my stomach take a plunge when it pulled alongside me and a black guy the size of size of a heavyweight boxer lowered his window.

"Get in stranger, we're going for a ride."

I obeyed.

My mind raced.

I was sat in the back of the Buick with a silent man wedged against me. He didn't need to sit so close, it was a large seat, but I guess he just wanted to make me edgy. I tried to resist it as we rumbled down narrow streets and through underpasses, and eventually came to a stop outside a large, sand-coloured building downtown.

They were detectives. When they showed me their badges I knew it wasn't good news. I did as I was told, knew that they were saving good-guy bad-guy for later.

I was pushed towards the building, and for a minute I thought of running. I wasn't in cuffs, and the push put a few yards between us, but I didn't know the area, and the black guy looked like he could run a few yards if he had to.

I wasn't booked in. The desk sergeant barely glanced up as I was propelled past him. I was taken instead straight to a room in the basement.

The room was austere. I looked around and saw minimalism, but I didn't think it was a fashion statement. It didn't strike me as an interview room. There was no microphone, no one-way mirror, but I sensed the good-guy bad-guy might still play out. The walls gleamed that grey sheen that you knew would wipe down, would wash off what happened in here, like a reminder board. A bare table and three chairs occupied the centre of the room, but everywhere else was empty. If it was meant to intimidate, it worked. I tried hard to look relaxed, but my insides were tearing themselves out. I concentrated hard on not thinking ahead, tried to deal with the here and now instead.

The big black detective had gone to get coffee, leaving me with a sharp-looking young detective. He was dressed all in black, from his thin jumper to his denims to his waist-length jacket. His hair was short, but it was no military cut. The way he just stood by the door made me think he was of a lesser rank than the black detective, and he just stared at me through deep brown eyes and a sharp twinkle. His gaze was deep and hard to work out.

The black guy was easier. His suit was functional, grey and unassuming. It told me that he had a life outside of his job, that he had other things to think about than how he looked when on duty. He had the look of a family man: well rounded and content, his greying hair happily receding and lines that looked like he smiled a lot. I was hoping I would get to see some of that.

"What's going to happen?" I asked.

I was met with a smile, but he just said, "wait for the lieutenant," and kept his pose by the door.

I tried hard to look casual. I cast my mind back to my courtroom days, when every nerve was stretched with terror but still I displayed just calmness, confidence, serenity. I thought of the oldest technique in the book: nonchalance. Nothing puts someone at an advantage with greater effect than an air of ambivalence. I was meant to be scared, for what reason I didn't know, but I hadn't been invited over for tea. If I looked scared, the battle was over.

I looked over at my guard, leant back in my chair, glanced at my watch, and shrugged my shoulders and smiled. "It's turning into one hell of a day," I said, and gave a small laugh.

"It's about to get worse."

I shrugged again. "Yeah, whatever."

I was relieved when the black lieutenant returned with coffees. The other detective was too cool, too calm. He knew what lay ahead. I didn't. I picked up one of the coffees. It was hot and strong. I tried to match it.

The black cop sat down, leant back and put his hands in his pockets. This had the effect of splaying his jacket, and for the first time I saw his gun. No, I'll go further. It was the first time I'd ever seen a gun so close. It nestled under his arm like a cobra ready to pounce, an unspoken menace.

I leant back again in my chair and tipped him a 'cheers' with my cup.

He gave me a surprised look and then started the conversation.

"I want you to tell me what you're doing here. Take it nice and slow, we've got time." His voice was quiet but firm, his manner businesslike. He rocked back in his chair and took a slow drink of his coffee.

I was surprised. I wondered if this was an immigration enquiry. Then I looked around the room again. It definitely wasn't an interview room. I wondered if it was a room they used for taking written statements. I thought of clues to help me work out what was going on. If I was in England, I would have been booked in, a custody record opened. I would have been cautioned, told of my rights, and then the interview would have been tape-recorded. I didn't know exactly what went on in American police interviews, but I was sure some of the English experiences must be similar. Then I remembered something I'd read seen in movies.

"Aren't you supposed to read my rights?" I asked. I said it confidently, trying to be the lawyer I once was. "Give me a phone call?"

The detective smiled. Like his colleague's, it was too calm for my liking. "And why would I want to do that?"

"Because if you don't, everything I say to you will be inadmissible. We might as well not be having this conversation." I was gambling on being right. Actually being right is never important. What is important is making the other side believe that you might be.

He wiped his forehead. "Shit, I forgot about that," and then he gave a theatrical thump of the table. "That's right, as a citizen you have rights," he said, nodding. "I should have remembered." He shook his head. Then he leant forward fast, his face in mine, and gave a low snarl. "But you are not a citizen are you." It wasn't a question. I suddenly realised I was a stranger. The language we shared, nationality we didn't.

"Well, can I ring the British Consul then?" I asked. I folded my arms.

"And shall I ring the US Immigration Service?" he asked menacingly, and with that he gave me a stare that would freeze fire. He stood up and over me. "No. I'll tell you what we will do. You will talk. You will tell us what you are doing here. You will tell us where you have been, where you are going when you leave here, and how long you will be in Boston for." He leant forward on the table, big hands shaking the tabletop so that my coffee spilled from my cup. "And trust me, you will tell me."

I looked at him, and then back at the other detective, and then back at the table. I seized on the indication that I would be leaving here. My confidence grew by inches, but only inches. "Why don't we introduce ourselves first," I said, trying some disarming tactics. "I'm Joe Kinsella, although I'm sure you already know that."

"Yes, we do." The response was terse. The black detective stared me out. I tried to meet his gaze, but the eyes were too dark, too much menace. I could feel my nerves jangling once more, but I relaxed slightly when the tone of his voice did. "I'm Lieutenant Cornwell, and the other guy is Detective Lehane. I call him Robert. You will call him Sergeant."

"Did you say Cornwell?" I asked, "John Cornwell?" I remembered the name from the newspaper. He was the detective in charge of the hunt for Sarah.

"Yes, it's John Cornwell."

That answered my main question: why have I been brought here? I knew now it was to do with Brad, or Sarah. "What do I call you? Lieutenant?"

He thought. "You can call me nothing until you tell me what I want to know."

I thought long and hard about what I should do. My eyes wandered around the room, but I knew I had little choice. I wondered how honest I should be. John had only hinted at Immigration, but I guessed that they already had an idea what I was doing in the United States, so there was no point in being too evasive.

"I'm a private detective," I said. When I saw the look in John's eyes, I realised that it hadn't gone down well.

He leant forward and set his cup down on the table. He stared at me with menace once again and the confidence I'd grown dissipated with the coffee steam into the room.

"What are you doing here?" he asked, but he said it slowly, coldly.

I thought about what to say, wondered about how much they knew. I'd only shared it with a few people. I began to wonder at how small this big city really was.

I decided that truth was probably the safest of the options. Or at least an edited version. My advice to clients had always been not to say too much. Say just what you need to say and nothing more.

"I've been asked by Sarah Goode's parents to come here and try and find out what happened to their daughter," I said. I shrugged as if to say there was nothing more to say.

John Cornwell sat back in his chair once more. The sergeant came over to the table and sat down. I was starting to feel hemmed in. The room shrunk and I felt my chest tighten.

"Who is Sarah Goode?" John asked.

"C'mon, you know who she is," I replied. "I remember your name from the newspaper. You're trying to catch her because you think she killed her boyfriend, because you think she's a murderer."

"I know what she is. I want to know who she is, who she knows, where she goes."

I thought about what he was asking. It was clear that she was still the suspect, the target. I reflected on how little I knew. "I don't think I can help," I said nervously, and then by way of afterthought, "client confidentiality."

"I thought her parents were the clients," came the reply, low and quiet, and somehow it sounded meaner for it. "That's what you said. You said Mr and Mrs Goode had asked you to come over here to find out what happened to their daughter. Are you lying to us? Is Sarah paying you to get her out of the country?" He spat the words out, and the venom didn't have to travel very far to reach me. I felt every word.

"No, no," I said quickly, "of course Sarah isn't the client, but everything I know about her I've been told by her parents. That's where the client confidentiality is."

"And what professional rules would you breach by telling us, Mr Kinsella?" John said, rich with sarcasm, "The Guild of Private Eyes? The Raymond Chandler Fan Club?" He paused for a moment before continuing. "Let's get one thing straight here," he said, pointing. "You are here on business. You know that, I know that, you have just told me that. You talk about clients, and you talk about confidentiality. You are no tourist. But the Immigration Service doesn't know that. They think you're swanning around North America soaking up the sights, snapping happy snaps with that box brownie of yours. But you're not. And if they find out why you are here, they will bust your ass so hard you'll wish you'd never boarded that plane." He paused to let his words sink in. "Now, why don't we start telling some truth here, and if you do, you can go back to your sightseeing. It's your call Mr Kinsella."

I realised I was in difficulty. I glanced around the room as if I expected to find some solution painted on the grey walls. Of course, there were none. It had to come out.

"As far as I know," I started, "she is just a normal young woman doing her college work." I received a nod that I should continue. "Her parents say she was happy, enjoying her year in Boston. She'd made a few friends, and I assume you know about Katie."

"Tell me about Katie," John said.

I gave a look of surprise. "Is she a suspect?" I asked.

He grew impatient. "Just tell me, goddammit!"

86

I sighed and continued. "She seems a nice young woman, enjoys normal things, baseball, her family, her coursework. She said she was close to Sarah and knew Brad, but they had their own circle of friends, to a degree."

"What did she think of Brad?"

"Just the usual things," I replied. "He was her friend's boyfriend, and I think they got on with each other at that level. She didn't seem to have any dislike for him, or at least none that I could guess at. It was just a routine thing, you know, he passes through the house, they talk, she goes away, he dies. Nothing more to it."

"Where had she gone?"

"When?" I queried.

"The night of the murder. Where was she?" John sounded insistent.

I felt a chill. What did they mean? Was she a suspect? "I would have thought she'd already told you," I said cautiously.

"I know what she told us. I want to know what she told you."

I could see the way the conversation was going. They were checking out alibis, weren't sure of Katie. I thought about her story, the vacation at home, the grisly find on her return. I thought about her closeness to her father. Would he cover for her? Could she have done it? I decided on caution.

"She hasn't told me," I lied.

"Mr Kinsella," John Cornwell said, mock disappointment rich in his voice, "I thought we'd agreed on co-operation. Are you trying to tell me that you've spoken to Katie Gray about Sarah Goode, and about what may or not have happened, and you didn't ask where she'd been before she found the body?"

"Why? Did Katie find it?" I said with surprise, but realised instantly I'd gone too far.

John Cornwell jumped up, kicked out at my chair, and before I knew what was going on, I was lying on the floor, listening to the sound of the chair coming to halt against a distant wall.

"Now why we don't just stop fucking around!" he shouted. It wasn't a question. "We ask questions, you will fucking answer them. If you don't, you'll find your ass waking up in the County Jail. And do you know how popular a pompous English guy like you would be in there? Many of them won't have tasted English meat, and they'll know you won't have had American."

"But why the fuck would I go to the County Jail?" I shouted. I was angry, the pain of the landing raising my mood a notch.

"Police assault would be a good start," he hissed.

"But I haven't assaulted anyone."

"That's not what the report will say." And with that he grabbed me by my shirt collar and hauled me to my feet. "Why don't we just quit fucking around?" Again, it wasn't really a question.

I was shoved back into my chair, and I felt the tug of friendship when Sergeant Lehane put his hand on his colleague's arm and nodded him calm.

"I'm sorry Mr Kinsella, but the lieutenant can get a bit impatient. I tell him that isn't the way, that co-operation is always better, but he sometimes gets ahead of himself. Now, where were we?"

I took some deep breaths. My racing heart deafened me for a moment. "We were talking about Katie," I said quietly. My chest hurt with anger.

"That's right, we were talking about Katie. Tell me, Mr Kinsella, where did she tell you she was before she found the body? She did tell you she found the body, didn't she?"

I nodded a yes.

"Good. So where was she before she found the body?"

"Wichita," I said. "She'd gone to Wichita, gone to her parents' home. She says she got in on an evening flight, spent the night watching television, and then she went into Sarah's room." I paused. "That's when she found Brad."

"Why did she go into Sarah's room?"

I was starting to feel weary. "Can't you ask her that?" I pleaded.

I saw the lieutenant begin to rise to his feet, but a touch on his arm kept him at bay.

"Okay," I said in resignation, "she says she went in because she felt something just wasn't right. All the signs were there that Sarah and Brad were staying there, but she'd heard nothing from them. She says she walked in and just saw Brad, on the bed with the knife in his chest."

I watched the two officers exchange glances, and the lieutenant gave a slight nod.

"Who else have you spoken with, while you've been in Boston?"

I shrugged my shoulders. "No-one really," I replied. I gasped as the lieutenant grabbed me by the neck.

"I'm having to use reasonable force here to defend myself from your attack," he hissed. "Do you get my meaning?"

I tried to keep my focus. "Get the fuck of my neck," I hissed. I struggled to get my words out from a choking throat.

"Tell us about Brad's friend, Paul Blincoe," he asked.

I looked at him, and I saw that he knew. I raised my hands as if to say I'll co-operate, and a nod from the sergeant brought the lieutenant's hands off me. "Okay, okay," I gasped, my anger spitting the words out, "I spoke to him. He didn't have much to say, just told me a bit about Brad, just general stuff. You know, that Sarah was just a girl he was seeing, nothing serious, and that he thought she had probably killed him."

"Why did he think that?" the lieutenant asked.

"For the same reason as you, that she's the obvious solution. He didn't provide me with anything that would help me find her. We had a brief chat and then I left, that was it."

"Tell me about the Professor at the university."

Now I was getting very nervous. How could they know I'd spoken to him? He was not an obvious choice to pluck out of the dark. They must be following me, or getting information from somebody. And then I wondered why they would be following me. I'd arrived more or less unannounced and only seen Katie on a few occasions. They have either an informant, or they are following Katie. Perhaps Katie is the informant. I suddenly felt lost and unsure.

"He just gave some background, you know, how Sarah had been doing at university. He didn't tell me anything I didn't know already."

"Why were you following Jimmy Walsh?"

I stalled. I knew how it would sound. Eventually I said, "Professor Lowenski told me that Sarah had a friend who wasn't from the university, that's all. Katie told me who he was. I was just checking him out."

"Who else is there? Who else are you going to check out?"

"No-one, no-one at all. You've just named them all."

I felt my head bang on the desk, the lieutenant's hand around the back of my neck, pushing down. I tried to pull my head up but couldn't. I thought about kicking out, giving his shin a good bruise. I felt his breath in my ear. "Fucking tell me," he hissed.

I twisted my head round so I could look him in the eyes. I relaxed my body and tried to sound calm. "I haven't spoken to anybody else, and I've no plans to speak to anyone else," I said quietly. "Believe me or not, that's your choice, but that's the truth."

My head banged one more time on the desk, and then I felt his grip loosen. I raised my head and felt a tingle on my lip. There was blood and a small cut. I dabbed it with the palm of my hand.

"So much for American hospitality," I said, sounding bitter.

"Ah yes," the lieutenant said, "truth, justice and the American way." He considered me for a moment. "Do we have it now? Truth?"

I felt my lip. "Fuck that, I could sue for this."

He smiled. "Proof might be a problem. No-one knows you're here. You weren't booked in, you're not under arrest, and you lied your way into the country."

"Fuck you," I muttered under my breath. Again, I saw the lieutenant twitch in his chair, but the sergeant touched his forearm lightly and he stayed put.

The two police officers looked at each other in a silent conference. I could make out the slightest shakes of the head, the odd raised eyebrow, and then the lieutenant spoke again. "You can go now, Mr Kinsella. We're done with you here."

"What, you mean I can go?" I asked incredulously.

"Do you want to stay?" Sergeant Lehane asked quietly.

I shook my head.

"Just get the fuck out of here then," the lieutenant barked. "But let me warn you, if you get involved in this investigation, I will personally bring you down. That is a promise. Now, goodbye."

Sergeant Lehane looked at me.

"Mr Kinsella?"

I looked at him, wondered what was coming.

"See the city," he said. "Travel round, go up the Cape, sit on a beach." He paused. "Just stay out of our way."

I gave a thin smile and stood up, heading for the door.

I was in shock. I expected one of them to lock the door before I got to it, some kind of psychological ploy, but as I left the room I was aware only of their stares of dislike and a growing sense of relief.

I was soon back on the streets of Boston, and after a couple of wrong turns I eventually worked out where I was. I caught the Red Line to Harvard, went back to my hotel, and had a long bath.

I needed it.

# Nine

I was startled awake by a light tapping on the door.

I glanced at the clock by the bed and saw that it was one thirty. Who the hell could it be at that time of the night? I'd only been back from the police station two hours, and I was whacked. The tapping continued.

I thought about the two policemen from earlier in the evening. It could be some sort of psychological ploy designed to grind me down, to get me out of the way of their investigation.

I thought about shouting out, to try and get a clue before I went to the door. I lay still. For a moment I could hear nothing. I tried to listen out for breathing, for a voice, a clue. The tapping had stopped. I wondered if it was just something from my dream, something my mind had carried on when I was awake. I rolled over and the rickety old bed creaked. The tapping started again.

I looked towards the window. There was a fire escape gantry running outside, and as I craned to look I saw that it led to metal stairs at the side of the building. I knew that whoever was outside knew I was in. They would have heard me moving about. In my half-sleep, it seemed a good idea to get out of the way, to go underground for a while. I was about to pull some trousers on and see if I could open the window, when I heard a familiar voice whisper, "Joe? Are you there, Joe?"

I jumped out of bed and opened the door a crack. When I saw who it was I felt relief: it was Katie. And she was alone.

I opened the door to let her in, not caring that I was only wearing boxer shorts and a t-shirt. As she came in, I noticed a worried look and a smell of alcohol. And she seemed upset.

"What is it?" I asked, worried.

Katie walked in to my room pre-occupied, her mind elsewhere.

"I'd just got back," she said, sounding strained.

My mind had jerked awake by now, and I shuffled into a pair of jeans I found by the bed. I turned the light on and noticed her eyes had red rims underneath, as if there had been tears.

"Whoa," I said, grabbing her by the arms. "What's wrong? What's happened?"

She wiped her eyes and took a huge breath, as if the concern had just tweaked open the floodgates slightly, but then appeared to steady herself.

"I'd just got back," she continued. "I'd been for a drink with some friends from class, and when I came in I found this posted through my door," and with that she pulled a folded piece of paper from her pocket. She passed it to me, and I sat on the bed by the light to look at it.

It was another letter from Sarah.

I looked up at Katie. "How long were you out for?"

She shrugged. "Not long. A couple of hours."

"Hand-delivered?"

She nodded.

"Have you asked around the neighbours? You know, did they see who delivered it? Did they hear anything?"

Katie shook her head. "I just came here when I saw it."

I looked at the letter. It had been hand-delivered. So she was still in the city.

I knew I had to read it, but at the same time, I didn't want to. I didn't know where it would take me. I'd had the warning from the police and I just wanted to let a sleeping head sort out the jumble, to see what it told me in the morning. If I read the letter, I knew I would keep on.

I looked at the letter again, and then back at Katie. She looked vulnerable, hurt, lonely.

I opened the letter and read it.

*"I have made contact with the devil. I have hurt that child. I have desired that child to look upon me and the child was tormented. I torment that child. I am not willing to mention the word God and I answer in a very wicked, spiteful manner.*

*I will and command you that you safely conduct the said Sarah Goode to the place of execution and there cause her to be hanged by the neck until she be dead and you are not to fail at your peril.*

*Sarah."*

My stomach lurched.

I put the letter down and rubbed my eyes. It felt like the whole situation was moving away from me. This confirmed the obvious,

93

that Katie had gone mad and killed Brad, but the obvious seemed incredible.

I looked at Katie. She looked near to tears. I went to her and held her. I felt a twinge of shame when I enjoyed the feel of her arms around me. It felt wrong, inappropriate.

"What does it all mean?" she said through tears. Her head was on my shoulder, my hand holding it there.

I didn't know the answers. It was all too obscure. It wasn't like looking through a mist, because I couldn't even see an outline. It was like looking into deep darkness.

"I don't know, I don't know," I replied softly, trying to be a comfort. "Sometimes trying to work out what things mean is too difficult. Sometimes it's just better to see it how it is."

"And how is it?"

I pulled away from her. I still had the letter in my hand. I sat down on the bed and tried to make sense of it all.

I read again the references to hurting *"that child"*.

Was she referring to Brad? Is that how she saw him? He was her child; she was in control. Or, at least, so she thought.

Or was Sarah that child, describing her own inner turmoil, battles between her good side and her bad side?

I strolled around the room, pulling at my lip, reading the letter. Maybe I was reading too much into the syntax? But I got the impression that the words must be important. Why else would they be so strangely constructed, the language used, the change from first person to third person?

I read the last paragraph again. A request to take her and hang her. No, not a request, an order: *"I will and command you."* And the warning that *"you are not to fail at your peril."* If Sarah wrote all this, has she recognised that she has done a bad thing and deserves to die? She can't bring herself to kill herself, but wants others to do the job for her. And by warning that to fail is to fail at peril, she is saying the task must be carried out. And if it isn't, will more bad deeds follow? What is the peril?

I sighed and ran my hand through my hair. I was being paid to find her and give her a credit card, not chase down her demons and deliver her to her own judgement day.

"Well?" Katie asked. "What do you think?"

94

I didn't know what to say. I wasn't really sure what I thought. But the look of helplessness on her face made me tell her how I saw it.

"It sounds like a confession," I said, with tinges of regret. "Another one, from a woman who is having serious mental problems. And a suicide note. She wants to die, but she wants us to do it for her. If we don't, shit happens. If Sarah wrote this, and you think she did, she has gone."

Katie nodded solemnly, as if I had just confirmed what she had been thinking on the way over. She looked at me. "Can we get her back, bring her back from wherever she has gone to?"

I shrugged my shoulders and smiled. "Who knows? But, I suppose we can try."

I was pleased to see her smile.

"It is her handwriting," she said, looking at the floor. The smile disappeared again. "Poor Sarah," she said sadly, simply. "What are we going to do?"

I stood up and held her again.

"We'll do something," I promised, "and that's what counts." I knew what this meant now. It meant that I couldn't leave it alone, as I'd told the police I would. It meant I would contrive to spend more time with Katie. It meant Sarah was in grave danger.

Katie was shaking her head. "I just don't accept this," she was saying. "It just isn't her. That's what keeps me going, the knowledge that there is something more to this. If it had been that simple, I would have seen the signs."

I just smiled. If it was only that simple.

"One thing bothers me," I said. Katie looked up. "Why tell us? It doesn't make sense. If she wants to die, why tell us? Why not just do it?"

"Perhaps it's a cry for help," Katie said. "Isn't that what they say, that self-harm is a form of self-publicity, a plea for understanding? Maybe she wants me to find her, and she is scared, so she tells me what she intends to do."

I shook my head. "I don't go with that. If she's making a cry for help, she doesn't give away many clues. This is a big city, and there is nothing here that would hint at her location. No, it's something more than a cry for help. Look at the language used. Take it from an Englishman that this is not normal spoken English. *'Until she be dead.'* It sounds historical, some kind of Tudor-speak, or later. You're the historian. What does it say to you?"

Katie shook her head. "I don't know. Perhaps that's where the message is? Perhaps I'm supposed to work out where it's from, and then that will remind me of something?"

"What period of history do you study?"

"The modern histories," she said. "You know, the 60's, the Kennedy's, that kind of thing. This letter doesn't remind me of anyone or anything. It just sounds like a suicide note from a very disturbed person."

I nodded grimly. "There's just one thing I'm going to have to do then."

"What's that?"

"Go see Professor Lowenski again, first thing in the morning. Whether it lands me in the County Jail or not."

Katie looked puzzled at the last remark but nodded that she agreed.

"Will you do one more thing for me?" Katie asked.

"Yes, anything."

She looked bashful and nervous for a moment. "Move into my apartment. This was hand-posted. Sarah may have keys. If she wrote this and she thinks I've betrayed her, I am in danger. If someone else wrote it, I am in grave danger."

I didn't have to think about it for long. I forgot my concerns about her in the police station, that she may be a suspect. The tearful woman who was standing in my hotel room didn't seem a threat. She seemed vulnerable, alone, and I wanted to be there for her.

I grabbed my coat, pushed clothes and my toothbrush into a bag, and we headed out into the night. I would check out and collect the rest of my things the next day.

We wandered towards Harvard Square, through a dark and deserted Harvard Yard. The trees blew softly in the night's breeze and I wondered what sounds Sarah could hear. Was it the same breeze, or was she overwhelmed by the noise of her own thoughts and guilt? White noise, screaming through her? I looked at Katie. We hadn't said much since leaving my hotel, and I wondered what sounds she could hear. Was it the breeze too, or was she replaying the final days of her time with Sarah, searching for some hint, some sign that something was not right?

As we left Harvard Yard, we hailed a cab, and as we were getting near to Katie's apartment, I finished telling her about the events at the police station. She didn't say much. I finished by telling her that Jimmy Walsh must have called the police. I told her he had spotted me.

Katie smiled at that. She'd forgotten to tell me, there was never a chance, that he had spotted me on Boston Common, rushing around with a camera. Katie had tried to persuade him that I was probably just a tourist, but Jimmy had said he would waste my time for a while. He thought I was probably a reporter, trying to do a report on Sarah's friends.

As we clambered out of the taxi, I was laughing. The whole day's endeavours had been shot to pieces at the start, but I hadn't realised.

As we climbed the steps to Katie's building, I remembered about her trips round the local courts. I asked her if she had found anything out. She shook her head. "No, nothing doing, although I think I prefer that answer."

Back at square one.

We were soon in Katie's apartment, and I wondered where I would be sleeping. This was answered when Katie came from her room holding a duvet and pillow. It was the couch again. She gave me a finger wave and a smile before she went to her room, and I was left in the dark with just my thoughts and doubts for company.

I thought about the letter again. There was something I wasn't seeing. It had to mean more than what it appeared to say. If the first letter was a confession, why make it so crazy? And if the second one was a suicide note, why not just say that? Katie was right: a suicide note can just be a request to stop the suicide. But if that was the case here, then why not give some clues? Why be so damn cryptic?

I began to work my way through the options. There were only two: it was either a suicide note or it wasn't. It was either a confession or it wasn't.

If it was a confession, why not be clearer? If it was a suicide note, why be so damn mysterious about it?

So if it wasn't a suicide note or a confession, what was it? And what did the first letter mean? If it wasn't a suicide note or a confession, it must be some sign, some pointer to where all the answers lay.

I tried to think like a lawyer. I could only find the answers to the riddles if I was analytical, tried to work through the options. All a defence lawyer does is try and explain accepted facts in a different way, see if they can point to a different conclusion. The defendant might be identified, but how good was the lighting, was it based on just a fleeting glimpse? Could forensic analysis point to other explanations? Can the forensic evidence be as foolproof as it seems?

I tried to imagine that I was defending Sarah, and that the letters were evidence in the case. What would I do first?

I smiled into the darkness; the answer was obvious. I would ask for proof that Sarah had written them. That would be the first hurdle for the Prosecution: you say my client wrote the incriminating letters: you prove it. I only had Katie's opinion that it looked like her handwriting. Could it be forged?

I put to one side any thoughts of why anyone would want to forge the letters and went to Katie's room. It was my turn to knock lightly.

I heard Katie shuffle her way to the door.

"Do you think you'd be able to do me a copy?" I asked when Katie's face emerged. "You are going to have to give the original to the police. Can you copy it like the other one?"

"You've got the copy," said Katie. "I thought you would tell me to hand it into the police, and if I did, I didn't think it would help you if your fingerprints came up on it." She pointed at the piece of paper I was holding. "I ran that off earlier. The original is in a drawer."

I could have kissed her. I smiled instead. It hadn't occurred to me what the police would do if my prints were all over it, the prints of the mysterious Englishman sent over by her parents to find Sarah before the police did.

"So you've got this image saved on your computer?"

Katie nodded.

"Good. I just thought of something. Can I use your telephone?"

Katie pointed towards the telephone. England would be five hours ahead, with people sat around breakfast tables.

I was very quickly listening to the two-ring tone of an English telephone.

"Hello," came the response, surprisingly clear. It sounded like she was in the room next door.

"Lucy? Hi, it's Joe. I'm glad I caught you before you went to work. Can you get hold of a handwriting expert from Manchester? Lloyd Chatwin? Get me his phone number. He'll be in that directory of experts you keep."

"Why? What's all this about?"

"Look, he owes me a couple of favours. Just tell him Joe Kinsella is calling one in, and it's urgent. Get his e-mail address and tell him I need something doing today. You'll need to fax him some documents as well."

"Like what?"

"Like copies of letters you're going to collect on the way to work and fax to him," and I gave her the address of Sarah's parents. "This is urgent, Lucy, it needs doing today. No, it needs doing this morning, first thing. Get me Lloyd Chatwin's e-mail address and ring me back. Is that okay?"

"Yeah, yeah," Lucy said, "I'll leave now. Oh, by the way?"

"Yeah?"

"I'm fine. Thanks for asking?"

I laughed and blew her a loud kiss.

I gave her Katie's phone number and was about to hang up when I heard her say, "Joe?"

"Yeah?" I answered.

"This is an international number. Where the hell are you?"

"It's a long story," and with that I hung up.

I smiled to myself. It was good still to have contacts in the legal profession. I did a lot of work for Lucy's clients. I didn't think she would mind helping me out just the once.

I sat down next to Katie. She was sat at one end, her knees drawn up to her chest. She hadn't bothered getting dressed. She was huddled in a t-shirt and knickers, not bothered about covering up.

"We've got a long night ahead," I said. "Are you sure you feel up to it?"

"No, I don't think I am, but I've gotta do it." She spoke quietly, thoughtfully.

Lloyd Chatwin is a handwriting expert. I'd used him in some fraud cases when I was still a lawyer and his findings seemed reliable, certainly juries thought so, and many acquittals were won on the back of his evidence.

Katie leant her head on my shoulder and interrupted my train of thought. I felt myself tighten. I sat as still as I could, and within minutes she was breathing lightly, dozing peacefully. I wanted to kiss her asleep, just once, a peck on her forehead, a comforter. I made do with a smile.

Despite my best efforts, I joined her in light slumber, only to be awakened by a long ring. In my half-sleep I thought it was on the television, an unfamiliar dial tone, heard only in films, one long ring, pause, one long ring. I realised then that it was Katie's phone, and I remembered my plan. I leapt for the phone, leaving Katie sprawling on the sofa. As I heard Lucy's voice, I smiled an apology at Katie and felt pleased when she smiled back.

I put the phone down. Lloyd Chatwin had an e-mail number, he would do whatever I wanted, and he would try and get it done in the next few hours. We were blessed by the time difference; we might have all the information we needed before daylight hit Boston.

The e-mail was sent, the copy of the letter sent with it.

"All done," she said, sounding tired. "Can we go to sleep now?" She gave a weary smile. It was four fifteen. Katie looked tired. Those dancing eyes had gone dull, her face drawn and pale.

"Yes, go to sleep," I said, and this time I did lean forward and I kissed her lightly on the forehead. It seemed right. She smiled and patted me thank you on my cheek.

I returned to my sofa and tried to get back the sleep I'd found before Katie had knocked on my door.

# Ten

My back creaked when I woke up and the light shining through the window made me wince.

I couldn't hear anyone else in the apartment. I glanced at the clock. Nine-thirty. Then I saw a handwritten note: *"Gone for a run (Nickerson field, if you fancy it). Back around ten-thirty. Help yourself to breakfast. Katie."*

I didn't fancy it. I hadn't been for a run for two years. When I'd first moved back to Morsby, I used to run along the sea-front. It was a straight mile and a half, flat black tarmac and a sea-breeze, but the first winter back home killed it off. The winds cut too much and the rain blew in so hard it made my legs raw. I took to a good breakfast instead. It showed.

But then I thought about Katie, took a look outside at the sunshine, and decided it would have some therapeutic value. I dived into my bag looking for a pair of running shoes, I knew I'd packed something comfortable, donned a pair of jogging pants, checked the map, and headed out.

It didn't take me long to get to Nickerson Field. It sits in a side street, part of the University campus, near the river and just away from the build-up of traffic on Commonwealth Avenue.

Nickerson Field isn't really a field, not in the real sense. A field to me is grass and wild flowers and pollen blown by a breeze. This was an athletic track and a football field, with seats and a brick building fronting it, twin-gabled and a row of arches. But I suppose Fenway Park isn't a park, not in the sense that I knew it anyway.

I wandered behind the frontage and by the side of the bleachers. I came out into the sun and was faced by the vivid green of an artificial football field and the false red of the athletics track. Traffic flowed behind it, over a road bridge, and the morning peace was broken by the impatient bleating of car horns.

And then I saw Katie.

She was running gently around the track, on the opposite side of the field to me. Her blonde hair was tied back by a black clasp, so that her ponytail swished and bobbed behind her in time to her steps. Black cycle shorts hugged her closely and a short black vest both pushed her out and kept her in. As she ran, I could see her stomach glistening with sweat and the muscles in her legs defined and redefined themselves with each step.

As she ran, I felt out of shape. I would have to do something about that. She looked young, in trim, beautiful. Maybe a run wasn't a great idea.

I turned and began to shuffle away, but then I heard her shout, "Joe? Is that you, Joe?"

I turned around and saw that she had made it around the curve and was now by the fence below the seats. I smiled and waved and began a slow saunter down to meet her.

As I reached the bottom, she had reached into her bag and was pressing a towel to her face. We met over a low concrete wall.

"Hi," I said, somewhat meekly.

She laughed.

Sweat was dropping off her chin and her cheeks were flushed exertion red. I glanced towards her naked stomach, and saw that it was washboard flat. I looked back up again and saw stray blonde hairs stuck to her forehead. She lifted a bottle of water to her lips and brushed the hairs away with her spare hand. When she had finished drinking, she looked at me and smiled.

I melted.

She reached her hand out and put it gently on my stomach. "You can stop holding it in, if you want."

I hadn't noticed I was, but as I looked down, I could see the front of my t-shirt flapping in the breeze, held in place by soft golden fingers.

I looked up again and our eyes clashed. I think she held my gaze for a moment, but then she gave my stomach a playful pat and wiped her face once more.

"It makes you more real," she said quietly, and her smile was broken by a soft bite on her bottom lip as she spoke, all coy and young.

One of those moments had taken place, when we'd each taken a step over the barrier that divides friendship and intimacy, but I felt myself stepping back. I should have stepped forward, come up with a devastating remark, or a touch that tumbled her into my arms, but I didn't. I gave a half-smile and looked around.

"Do you come here often?" I asked.

Katie giggled. "Good line."

I laughed and nodded. I ruffled my hair. "Sometimes they work."

Katie put the towel down and turned away from me.

"C'mon," she said. "Let's run."

I watched her set off at a slow canter. I thought about it for a moment, before clambering over the wall and setting off after her. By the time I caught her, she'd slowed to a slow jog. She looked across and smiled, and then looked forward again.

"Good field for a college," I said, for want of anything else to say.

"It's an old baseball field," she said, as we rounded the bend and onto the back strait. "Boston Braves. Used to be in the Majors.

I looked around. "What happened," I asked between deep breaths, "not popular enough?"

She shook her head. "Worse than that," she said. "They left town."

We carried along the back strait and started the bend. I didn't feel too bad. My lungs had found a rhythm and the pace was slow enough for my legs.

"What are you hoping for?" I asked, puffing lightly. "Out of all this mess, what do you think would be a good outcome?"

Katie didn't answer for around one hundred metres, and I thought I had upset her, but as we came off the back strait and into the bend, she said quietly, "that depends on Sarah. If she killed Brad, I hope she is caught. I want to know what brought it on, why nobody warned us."

"And if she didn't do it?"

Katie gave a half smile. She didn't have to say anything. She didn't really believe there was another answer.

We continued our run in silence. I managed another lap before the lure of her water bottle became too great. I sauntered off the back bend and leant against the wall, wiping my face with her towel. When she joined me, I held up my hand in friendly apology and passed her the towel. She took a long deep breath and pressed her face into it.

"You can't really change a person," she said quietly, "not inside. A good person stays good. A bad person stays bad. I just want to know which one Sarah was."

I looked at her, panting. "We'll try and find out."

"Do you know what I want, more than anything?"

I caught her eyes. "Tell me."

She took a deep breath. "For Sarah to stop being important. Just for life to be normal again."

I nodded. I understood.

Katie smiled and began to walk up the steps away from the track.

"We'll do this again," I said.

"You bet."

Sarah lay as still as the silence that had gathered around her when the door opened.

She counted. The door opened, a pause. Then footsteps entered the room. One, two, then three. Then the pause, and then a small metallic clink as the tray went to the floor. Then the small grunt as he straightened himself.

Sarah felt her spirits lift. She had been counting. Three seconds, that's what she figured. Three full seconds from the third step landing and the end of him straightening himself. Could she do it? Could she get from the bed to him in three seconds without him reacting?

Sarah felt depression smother her once again. Of course she couldn't. He would whirl around at the first rustle of the sheets, would be ready for her before her feet hit the floor. She could always just try and use the full element of surprise. His mind might not react to what his eyes were telling him, that his captive was turning captor, that she was trying to trap his head in her sheet.

Sarah realised that the door hadn't closed, which meant he was still in the room. She turned over slowly, peeping over the blanket. Yes, he was there, watching her.

"Enjoy your trip?" he asked mockingly. And then he began to laugh, a raucous noise echoing around the steel confines like a roulette ball.

Sarah sat up, letting the blanket fall to the ground.

"Why did you do that?" she asked quietly, almost politely.

He smirked. "It livened things up for a while."

He didn't seem to be in a rush to leave.

"Why are you doing this?" Sarah asked, gesturing around the steel walls. "Why are you holding me like this? I've done nothing to you."

He walked over to the bed slowly. Sarah scuttled back onto the mattress, tried to sink back into the wall. He stood at the side of the bed and smiled malevolently. He reached forward and tried to stroke her hair. Sarah backed away, frightened.

He snatched his hand out and grabbed a handful of hair. He pulled her head to the bed and knelt down. Sarah screamed in pain. His hand strained as he pulled her hair tighter against her head, Sarah's hands flailed at his, trying to break free, crying out.

He put his mouth to her ear and whispered, "I do it because I like it." And then he kissed her lobe gently, catching it between his teeth, nibbling gently.

Sarah froze. She didn't like the overtones. She had dreaded this moment. She had wondered since her capture whether they were going to use her, and expected it. But now it was in the here and now, she froze, her breath catching, revulsion coursing through her.

He stood up and stepped away from the bed.

"Enjoy the food," he said, laughing. "It will be the last for a few days."

And then he left the room, leaving Sarah holding her stomach with one hand, the other trying to wipe the remnants of him from her ear.

Then she rushed up and ran to the toilet, just making it before she vomited.


"You've got mail."

It was an electronic voice, so I knew it could only be one thing: it was the computer speaking through Katie's open door, and she had turned the volume up to make sure we heard it. I glanced at the clock. It was ten-forty. It would be afternoon in England.

Katie strolled from the kitchen, still towelling her hair, wet from the shower. I followed, trying not to barge into her bedroom.

"There you go," she said, and moved out of the way to let me see the screen.

I scrolled through the document and smiled. Lloyd had dressed it up like a professional. Placing of signature, margins, matching zone characteristics. But it all said one thing: it matched. Sarah had written the letters.

I turned round to Katie. "We've got a match."

Katie nodded and then reached for her hair dryer. She hung her hair down to dry it and looked away. I knew what she was doing. She was hiding in the noise. She was beginning to seem laden down, showing shades of vulnerability, as if she was slowly wearing down, becoming threadbare. And I knew what she was thinking: knowing who wrote them doesn't make it clearer about what they mean.

I left her to her own thoughts for a while, before she shouted above the noise of the dryer, "what do we do now?"

"You take the original to the police," I said. "Don't make concealing evidence another problem. Tell them everything you know, but don't mention that you've seen me or that I have seen the letter. Particularly don't mention Lloyd's opinion."

"So you mean don't tell them anything I know? Just be a good girl and play messenger?"

I shrugged an apology. "I know, I'm sorry. I'm not quite ready to go home yet, but the police may disagree."

"What are you going to do then?" Katie asked.

"Just see what Professor Lowenski thinks. I want his opinion on the wording of the letters. If it does have some historical significance, he may be able to tell us. Sarah must be saying something in these letters, but I can't think what. It's old-fashioned language and Sarah is a historian so there might be a connection. And if he can't see it, the hidden hint must be so far hidden that it can't be a message to us from Sarah. It may be exactly what it appears to be: a suicide note."

"Is that what you call leaving well alone?" she said smiling. "I'm not surprised the police want you on the next plane." When I simply smiled back, she asked, "meet you at lunchtime?"

I smiled again. Why not?

*        *        *        *

I stood outside Professor Lowenski's office. I listened at the door and I could hear faint singing, but it consisted of words I couldn't make out and the occasional curse that I could. I wondered whether he was tidying up. I hoped he wasn't; it would leave him with little time to deal with me.

I knocked lightly. I heard the singing stop and all went quiet. I knocked again, and within seconds the door flew open and I found myself again looking at that tangle of grey hair and long limbs.

He looked at me blankly.

"Good morning Professor Lowenski," I ventured. "I hope I haven't disturbed you."

A look of recognition flickered across his eyes. "Ah, my English friend, good morning to you too. Come in, come in." And with that he stood aside, and I saw instantly that he hadn't been tidying up. If anything, it was worse. His desk had attracted more open books and I saw that the small sofa held a blanket and pillow.

I looked at him. His hair was pointing skyward and his shirt looked like he'd been wrestling in it.

"I hope I haven't come at a difficult time," I said. It looked like I'd arrived in the middle of a domestic crisis.

"No, no," he said loudly, shoving me towards a footstool positioned in the corner. "Make yourself comfortable. I'm working on a thesis and I found myself working late."

"What's the thesis on?" I asked.

"Oh, I couldn't say," he said. "Academia is like the fashion world: it's not what you say that counts, it's saying it first."

"And you think I might steal your theory?" I asked.

He laughed. "Of course not, but loose talk is dangerous on this campus."

I smiled.

"The question is, what can I do for you?" he asked.

"I'm hoping you can help me on something," I said.

His look darkened. "Oh, I don't know if I should. Aren't the police still involved?"

I nodded. "The police will always be involved." I pulled out the copies of the letters sent by Sarah and passed them to him. "I just want you to cast your mind over these," I said, "if you have time, that is."

He looked at the paper with distaste, but I could sense an irresistible urge to open the folds and see what had brought me to his office again. I watched him sway like willow in the wind. He was reluctant to get involved, but he had a natural inquisitiveness, wanted to know what it was all about.

"What are they?" he asked quietly. He looked at them, but not at what they contained, as if it would somehow spoil a big surprise.

"They were sent by Sarah to Katie, her flat-mate. I would like your views, if you don't mind that is."

"Do the police know about these?" He handled them now as if they had just burst into flames.

"Yes. Katie is taking the most recent one to the police this morning."

"Do the police know that you have copies?"

"I told Katie to be honest with them," I said, which was more than I was being with Professor Lowenski, speaking in half-truths.

"Why do you think I can help?" he asked, whilst starting to slowly open the copies, his eyes not yet glancing downwards, but his hands unable to resist the temptation to look.

"It's the language used," I said. "I don't know, but it's just not modern English. It feels old, but I can't work out why Sarah would write anything using language like that. I know she was an historian, and Katie thinks it might be a sign, a hint as to where she is, but I'm not too sure."

"If it is a sign," the professor said warily, almost dropping the pieces of paper, "I'm not sure I should be helping you. What if you go and help her leave the country? I'll be an accessory to that. Oh, I don't feel good about this, Mr Kinsella. I don't feel good." He put the letters on the desk and started to run his fingers through his hair, and then he tutted as his long fingers became knotted in his locks. "No, no, this isn't good, not good at all."

"It won't put you at risk to at least read them, would it? What if Sarah is in danger? What if this will help get her out of danger? How will you feel if you have done nothing to help?" I paused, and Professor Lowenski didn't have a response. "Just read them and tell me what you think, that's all I ask."

He looked at me, his curiosity visibly bending his will. He still said nothing, but he did reach for glasses that were lying across open textbooks on his desk and picked up the letters. He gave me another look, took a deep breath, and then opened the folded copies.

He read silently, and then his forehead creased in puzzled furrows. He read them again. "H'mm," he said, "I see what you mean."

He took his glasses off and twirled them in his hand.

"What do you think?" I asked hopefully. "Does anything spring to mind?"

The professor put his glasses back on the desk and studied me. I'm not sure if he was checking for signs of madness or just thinking about his response, but I could tell something had occurred to him.

"There is something," he said eventually, "although it might be just coincidence. It is something I thought of when Sarah first came here. I think I may have even teased her about it. It's not really my field of expertise, but I'm sure it would occur to most historians, serious historians, in this part of world."

"What is it?" I asked. My curiosity was beginning to spill over into impatience, fuelled by a lack of sleep and the threat of police attention. "Just tell me, please."

"No, no," he said, shaking his head, "it's ridiculous." He stood up and walked over to his window. He stood looking out, but I could tell he wasn't seeing anything; except a jumble of thoughts trying to slot into order. "Why would it have anything to do with anything?" he muttered. "No, no." He was clearly talking to himself.

"What is it Professor Lowenski?"

He looked at me blankly, his mind still occupying his energies.

"Whatever has occurred to you, it is more than I have. I do not know what this all means, and I don't even know where to start looking." I realised I'd caught his attention again. "I've been in Boston a few days, and so far all I've gained is a closeness to Sarah's flat-mate I didn't expect, an insight into baseball, and an arrest and threat from the Boston Police Department. If you can tell me anything that will point me in a new direction, whether wrong or not, I will be eternally grateful."

He whirled round at that. "What happened with the police?" he asked. He looked suddenly serious, perturbed.

"Is it important?" I asked.

"You are a guest in this country. I would hope you were treated with courtesy. These things do concern me."

I told him of my arrest and treatment in detention. He didn't look amused. I thought I even detected a moment of resolve. "So much for the 'special relationship'," I said bitterly.

He sighed, and then said, "I'm sorry about that, Mr Kinsella."

"You've nothing to be sorry for, professor." I tried to get his attention back onto the letters. "You were about to tell me what the letters reminded you of."

"That's right, that's right," he said. He paused, and then asked, "have you ever heard of the Salem witch trials?"

I looked blank.

"1692," he continued. "Young girls in Salem, about thirty miles north of here, accused many local people of witchcraft. The local judiciary took them seriously, and many people were imprisoned, many were killed."

"I think I've heard something about it," I said, scratching my head, "but where does this tie in with Sarah?"

He smiled. "Sarah Goode might be an attractive young English student, but she has a namesake. Oh, the spelling is slightly different, but it is essentially the same."

I was leaning forward now. I knew whatever was coming might be something important.

"Sarah Good," he continued, "was a Salem witch, one of the first to be accused, if I remember my history correctly."

I was shocked. And amused. A witch? Must be coincidence. My mind filled with pointed hats and broomsticks.

He caught my look. "I said it was stupid."

I thought about it and realised he was right. It sounded irrelevant, an amusing coincidence, but he had warned me it did. "But why do you think of it now?" I asked. "You knew before her name was the same as a historical witch, so why does it seem more relevant now?"

"It's just the wording of the letters. The language used wouldn't be unheard of at the end of the seventeenth century." He paused and looked at me. "They remind me of something."

I leant forward, curious.

"Legal documents," he continued, passing me the first letter sent by Sarah. "The Salem witch trials were legal trials in a very real sense. People gave evidence, judges presided, sentences were passed. And how do you think the proceedings were commenced?"

I shrugged. I didn't know.

110

Professor Lowenski smiled. "People who thought they were being bewitched by these wretched women filed a petition making their allegations. Arrest warrants would then be issued on the strength of those petitions. Look at that letter," and he pointed at the first letter. "It sounds like an allegation, like a petition. I've seen a few old trial documents, and that has the look of one."

I read Sarah's first letter again:

*"They said Sarah Goode was of so turbulent a spirit, spiteful and so maliciously bent, that her detractors could not suffer her to live in their house any longer. Ever since these detractors turned her out of their house she has behaved herself so crossly and maliciously. She must kill somebody with a knife. If you take her life away, God will give you blood to drink."*

I wasn't convinced. "It sounds more like a comment on fact and then a threat."

He raised an eyebrow. "What do you think a petition is? It's a simple allegation, a comment on fact."

He looked at Sarah's second letter, the one delivered the previous day, and then passed it over to me. "Read that one," he said.

I read it again.

"Look at the second paragraph."

I did.

*"I will and command you that you safely conduct the said Sarah Goode to the place of execution and there cause her to be hanged by the neck until she be dead and you are not to fail at your peril."*

I looked at him expectantly.

"That sounds like the passing of a death sentence, or even a warrant. I don't know what the first paragraph means, but that sounds like a sentence of death."

He looked thoughtful again. "I find this most unsettling," he said. He looked at his lap for what seemed like the whole morning, although it was probably no more than a minute, before saying, "will you leave these with me?"

"Of course, of course," I said, "that's why I brought them to you. What are you going to do?"

111

"I'm going to look into this, see if I can find anything out. Can I call you later?"

"Yeah sure."

"I didn't know anything about these letters," he said. "It might have helped."

I shrugged. "There was no reason why you should."

He nodded, and I seemed to lose him as he retreated to somewhere not in that room.

I sat there for a further five minutes before I realised I was expected to leave. I think he thought I had done, he'd just stared into space for most of that time, so I made to go to the door, remembered he didn't have my number and so I scrawled Katie's phone number on a piece of paper and put it on his desk, and then made my way out of his room.

The corridor was busier now, students heading to lectures, all textbooks and earnest looks, but my mind was elsewhere. About thirty miles away, to be precise.

I sat on Boston Common some time later with a cream cheese bagel, a large Coke, and a busy mind.

I'd already dismissed what Professor Lowenski had said. Witches? It was ludicrous. I couldn't think how it would fit into what I knew about Sarah. Everything I had heard about her made her seem like a normal young student: studied hard, played when she could, and just enjoyed life. It made absolutely no sense.

Even though I thought it was nonsense, I had left Professor Lowenski's office and gone straight to the library. It niggled me. Something unsettled me, and it was tap-tap-tapping away at the back of my head. I knew I had to dismiss it before I carried on.

I'd spent a couple of hours skimming through books, and now I was sat on a bench on the Common, bespeckled with the beginnings of afternoon rain waiting for Katie. A strong breeze had picked up and my Coke was acquiring rings as it rocked on the bench. I could feel ancient oaks rustling around me, and shoppers and tourists rushed along the paths to get away from the impending storm. As I looked over towards the Charles Street corner I saw

Katie trotting along, her jacket pulled across her chest and her bag held in front of her to stop the wind blowing it open. When she saw me she gave a wide smile.

As she got closer she said, "hi Joe, sorry I got you to meet me outdoors. I thought it was going to stay dry."

"That's no problem. Coming from England, I've got used to the rain. Do you want to go and get something to eat? My lunch was losing its appeal with the weather change."

"Sure. I know a great little place just up Charles Street from here. Does that sound alright?"

"If I'm with you," I said jokily, "it sounds perfect." And I was pleased to see her laugh.

We wandered up Charles Street together, past art shops and coffee bars. The close-knit brick paving was slippery due to rain and the trees brushed water onto my clothes, but I didn't mind. The streets seemed less frantic here, shoppers browsed rather than rushed, and I enjoyed Katie pointing things out to me. The purple windows, the narrow side streets, the more bohemian feel.

We ended up outside a wooden-fronted bar with pale ale and Guinness signs in the window.

"I thought you might be getting homesick, so I thought you'd like to come to an English-style bar," said Katie.

As we went in I noticed the beer mats and the dartboard, but elsewhere a long, wooden bar glowed with polish, high stools pushed against it. A young man with shoulder length hair and a surfing t-shirt was cleaning glasses at one of the bar and when he saw us he wandered over. It seemed very American.

"Hiya, you guys, what can I get you?"

"Two chillies with cheese, and two Sam Adams," Katie said with some authority.

"You've got it," he responded, and with that he wandered off to arrange our lunch.

I sat next to Katie at the bar. "How was your morning?" I asked, just as our beers arrived. It had been agreed that she would take the letter to Lieutenant Cornwell in the afternoon, there'd been lectures in the morning, but dinner with me was offered first, and I accepted.

"Oh, you know, the usual," she replied. "It's funny, but just as we seem to spend all our time talking about Sarah, it's only now that people at college have stopped asking me how I'm doing. Like enough time has passed for things to be normal again, you know, the way these things move off the front pages."

"Is that good?"

"Sure it's good. As I've said, this tragedy didn't really happen to me. I'm not the one that was killed, and I'm not the one who has disappeared. Although I pray nothing bad has happened to Sarah, I want things to be normal again. I'll have exams shortly and I've assignments to complete. I found this tragedy, but I'm not part of it, and I want my life to go back to normal; there's a lot of it left."

"But will you still help me?" I asked. "I don't want to lose a sidekick."

"Sure I'll help you," she replied, tapping me playfully on the arm, "but I just want other things in my life to carry on happening." She paused to take a pull at her beer. "So why don't we start today, start over, and talk about us as people, rather than us as bit-players in someone else's drama?"

I clinked my glass against hers. "That sounds just fine." I didn't think that. These conversations always end up as an outpouring of problems, or the confessions of sins for which absolution was long since granted. But it was Katie's conversation and I didn't want to persuade her away from that.

"You start," she said.

I shrugged my shoulders. "Where?"

"How about what led you to become a private detective?"

I smiled and sighed. "Now, that is a sordid tale. Are you sure you want to hear it?"

She nodded and smiled.

"I used to be a lawyer," I said simply.

Her eyes widened. People always seemed impressed, although I've never really worked out why. A law degree hadn't seemed particularly hard, certainly no harder than I imagined an English degree or history degree to be, and the rest was just following the natural route from college to job. But for some reason, it still commanded respect.

"I was struck off for attacking a client," I continued, "so I became a private detective. It's as simple as that."

Katie looked aghast, so I spent ten minutes as we waited for our chilli giving her the rundown on my fall from grace. I tried to paint myself as the victim, but I could never get away from the fact that I'd fucked up my career choice.

"Are you happier now?"

"Than when?" I asked. "Than before I messed up, or after?"

"Before, I guess."

I took a drink of beer. "I don't know. I like the lack of complications, the freedom to choose, but I miss the money and prestige. And it feels like I should still want more. At thirty-five it seems like I've settled for what my life has become, and that disappoints me. But at the same time, I've got everything I wanted when I was a lawyer. I've got plenty of free time, and I don't worry about what people think of me."

"Do you really not care what other people think of you?"

I thought about my answer, about the way I always wanted to say to people that I used to be a lawyer, but then had to stop myself because there wasn't a happy ending.

"Yes, I probably do," I conceded.

"That's sad." She cocked her head and looked thoughtful for a moment. "If it helps, I think it makes you interesting. But the question is really, what do you think of yourself?"

That was a harder question. Introspection was never a good thing, particularly if you knew the answers weren't likely to be favourable. I knew it was time to hide behind the English reserve. "I think I'm a private detective in a beautiful little town by the sea, and I'm happy with that."

Just then the bowls of chilli arrived and I was able to lose my cross-examination in the food. It went well with the beer, and I'd been eating for a while before I realised I hadn't asked Katie anything.

"Where do you see your life going?" I asked.

Katie paused for a moment. "I just want to get beyond this semester. There are too many issues to resolve to think too far ahead."

I nodded silently, trying to show empathy. I couldn't have any idea what she was going through. I'd never seen a dead body in my life, never mind discovered a bloodied corpse within the walls of my own home, so I did have difficulty knowing how she must be coping.

"How about friends?" I asked. "If you don't mind me saying, you seem something of a loner."

Katie shook her head and gave a small laugh. "No, no. I like to think I've plenty of friends, although sometimes it doesn't seem that way. Since Brad was found, people have been reluctant to call round. There was some ghoulishness at first, folks wanting to see the death scene, but now people have backed off. The shock has died down so people are only left with doubts and concern. The apartment is now the place not to be seen in. But I have friends from class, and I know people in bars. I get by."

A natural pause arrived and we both carried on eating, but I watched her. I saw her eyes occasionally go distant, her spoon sometimes go still, and I could tell she was a little bit lost, perhaps hanging on for the summer when she could go back to Wichita where her daddy would protect her. Next semester would come and all this would be forgotten. Perhaps a new apartment, perhaps even a longer stay in Wichita, although I thought I detected a will to not let this thing beat her.

I had to get her back onto Sarah. I needed her help, and if she agreed, we would get to spend the afternoon together. I knew I could do things without her help, but you have to seize your chances when they arrive.

"I saw Professor Lowenski this morning."

She looked at me interested.

"He had some interesting information."

"Go on," she said quietly.

I wiped my mouth with a napkin. "Sarah shares the same name as one of the Salem witches."

Katie looked faintly amused. "As a piece of historical trivia, I'm sure it made for an interesting conversation, but you'll need more than a magic spell to find her."

"He also told me that he thought the two letters sent by Sarah sounded like legal documents, the sort they would have used in the witch trials."

"It means nothing." Katie dismissed it with a wave of the hand, but her eyes flickered something deeper. The amusement wavered, and I thought the flicker was of someone who had just seen the bigger picture that she hadn't been able to see before, like a child who takes her nose from the mirror and takes a proper look at herself.

"Why did the professor think it was relevant?"

I watched her. "I'm not sure that he did."

"1692," she said, looking worried. "1692. The year of the witch trials in Salem. It would fit in with the type of language used. It

116

sounded like it was from that era. I should have thought of it before."

"But it's not your period. Why should you have known?"

"Because I've been to Salem, I've been to the Witch Museum, with Sarah. We had a couple of days off from class and it was Halloween, so we thought it would be fun to go to Salem, because of the witch thing. We had a look round, did the tourist thing, spotted her name around. We ragged her, played around over a few drinks, you know, making ghoulish noises and fooling around. I can't believe I didn't think of it when I got the letters."

I narrowed my eyes. Had the letters been a sign? Were they referring to somewhere they'd been together, where I'd still be able to find her? "Who went? You said 'we' ragged her?"

"Oh, just Sarah and me, and a couple of guys from class. And Jimmy Walsh. He was starting to hang around then, and he came along for the ride." Katie became thoughtful. "Now I look back, I think it may have been Jimmy who suggested it. That's right, we were sat in a coffee shop on Newbury Street, talking about Halloween, when he said Salem was supposed to be fun, you know, with the witch connection. It was about the only good idea he ever had. We had a few beers that day and had a good time. It was great, a cool day."

"Was Salem anything special? Do you think she may be sending you secret messages? You know, 'I'm in Salem'?"

Katie shook her head. "No. It's a nice town, things to see, but we just went to the museums and a couple of bars and came back. We ended the night on Boylston, like we always did, but it was fun. No, if she was trying to send me secret messages, she did too good a job. Like the name, it could just be coincidence."

I nodded in agreement.

"Katie, I need you to do me a favour, to help me out."

"How?"

"Get me into the college library. I've got a couple of ideas I'd like to look into."

"Sure. Do you want any help? I have no more classes today. Lieutenant Cornwell can wait."

I smiled. I was glad she asked.

117

# Eleven

Katie and I decided what to do as we finished our beers.

Katie would take the first letter and I would take the second. We would split up and see if we could find anything. As we walked, I thought about the possibilities.

Sarah might be sending messages, but it was too damn cryptic. She may well have just lost her mind, a mental implosion that started with Brad's death and ended with an obsession that she was an evil person. Had the Salem connection eaten away at her after Brad's death?

It was third option that gnawed at me, that Sarah hadn't killed Brad, that she was in danger, and that her connection with Salem was a key to why she had become involved in the first place. That haunted me, because it came with added guilt. What had I been doing while Sarah needed help?

Whatever the reason, or whether there was any connection with Salem other than coincidence, I needed more background on Salem. So I'd done some reading on Salem that morning.

In 1692, a group of young girls began to play act, babbling and fitting, and then they accused three local women of bewitching them, one of them being a local beggar, Sarah Good. It must have been a good game, because then they turned on other people in the town, until there were twenty-five deaths and one hundred and fifty accused. Sarah Good was hanged for witchcraft on July 19.

What I couldn't work out was why someone would regard events from over three hundred years ago as a catalyst for disaster.

I listened to Katie chatter as we walked, her skip as she talked a distraction from Salem. But time played that trick, and as we wandered through the university grounds, our conversation fell quiet. She said hello to people she knew as she passed, but I saw a look in their eyes, a wary look. No more the sweet girl from Wichita.

We ended up in the University library, deep in the history section. There were students sat around desks, surrounded by piles of books and serious looks.

"What are we looking for?" Katie asked.

I shrugged my shoulders. "Anything, just anything. Let's start with whatever we can find on Sarah Good, the old Sarah. Look for documents that might give a clue as to where those cryptic letters might be from."

We both went hunting through rack after rack, shelf after shelf, of books. I found the Salem section, and noticed with some dismay how well studied this area is. Line after line of perspectives on the trials, transcripts of evidence, studies of the reasons and theories behind the reasons.

I returned eventually with an armful of tomes; three volumes of a verbatim account of the trials, or at least as verbatim as you could get before the days of stenography, and two books on the characters and personalities of the trials. I couldn't see Katie when I returned to our table, so I ploughed through the books on my own.

I reached into my pocket and put Sarah's second letter on the table. I read it again, shaking my head:

*"I have made contact with the devil. I have hurt that child. I have desired that child to look upon me and the child was tormented. I torment that child. I am not willing to mention the word God and answer in a very wicked, spiteful manner.*

*I will and command you that you safely conduct the said Sarah Goode to the place of execution and there cause her to be hanged by the neck until she be dead and you are not to fail at your peril.*

*Sarah."*

I gave a weary sigh

I looked once more at the pile of books and began reading.

They made tortuous reading. I found myself drifting as I read, thinking about how Sarah's parents must be feeling back in England, wondering what Sarah was doing at that moment as I sat huddled over dusty pages reflecting on events of three hundred years earlier, and I wondered what Lieutenant Cornwell would do to me if he saw me now.

I began to flick, racing through transcript after transcript, facsimile after facsimile, my eyes glazing, until I stopped dead when I saw the name Sarah Good and copies of some documents. I couldn't make out what they said, the old scrawled black pen too untidy to make out words recognisable to modern eyes. I found myself scanning the text underneath, and then I found it.

Mental fireworks deafened me. I looked up, certain everyone had heard them, but all was quiet.

It was just a phrase I recognised. I had been making my way through the documents in Sarah Good's case, my mind elsewhere, when I spotted words that rang familiar. I turned again to Sarah's letter and read the second paragraph, my hands fumbling with the paper:

*"I will and command you that you safely conduct the said Sarah Goode to the place of execution and there cause her to be hanged by the neck until she be dead and you are not to fail at your peril."*

I looked now at the text in front of me. It was different, I knew that, but it was the same. It was virtually the same. I had to look for the words, and I almost missed them, but the title of the extract reminded of Professor Lowenski's words, that it sounded like some form of warrant. As I was scanning page after page of accusations against Sarah Good I came across it: the death warrant of Sarah Good. The old witch of Salem was named with four others, but I spotted a familiar phrase:

*"to will and command you ......safely conduct the s'd Sarah Good ......From Maj'ties gaol in Salem afores'd to the place of Execution and there cause them and Every of them to be hanged by the neck until they be dead and ......hereof you are not to fail at your perill."*

Libraries are quiet places, but all I could hear was the deafening noise of adrenaline, that rush of excitement. I knew I'd found something, and I wanted to make some noise in the library, jump and shout, grab Katie, but as I looked up from my book I still saw just a room full of studious faces pouring over routine textbooks.

But it had confirmed one thing: the Salem connection was not a coincidence. The letter from Sarah had paraphrased part of the death warrant relating to the old Sarah Good. It was close enough for me.

I leant back in my chair and let my hands ruffle my hair. I wondered whether a giant leap had been made, but as I cheered to myself, a cold, hard reality hit home: the end to the story. Sarah Good, the convicted old woman from centuries before, had died.

The warrant had been carried out, and on July 19<sup>th</sup> 1692, Sarah Good had indeed been hung by the neck until she was dead.

I returned to the books in front of me. I could feel my dinner begin to churn, my breath begin to shorten. I turned page after page, looking for Sarah's name, trying to see words and phrases that might leap out at me. As I scanned I pitied anyone having to study this, but I knew the key was in there, it was just a matter of finding it.

I looked up and saw Katie pass an aisle, recognised her along the narrow racks, and I saw how buried she was in the book she was carrying. I returned to my own study, wondering whether she had found something, and just as my own mind began to speculate and wander again I saw Sarah's name. The transcript of her evidence.

I felt my chest tighten, the acid burn.

I skimmed quickly, wondering what I would find, when again I knew I had found it. I sensed the hush retreat as my mind screamed at me. I was getting somewhere, I knew it, although I wasn't sure where. Page after page rushed past my eyes as I looked for more signs, and the more I looked, the more I saw. I scribbled fast, made notes, flicked page after page over until I thought they would rip and tear in front of me.

I grabbed my papers and went to Katie, rushing through the library like a thief.

I found her with a look of shock on her face. I wondered if she had found the same.

"We need to go," I whispered urgently into her ear, and I was pleased to see her grab her papers and follow me out.

We ended up in a fast walk through the Back Bay. My mind was still racing, and I didn't want to speak until my mind had assembled all I'd found into something real.

"Why the rush?" asked Katie, interrupting my train of thought.

I looked at her. "The Salem connection is no coincidence," I shouted at her. I sounded breathless.

"What do you mean?" she asked quietly, although I could tell it wasn't a simple question. She said it quietly, nervously, as if she didn't want me to confirm what she was now suspecting.

She pulled me into a coffee bar and we sat down. Coffees were ordered, and then she said, "talk to me, Joe."

"Okay, okay." I spread my papers over the table. I thought how best to approach this, then realised that direct was the best route.

"Do you remember I told you that Professor Lowenski thought the letters had a legal feel to them, that they sounded like some form of warrant?"

Katie just nodded.

"Well, he was right."

I placed Sarah's letter on the table.

"I found this first," and I showed her the passage from Sarah Good's death warrant. "See how close they are. The spellings are modernised in Sarah's letter to you, but the words used are too alike to be just coincidence. Same name, same phrase."

Katie looked dolefully at me, not showing the excitement I was feeling.

"So next," I continued, "I carried on rushing through the volumes, when I came across the transcript of Sarah Good's evidence." I paused for breath. "The phrases from Sarah's letter are taken from the trial of Sarah Good, just twisted and given a different meaning.

"Look at this sentence from Sarah's second letter, '*I have made contact with the devil.*'" I pushed my scrawled notes in front of her." And now look at this quote from the trial," I said excitedly, "*'have you made no contract with the devil?'*" I smiled at her in triumph. "Can you see?" I said, "can you see? They are almost the same."

I paused to look at Katie. She looked serious.

"That quote is from Sarah Good's trial," I repeated, "the witch Sarah Good, back in 1692, before she was convicted. There is a slight difference. In 1692 Sarah Good answered the question in the negative, and the letter to Katie changed her answer to yes, but it's near enough."

I scrabbled through the papers again. "Look at this one. In her trial, Sarah Good is asked why she hurts the children, and she answers, '*I do not hurt them.*' She is then asked, '*Why do you thus torment these poor children?*' and she responds, '*I do not torment them.*' Sarah Good denies the allegations put to her. Katie, look again at Sarah's letter to you. The same as before. The words are nearly the same. It is just the answers are turned around. In her trial, the old Sarah Good denied hurting or tormenting the children. In the letter to you, she says that she did. Look," I said, pushing

Sarah's letter in front of her again, "she says *'I have hurt that child,'* and *'I torment that child.'* They are so similar in wording, there must be a connection. The denials are just changed to confessions."

"What about the rest of the letter?" Katie asked quietly.

"The same, the same. Just accusations turned into confessions. In 1692, Sarah Good denied everything. Now, she admits them."

I was excited. The coffee had arrived but I hadn't noticed. I was talking too loud and shoving pieces of paper at Katie. She didn't share my excitement.

"What's wrong?" I asked. "I thought you would have been pleased. You know, starting to make progress."

"Don't do it for me, Joe," she said softly. "Do it for Sarah, or because it's your job, or even for yourself, but don't do it for me."

"What do you mean? I don't understand."

"Joe, this isn't good news. If you are right, that there is a connection with the Salem witch trials, for Christ's knows what reason, then something is seriously wrong. It can only mean one thing: that Sarah is in deep trouble, in great danger, either from herself, or from whoever is behind all of this. That is not a reason for me to be pleased."

I felt guilty and short-sighted when I saw a look of strain dull her eyes.

"I just want all of this to be over," she continued. "Before today it all looked like a crime of passion, a moment of madness. I could deal with that. We all feel passion. We do things we regret, bad things. I can deal with that, can empathise, but what I can't deal with is talk of witches and ancient trials and executions. This is not Puritanical New England. This is Boston, in the twenty-first century."

I put my hand on hers. It was a tender gesture, one I'm not used to making, and I was pleased to see her take it that way.

"I'm sorry," I said. "Perhaps I've got a little carried away with myself. But tell me this: why aren't you dismissing it out of hand? If it bothers you, it must be because you believe there might be something in it."

Katie didn't say anything. She moved her hand from under mine. Something was wrong.

"What did you find, Katie? What did you find?"

She looked at me. I could tell her mind was flying.

"I found the same as you," she said quietly. "Just the same."

I struggled to contain my excitement. "What do you mean, the same? What did you find?"

She delved into her bag and passed her notes over. "I found it all straight away. I just didn't know what it meant."

I looked at her writing. Katie was much neater than I'd been. She'd written the whole letter out again, as if seeing it in her handwriting would make things easier. Then arrows led me down the page to where she'd copied extracts. I saw her handwriting get larger as her findings increased, as if she was trying to get it all down as quickly as possible before the chance slipped away. I felt my eyes widen as I read.

"This is no coincidence," I said in astonishment.

Katie looked at me with sadness. "I knew it meant trouble. When you came over I hoped you'd found something different. I was wrong."

"But Katie, this gives a direction." I squeezed her hand this time, more excitement than tenderness. "There are two possibilities. That Sarah is doing all this through some form of madness. If she is, this may help us find her and get her the help she needs. If someone else is behind it, then this may lead us to that person."

"What do you think is going on?" she asked. She sounded lost.

I shrugged my shoulders. "At the moment, I don't know. Let's look at what you found."

I looked first at Sarah's letter:

*"They said Sarah Goode was of so turbulent a spirit, spiteful and so maliciously bent, that her detractors could not suffer her to live in their house any longer. Ever since these detractors turned her out of their house she has behaved herself so crossly and maliciously. She must kill somebody with a knife. If you take her life away, God will give you blood to drink."*

I looked at Sarah's arrows and jottings, and I saw some scribbled down quote from somewhere:

*"...that said Sarah Good was of so Turbuland a Spirrit, spiteful and so Mallitiously bent, that these Deponants could not suffer her to Live in their house any longer. ......ever since these Deponents*

*turned her out of their howse she hath behaved her selfe very crossely and Mallitiously......."*

I felt that same cold shiver, that same rush. Something was going on here, something revealing, important.

I looked at Katie, who was looking into her coffee.

"Where is this from?" I asked.

Katie looked up solemnly. "The petition against Sarah Good by Samuel and Mary Abbey. It was the petition that started the legal proceedings against Sarah Good. They outlined the allegations and what each petitioner would say. Samuel and Mary Abbey weren't the only petitioners against Sarah Good, but they would have affected her the most."

"Why? Who were they?"

"I was just finding that out when you came over," Katie answered. "They took her in, gave her a room, about three years before the whole witch thing blew up, but the Abbey's evicted her. By the time of the witch trials she had been reduced to begging for food, so she made an easy target for the young girls making the accusations of witchcraft. The Abbey's asked her to leave because, in the words of the letter, she *'was of so turbulent a spirit, spiteful and so maliciously bent.'*

"The Abbey's joined in the case against Sarah Good by claiming that since being asked to leave she, and I quote, *'behaved herself very crossly and maliciously.'* It wasn't the only petition against Sarah Good, but it was the most personally connected."

"So," I said, "in sending these letters, Sarah, for the first part of the first letter, uses the beginnings of the legal proceedings against the witch Sarah Good. Twists the words, but unmistakeably uses them. Am I right?"

Katie nodded. "That's how it appears."

"What about the second part, the bit that reads, *"She must kill somebody with a knife. If you take her life away, God will give you blood to drink."*?

Katie leant over and pulled out a piece of paper from the middle of the pile. "I didn't find the sentence, *"if you take her life away, God will give you blood to drink,"* but I found the first part, the part about, *"she must kill somebody with a knife."*

I was excited now. That was a telling comment. It had a direct connection with the method of Brad's death.

"Where is it from?"

"From the evidence given at Sarah Good's trial by Tituba Indian."

I wrinkled my nose. "Who the hell was she?"

Katie smiled. "Perhaps the start of the whole sorry saga. Tituba Indian was a black housemaid who used to spend her time with the bewitched children telling them tales of Caribbean sorcery. The girls were so taken with these stories that they started acting bewitched. From this, the accusations were made."

"Did Tituba stand trial?"

"Oh yes, although she didn't hang. She escaped the noose by confessing the sin of witchcraft and giving evidence against the other people accused."

I smiled. "And one of the victims of her evidence was Sarah Good?"

Katie nodded again. "Yes, you've guessed it. Tituba Indian states in her confession of witchcraft that *'Good tell her she must kill somebody with a knife.'*"

"What about the last sentence, that," and I paused while I found the note of the last sentence, "that *'if you take her life away, God will give you blood to drink.'*? You said you couldn't find anything out about that one?"

Katie shook her head. "I couldn't find that one, but we weren't in that long. Shall we go back?"

I was deep in thought, my mind turning over solutions and possibilities like a blackjack dealer.

It was my turn to shake my head. "No, no. There's somewhere else I need to go. Why don't you go and see Lieutenant Cornwell, take him the letter?"

"Do I tell him about all of this, about what we've found?"

I thought about it. I realised suddenly that this might have occurred to the police. Their local knowledge will be better than mine, and I was sure there would be experts who would look at the formation of words, of sentences, and who would realise the connection.

But then I thought about why I wouldn't want it mentioned. Personal reasons only. To keep the police off my back, to claim the glory for myself. Those weren't good reasons.

"Yes," I answered, "you should tell him. Just keep my name out of it. You can take all the credit."

Katie smiled. It wasn't a beam, just perhaps a smile of realisation, that although she would rather it would go away, it wasn't going to do that. And Katie knew that she would always do the right thing. She was right to smile.

"I wonder what it all means?" said Katie, almost to herself.

"Does it have to mean anything?"

"Of course it does. There are so many questions, but perhaps the first should be, why were those particular passages chosen? There are volumes and volumes written about Salem and witchcraft, so why pick on those?"

I looked at the notes. "We might find out later, but at the moment, I don't know." I scratched my head. "I don't think we'll receive any more anyway, so if we are not clear from these, we never will be."

Katie looked puzzled. "Why don't you think we'll receive any more?"

I looked at Katie. She had suffered enough. But my mind had flipped the cards and come up twenty-one.

I sighed. "Think about it. The letters have gone full circle, gone through the whole legal process." I pulled out the copy of the first letter written by Sarah. "This letter starts with an extract from a petition against the old Sarah Good. It started your letter, and it started the chain of events for Sarah Good back in 1692. The next sentence is taken from evidence against her, from the mouth of Tituba Indian. Then go on to the second letter, the one I looked up." I pulled out the copy of the second letter, the one I'd been working on. "We move straight on to a twisting of the evidence given by Sarah Good herself. We are in the next stage of proceedings. We have had the allegation, then the evidence against her, in the first letter. Now we are onto the defence evidence, answering the allegation, in the second letter."

"Except," Katie said, understanding my thread, "the modern Sarah Goode confesses, says she did hurt that child."

I nodded grimly. "Maybe why the letters were sent in the first place, to confess. She sends a letter to point to the allegation and evidence against her, perhaps in the early stages of Sarah's decline, the early signs of paranoia, of self-blame. Not ready yet to confess, she just wants to blame herself. Then the decline hits a lower level, and so she confesses. Perhaps she has sunk into a delusionary existence, somehow using an ancient coincidence to explain to

127

herself why she killed Brad. She seeks absolution in confession, and so twists the testimony of 1692 to complete the legal scene."

Katie looked upset. I could see her becoming distant, looking scared.

"Are you alright?" I asked.

"I'm worried," she said, her voice trembling. "Because look at what she has written, and look where she sent them. The first letter is taken from a document made by the people who evicted the witch Sarah Good, who took her in but then couldn't put up with her strange ways. That eviction sent Sarah Good on her begging route again, made her an easy target for those little girls calling people witches, and ultimately led to her death." Katie looked at me, and I thought I could see a trace of fear. "That letter was sent to me. I took her in. Did Sarah think I wanted her to leave? Is she blaming me for Brad's death? Is she coming to get me?"

I placed my hand on hers again. "No, no," I said softly. "Whatever happened, it wasn't your fault. Whoever made those letters may have just plucked those passages because he or she liked the sound of them. Any interpretation that can connect to you will be just coincidence."

I wasn't convincing her. I'd told her that there would be no more letters because I could see a thread running through them. I was asking Katie to ignore that thread and just see it as coincidence again.

"But Joe, coincidences are starting to add up here," Katie cried. "Sarah's connection with the Salem witch trials was just a coincidence until we spent the last hour or so in the library. We shouldn't dismiss coincidences. I might be in danger."

I squeezed her hand tightly.

"Whatever may happen next, I won't let anyone hurt you. You have my promise."

Katie just looked at the table.

I dipped my head so that I was able to catch her eyes and I smiled. I was pleased to see her smile back.

"I promise," I said, "I won't let anyone hurt you. Do you believe me?"

Katie nodded silently and smiled again.

"C'mon," I said, cajoling, "we've things to do. I'll get the bill, you gather your senses, and I'll see you back at the apartment later."

"Where are you going?"

I tapped my nose. "Just something I want to keep to myself for the moment. I'll speak to you later."

As I was settling the bill, Katie asked, "what about the last part of the second letter? You told me where much of it came from, but you didn't mention the last part, the bit about the hanging. You said the letters went full circle, that we wouldn't get any more letters from Sarah. We've had the allegation, the evidence, then the defence case. Where did that last sentence come from, that about taking her to be hanged by the neck until she is dead, and not to fail at your peril? Did you find it?"

I was quiet for a moment. I knew what the answer would mean to her. I had shown her the passage, but not told her where it was from.

My eyes must have given her the answer. Her hand shot to her mouth.

"It's from the death warrant," she exclaimed, "from the warrant that allowed Sarah Good to be killed."

I nodded.

Katie sighed heavily. "And Sarah Good died," she said softly, almost to herself.

I just nodded, and then watched Katie walk away in the direction of the police station with her head tilted towards the floor.

I wished for a moment that Professor Lowenski hadn't made the connection, that this was all still a blissful mystery. But then I realised I might as well wish for Brad to be still alive and for me to be still in Morsby, peering into parked cars and serving court papers on violent ex-husbands. I was in Boston, and the connection had been made.

I went in my own direction, wondering what I would find next.

Sarah's ears pricked open when she heard the key in the door. She didn't know how long it had been now. There were no distractions, just time passed by making paces and lying in bed, dreaming about outside.

She gripped the bedclothes tight, eyes shut, trying to make like low, steady breaths. This could be it. She listened for the steps as he came into the room. Three steps, the food goes down, just a few seconds to get out of bed and get the sheet. Sarah was poised and ready.

The footsteps came in slowly, deliberately. This wasn't the same as last time.

Sarah's breath quickened. Something was different. This wasn't for food, no supplies coming in.

Sarah wanted to be asleep, but curiosity won her over. What was different?

She opened one eye. She winced in the bright light. She then shot back across the bed, surprised at what she saw.

He was stood over the bed, right by her, a smell of overwork and stale sweat, mixed in with a metallic, oily smell.

But it wasn't the smell that made her scuttle backwards. It was something else entirely. Sarah was made scared by a look in his eyes, one that she had expected since her capture, but not one she had ever wanted to see.

It was a look of want, mixed with distaste. He wanted her, and he was going to have her.

He knelt down by the bed, unfit knees creaking in the packed silence. He leant forward towards her, breathing through his nose, as if trying to smell her, trying to make something of her become part of him.

Sarah sat back against the wall, legs kicking away the sheets, then she pulled them up to her chest, protective style.

He reached out, trying to tease some hair into his fingers.

Sarah brushed his hand away.

"Why are you doing this?" she screamed. "Leave me alone. Do you hear? Just leave me alone. Not this."

He smiled. It was what he wanted. His breath quickened as Sarah began to sob.

He stood up slowly, then climbed onto the bed with her, blocking her in against the wall.

Sarah put her face in her hands, knees drawn tight into her chest, pressed together, a low cry escaping through gritted teeth.

Sarah didn't see his hand go to her shirt. But she felt it. Sarah felt those hard, calloused hands, those iron fingers. She froze. Her hands fell away from her face and she looked at him, letting a long moan. "No, no, no, no," she cried, tears streaming down her face.

One button was flicked open.

His hand went inside her shirt and cupped her. His fingers mauled her as if expecting a response, but there was nothing, except cold, naked fear.

He flicked open another button.

And then another.

The shirt flapped open, revealing her bare chest, her nipples hard through the cold.

Sarah looked at him. His eyes were wide and staring, his mouth open, breathing hard. That was the last time she looked at him. She cast her eyes to the ceiling and tried to hide.

He ripped off the shirt and threw it on the floor next to her, then grabbed her hair and threw her face down onto the bed.

Sarah went dead inside when he undid her jeans, panting in her ear like a dog. Whenever she'd thought about these things, she'd always thought about a fight, a struggle, knowing that she would never give herself easily. But now it was here, she'd given in. The tears had stopped, her emotions turned off. It was as if she had tuned into a different channel. Perhaps because she had been expecting this, and now it was here, happening right now, she was able to deal with it. But she knew she wasn't dealing with it. She was switching off, but she didn't know if she would ever come back on again.

When he got behind her, kicking her legs apart, Sarah didn't cry or shout. She was limp, passive. Even when he grabbed her hair from behind and put himself inside her, she didn't scream or thrash. She just stared at a spot on the wall, grimacing with the pain and the awareness of what was happening to her, but she was beyond tears.

It was over quickly.

She became aware of his sobs as he lay on top of her, crushing the air out of her and pushing her face into the sheets.

He stayed like that for a while, before he moved her hair to one side, and kissed her tenderly on the back of the neck.

Sarah didn't move.

He clambered off her, fastened his trousers, and stood over her.

Sarah could hear him panting, could hear his hand wiping his brow. She wanted to turn round and scream, wanted to hurt him like he had hurt her, kill him maybe.

She didn't do any of that. Instead, she lay there on the bed, naked, staring into nothing. She knew his eyes were on her, but she felt lifeless, uncaring, unable to do anything about the hatred she felt inside.

He kicked her in the ribs. Just once, but hard. Sarah hardly moved. Sarah hardly cried out. She just curled up tighter into a ball and began to rock gently, her eyes glassy and dull.

He walked out of the room. When the door shut, she began to feel the pain. And when the sobs came, they came in a wail, like a long scream, and she didn't know if it would stop.

# Twelve

Day was surrendering to dusk when I returned to the apartment. Gnats caught the fading sunlight and danced between the trees, and there was a hum as people made the most of the few moments of daylight left. I'd worn my shirt into my skin and I needed a drink.

I should have felt good. We'd made a connection, found a link that might mean progress, but things were turning out different to how I thought.

"Is that you Joe?" It was Katie, shouting from her room.

I waved my hand wearily. "Yeah, hi," I said, and flopped onto the couch. Baseball was on, the Yankees at Cleveland. I lay there for ten minutes with my eyes closed. My mind raced and dipped and bobbed. I'd found out too many things. I tried to make it go still, but it wouldn't. My thoughts turned to witches and captive women and screams and then failure. I wondered what Sarah must be going through, and how I'd agreed to try and end that hell. Well, hell had just got hotter, and I wished I hadn't seen it.

My eyes flew open when I felt Katie nudge my leg. "You look shot, Joe," she said.

I smiled in agreement. "I feel it." I lifted myself up. "How did it go with Lieutenant Cornwell?"

She raised her eyebrows. "He didn't seem pleased, as if I'd just made his day a little harder. We had a talk and he asked about you."

"What did he say?"

"Nothing. He said I'd been very helpful, and then ushered me out."

"Is he coming to deport me?" My question was only half in jest.

Katie laughed. "Not yet, I don't think. I said you were just seeing the sights, and then reporting back to Sarah's folks once she was caught. You know, a paid vacation." She smiled. "I don't think he bought it."

"Well," I mumbled, "he might soon realise that."

"What do you mean?"

"Oh nothing. I've just had a long afternoon."

I sat up and looked over towards Katie. I was surprised to see Danny stood there, the person from the bar where Katie worked. He nodded and smiled.

"How are you doing, Mr Kinsella?"

I nodded and smiled back. "Okay, thanks."

Katie looked at Danny. "He just called by to see how I was doing."

"A lot of people at the bar are worried about her."

I smiled again. "It's nice to be thought of."

Danny nodded, then stepped away from the kitchen. "I'll get going, Katie. Don't make yourself a stranger at the bar. People miss you."

I waved as he walked towards the door. I felt bad, because it felt like I'd intruded, come in halfway through a moment, but then I was glad at the same time.

When he'd gone, Katie asked, "where've you been today?"

"I'll tell you later," I said. I didn't want to shut her out, but I needed to get straight in my head what I'd found out that afternoon.

I'd been to the Boston Globe offices, a neat collection of computers and paper, and done some searching, with the possibilities flying around my head.

I'd discounted the possibility that it was an unconnected coincidence, the similarities between Sarah's letters and the Salem documents were too great. Katie didn't think they were hidden hints to Sarah's whereabouts, as they were too obscure. That left the possibilities that either Sarah had gone mad, or someone even crazier had targeted her because of her coincidental connection with the Salem witch trials. It was this last possibility that I went to the Globe offices to disprove. I almost wished I hadn't. I'd spent three hours in the Globe archives with a very helpful clerk, going through years of newspapers, cross-referencing and photocopying and tearing my hair out. I'd returned to the apartment with a bundle of papers and a headache that would fell Hercules.

I hauled myself up wandered over to the window, just for something to look at, to give my mind a rest.

I heard the patter of feet. I looked round to see Katie walk to the bedroom. I looked away, but then the door buzzer went.

"Can you get that, Joe? I'm getting changed."

"No problem," I shouted back, but when I opened the door, I saw that it was very much a problem. Lieutenant Cornwell and Sergeant Lehane were stood there.

My heart gripped me. What was the lieutenant doing here? I looked back into the apartment, looking for Katie. I couldn't see her. My stomach dropped like an elevator with a snapped cable. Shit.

I turned round and they both followed me in. I gestured for them to sit down, but they ignored me, and then shouted towards Katie's room that she had company.

I leant against a door-frame, not wanting to start the conversation. Katie came in and flashed me a look as if to say that the visit wasn't down to her. Sergeant Lehane was looking at photographs on the wall. Lieutenant Cornwell just glared at me.

Why were they there? Perhaps Katie had said too much in their meeting? Lieutenant Cornwell scowled a mean scowl. He was a man who preferred silence to fill the uncomfortable gaps, rather than words.

I broke the silence.

"I guess you're not here for tea."

Lieutenant Cornwell shook his head, smiling. It looked cold.

"Okay, let's cut to the chase." I looked at both police officers. "You're here about the letters."

The two officers exchanged glances, then Lieutenant Cornwell said, "maybe it's you and the letters that bothers us."

I shrugged. "Yeah, maybe, but I know more than you've been told."

Katie looked surprised. Sergeant Lehane turned round to look at me. Lieutenant Cornwell just smiled. "Good news then," he said quietly.

"Please sit down officers," Katie said anxiously.

Lieutenant Cornwell's eyes never left mine, but he sat down. Sergeant Lehane leant against the wall.

I took a deep breath. I thought the lieutenant was maybe enjoying himself too much.

"What's your spin on Salem, lieutenant?"

His smile broadened, like he was surprised to be answering the questions. But then he decided to play along.

"A whole industry," he said, "built on a year of utter madness three centuries ago. Wax museums, haunted houses, the full shit.

135

Anything thing with a space has the witch logo, even the police badge. It's crazy." He leant forward. His voice lowered, his eyes darkened. "And I think it made your friend crazy too." He said it with menace. He leant back and talked at the ceiling. "It takes just one trigger to go off at a time of weakness, just one, and all hell breaks loose."

Lieutenant Cornwell turned to Katie. "I've thought about what you told me this afternoon," he said, "all this witchcraft garbage. It's been swimming around up here all day," he said, tapping his forehead. He took a deep breath. "My sergeant thinks there is something in it, but he loves a mystery. I don't. I hate mysteries. I like clear signs, clues, forensics, confessions. Leave the mysteries to the writers and airport bookshops." He looked around the room, looking at me with something swinging between dislike and contempt.

"Is this normal procedure?" I asked. "Home visits?"

Lieutenant Cornwell said nothing for a while, and when he did, he spoke quietly. "No, this isn't normal procedure, but this isn't a usual box of ideas." He looked uncomfortable for a split second, the stern façade slipping and revealing uncertainty, but then he found a tough glare. "I want to know what else you know before I go to my captain."

I smiled. "Let's talk then."

Lieutenant Cornwell nodded slowly. "We need to find out more about Sarah," he said, "find out what made her so obsessed." He sighed, the tough guy letting go for a while. "There has to be some sign, some door into the darkness, and you people know her best. You are her closest friend," he said, gesturing towards Katie, "so you know her pretty well. We just need anything. Anything at all."

"Could you just tell me one thing," I interrupted. Something had occurred to me. "You're not asking me to leave, so how did you know that I knew all about the letters?"

Lieutenant Cornwell smiled. "Do you think I wouldn't consult the university when one of their students is involved in a murder investigation?" he said. "And do you think the university wouldn't tell me when something relevant came up?"

"Professor Lowenski?"

Neither police officer said anything.

"Okay, okay, fair enough," I said in exasperation. I was always going to get caught.

The lieutenant spoke to Katie. "Why didn't you tell me 'you' was a 'we' when you came round with the letter this afternoon?" he asked.

Katie just shrugged and said nothing. I was pleased at her loyalty.

"I've found some other things out too," I said quietly. "More than Katie knows."

"What do you mean?"

"Sarah hasn't gone crazy," I said, "although she might be in danger."

The two police officers exchanged glances again. They gave me the nod to continue.

I walked over to lean against the window. The view gave me another focus.

"I was trying to work out the options," I said. "I just couldn't go with the thought that a normal girl from a normal family would suddenly have an obsession with witchcraft and then start murdering people. It had that ring of the unbelievable about it. Why would this happen?"

Lieutenant Cornwell sounded unconvinced. "I'll tell you why," he said. "It gives her a defence. Sarah knows she shares the name, she knew before Brad died. They have a row, over what, we don't know, and she stabs him. Perhaps she didn't mean to kill him, but he dies. She panics and leaves. She knows she is in trouble, and that the finger will point at her, so what does she do? She makes herself sound like some crazy woman from the past and gets herself an insanity defence. Avoids hard time, and maybe even a plane ticket home to be treated in some soft English hospital." He stared at me. "Perhaps she even has some smartass lawyer telling her how to sound."

I looked at Katie. She was grim-faced. We'd both considered that view and dismissed it. But we'd only dismissed it because it was about Katie's friend. I wondered how Katie felt about it coming from a more cynical source. It gave it more gravitas. I wish I'd told her now about my afternoon's labours.

"You might be right, lieutenant," I persisted, "but what are the witchcraft options? We know that it isn't a coincidence, the letters tell us that. And we know the letters are from Sarah."

"How do you know that?" The question was brisk.

"It was my idea," Katie interrupted. I looked at her, startled but grateful. "Joe was here when I received the second letter," she said, "and I was worried about wasting your time. They seemed too cryptic. So I asked Joe if he knew anyone who could get a handwriting analysis done first, to confirm it was her writing."

"And is it?"

Katie nodded. "Yes, it's her writing."

I shot a glance at Katie, and when she caught it she acknowledged my gratitude.

Lieutenant Cornwell seemed satisfied. "Go on," he said to me quietly, "you were just curing my insomnia."

I ignored his sarcasm.

"Firstly," I said, "Sarah could have gone crazy, some obsession with witchcraft, and in her madness killed Brad. The letters are a manifestation of that madness. She is a dangerous woman, in particular to herself, and must be caught.

"Or secondly, she could have killed Brad in some lovers rage, and it could be this that has sent her over the edge. She's attached some weighty significance to the coincidence of her name, become obsessed with herself as an evil person, and her mind has travelled to some unravelled land, never to return."

"And I know reason number three," the lieutenant interrupted, the sarcasm still there. "She kills the fireman, decides she needs a defence, sees some crooked defence lawyer, and he says act crazy. She sends some well-researched letters and waits for a sympathetic jury. She's probably trying to grow long, unkempt nails and hair, will sit in court like some rocking hag, and eventually see out her days on chat shows as the woman who walked. Hey, she could be a female O.J. Simpson."

"That's not fair!" Katie shouted. "I know Sarah is a suspect, I expect that, but don't make her out to be a manipulative, cold-hearted bitch. She is still my friend, and I'm worried for her."

The lieutenant held up his hands defensively. "Okay, okay, I'm sorry. Perhaps I'm just getting old and cynical. I just forgot who I was dealing with here."

"No, you're wrong," I said, trying to retrieve the initiative, "that wasn't the final possibility. There is a more obvious one."

"Which is?"

"What if the witchcraft obsession is someone else's? What if Sarah is the victim of that obsession? Think about it. She comes from a stable background, she's close to her family, and there are no known mental problems. I know that before Brad was killed, Sarah was just an ordinary English girl involved in an ordinary relationship with an ordinary American guy."

I looked around. I had their attention. They knew I had something else to give.

"Sarah wasn't crazy before she met Brad, we all know that. To go from routine student to psychotic knife-woman in a few months makes no sense." I turned to Katie. "Did you notice any dark episodes? Any obsession with the witch trials."

Katie shook her head slowly and looked sad. "No, none."

"Did she indicate any prior knowledge when the day out in Salem was suggested?"

She shook her head again.

"And how did she take it when the coincidence of the name was pointed out?"

"Fine. She laughed."

"Good," I said. "Then we have to assume that she wasn't crazy before she came to America."

I began to pace.

"So could killing Brad have sent her over the edge? Well, I'm no criminologist, but I do know one thing: young women do not kill casual boyfriends without very good reason. They had only been dating a few months, and even then it wasn't every night, or even every other night. It was two unattached young people who found each other attractive and enjoyed each other's company, so they drank and ate together sometimes, and they slept together sometimes, but they were not so close that an argument would send Sarah into a blind rage. Do you agree with that Katie?"

Katie nodded. "He's right. I told you lieutenant, they were just a casual couple. If they'd fought, like seriously, she would have just ended it and got on with something else. Sarah was here to have fun, not get stuck in some serious logjam for a year."

I turned back to Lieutenant Cornwell. "So if we say it isn't fraud or madness, there is only one option left." I raised my eyebrows. "And that someone else is responsible for Brad's death." I paused. "It is the witch connection that ties Sarah into all this. And if that is the case, then Sarah is in great danger."

"You are grasping at straws, Mr Kinsella," Lieutenant Cornwell said, his voice thick with contempt. "If part of your brief is to try and distract the official investigation, then you'll get little help from me, except a lift to the airport."

"No, that is not my brief," I said firmly. It was getting to crunch time, so I had to somehow take control of the gathering. If the lieutenant wasn't impressed, I would have to do it all on my own. And I wasn't sure I could.

"I spent the afternoon at the offices of the Boston Globe, in the archive section," I continued. "I had to try and work through the alternative, the possibility that Sarah was the victim, not the slayer. I wondered whether someone had targeted Sarah because she shared her name with a Salem witch. I didn't buy the madness thing, so that was the other option. The letters were too close to the witch transcripts for it to be a coincidence, and I just couldn't see Sarah as the crazy one. Her profile didn't seem right. So I began to wonder: what if someone else is the crazy one, driven by some obsession with the witch trials?" I shrugged. "So I did some digging."

It was time to start my show. I reached under the table and pulled out my copied extracts from the Boston Globe.

"These go back thirteen years," I said. "Missing persons, murders, and suicides, scattered around the Greater Boston area. All different. Certainly no obvious connection, except that all the victims have the same name as one of the Salem witches."

I looked around at the group. Lieutenant Cornwell had stood up and was pacing around. Sergeant Lehane had stood away from the wall.

"Bullshit," Lieutenant Cornwell said quietly, as if he knew it was, but at the same time believed that perhaps it wasn't.

"No, it isn't," I said. I started to place copies of newspaper cuttings onto the table. "Bridget Bishop. Accused and hung in 1692 for witchcraft. Bridget Bishop of Brookline. Went missing eight years ago. Her husband went to work, and when he returned Bridget was gone. She turned up three weeks later, dead and hidden in undergrowth. Rebecca Nurse. Also a Salem witch. Also a teenage girl from Jamaica Plain, who ended up hanging from a tree, an apparent suicide." I had their attention now. Another clipping. "Anne Foster. Shared name again. Ends up dead, found in a fume-filled car."

"Suicide?"

I shook my head. "The detectives at the time didn't think so."

I threw the rest of the clippings on the coffee table. "Starting thirteen years ago, thirteen people have been found dead. They all share the name with a Salem witch, they all died. One a year."

There was silence in the room for a while as everyone looked at the clippings. No-one touched them.

It was the lieutenant who spoke first. "You could probably pick any name, and someone will share that name. And you're always going to get deaths; it's part of living. You are grouping together isolated incidents and trying to make a pattern."

"Come off it, lieutenant. You were happy to accept a coincidence to show Sarah was a deranged killer. Why won't you accept a coincidence, a collection of coincidences, to show that she isn't?"

He squared up to me. "Let's get one thing straight. I do not explain myself to you, or anyone else like you. I am answerable to my superiors and the people I serve, that is it. Period."

"For Christ's sake lieutenant, I'm not being critical. I'm trying to prompt an open discussion, to try and sort this mess out. I have spent the afternoon at the offices of a large Boston newspaper, digging out articles on murders and suspicious deaths, and the clerk knew all I had was a list of names. Do you think she will have failed to mention it to her colleagues? If you aren't interested, I'm sure a crime journalist will be."

He snarled his teeth and began to point.

"And before you threaten to deport me," I interrupted, now getting angry, "I can just give all this to Katie. I'm sure she'll do her civic duty. I could e-mail it to her from the safety of my little house by the sea. Or even straight to the Globe. You couldn't touch me there. Remember, I have a different job description to you. I don't give two fucks for the reputation of the Boston Police. I just want to do my job, which is to find Sarah, by fair means or foul. If you won't listen, I'll find someone who will. So perhaps it would be better to have my co-operation over here, where you can keep a check on me."

"I am not going to bargain with you," he bellowed. His teeth were bared, but he looked like a man who thought it wouldn't be a good idea to create more problems.

"I'm not saying you should. I'm just saying you should hear me out, and if you accept what I say might be right, we could perhaps work together, or at least allow me to keep close by."

"This had better be good." Everyone looked round. It was Sergeant Lehane. He had his arms folded, still dressed in black, his eyes dark and intense.

Lieutenant Cornwell stared at me, and then looked back at Robert. "He's saying we've all missed a serial killer, obvious only to some private dick from overseas, and that this killer goes around on a massacre-fest based only on someone's name. It's bullshit."

Sergeant Lehane shook his head. "Any more than Albert De Salvo, or Ted Bundy, or Jeffrey Dahmer? What if he's right and we do nothing?" He raised his eyebrows. "We're stone dead, that's what. Boston Police face a lawsuit if anyone else of a similar name is killed in the future, or if Sarah is killed and you had enough time to save her." He nodded at me. "Hear the man out."

The lieutenant looked at me. I could tell he was wrestling with his professional pride, and weighing it against a crackpot theory and a bag of news cuttings.

I was relieved when he looked at me and said, "go on, tell me what you've got. But if I find out you've been dry-shaving me, I'll personally escort you to the airport."

I nodded to indicate I understood. I breathed a large sigh and began to address the group.

"You've heard the general picture. A collection of suspicious deaths involving women who share the name of a Salem witch."

"Did you find any witches whose names didn't get a hit?" John Cornwell was going to scrutinise everything to try to find a hole.

"Of course, although I only looked in the Boston Globe archives. The women and discoveries aren't confined to Boston, so a wider net might catch more matches. But I didn't find any dead Martha Cory's, or Mary Easty's, or Tituba Indian's, although the last one didn't surprise me. I didn't work through all the names though, there just wasn't time, but I knew I'd got too many hits for there to be a coincidence. What I did do though, just to try and disprove my theory, was pick out twenty names at random from the telephone book. I picked English-sounding names, to keep the comparison with the Salem witches, and I ran those through the archive computer. Do you want to know how many hits I got, on suspicious deaths?"

"Go on." The lieutenant had now sat down near me, leaning forward, trying to get near to my file.

"None," I said. "Not one. This is no coincidence, lieutenant, no coincidence at all. Once I'd got enough to persuade me I was onto something, I began to go through the follow-up stories, trying to find out a bit more about each one."

Lieutenant Cornwell sat down. "Shit," he exclaimed, shaking his head. "A serial killer. A fucking serial killer. And witches." He sat back, suddenly looking tired, exhaled deeply, and then for the first time I saw him smile at me. It was only a half-smile, a smile of truce rather than friendship, but it was a start.

"Do you want me to go through all these?" I asked, pleased to see a breakthrough. "Or do you want me to come into the station tomorrow?"

He looked at me. "You keep the hell away from my police station. They already think I'm a strange motherfucker. How do you think they'll react when they find out I'm on a witch-hunt, a real witch-hunt?"

"So what do you want me to do?" I asked. "I collected a lot of information, but I don't just want to hand it over without taking copies."

Lieutenant Cornwell stood up again and clapped his hands together. "I'll tell you what we are going to do. First, we are going to order some pizzas; this is going to be a long evening. Then we are going to go through what we know about each one and see what we can come up with."

"What about confidentiality?" I asked. "You know, these are police cases."

"Why is it confidential? You're telling me, not the other way round, and this is a time for ideas. But let me assure everyone here," and he passed round a stern glare, "if what we discuss here goes beyond the bounds of this room without my permission, whoever is the cause will have me to deal with, and then they'll wake up in jail. Is that clear?"

It was clear.

Within fifteen minutes the apartment was thick with the aroma of Italian herbs, pepperoni, and American beer. I alternated between reaching for a slice and sifting my papers into some semblance of order. They were kind of together, but now I was doing a presentation for a professional audience, so it had to be right, it had to flow and follow a pattern that would seem logical. I knew that if I didn't get it right, Lieutenant Cornwell would leave, go back to his duties, and the search for Sarah Goode would find itself in a mud-rut, wheels spinning.

I raised my hands to get everyone's attention.

"Go ahead, Mr Kinsella."

"Call me Joe."

"Excuse me?"

"Call me Joe."

The lieutenant shrugged agreement.

"Shall I call you John?"

"Is that an ex-lawyer's way of saying that if we become buddies, I might get off your case?"

I must have looked surprised, because the lieutenant then said, "I know all about you. I made some phone calls." He smiled. It was his moment. "You fucked up, but you did it good."

I shrugged and smiled back. We'd found some common ground: he didn't like criminals, and I'd assaulted one.

Lieutenant Cornwell raised his hands in surrender. "Okay, John is fine," and he jerked his thumb towards Sergeant Lehane. "And that is Robert." He raised eyebrows. "Can we get down to business? Who was the first?"

I reached for my pile of cuttings and rummaged through the cuttings. "Here we are. Mary Bradbury, from Saugus. Jumped from the Saugus Town Hall tower thirteen years ago. Thirty years old." I looked at a picture of a smiling woman, long blonde hair, head thrown back. It seemed such a waste. "The citizens of Saugus went to bed with one night with no mysteries, then woke up the next day to find a naked woman had thrown herself from the Town Hall clock tower"

"Naked?"

"So the papers say?

"What did the family say about it?"

I rummaged again. "No direct quotes. She was married, one child, a boy. Her husband just said that he wished to be left to get over his grief undisturbed."

"What about suspicious circumstances?"

144

I shook my head. "Just that Mary Bradbury had been suffering from depression, and that everyone who knew her were shaken by her death. Nothing about how she got onto the Town Hall roof, or where she had been before then, or why she would be naked."

"Had there been any sexual assault?" It was Robert.

"There's no mention of it," I replied, and then looked back to my notes. "The next one I found was one year later."

"That's quite a gap for a serial killer. They tend to go in quick clusters."

"Maybe, but if my theory is correct, then the motivation is governed by circumstance, not by desire. He has to wait until someone with a corresponding name becomes known to him, or some other detail that fits into a patchwork of his own devising. He may not just go from names, but I've only looked for a link with names. He might attack when there is any link with the Salem witch trials. There could have even been other killings in that period by this person that aren't connected to the witch trials."

"That is true," Robert agreed. "This could be his preferred methodology, the wait and search and planning his kick, but if he has a murderous psychosis, he might satisfy this by unconnected killings."

"Jesus Christ," John exclaimed. He ran his hands over his hair. "I am either on the verge of a career-making investigation, an undetected multiple killer going back years, or I am about to make myself the laughing stock of the force by chasing a set of spooky coincidences. Why me? Why the fuck me? I've got three children who will need college paying for in a few years time, and a wife I adore, and I'm going to risk all that is safe so I can chase shadows." He ran his hands across his face, and then laughed. "Fuck it. Go on, limey, give me the next one."

"Abigail Hobbs, a thirteen year old girl from Arlington. She went to hang out at a shopping mall, was meeting friends there. She never made it. She was found in the woods around Prankers Pond in Saugus two days later."

"Saugus again," Robert commented, chewing on his lip.

I nodded.

"How did she die?"

"She'd been anally raped and then strangled," I said, "but the forensics hit a wall. A condom and widely available lubrication jelly were used. Marks around the wrists indicated she might have been tied or cuffed with her hands behind her back. Friction marks on her knees, breasts and shoulders showed the sex act took place away from the pond, as it indicated some kind of stone floor. She was clearly pressed down, without her hands to support her. Prankers Pond was just a dumping ground. She was strangled using a thin cord, they believe during the act of anal intercourse." I looked up. "A young girl, killed like a dog on a choker."

I heard Katie gasp. I looked round and I could see she was becoming upset. Her hand was over her mouth, and her eyes were becoming wide and moist. I wasn't sure if it was horror at what happened to that young girl, or fear for Sarah, her friend.

"But they don't know exactly where she was taken from?"

I shook my head. "The police were appealing for anyone who had seen her after leaving her home."

John didn't want to dwell on that one. "Who was next?"

"The following year. Mary Lacy. A teacher from Dedham. She'd been working late at school in mid-winter. She had an apartment in the Back Bay. She'd often get the commuter train back to the Back Bay station, and then call in at a couple of bars on Newbury Street on the way home. An attractive, single woman, not long qualified. As far as anyone knows, she didn't make it to her train. It was a dark, wet evening, and she'd been taking a drama class. She finished after everyone else." I looked up from my notes. "What no-one knows is what happened after that?"

John's eyes were wide. "I know this one."

Robert was stood rod-straight, his jaw set.

I nodded grimly. "You probably do. The pupils came to school one morning three weeks later and found her head impaled on one of the railings outside school. It was on one of the quieter sides, so the adults going into the school wouldn't have noticed it. They just became aware of a commotion when some of the students came running towards the school building hysterical." I shook my head. "The eyes had been removed and the head removed at the neck by something heavy but blunt. Her throat was shattered, not cut. The police thought a blunt axe."

Katie shuddered and John looked cold.

"They didn't find the body," said John quietly. "I was on the murder team for that one, I'd just been made detective. No-one saw who put it there and we couldn't find anyone with a motive. The best we could come up with was a disgruntled former student, you

146

know, like giving the finger to the school, but nothing came up. We had to suspend the investigation eventually, and just pray to God that it didn't happen again."

"Well, it did," I continued. "The following spring. Susannah Martin. Mother of three from Waltham. Respectable, middle class wife. Husband went to work, children went to school, Susannah Martin went to her grave. Reported missing that day. Discovered four weeks later in a burning car in Newton. She had been killed by multiple stabbings. Her hands, her chest, her genital area. The newspaper described them as slashings in the main, but with a number of substantial puncture wounds that would have caused death. The police believed the fire was simply an attempt to frustrate a forensic search. The husband was a suspect, for obvious reasons, but there was no real evidence against him."

John nodded. "Keep going."

"Bridget Bishop. Woman in her forties, lived and worked in Brookline, ran a jewellers shop. Once again, one day she was there, then she wasn't. At the time she went missing, the family were more concerned that she'd had some kind of a breakdown. She was found three weeks later, hidden in undergrowth in Peabody, naked. She was covered in burns and puncture wounds, and the pathologist thought she had been raped, but again there was no forensic evidence that could provide any pointers. The final story on that talks of a dead-end investigation."

John nodded for me to continue, and I noticed he was making notes as I did so.

"Rebecca Nurse. A seventeen-year-old girl from Jamaica Plain. Parents had gone away on holiday, and young Rebecca had the house to herself. The neighbours were surprised she'd been left, because she'd been seeing a boy much older than her, and the parents didn't approve. The boyfriend wasn't immediately placed under suspicion, because he was a pleasant, middle class boy, whose parents had said he'd come home as normal, nothing to suggest that he'd been involved in anything bad." I looked around again. "She was found hanging from a tree in Needham, but it wasn't suicide."

"This person is dangerous, if you're right Joe." It was Katie who broke my dialogue.

I grimaced. "This is where I hit a snag."

147

It was John who provided the answer. "The boyfriend was arrested, tried and convicted. He's still in jail."

I nodded. "She was discovered wearing a shirt belonging to the boyfriend's father. And her own clothing, blood-stained and torn, was discovered in a locker at South Station. The key to the locker was in the boyfriend's drawer when his house was searched."

"I remember that one as well," John said. "The boyfriend's parents started to get a 'my son has been framed' campaign going. It didn't get anywhere. There was forensic evidence, the blood on the clothes was Rebecca's, and he couldn't provide an alibi for the night of the disappearance. Said he was out drinking with a man who, according to public records, didn't exist, and this friend was never seen again by the accused. If he was framed, it was elaborate and planned in advance."

"You know a lot about it," I said.

"I arrested him," John said simply, calmly, but I knew what he meant: you are questioning my judgement, and saying I locked up a man for something he didn't do. I knew I'd entered dangerous territory.

"Do you want to know the others?" I asked, getting ready to ride the storm.

"No," John replied. "Just tell me how many more you have"

I glanced at my list. "Six more, and Sarah. One a year, just about."

John nodded and looked thoughtful.

"I think we need to do some analysis," Robert said, turning heads back his way. "We need to formulate a modus operandus. We need to examine each one for indicators to a common theme, something to attach a description to, an educated guess at the make-up of this mystery killer. We can narrow this down. There are always signs. We've just never looked before." He paused. "Let's start with forensic knowledge."

I flicked through my cuttings. "I'm not sure I found any mention of forensics in the newspaper."

"That's right," John said. "I remember the headless teacher case, and the Rebecca Nurse murder, you know, the convicted boyfriend. There was nothing on the head. No fingerprints in blood, no hair samples, no skin in the teeth where she might have bitten to try and get away. We did find concrete dust in the abrasions on the

148

back of the teacher's head; it must have been the pressure on the floor as she was beheaded. But that was it."

"Wasn't there concrete dust on one of the others?" Katie asked, now taking a more active part.

I rummaged through the papers again. "Yes, here we are. The thirteen-year-old girl from Arlington. Found at Prankers Pond after being sexually abused and strangled to death. There were friction marks that looked like she'd been raped from behind, with her knees and body face down on a stone floor."

"Can't the dust samples be matched up?" asked Katie.

John shrugged. "Firstly, stone isn't concrete, and we don't know if there was dust in the girl's scuffs. You are only dealing with newspaper reports, not police documents. Secondly, it's a different police force handling the case. They may not like it if we burst in and try and take it over. The file will still be open, so we will have to tread carefully, but if there is dust, and we still have it, they could, in theory, be compared. But is that important? The immediate concern is to find Sarah Goode, not solve ancient murders. If we find Sarah, then we can look at things again, because Sarah will be with whoever did all this. What about the six you haven't mentioned yet? Any forensics? Any appeals for a particular type of suspect?"

I shook my head. "No. Women disappear, then reappear up to a month later, dead. Each time the police and family are baffled, although we are dealing with police forces in different areas, so a link presumably would not be made."

"So," said Robert, "we have to assume a degree of forensic awareness. He leaves no traces, except in the Rebecca Nurse case, where clues were left, but intended to convict another person. Are there any convictions in any of your other case studies?"

"No," I answered, "not that are reported anyway."

"Good. That helps us with the age. This person is likely to be in middle age."

"Why?" Katie asked.

"Because these are well-planned killings. Impulsive crimes are committed by younger criminals. The older criminals tend to more measured, more planned, less rushed. Like in all things, we calm down as we get older. Think about this case, Sarah's case. There are no clues at all. He tricked his way into the apartment, overcame a fit and healthy fire officer, likely to be younger than him, and then took Sarah, without leaving any hints as to his presence. It must have been well-planned."

"Perhaps he just had a gun?" I ventured. "Perhaps the first thing Sarah saw when she opened the door was a gun pointing at her face. She wouldn't expect it. She's English. When would she ever have seen a gun before? She may well have been quiet, shocked, leaving enough time for the killer to go into the room, see Brad there, and decide he would have to kill him in order to get away."

"That's a lot of surmising," said Robert. "Where did the knife come from? Do you think he wandered in, saw Brad there, asked to be excused so he could go and get a knife, and then returned to the room while Brad is still slipping out from under the covers? Not likely. No, there are too many things we don't know. I need to look into this."

John started to move around the room. He went to the window by me and looked out onto a night now dark. He gave me a glance, a shot right in the eyes, but I couldn't read him.

When he turned back to the room, he looked tired. "We're going to call it a night. I'm going to have a long day tomorrow, and I need to get things straight in here first," and he tapped his head. "I don't know where the hell all this is going to go, but I need to think, long and hard."

I decided to be bold. "And what do we do in the meantime?"

"You've no need to do anything. This is police work, after all." He sounded jaded, as if he was going towards an argument he didn't want to have.

I groaned to myself. I thought we'd been through this.

"It's police business," I said, "but I could make it press business. I don't want us to fall out over this, John, but I want to make sure I've done my damnedest for my client. Think about it. Take me along for the ride; you have nothing to lose. If I'm right, I've pointed you in the right direction and I should get some credit for that. If I'm wrong, all you've lost is a few hours chasing a frightened suspect who is probably only a danger to herself, and you can blame me for making you do it. What if I'm right, and Sarah's family hears that the man who gave the police the answer was cut out of it by those who believed she was the killer? The civil courts will have a field day, as well as your supervisory board."

I looked at John and thought I'd made a mistake. The mention of his supervisory board snapped him awake. His eyes were the colour of fire and I could see his fists clenching and unclenching. But I could see his mind working, and I sensed that his anger was because he knew I was right. It made sense to have me along, as a form of insurance.

"If you like, we could another meeting tomorrow, say three o' clock to discuss progress," I said, with the bravery of a foolish man.

I saw John look towards Robert Lehane, and they both came to silent agreement.

John gave a resigned nod. "Three o' clock it is then. Here. But I've some people to see first, so don't be surprised if I'm late."

I nodded, and the polite routine of goodbyes took place.

I watched them go, and then returned to the apartment. I could hear Katie in the kitchen so I slunk into the bathroom to calm down.

When I got there, I stared long and hard into the mirror. My hands shook against the edge of the basin and beads of sweat appeared on my forehead. I wondered whether I should just leave it to John and the police. I mean, what did I know about murder investigations and murderers? I'd had my shot at serious crime and blown it away in a rage. John Cornwell would know what to do. No, I'd done my bit. I'd made enquiries and pointed the police in the right direction, there wasn't much more I could do, at least not without getting arrested.

I stared hard into the mirror. Bright, brown eyes stared back, and I smiled at myself.

I knew I wasn't going to leave this. I felt a buzz I hadn't felt in years, that thrill of the contest, the rush of battle. I knew I wanted to be there, wanted to see my discovery end up in a glorious arrest, wanted to read the press plaudits, the grateful citizens of Boston. Something to be proud of.

I grinned at myself, and I saw an energy that lit up the shadows. I felt good.

I ventured back into the living room and found Katie sat on the sofa, head back, eyes closed. She looked like she might cry, but when she lowered her head, she just looked tired.

"Are you okay?" I asked. It was a pointless question, she clearly wasn't.

"Oh, Joe, why did all this have to happen? Why did it come to my life?" She sounded desperate, and as I went to her, she did begin to cry.

I sat next to her and held her while she gently rocked. She didn't hold me back. She just drew her knees to her chest, folded her arms, and lost herself in my clutches.

We stayed like that for some time.

I didn't want to say anything. If I disturbed her, she might move. Instead, I felt the warm glow of her head on my chest. I could smell that dark aroma of her hair, could just make out the perfume she'd worn out during the day. It was hard to be sure of all the sensations going through me, as I sat there with Katie in my arms, but it was like something I could sink into, as if I would wear her all night.

I started to doze, when suddenly I heard her speak, quietly.

"Who do you have, Joe?"

"What do you mean?"

"I have my father and family, and I have friends here in Boston, for when, you know, for when times get too tough. Who do you have, Joe?"

I rested my head lightly on hers. "I'm not sure I have anyone," I said. "I just go for a cold one and work things through."

I felt her head rest once more against my chest. She was silent for a while, and then she said simply, "that's sad."

I smiled to myself. We stayed like that for a few minutes longer, and then Katie asked, "are you on your own out of choice? Or do things just not work out?"

I gave a slight shrug, which Katie couldn't have seen. "No, some things just don't work out as you expect them."

I became reflective as I sat there, with a woman who twisted me around resting in my arms, and thought that I was just where I wanted to be. It didn't matter what happened, because right there, right then, I had all the comfort and warmth I could ever have wanted.

I felt Katie nuzzle once more into me and I felt the butterflies start.

It started as a mild flutter, like cobwebs brushing past, but the more I sat there, the more I could feel wrenching and twisting, as if a noise had disturbed a hundred.

I knew what I wanted to do. I wanted to lift her face to mine, kiss away the tears, and then carry her into the bedroom, door shut. Every pore tried to mingle with hers, until I thought we couldn't

152

have held each other any closer without merging, but still I felt apart from her.

I don't know what made her do it, but after we'd been sat like that for nearly an hour, Katie sat up and looked me in the eyes. I held her gaze, and I thought I could hear the hands of the clock splutter and grind to a halt.

And then she kissed me, and I felt the butterflies dance.

# Thirteen

I peered out of a dusty cab window at Lieutenant Cornwell's house.

John had telephoned in the afternoon. He wasn't ready for the meeting, was still collecting information, so we re-scheduled for the evening at his house. I glanced over at Katie and tried to give her a reassuring smile. I paid the driver and we both stepped out onto the streets of Somerville.

I was nervous. I felt guilty, ill-prepared. Katie and I had done little during the day in readiness for the meeting. We hadn't made love, it hadn't seemed right. Instead, we had lain in each other's arms, dozing, talking, taking Katie somewhere free of Sarah. When we left our bed, we went for a walk in the sunshine, sat on Boston Common, watched the buildings around it trying to crowd out the green, and it felt special.

But now we were at John's house, it was back to business, and I noticed Katie harden as the taxi pulled away.

John's house was a white timber-frame. I hadn't really known what to expect; we'd just jumped in a taxi and gone to the address given to us. Somerville was a collection of narrow streets and sagging porches, home for the academic fallout from nearby Harvard. Uneven sidewalks, old brickwork and subsidence, with ageing trees casting long shadows into the road.

As we approached the door, it was opened by an elegant woman, smiling, her tight afro cropped neat and short. A long flowing skirt trailed around smooth, dark legs. We followed her in and heard the lieutenant's voice boom from a room off to the side.

We detoured into a small study, cramped by a large wooden desk and books everywhere, and dominated by the hulk of Lieutenant Cornwell; or, as he was now, John.

I saw he'd cleared some room by the window, overlooking a small narrow gap between the houses, and outside I could hear the laughter of young children and the regular pat-pat of a basketball.

I sneaked a glance at the books. I hadn't considered his reading habits, but I was still surprised to see a policeman's bookcase filled with books on the arts and a smattering of the classics: Thomas Paine, the Complete Works of Shakespeare, Nathaniel Hawthorne.

154

The history of Boston was well documented, and the city's sports heritage dominated a full shelf.

The walls again surprised me. In between the sports memorabilia, pictures of Ted Williams, Muhammad Ali, Jackie Robinson, were tacked-on family pictures. Three small, laughing children crammed themselves around the neck of a younger, smiling John Cornwell. A much slimmer John Cornwell smiled on graduation day next to a young woman sporting the same gown and mortarboard. I recognised the face in the picture as the woman who had let us in. Elsewhere, children's paintings, showing mummy and daddy and the house and the dog, were pinned for display. It was the playroom of a happy man.

"You made it, good," John said, with surprising warmth. "I thought the meeting would be better here. If this turns out how we think it might, I'm going to see precious little of my kids over the next few months."

"And don't forget me," Mrs Cornwell chipped in, bringing a tray of coffee and cookies into the room. She was playing the little wife, but I guessed from the graduation picture and the mischievous twinkle she flashed John's way that she was only playing.

"How could I ever forget you," the lieutenant said, laughing and settling back with his drink.

She gave a flirty smile over her shoulder as she left the room, and I saw John's smile continue in her direction even when she'd gone.

John turned back to us, raised his cup, and said, "to business."

I watched the lieutenant on his home turf with interest. Gone was the suit and brusque manner. Instead, he was in a Boston Celtics t-shirt and seemed friendlier, more genial.

"Is Robert coming?" I asked, reaching for my second cookie.

Before John could answer, I heard the door go and then Robert Lehane came into the room. He smiled at me and then nodded at John.

"Good timing," John said, and then he settled back, still for a minute or so, just chewing slightly on the skin around his index fingernail.

I shot a sideways look at Katie. She smiled.

John sighed, smiled, and then said, "we might as well start."

He made an open-handed offer towards me. I held up my hand in refusal. "I've had a day off today," I said, somewhat meekly. "I thought the same as you: we might have a long haul ahead."

Katie glanced over my way. "Same here," she said, cutting off the question before it was asked.

I caught John giving us a look, one that wondered whether anything had gone on since the previous night. Perhaps it was the sideways glances? Perhaps it was the arrival together, the sitting together, or some unseen message passing between us both that said we two had become one?

John smiled almost imperceptibly to himself, but he said nothing. Instead, he leant forward and then grabbed a Cheetos box from under his desk, crammed nearly to the top with paperwork and files. I could see the sheen of photographs, yellow post-it notes indexing bundles, maps, drawings, bound reports.

"As you can see," he grunted, as he heaved the box into the middle of the room, "I've done a bit better."

I whistled. "How did you get all those? I thought your police departments liked to hang onto cases."

John smiled and nodded. "We do, but I had favours to call in, and I promised each department a seat on the podium if these are all connected." He raised his eyebrows. "If you're right, Joe, you've done well, but the price of your involvement is that the police get the credit. A joint operation, mutual credit, but the only people in front of the cameras will be from the police departments. Is that okay?"

I shrugged. "Just tell Sarah's parents the reality. Whatever happens, I live in a small town. Don't make it smaller."

He nodded. "No worries."

"So what have you got there?" Katie asked.

John looked towards the box. "Details on each one Joe mentioned last night."

"Did you get all that today?" Katie sounded incredulous.

"Oh sure, but it didn't take long. I spent two hours on the telephone when I got in last night, explaining to people what I wanted. It just took a few hours this morning, driving around and collecting copies of key documents. Most of it had been dug up prior to my arrival. I've spent this afternoon going through them."

John got up and stood by an artist's easel, like something he had pinched from a child's bedroom, a marker pen in his hand, and he turned over the front page of a large pad to reveal a list of names.

"These are the names given to me by Joe yesterday. I've been able to get some background on all of them, although," and he gave a hard stare around the room, as if he thought we were just there for the fun of it, "none of it must go any further than us in here.

"I thought the easiest way to do it would be to try and find a common theme linking all of them together," he continued.

"And did you?" I asked.

John sighed and gave a light shake of the head. "See what you think, but I don't think so."

He wrote down the names on the paper, but in four columns. "I've split them up, as they fall into four types: apparent suicides, savage unexplained killings, other deaths, and missing persons. We should look at each category and see if a theme connects those in the category, and if there is a connection, we'll see if we can connect the categories."

I saw Robert Lehane give a slight nod of approval, a half-smile.

John gave a look around the room. "I'll start with the suicides.

"There's the first one that Joe mentioned last night, the suicide thirteen years back, in Saugus." He gave a smile that seemed full of regret. "There is no doubt that this was a suicide."

"How so?" I asked.

"Because there were about twenty witnesses," he replied. "Mary Bradbury was a well-known woman, the unruly daughter of a local town official. From the age of fifteen, she'd go to bars where the owners weren't interested in asking for proof of age. She'd taken up with a local biker crowd, and her attraction to them was that she was young, attractive, nubile, and sexually promiscuous. From speaking with the chief of police in Saugus, who remembered Mary Bradbury from his days as a street policeman, she was a well-known local easy lay, and he mentioned one famous incident in a seedy bar just out of town, close to its motel strip. The police arrived, some people complained about a bar dealing in live sex, and found an eighteen year old Mary Bradbury lying on a pool table, wearing nothing below the waist but the hairy-assed guy she was humping, with the rest of the bar either cheering her on or standing there with their dicks in their hands, waiting their turn."

John shook his head. I guessed he had a daughter entering her teens.

"She was a mess in here," he continued, tapping his head with his finger, "who seemed to want to do nothing more than ruin her father's public reputation by destroying her own."

"So what happened?" asked Katie, her voice quiet, concerned.

"For a while, nothing. She starting dating one of the bikers more seriously and they set up a gas station and repair shop. They had a little boy, and for a few years she calmed down. But then she started drinking, seriously drinking. She became a well-known figure in bars again, and she would sleep around, although less publicly. And then she got depressed. She began to damage things. Police cars, municipal property, that kind of thing."

He shrugged sadly. "It seems she was just a fuck-up. She tried normality and didn't like it. And then one night, she drank herself to a standstill in a bar, bought some whisky, and carried it on outside. The police think this was all premeditated, because at around midnight she climbed up the side of the Town Hall building. There was some scaffolding there, just doing minor repair work. She reached the top and stripped naked. She gathered quite a crowd apparently, calling everyone 'cocksuckers' from the rung of the scaffold. The crowd that gathered all knew her. Some made fun, some told her to be careful, some just laughed."

John paused to gather his thoughts.

"What the crowd didn't know was that she'd taken a fifty foot length of thin wire up with her and hooked it around the scaffold pole. The other end was just looped through, and it was as sharp as cheese wire. She stood on the edge of the scaffold, made a farewell speech, something about "I am evil, I am death, but now I am at peace. I am alive," and then she jumped off. She'd put the loop around her neck." He exhaled. "It took off her head like a pea being popped from its pod."

Katie had her hand over her mouth.

"About twenty people saw her do it," John said, "so it's not a good start."

"Not everyone will be connected though," I said in mitigation. "It's the number of hits that I thought was unusual, not the facts of each one." I looked at John's easel. "What about the other two suicides?"

John cocked his head to one side and gave a slight grimace. "Those aren't so straightforward."

He reached into his box and produced, after a brief rummage, some photographs and some heavy, typed reports. He scattered the photographs, four in total onto his desk.

"Two from each discovery," he said. "Have a look, see what you think."

I reached the pictures first, but as I placed them on the floor in front of me I realised everyone was crowding round.

The first picture showed a woman in her fifties, sat in the front of a car, smiling almost peacefully to herself. Her lips and cheeks were an unnatural cherry-red, but otherwise she looked at ease. The second picture was from the same set, but this time it showed the whole car, and I could see the rubber hose going from the exhaust pipe, through the crack in the window at the top, from where I assumed it would bellow exhaust gases until the car was filled with enough carbon monoxide to kill its occupant.

I began to feel less confident.

The next set showed a young girl, possibly in her mid to late teens, hanging from the branch of a tree. Her feet dangled only a couple of inches off the ground, and nearby a thick stump lay discarded. Her tongue protruded from her mouth like an unwelcome guest, and her eyes were staring.

I put the photographs down, feeling strange that I should somehow be disappointed by all this. Perhaps my worst fears weren't to be realised.

But then I glanced back at the photograph of the young girl, the limp form suspended in mid-air. Something about her clothing bothered me. She was wearing a lilac shirt and jeans, and they looked dishevelled, but they didn't look quite right. The jeans looked okay, although I thought her zip looked undone.

I looked towards Katie and shrugged the question.

Katie looked at the photograph, and then at me, and then frowned, and then looked back at the picture. I saw it dawn on her. I leant forward.

"It's the shirt," she said quietly, unsure of herself. "It's the shirt, isn't it?"

John smiled, and then nodded.

"The buttons are done up wrong, out of line," Katie continued. "One side at the open neck is all rouged up, and at the bottom there is extra button or two." Katie looked at me, and then at John. "Somebody else dressed her."

John nodded. But his face looked drawn for a moment, tired, as if he didn't want to think about this anymore.

"She was murdered, wasn't she," I said.

John nodded.

Then I heard Katie gasp.

"It's the one you mentioned yesterday," Katie said, her hand over her mouth. "The boyfriend did it, the guy you arrested and who is still in jail."

John gave a laugh, but he wasn't laughing. "That's what the jury thought." He looked at me. "You see, Joe, a lot of old wounds are going to be opened up here. The boyfriend is serving his sixth year of a mandatory life sentence. The girl's parents have moved on. They've got someone to hate, a focus for their grief, and there's a chance I'm going to have to go to them and say we got it wrong." He shook his head. "In a small way, I hope you are wrong Joe, I really hope you are wrong."

"Was it the shirt that gave it away?" Katie asked, eyes twinkling.

John nodded. "It's what made us look more closely. On the post-mortem, it became apparent that she'd been strangled with a thinner cord a few hours before being strung up. You see, there are two types of knots: fixed and sliding. If you look at this knot," and he pointed to the photograph, "it's a fixed knot, where the body just hangs in the loop and victim is killed by the weight of the body against the rope. A sliding knot, however, closes against the neck as the weight takes effect, so it's the tightening of the rope that causes death. Think about the actions of the rope, they are different, and they cause different grooves in the neck. In a fixed-knot hanging, the rope will cut deep furrows into the skin on the neck as the body weight takes hold. However," and this is where he paused, "the groove will follow the direction of the jawline, as it's the jawbone that acts as a brake, keeps the rope around the neck." He paused again. "We found something different."

I could almost hear the silence in the room. John had worked on this case, knew all the intimate details, and I could tell he hadn't needed to revise the file to know the facts.

"There was a deep, narrower furrow running across the front and around the neck itself, not the jawline, as if it was the application of pressure rather than the weight of the body doing the work." He looked around the room. "That's not a fixed rope hanging. That's strangulation. And we found scratch marks around a deep ligature mark. That ligature mark wouldn't have been very noticeable at first, very pale, but later on it becomes brown and dry. We found fibres under Rebecca's fingernails, and we find those same fibres in the scratches around the ligature mark. We matched those fibres to the cord from a robe belonging to Rebecca's boyfriend. Rebecca had been strangled with the cord, and had struggled trying to get it from around her neck. The marks wouldn't have been that clear when the attempt to make it look like suicide was made, so whoever did it wouldn't have known the difference would be so easy to spot."

"So the boyfriend was arrested," I said matter-of-factly.

"Not straight away. But his mother almost passed out when she was shown the shirt. It was one of her husband's shirts. We went through the house, and became convinced it was the murder scene. Fibres from the carpet matched fibres found in Rebecca's hair. That's when we found the cord, hidden under the boyfriend's bed. We also found a key to a storage locker at South Station. In the locker we found Rebecca's own torn shirt." John shook his head. "This is cut and dried. We had a victim who was killed in the bedroom of the accused, by something belonging to the accused, and discovered wearing something belonging to the accused's family. He said he had an alibi, but when we checked it out, the guy didn't even exist."

"This guy is clever." It was Robert.

We all whirled round.

John paused for a moment. "Go on," he said quietly. He was defensive, but I could tell he respected Robert.

"Think about it," said Robert. "Having the forensic knowledge to make a murder look like a suicide is one thing, but to make a murder look like a faked suicide is another. And to do it to frame someone else. Wow, that is marvellous." He shook his head. "The shirt is a wonderful touch. It must have been pre-planned to go to the trouble of hiding the other shirt and leaving the key behind, and to pinch his father's shirt. But to do the buttons up wrong was a lovely touch. He knew you'd notice it, as if he couldn't risk an autopsy missing the truth." Robert looked at John. "Was she a virgin?"

John nodded.

"Was the boyfriend?"

John shook his head. "No."

Robert almost smiled in admiration. "The perfect victim. Who wouldn't suspect the boyfriend? Wants sex, doesn't get it. Head rage, sexual fury, call it what you want. Panics. Tries to fake a look-alike suicide, spotted, caught, convicted."

"But if she was killed by someone else," I said, "she wasn't selected as a desirable victim. She was killed because she was called Rebecca Nurse."

Robert shrugged. "But who she was might have determined how she died."

"So if there are clues here, are there any other clues in the other ones?" I asked.

John pointed to the photos. "Be my guest."

We all leant forward, and once again it was Katie who spotted it.

"The woman who gassed herself in her car. She's in the passenger seat."

John smiled.

I hadn't noticed that. Because everyone drives on the left at home, the victim was sat in the seat where I would normally expect to see a steering wheel. I looked closer. Katie was right.

"Is there anything unusual in that?" I asked.

"Have you ever touched a hot tailpipe?" John raised his eyebrows. "If the engine was running before she attached the hose, it would have jerked her out of her melancholy pretty damn quick. No, she would have to have put the hose around a cold tailpipe, climb back into the car, switch it on, and then clamber into the passenger seat." He shrugged. "Unlikely, you would think."

"Particularly as the passenger door was locked." I could just make out that the door lock was not as depressed on the driver side, the little black lug pointing away from the upholstery. The passenger side's door had an unbroken line against its window. "Clambering over was the only option."

John stood up and walked to the window. He looked like he was listening for sounds outside, but things had gone quiet.

"We mustn't forget that these are only theories," he said quietly. "The woman who gassed herself in her car did exhibit unusual features. She was in the passenger seat, and the autopsy report thought that the carbon monoxide ingestion had been slower than you'd expect from an automobile suicide." He turned around, his hands in his pocket. "If the fumes are inhaled over a long period of time, there are usually no signs of a struggle, and you get that flushed look you see on the photographs. However, if it is rapid, as in an automobile suicide, you often get convulsions and evacuation of the bowels." John looked grim. "It's not always the dignified death people think it is. They aren't always found in pleasant sleep. No, their last appearance on the planet is often in ruffled clothing, sat in the waste of their last meal. Not nice." He shook his head and shrugged. "But she was a tall woman, and it may have been that sitting in the passenger seat gave her more room; no pedals in the way. Or perhaps she wanted to be a bit further away from the hose?" He paused. "But what I haven't mentioned is that her only child was killed in a hut and run accident two months earlier. If anyone was a candidate for suicide, she was. And although her post-mortem appearance suggested a slower exposure to carbon monoxide, it wasn't that inconsistent to cause any problems,"

"So what you are saying," I said, trying to pin John down, "is that we have a murderer convicted on good evidence, and two obvious suicides?"

John nodded. "Other than the coincidence of the names being connected to Salem witches, that's exactly what I'm saying."

"It still fits though." It was Robert again. "Perhaps I'm just trying to make trouble, but they could still be connected." He stood up. "Think about Rebecca Nurse and her convicted boyfriend. Is it ridiculous to think that someone killed Rebecca in his room while he was out, and then framed him? Once you're in the house, everything is there. The fibres from the carpet, the cord from the robe, the father's shirt. All you need to do is put the shirt on wrong, plant the key and hide cord, dump Rebecca's shirt in the locker, and wait. The police will either think it is suicide or go to the boyfriend. The set-up might have just been a form of insurance, to deflect attention away from any mysterious strangers seen in the neighbourhood."

"But what about the false alibi?" John asked.

"What if it isn't false? What if he was taken away from the house to allow the killer time? The name of the alibi will be false, but he won't know that. He is fitted up, every angle covered." Robert shook his head almost in admiration. "Clever, very clever."

John had his hands on his hips. "Do you really think that's what happened?"

Robert smiled. "I don't know. But is it impossible? If you were intending to kill a particular person, planning and waiting, is that scenario so far fetched?"

John said nothing.

"What about the woman in the car, the one who gassed herself?" Katie asked. "We are dealing with a house of cards here. There either is a link, or there isn't. It's unlikely only one or two will be linked with the Salem witches. It's all or nothing."

Robert shrugged. "Is it so hard to gas someone, drive the body somewhere and leave it? I wouldn't have thought so. Put her in a room, run some carbon monoxide through it. The concentration will be low, so she'll just get drowsy and then fall asleep. Couldn't be easier. And it would explain the autopsy findings."

Katie suddenly went white. "There is one other thing," she said quietly, almost whispering.

We all looked at her.

"The alibi." She looked at John, and then at me. "It means there are two of them. One with the boyfriend, and one with the girl."

Robert smiled. I heard John groan.

It was going to be a long night.



Sarah was in the shower when they both came in. She had been in the shower for a long time, but she hadn't been counting. She'd sat on the floor, the water washing over her, each drop trying to wash him away and down the drain.

She didn't move when they came in. She didn't care what happened now. She was seeing everything from a distance now, not tuning in.

She was grabbed roughly by the arms and hauled to her feet. She felt a hand grab her around the throat and push her against the wall. Then she felt her legs kicked open. Rough hands fumbled with her, and she felt something inside her. She stared ahead, cold. She thought it was him again, but when she was led by her arms towards the door, whatever was put there stayed there.

She felt handcuffs wrap themselves around her wrists, bound together at the front tightly. Then a plastic sheet was placed over her head and she was taken out of her prison.

Sarah winced when she got outside. It was cold, and she could feel rain beating on her naked legs. She looked at her feet and saw darkness. It was night-time. Cool mud washed between her toes and she stumbled on a fallen branch.

She was put into the back of a van and placed on the floor. She felt her cuffs become attached to something on the floor, and when the rough hands let her go, she couldn't move her hands away.

She was bolted to the floor.

The van started and she left her prison.

We'd taken a coffee break.

I was sat in a corner, staring at the floor. Robert was deep in thought, his fingers pulling at his lips. John had gone to say goodnight to his family.

I glanced over at the photograph of young Rebecca Nurse and wished she could have wielded a sign, a clue. Anne Foster just seemed sad. If I was right, I wondered how bad the last couple of months could be of one's life. First your only child, and then death for yourself. Even if I was wrong, it was a cruel way to end two lives.

I looked towards the window. The night had arrived, and the rain hit the window hard like a scattering of pebbles. It was not a night to be homeless, and I wondered what sort of home housed Sarah.

Katie was stood at the window looking out through the streaks of water. I wondered how all this was for her. She had carried on with her life, but it was still her friend who was out there, missing, and it was still in her apartment that someone was killed.

I went behind her and put my hand softly on hers. I felt her squeeze and grip my fingers, and then she turned round and gave me a moist smile. I could tell it was difficult, but I sensed also a determination to see this through, as if that was the best way to deal with it.

Katie mouthed the words, "I'll be alright." I smiled at her, and then turned back to where Robert was sitting.

I couldn't help liking Robert, despite my arrest. He was cool, calm, much different to John Cornwell. He was sat back, legs crossed at the ankles, his fidgeting the only sign of his mind working. If John was high speed, Robert was a cruiser.

He caught me looking and smiled.

"Bit of a hobby of yours?" I asked.

"Huh?"

"Criminology, psychology, whatever you want to call it? You seem to have a take on this."

He laughed. "Call it a professional interest."

"So what is your take?"

He thought for a moment, and then said, "highly organised, each crime scene planned in advance, forensically aware. They'll be difficult to catch."

I exhaled. This hadn't been what I expected when I left Morsby a few days earlier. "What makes them, killers like this?"

He sat back. "We all know what kind of people are serial killers. Spotting them in time is the hard part. Serial killers are born, not made, but something has to trigger them. Their upbringings seem okay on the outside, with parents still together, stable families in nice neighbourhoods. But their lives tend to be fucked up on the quiet: family histories of psychiatric disturbance, alcohol and drug abuse, with sexual violence in the home, but we don't always know that. They retreat into fantasy, an escapist world they create, and they play out hostilities in this world. Then there is the trigger, something that makes them step out of the fantasy world and start killing in the real world."

"What, so there might be potential killers around that just haven't been triggered?"

Robert nodded. "Think to wartime, those acts of brutality committed against civilians in the name of revenge or cleansing. Ordinary people do that, not just generals."

"So how do you spot these people?"

He shrugged. "You don't. You play the percentages game. You take the usual characteristics, depending on the type of killer, and create a profile. It helps you rule people in or rule them out, or helps you work out how to catch them if you think you know the identity of the killer. But can I let you into a secret?"

I nodded.

"It doesn't catch anyone. Think of the big ones: Ted Bundy, Jeffrey Dahmer, John Gacy. All caught by chance. Ted Bundy wasn't caught by a profile. He killed at least twenty-three people, but ended up in custody for firing at a patrolman when he was driving a stolen car. John Wayne Gacy was arrested because he was the last person seen speaking to the final victim. He had his victims buried beneath his floorboards, and the police had been in the house, but it wasn't the profile that caught him. It was just good old-fashioned police work. Wherever you look in recent times, it isn't the criminal profile that catches the man, but witness testimony, or forensic evidence."

"But there must be other types of killing, you know, just crazed murders. Not just these organised murders you talk about."

Robert nodded. "Yeah, sure, a disorganised killing, but it's not what we have here. A disorganised killing is unexplained savagery, random in style, and usual scattered with clues. A blitz killing. If you want to know what kind of killing it is, just look at control. The organised killer uses restraints, controls, he is in control. The disorganised blitz killer doesn't. He's out of control."

"You said "he"," Katie said. "Is it always a man?"

Robert turned to her and smiled. "Always, where there has been an obvious murder. There are female serial killers, but they kill in a different way. You know, the nurses who kill while on duty. Female serial killers murder passively. Men kill."

I was about to ask more, when John walked back into the room.


The journey lasted around half an hour.

Sarah could hear other traffic passing the vehicle she was in, ordinary people going about ordinary things. She was naked, trussed to the floor, scared, covered in plastic sheeting.

Sarah sensed she was on some kind of an interstate. The ride had started bumpy, and when it went smoother, it became stop and start, as if the van was stopping for traffic lights or junctions. But for the last fifteen minutes or so, the ride had been smooth and constant, a steady purr, broken only by the swoosh of an occasional passing vehicle.

Sarah wondered about where she was going. Was she going to be left somewhere, left to stumble into the nearest police station, her captors long gone, whereabouts unknown? He'd used her now, so he had finished with her. Sarah didn't think so, she'd seen too much, but the possibility kept her head clear, the hope that the nightmare was soon to end.

She sensed the engine change its pitch as it decelerated, and then she felt the van lurch to the right as it came off the interstate.

Sarah sensed the journeys end.

John came back into the room with fresh coffee. The huddle around Robert broke up and once more, John had the floor.

John looked tired. Mrs Cornwell had looked into the room some time ago to wish us all goodnight, and as the sounds of life fell still I became aware of how late it was.

"C'mon, you guys," he said, "let's chew through the rest of it." He was running his hands over his cheeks as if he was feeling late stubble, and I could see the effort of a long day taking its toll.

I dropped my hand from Katie's and raised my eyebrows at her. She smiled and nodded, and we returned to our seats.

John went to his easel and pointed out the name of Bridget Bishop. He gave the easel a bang with his fist. "Bridget Bishop. Ran a jeweller's shop in Brookline, went missing for three weeks, and was discovered in Peabody, hidden in undergrowth."

"How did she die?" Robert asked.

"Strangled, eventually," John replied, "but she was tortured first. She was covered in small burns, slashes and puncture wounds. Never bad enough to kill, but some were scabbed over. They would be consistent with self-harm, but also consistent with torture." He looked around the room and gave a small smile. "I might go with your theory on this one."

I felt a surge of hope. I could tell John was in a rush. "What else is there?"

John rummaged once more through the box, and pulled out some typed sheets. There were no photographs this time.

"Abigail Hobbs." John looked at Katie and gave a look of apology. "We talked about this one last night, the thirteen year old girl found at Prankers Pond, naked from the waist down, hands tied behind her back, thin cord around her neck. She'd been anally raped, and strangled during the act. The rape and murder took place somewhere else. Prankers Pond was just the dumping ground."

Katie nodded grimly, but I saw her steel herself, and I knew she was going to be alright.

"This is the one that shows a link," Robert said. "It's the first death in this bundle after the suicide in Saugus, you know, the woman from the clock tower, and so the first two in the list have Saugus connections."

"What was the feeling at the time?" I asked. "Did anyone make a connection with Mary Bradbury's suicide?"

John shook his head. "Why should they? One's a local crazy doing a double twist and swallow from the town hall, and the other's an apparent sex attack on a young girl."

Robert sat forward. "Don't always assume an act of buggery is a sex attack," he said quietly. "Anal rape is a particularly savage form of attack. If the attacker wants sexual gratification, there are other ways to achieve it. To bugger someone is to humiliate them, because of its savagery, its anger. The motive may have been to humiliate, to degrade. If that's the case, it isn't necessarily a sex attack."

Everyone looked at Robert with puzzlement.

"Isn't a sex attacker someone who uses sex as a weapon, as a form of attack?" asked Katie, clearly not agreeing with Robert.

Robert thought for a moment before continuing.

"Think of Albert De Salvo," he said. "They called him the Boston Strangler, not the Boston rapist. He used objects in the sexual humiliation of his victims, often after death. His first two victims were sexually assaulted using bottles, intact ones. His final victim was found with her buttocks propped on pillows, sat back against the headboard, with semen running from the corner of her mouth and a broom handle sticking out of her vagina. A greeting card saying 'Happy New Year' was propped against her foot. All this was positioned so that it would be the first thing to greet someone when they opened the door."

Robert shook his head.

"Albert De Salvo did rape and strangle many people in between, and did boast of an insatiable sexual appetite, but to me those killings have the mark of sadism and hatred, not sex. Sometimes sex is just the expression of the hatred, the anger, and not the motivator. It's the control, the power, the infliction of pain, the degradation that motivates. A sex attack is one where the sex is the motivation. You hear of rapists who apologise to their victims immediately afterwards, or who drive them home. That is a sex attack, as the attacker wanted sex. This girl at Prankers Pond. That isn't sex, its anger. I don't suppose De Salvo had an overwhelming desire to fuck someone with a broom handle. It was a humiliation thing. This sounds like the same."

"Does it matter what label it has?" Katie asked bitterly. "It's still a man using his sex against a woman."

"The label is vital. Someone who attacks with sex as the motivator will be sexually dysfunctional in some way. The desire for sex overwhelms everything else, so you can already guess what sort of person this might be. Someone who uses sex just as a form of attack poses different questions and will provide different answers. He might be in a stable sexual relationship, might be a normal married man. His desire to inflict pain is what motivates, and sex is just the most severe way to do it. Get the label right, and you can look in the right places."

"So what you are saying," John intervened, "is that we shouldn't rule it out because the suicides weren't sex attacks, that this girl isn't necessarily different from the others?"

Robert nodded. "Something like that." He paused. "Is it the only attack with a sexual element?"

"No. Around eighteen months ago, Liz Proctor worked at a late-night convenience store. Didn't make it home after a shift. Found in a dumpster three days later. She'd been raped and then bludgeoned to death. A couple of homeless found her. She was a mess; I've seen the pictures."

"Where did she live?" Robert interrupted.

"Dorchester Heights."

"Where did she work?"

"At a liquor store in Dorchester."

"And where was she found?"

John shrugged. "Again, Dorchester."

170

"There was another one that year?

"Yes."

"Was she black?"

John nodded.

"Is she the only black victim?"

John nodded again.

Robert looked deep in thought.

"Is that relevant?" John asked.

Robert looked at John, but then he just waved him away. "I'm just musing to myself," he said quietly.

I looked at Katie and saw she had her knees drawn up to her chest, defensive-like.

"Do you want me to go on?" John asked. She gave a slight nod.

"Mary Lacy was next. You know, the teacher from Dedham who wound up with her head on a pole outside the school."

Katie waved him on.

"The one after that is Susannah Martin, a middle-aged mother of three from Waltham. Her husband went to work, and when he returned she wasn't there. The kids were all at school, so it was a few hours before anyone discovered she was gone. We found her a few weeks later in a burning car in Newton. She'd died from multiple stab and slash wounds. We think the fire was just to frustrate forensics. If we have the complete list, Susannah Martin was the killer's longest guest at that time. Perhaps he hadn't perfected his forensic-free technique. Before Susannah, there'd just been the girl found at Prankers Pond, the Saugus suicide, and the teacher with her head on a pole; and if you remember on that one, we never found the torso."

"How do you know the victim simply didn't burn to death?" I asked. "I mean, wouldn't a fire destroy much of the evidence?"

"There was no tissue reaction," John explained. "If someone is alive in intense heat like that, you distinguish pre-death burns from post-death burns by a dissection of the tissues around the burn. If the victim is alive at the time of the fire, there is a reaction in the tissue cells, as the tissues are still alive to react. In a very high temperature situation, as in this case, the tissues can rupture, and splits appear that look like slash wounds. There were no tissue reactions in these ruptures, so the pathologist decided that Susannah Martin was already dead when she was placed into the car."

171

"How was the pathologist able to say the other injuries were slash wounds then, if the fire leaves slash-type wounds?" I asked.

"Do you really want to know?"

I nodded, unsure.

"Because the slashes and stabbings were deep, very deep. They had cut into the bone, and so whatever was used was big and sharp."

I saw Katie rub her forearms and shudder. I thought perhaps I didn't need to know.

"Okay, okay," I said, "we're getting somewhere now."

John raised his eyebrows at me. I could tell that he didn't necessarily agree with me. But I could tell he was keen to keep going.

He skimmed through his list, putting papers to one side, taking some time to sort his paperwork out. He eventually worked out which one he wanted.

"Abigail Faulkner," he continued. "Only three and a half years ago. There'd been some missing persons in between, and the couple of faked suicides we talked about earlier, but this was the next obvious murder. A young mother of two boys. Her husband had taken her two boys to a Patriots game. They lived in a quiet suburb, typically middle-class, and no neighbours reported anything unusual, no lurking strangers. She just wasn't there. She turned up two weeks later, buried in a shallow grave in Braintree, still smouldering from the application of gasoline and a match." John paused. "The pathologist thought she'd been alive before she was set alight."

John caught my enquiring look, so he explained.

"She was found on her back in a small ditch, in a fighting stance, you know, like a boxer's stance. It's caused by the muscle proteins coagulating in the heat, causing the muscles tissues to shorten and contract. The body becomes foetal again." John looked around. "Whoever did this put her into a shallow pit, poured gasoline over her, and threw in a flame."

I shuddered. I wondered about Sarah. What hell was she going through? I thought of Sarah's parents. Their worst nightmare was that Sarah had killed Brad and would be locked in a cell for many years. I suspected that would be the option they would choose if they knew the alternative.

"That sounds pretty bad." It was Katie.

172

"You haven't heard the worst," John continued. "There'd been a tape made of her screams. Whoever had her called her husband from a phone by the side of Highway One and played it down the line. He'd kept on playing and rewinding and playing until the husband put the phone down."

"Is there a tape of that call?" I asked.

John shook his head. "No-one knew then she'd been abducted, so there was no wire-tap. The husband got the number by doing caller-ID. The papers say he was a mess. He could never describe how her screams sounded. Just said it was like something he hoped he'd never hear again."

John threw the papers back into the box and shook his head. "We might have got somewhere with that one, but with no forensics, we were relying on a member of the public calling in with information. There we hit a snag. The media weren't too interested, as there was nothing to play on camera. Same old story. It's not how good the story is, it's just how well it can be told, and a picture always says much more than somebody telling the tale second-hand. It didn't get the coverage it deserved, so the response was small."

"So what have we got?" I asked, concerned. I'd listened to descriptions of murders and possible suicides, but I hadn't heard any link to bind them. Robert was clearly working on something, his silence and grim expression said it all, but for the moment he was silent. All that bound them was the lack of a murderer, and even that wasn't true in all cases, as there was a murderer sat in jail while we ruminated over his crime, and the lack of forensics. The method was different in each case, or so I thought, and as I looked back on my great scheme, my great idea, it all seemed a little foolish.

"We don't have anything, do we," I said glumly. "They're all different. Apart from the name connection, there are no similarities."

I felt like I'd wasted some days when I should have been chasing real clues, not the jumbled thoughts of someone finding leads that aren't there due to a lack of anything else. I felt Katie's hand touch mine.

John shook his head and shrugged. I thought I saw relief in his eyes. "Sometimes coincidence can be cruel."

Robert stood up and walked over to the table. He picked up the papers and began to leaf through them quietly. A look of concentration furrowed his brow. John looked towards him in a way that said, 'don't piss me off, man.'

He stood up and looked around the room.

"I'm not so sure," he said, stroking his chin absent-mindedly. "I'm not so sure."

I saw John sink into his chair and felt Katie's hand once more clasp mine.

# Fourteen

Robert stood facing us all, stroking his chin and looking at nothing.

"What do you mean, you ain't so sure?" John exclaimed, now stood up. "If you can find a common theme to all these," he said, waving pieces of paper in his hand, "you are as mad as that limey bastard," and he flicked his other hand my way.

Robert looked at John and John fell quiet. Katie's arms had dropped from her knees, and she was staring open-mouthed.

"You are looking at it from a different angle," Robert said quietly, "the wrong angle. You are looking for something to link what he did, not why he did it."

He smiled an apology at John and then said, "linkage blindness. It's what allows serial killers to tot up their totals. There is usually a link somewhere, something to show that the unexplained deaths have a connection to each other. It's a fact of life, John, that too much attention is paid to what is done, and not enough to the why. We've spent the last few hours talking about the lack of a link because his MO, the modus operandi, is different in each one. That's wrong."

I looked at John and saw a quiet fury, but I saw also a willingness to listen, a silent respect.

"The modus operandi changes each time, it has to," Robert continued, "or else the fantasy becomes stale. The MO is just what he does to carry out the fantasy, and as he gets better at it, the MO will change. Or else, circumstances will dictate a change. So if you only look at the MO to find the link, you'll miss it, because it will evolve and change with each murder. You take a serial rapist who always takes his victim to a secluded spot in a blue van, and then ties her to a tree using garden twine before raping her, most people would say the seclusion, the van, the tree, the twine were the things to examine, because those things constitute his MO." He paused to cast his eyes among us before shaking his head. "Those people would be wrong. Those things, the seclusion, the van, and everything else, are just what he needs to carry out the fantasy. Those things will change, the modus operandi always do. It's an evolving, growing thing. The seclusion is necessary for the outdoor

175

crime, the tree is needed to anchor the victim, the van is just transport, the twine is just what he has handy. No, what is important is his signature, those things that motivate the crime, not how he makes he fantasy real. Why outdoors? How was the victim restrained? In what position? Were there any further injuries, any specific types of mutilation? What did he say during and after the rape? Was it slow and prolonged, or was it fast and frenzied? Did the victim's clothes stay on, or did certain articles always come off? Those are the signatures of the offender, and that's where the links are to be found. The rapist may rent himself a hunting lodge, he may trade in his van, he may run out of garden twine. The MO will change in time as he finds better ways of committing the crimes, but the signature, the reason for the fantasy will stay the same. The victim will still be restrained in the same position, the act of rape will still take place in the same way, because those facts make up the fantasy. The signature never changes, and focusing on just the MO misses links between other crimes. Linkage blindness."

"That doesn't answer the big question," said John questioningly. "Which is, what is the link between the killings? Are the signatures the same?"

"Captivity, torture, and vanity," Robert said quietly, "and the witches of Salem."

John raised an eyebrow. He tried to flash that look of disbelief that he'd first given me, but I could tell his respect for Robert overcame it. If Robert gave it credibility, then maybe it was credible.

"I know, I know, that last one sounds crazy," said Robert, his hands up in apology, "but if they are all connected, he is motivated by some link with the Salem witches. And you only have to look in the newspapers every day to see that life throws up things beyond comprehension all the time."

John muttered something about us all being crazy bastards, but he didn't ask us to leave, and he stayed to listen what was being said.

"Think of the underlying facts in each one," Robert continued, "or at least a best guess. They were all missing for some time, so the killer wants to spend time with his victims. What for? Revenge? Who knows? But the captivity is important to him. He wants to spend time with his victims. And the periods between disappearance and the discovery of the body have increased. His

176

enjoyment of the captivity is now more fulfilled. And the victims are tortured. Some of the bodies showed old injuries, as if death was just the last act, not the only one. We can't know about the teacher with her head on the pole, but I would have thought it impossible to just cut someone's head off. Some form of restraint will have been used, and I think you said the head was hacked off with a large blunt instrument. That would have involved downward pressure, and so she was restrained. If she was restrained, she was probably tortured. Even the young girl found at Prankers Pond had been killed somewhere else, pain inflicted before the body was discarded."

"What about the girl killed by her boyfriend?" John said coldly. "That was a straight killing."

Robert smiled. "But he didn't repeat the formula, did he? Perhaps the lack of any period of captivity took away the pleasure, took away the whole reason for doing it." He picked up some paper to hold while emphasising his point. "But you did spot the set-up, so he was able to get some vicarious recognition. That's the vanity part. You were supposed to spot the set-up and admire his technique. The other fake suicide, you know, the woman found in the car, was easier to spot, because the body was displayed when it could have been buried. And the others, the head on the pole, the burnings. All displays." Robert glanced around slowly. "But you didn't go one step further and spot that the boyfriend had also been set up, the more subtle display. You never really got round to admiring him, not properly, and no-one spotted the link between the deaths. That will be why he has resorted to the letters. He's trying to make it easier for us. Again, vanity. He believes he has a superior intelligence, so he is trying to make the link more obvious to us lesser mortals. But the most important thing is that he wants us to appreciate his intelligence." Robert paused, and then asked, "do you remember Ted Bundy?"

"Of course I do. Most people do."

"And as a police officer, what do you recall most about him? The long list of victims?"

"No," John replied, seeing Robert's direction. "I remember the arrogant way he thought he could get away with it by conducting his own trial, strutting around in that bad grey suit."

Robert smiled. "That's right. You remember the strutting, the calmness, the cold-bloodedness. He never thought he would win an acquittal, but in the process of being convicted he wanted the world to know how clever he was. Even when asking questions, his main purpose appeared to be to get the officers to explain how cleverly constructed the scenes were, so we could all share the admiration that he had for himself. I think we might be getting a bit of that here, but he is worrying that the links won't be spotted."

"It's an extreme way to get respect," I said. "Does he really enjoy killing that much, that it is the best way to get attention?"

"Just the opposite," Robert said, shaking his head. "I don't think he enjoyed killing at all. Think of the way they died. They all suffered at arms length. Strangulation with a cord, a match being thrown onto a gasoline-soaked victim, a slow asphyxiation. Even the death of the young girl involved a condom and then restraints to kill her. None of the deaths involve the direct application of the killer's hands to the victim. And that must mean that he doesn't want to kill the victims, but knows he has to. He could be identified, or perhaps he feels their usefulness has ended. The disposal of the bodies is used to display his intelligence, but I think the death itself isn't an enjoyable experience."

"So where do we go from here?" asked John, not happy at being told that he'd been getting it wrong.

Robert must have sensed his mood. "Don't blame yourself, John. It isn't your fault, it never was. The links weren't obvious. It's only the letters he's sent to Katie that gave any clue."

John didn't say anything. He just gave Robert a steady glare, like a boxer during the pre-fight warm-up.

"Where do we go?" I asked, trying to keep the discussion to the matter in hand.

Robert looked away from John and at me, and then at everyone in the room. "We look at what sort of person he might be."

Robert went to the easel and turned over a fresh piece of paper. "Let's see what we can work out about this guy, and then see how they fit the facts of all the murders. Try and disprove a link, find a thread of thought that breaks the link and we'll forget all about it." He paused to look around the room. Everyone was watching him expectantly. He smiled briefly. "We know he is white, middle-aged, and with hardly anything of a criminal record. That fits all of them."

I almost choked on my coffee. "How the hell do you know that?" I exploded.

Robert shrugged his shoulders. "The white bit was easy: all serial killers are white, at least they are in the Western world. If the same person committed all these, he is likely to be white."

"Yes, but hang on," John interrupted, "you have the equation the wrong way round. You need to find the connection before you can attach a racial description. If these aren't connected, the racial make-up of serial killers is irrelevant. Some of these killers may be white, some may be black."

Robert nodded. "I agree, but look at the facts of each one. What strikes you about the racial make-up of each victim? And the victim is usually the biggest clue in any crime." He paused. We all knew the answer, but we wanted to hear someone say it. "Each one was white," he said, "apart from one." He looked at our expressions, letting our expectations build before continuing, "and each one must have been abducted from her own neighbourhood, or near enough to it."

"How do you know that?" I asked. "Do you know something about all these?"

"No more than you do."

"Then how do you know where these people were taken from?"

"Think about it," he said. "Work it through logically. No-one has mentioned any reports of people being abducted in public, no struggles into waiting cars, no muggings in malls. These are all unexplained absences."

"Apart from one," John mumbled, referring to the one he'd explained to a jury.

Robert ignored him, save for a quick glance in his direction. "If they weren't taken from a public place, they must have been taken from their own neighbourhoods." He smiled. "And you can say what you like about progressive America, but we all know that neighbourhoods still define themselves on racial lines. And are there any reports by neighbours of a black man loitering?"

John shook his head slowly.

"Well, there you have it. You have a white teacher, a white jeweller, a white suburban mother of three, a white teenager, a white bereaved mother."

"Hang on," I interrupted. "What about the woman from Dorchester? You know, raped and bludgeoned and found in a dumpster? She was black."

"She wasn't the victim of the same man."

I opened my mouth to protest, but Robert raised his hand.

"Please be patient," he asked.

"We know that all the other victims were from middle-class white backgrounds," he continued, "and they were taken from white neighbourhoods. And I think they were tricked into going somewhere, not taken by force."

"How the hell do you know that?" asked John, starting to sound exasperated. "We don't really know where they were taken from, or whether there was a struggle or not."

Robert nodded. "I agree, but if the person went by force, don't you think they would create a fuss. I use the word consensual to mean there is no evidence that they were physically grappled into going. If that had happened, surely someone would have seen or heard something? No-one did. How much more likely is it that someone would have reported it to the police if they'd seen a black man forcing a white neighbour into a car, or down the street? Which means that they weren't taken from busy areas, as there were no struggles reported by witnesses, and therefore they went willingly from their own community. And think of this: would a middle-class white woman go anywhere with a black man, or Hispanic, or whatever, if that person was unknown to them?"

He was met with a chorus of silence. Robert answered his own question. "No, that person wouldn't. And that's why I rule out the Dorchester killing as part of the same series. She was black in a black neighbourhood. The rest are white."

"And there's another thing."

It was Katie. We all looked round at her.

"Go on," said Robert.

"Well, if we take the woman from Dorchester out of the frame, it is one victim a year. That was the only year where victims doubled up."

Robert nodded. "Makes it relevant."

"So," I queried, getting back to the earlier point, "it's a general rule that the victim matches the racial background of the attacker?"

Robert grimaced. "If the victim was taken by trickery, not force, then yes. We have no reports of the victims being taken by force, either in public or in their neighbourhoods, so we have to assume some trickery, some subterfuge on the part of the killer. That, in turn, suggests they were from the same racial group as each other."

He turned to address the whole group. "Look at any case study involving serial killing, and we are talking about a serial killer here, a serial killer and subterfuge, and you will see similar social and ethnic backgrounds between killer and victim. Being inconspicuous in a social group is the disguise, the ability to move freely, to be able to deflect suspicion on the part of the victim. The subterfuge is the killer's get-out clause. If events don't go as planned, there is always an opportunity to back out, to retreat. It gives them time to win their victims over. So think about it: he is less likely to go into a strange neighbourhood if he knows he is going to be prominent. Any trickery, any attempt to gain the trust of the victim would fail. So we have to assume that the killer in each case is from the same social background as the victim: which is white and middle-class."

"And that's why you rule out the blue-collar black woman from Dorchester?" I asked. "Because the killer knows he would stand out in a black neighbourhood?"

Robert nodded in agreement. "And also because the victim would be less likely to trust him."

"So," John said, trying to make sense of it all, "as all the victims, apart from the Dorchester victim, have the same racial and social characteristics as each other, they could feasibly have been killed by the same person?"

Robert nodded again. "Certainly. At stage one, there are similarities. The woman from Dorchester could just be an unhappy coincidence of the name connection. There has to be at least one coincidence in this bunch."

"And as the victims are white, the killer is going to be white, and this would fit in with the fact that serial killers are invariably white?"

Robert smiled in agreement. John sat back in his chair and considered this for a moment.

"Is that really right?" I asked, somewhat incredulous. "Are serial killers always white?"

"Yes," Robert answered. "Invariably."

"Why is that?"

Robert shrugged. "If we knew that, we would find the key to why killers kill. It's just one of life's great mysteries. All we know is that the statistics say one thing, but we just don't know why."

"Okay, okay," said John, "let's rule out for the moment the Dorchester killing. It is different, in a way, as it seems less calculated, less risk-free than the others. There is more scope for forensic analysis, more chance of being seen, either dumping the body or doing the taking. What we have is a white man capable of subterfuge."

Robert nodded in agreement. "As I've already said, no-one has reported a woman being forced away from the scene of their suspected abduction. That suggests the other identifying feature I mentioned, and perhaps the most important." He looked around to make sure he had our attention. He had it. "He has limited criminal history."

"I would have thought it pointed to the opposite conclusion," I said, confused. "Surely it would only be an experienced criminal who would be able to work out how to go about undetected?"

Robert shook his head. "Just the opposite," he said. He turned to John Cornwell. "John, what strikes you most about criminals?"

John snorted. "Stupid fuckers most of the time. Wouldn't know the perfect crime if it bit them in the ass."

I smiled to myself, feeling things click into place, making sense. John was right. It's not often that dazzling detective work solves routine crime. Most victims know their attacker.

"Does this fit into the 'same social grouping' thing you were talking about before?" I asked.

Robert smiled. "Exactly right. Criminals generally fall into one category: socially and economically deprived. So when they are at work, they want to be comfortable, feel familiar in their environment. And they know they would be spotted instantly roaming the affluent suburbs for a victim, or an empty house, an unlocked door. So they stick to their own. It's one of life's great ironies: the less you have, the more likely you are to lose it. And the same rules apply to serial killers as they do for street level criminals. But you are missing the other most obvious point."

I looked blankly.

"They were all caught. You'll remember I said that they'd have limited criminal history. The important word is 'history.' It doesn't mean he isn't a criminal, just that he hasn't been caught."

"And that he falls outside of the profile of the petty criminal, so wouldn't attract detection," I contributed. "Because he's white and middle class."

"You've got it. Everything points to him being white and middle class, and that in itself creates different problems."

I sat back wearily. This was getting tiring.

John fell silent to let another truth hang in the air: until he makes a mistake, he is untraceable.

I reached for some more coffee. We all knew that if my guess was right, I had still got us no nearer to finding Sarah. The dialogue from before still hung heavy. No neighbours had reported anyone being taken from the victims' property by force, and there was no sign of forced entry at any of the properties. Including Sarah's.

I watched John as he stood up and walked to the window. He took his coffee with him, but he didn't look like he was going to drink any of it. He went to the window and looked out, trying to peer through the reflection of the lit room and into the dark wetness outside.

Until that point, my relationship with John hadn't been good. We'd spent most of our time disagreeing and engaging in an atmosphere of mistrust. But as I watched by the window, I suddenly felt for him. I could see it in the way he stood, the way his eyes didn't gleam like they had earlier in the evening. It told me that he knew he might have made a mistake, might have ruined someone's life because he didn't spot what could have been obvious. There was a young man stuck in prison, and the real killer stayed free, and he had killed again.

I joined him at the window while Robert shuffled some of the papers, reading quickly, scratching his head and sighing. I took the coffeepot with me and topped up John's cup. He looked at me, and I could see sadness blink back, just for a moment. It was one of those unspoken things, the sigh behind the eyes, but I saw it. He nodded a thank you, I didn't understand what for, perhaps just for the coffee, and gave a smile of regret. I smiled back, and then his hardness returned. It was a tensing of the shoulders, a heavy breath, but I saw John the homicide detective return. But I no longer felt like John was the enemy. We both knew that there was a greater enemy out there somewhere, somewhere beyond that rain-streaked pane of glass and amongst that darkness.

I returned to my seat and John stayed by the window. When I sat back down the discussion started again, as if my brief departure had put the whole thing on pause.

Katie spoke up. "So there is a prospect that he's tried it with other people who have names the same as the Salem women, and backed off?"

Robert looked thoughtful, and then answered, "yes, quite likely, although his preparation time is lengthy. Look at the facts of the case you are really concerned about: Sarah Goode. The snatch took place at just the time that you were home in Kansas. That must be more than mere chance. It suggests that he has been watching, or even perhaps knows you."

I saw Katie bring her knees to her chest again. I wanted to protect her, wrap myself around her and stop her from hurting. But I knew she didn't want that. I could see her trying to get through this, to deal with whatever it was she had to deal with, even if that meant knowing someone had been watching her apartment.

"This isn't just a case," Katie said quietly. "This is my friend."

Robert chewed his lip for a moment, and then held his hand up. "You're right, I'm sorry." Routine professional detachment, he meant to say, but I was glad he didn't.

"It wasn't a very good plan," I said. "What about Brad? If you plan to take someone against their will, you don't take them when they have a fit and trained fireman in attendance."

"Well," Robert replied, "that implies he was working from knowledge of their movements rather than actual observation. If he'd watched them, he would have seen Brad go in. That suggests he knew Sarah, and so knew Katie would be out of town."

I stepped in quickly to distract Katie.

"So we know he is white, middle-aged, and middle class," I asked. "Is there anything else we can find out?"

Robert looked thoughtful and reached forward for the paperwork. He shuffled pages around and looked at photographs. He then sat back and thought some more. Eventually he looked around the room and said, "I can probably guess where he lives."

I felt the intrigue buzz through the room like a chainsaw.

"How can you do that?" John asked, whirling round, his surprise lighting his fires again.

I wondered how reliable this must be if it was new to John, but then I remembered that John respected his opinions. He had asked him how he knew, not just dismissed him.

"The circle theory," Robert replied.

I looked quizzical. "So how does this theory pan out?"

"Put yourself into the mind of an attacker," Robert said, "a killer, a rapist. If you wanted to do the crime and get away without being identified, where would you do it?"

184

I scratched my chin and thought for a moment. "As far away from my own home as possible, I suppose."

"That's right," Robert agreed, "but what if you wanted to do it again? Would you return to the same place?"

I shook my head.

"Right again. It would be in peoples' minds. They would be on their guard. But you still wouldn't do it near your own home, would you?"

I shook my head again. "No, I'd go as far away again, but in the opposite direction."

"To throw the police into confusion?"

I nodded.

"Well there you have it," Robert said, with a note of triumph. "You've just created the diameter of the circle. Your instinct was to spread the attacks apart, but as far from your own home as possible. Think how that would look if there were a few attacks, how they would look on a large map. They would form the circumference of the circle, and your home would sit right there, right in the middle, as far away as possible from each attack."

I sat back with a smile. I was impressed. A killer drawing a big arrow to his own home, created by a desire to do exactly the opposite.

Robert smiled. "It's what profiling is all about. We ignore what the killer knows we can see, and try to look at things he doesn't realise we can see."

It was John who burst the bubble.

"That was fascinating, most fascinating," he said, "but aren't the locations here pre-determined?" He looked around the room, his eyes alive again. "If I'm understanding this right, the only link between these incidents is the name connection to the Salem witches. That means the locations were pre-determined by someone having the same name as a Salem witch, not the killer's choice of location. The killer's subconscious is not part of the equation."

Robert smiled. "I agree, insofar as the snatchings or captivity is concerned. But what about disposal of the body? That isn't pre-determined."

John couldn't stop himself from smiling. "And if I get my map out," he asked, "we can work out where he might live, is that what you are saying? We look at where he left the bodies?"

Robert nodded in agreement. "A basic version of the theory, but we don't have too much to work on."

John left the room to go map-hunting.

"Aren't you worried that we might be getting it wrong?" I asked.

Robert smiled, a comfortable smile, and I wondered whether he had ever worried about anything.

"Everything has to be tested sometime."

I was thinking of a response when John came back into the room with a large foldaway map slowly unwrapping itself as he crossed the room.

"I think this should do us," he said to himself, and then he placed the map on the floor.

I found myself looking at a large street map of the Greater Boston area, wondering if the answer lay in that giant noughts and crosses puzzle. I could see some of the town names I'd heard staring out at me in large capitals. I could see the circle they drew and I began to understand the theory.

I looked at Robert. "So what you are saying is that by looking at this map, we should be able to work out where he lives."

Robert looked at the map and grimaced slightly. "I wouldn't put it so positively, but we might get some ideas."

"C'mon, c'mon," John harried, "let's get moving."

He made towards the map with a black marker pen. "Give me some locations of bodies," he barked.

I shuffled through the papers that were still on the desk. I stalled as I rummaged, and then said, "okay, here we go. The young girl was found in Saugus." I shuffled some more. "The jeweller was found in Peabody." I noticed then that John was underlining the relevant towns in black, and I could see the even spread. "Then we have Newton, Dedham, Needham." I reached for more papers. "Woburn, Reading, and Waltham."

We'd only discussed in detail a few of the murders, but as I reeled off the names of the towns, I looked down on the map and saw the spread.

Boston sits in a bay surrounded by a conurbation of independent towns and communities, fanning out in a big semi-circle. As I looked, I saw that the towns did indeed follow a pattern. They encircled the Greater Boston conurbation like the infield facing home plate. None came near to the city, yet none retreated into the countryside to break the line. But one thing did stand out as obvious. Blatantly obvious.

"I don't think it's hard to work out the circle," I said.

John and Robert looked at me and nodded.

"The I-95," John said quietly. "There's no need to draw a line. The interstate does the job for us."

Robert nodded. "There's your second link," he said. "You already had the coincidence of name, but now you have that the bodies were all found near the interstate."

I raised my eyebrows. "So the answer is?" I asked, perhaps already knowing the answer.

It was John who spoke. "The killer lives within the I-95," he said slowly. And just when I was starting to look triumphant, he added, "along with nearly everybody who lives in the Greater Boston area."

I deflated again.

Robert spoke, and he lifted my spirits. "We can be a bit more precise than that."

John looked at him and raised an eyebrow. I held my breath until I'd heard what he had to say.

"If these crimes have been committed by the same person," he said, looking around, feeling the moment, "he doesn't live within the loop of the I-95; he lives by the I-95."

My eyes hurtled to the map, and I saw what he meant. All the places where the bodies had been found were close to the I-95. The I-95 circled Greater Boston as if it was holding it all in, protecting the rest of Massachusetts from the urban over-spill. But those places where bodies had been found hugged the rim, rather than nestled within it.

"You were right," I said, scouring the map for potential starting points. "People reveal as much by trying to stay hidden than they do when they don't." I looked at Robert. "So all we do," I continued, "is look in the towns around the interstate?"

Robert nodded in agreement.

"Although," John said, trying to put over a note of caution, "what are we looking for? Any profile of this person will say that previous police involvement is unlikely. What do we do? Hang around the suburbs, stopping to ask every middle-aged white male if they have a thing about witches?" He shook his head. "We need something more."

Robert looked distant, deep in thought. He was looking at the map, and then glancing towards the photographs, and then back at the map. He rummaged through his hair and stroked his cheek.

"Are we agreed," he finally said, "that he has sweet-talked his way into these peoples' lives before taking them away from them?"

John stayed silent.

"So all we need to do now is work out why anyone would have any kind of fixation on the names of Salem witches."

John was looking at the floor, watching his toe nudge and play with non-existent scraps of paper. He was starting to look frustrated, edgy.

"This is not my idea," John said quietly, "and I'm not agreeing anything yet. I've got a conviction for murder on my career record, and I have seen nothing here that would change my mind, nothing that would make me feel the conviction is unsafe. And we have a young English girl," and he glanced towards Katie apologetically, "who disappeared at the same time as her boyfriend was dead in her bed, re-appearing only in the shape of kooky letters containing some form of confession." He glanced around the room, but his gaze rested longer on me. "What you have," and now he was looking directly at me, his mind clearly ablaze, "is a link with a few deaths, based only on the sharing of a name with a long-dead Salem witch."

"Oh, c'mon," I said, defensively, "what about those kooky letters? Those themselves connect to the Salem witches, because they are taken from the transcripts."

"And how many other cases have such letters in them?" He looked at me hard and then answered his own question. "None, that's how many. And how many of these connected murders are similar? We have a woman who jumped off a clock tower. That can't be murder. We have a young teenager who was sexually attacked and killed, and call me brutal, but that sounds to me like your normal sicko child killer. We have a teacher killed and decapitated, and a young woman proven beyond any reasonable doubt to have been killed by her boyfriend. I don't see too many connections there. Some of the other deaths may seem similar, but you can't pick and choose which ones apply and which ones don't. You're basing all of this on an excessive coincidence. If you take a few out of the equation, the coincidence isn't so unusual after all." He sat back in his chair still glaring, but his tirade winding down.

"There just isn't anything. Sarah Goode is still wanted for the murder of her boyfriend, and I'm going to keep looking."

I noticed Robert was smiling. "Are we quite finished?" he asked, in a slight mocking tone.

John just waved his hand dismissively.

"Are you dismissing this out of hand?" Robert asked.

John shrugged, then kicked the wall beneath the window. "You know I'm not, you crazy bastard. But we have to think about prioritising our resources, and I think they are best spent looking for a missing murder suspect, not trying to solve old murders and freeing convicted killers."

"It's the first time you've called Sarah a murder suspect," Katie said softly. "You've always said before that you've got an open mind." Katie looked sad. "You don't, do you," she said rhetorically. "You think Sarah did it."

"I'm sorry," John replied sheepishly, "but you give me something to change my mind, and I'll change it. Something real, not a night of theories. I'm not inflexible, I'll admit mistakes, but I need something more solid, more certain, before I go hurtling to my captain."

"What about all this?"

John shook his head. "I'm sorry, but it's just not enough. A collection of coincidences and unconnected murders does not make Sarah Goode seem any more innocent."

I looked at Robert. He was sat back in his chair, massaging his eyelids.

"It's been a long day for you," I said.

He smiled and nodded. "And it's going to be another long one tomorrow. But hey, it's all part of the game."

I smiled back. But I wanted his views. John wasn't swayed, and his views on Sarah were now quite clear. I wasn't sure myself, but it was the only thing I had to go on. If John were right after all, then I would never find her. If she can avoid the police, she can avoid me.

"What do you think, really think, about all this?" I asked.

Robert studied me for a moment. I could tell he was weighing up his views, and also whether he should give them.

"There is something not quite right about this," he said quietly. "There are too many similarities, too many differences," and he smiled, "but there is something. All the victims share a common link, their names, and the same type of person was involved in each."

"So where the fuck do we go from here?" John asked.

"Your captain?" I suggested.

John shook his head, looking weary. "Not yet. When you've all gone, I'll make some phone calls. It's still all or nothing, so I'll stick with the I-95 theory. I'm going to call the police who run the towns on the interstate. Ask them to find to keep an eye on any suspicious activities and ask them to check their records for any outstanding murders or missing persons. If any more coincidences come forward, I'll go straight to my captain. If not, I'll sleep on it and decide what to do tomorrow."

"Do you think that you're right?" I asked. "Deep down, do you dismiss all this as coincidence?"

John reflected on his answer for a moment.

"No," he said eventually, "I don't dismiss it. I think I'm right, but not sure."

"What should we do?"

John stared at me. "You should look after Miss Gray. These are difficult times. Try and make them easier for her."

I looked over at Katie. She looked strong, but it was only a look. I smiled at her. She smiled back.

John stood up. "Come on, I'll kick you fellas out. I've got some calls to make. I've let you run this crackpot nonsense by me for twenty-four hours now. Give me one nights sleep on it, and I'll make a decision in the morning."

I wiped my eyes. That seemed fair enough.

As we headed for the door, I felt Katie grip my hand, and as I looked down at her, she put her head against my arm. Without thinking about what John would think, I reached down and kissed her gently on the top of her head.

We left linking arms, going out together to wait for John Cornwell to do his job.

Sarah was pulled from the van. She scraped her feet on tarmac, wincing, and was then lifted and dragged until her feet hit grass.

190

She felt herself being propelled along mud and grass, and could hear the feet of those with her splashing in water. She was by a lake or river. Her feet were moving fast along wet grass, slipping and trying to keep up, breathing heavy, her hands in cuffs, the plastic sheeting still wrapped around her head. Her breaths were thrown back around her face, hot and wet.

Her captors were silent. The water filled the gaps, lapping softly against its shore, providing a tranquil backdrop for a feeling of absolute dread.

Sarah was still hopeful. Was she about to be left? There had been too many opportunities back in the room to kill her. Any time, she could have been tortured, killed, dismembered, disposed of, never seen again. But now, she was back in the open. Cars could be heard in the distance, and when she looked down, she thought she could see streetlights reflected off the water.

They ran for a few hundred yards. Her chest ached with running, her legs going weak. Then they stopped.

The plastic sheet was torn off her head. Sarah blinked, tried to wipe her eyes, but her hands were still cuffed tight. Once her vision had cleared, she saw the gun. It was pointing straight at her, the barrel an inch from her eyes.

"Even the start of a scream, and I'll blow your brains out."

Sarah stayed silent, transfixed by metal. Then she heard a noise, and when she looked to the left of the gun, at the other person with her, she saw a video camera. He was filming her. Sarah flashed back to the screen in the room and began to cry.

"If you don't struggle, we'll take your cuffs off."

Sarah didn't say anything. She sank to her knees, tears streaming down her face. She didn't feel the cold of the night, the rain pouring over her naked body. She felt only the certainty of what was going to happen.

The gun was lowered as the younger one knelt down beside her, took a key from his pocket, and undid the handcuffs. She rubbed her wrists slowly and then went to wipe her eyes. She felt the hard metal of the gun against her temple. Sarah closed her eyes, gritted her teeth, and waited for the bang. At least it would be quick.

"Do you want to know what you've got between your legs?" he asked.

Sarah said nothing. She remembered him putting it there, his rough hands, his force. She could still feel whatever it was inside her.

The gun jabbed her in the temple, making her look at him.

"Gunpowder," he said simply. "I'm experimenting, branching out. Gunpowder, packed with ball-bearings, stuffed into an unlubricated condom." He smiled. "Like a small bomb."

Sarah's mouth dropped open. She went pale, cold. She began to sob, knowing what was coming. She thought of her parents, thought of home.

"That little blue string you've got?" he said, grinning now.

Sarah's head hung down, tears falling onto the grass.

"A fuse." And he began to laugh.

Sarah began to panic. It was all moving too fast. She tried to get to her feet, but she heard movement, heard a shout, then felt the splash. It was petrol, the stench sweet in the clean air. She knew what would be next. Her hand reached down between her legs, scrabbling to pull it out, screeching in terror. She knew what was happening, reality flooded in, but then she saw him flick the lighter into life.

She screamed. He laughed. Then the flame came arcing towards her, spinning slowly, yellow and blue stars dancing in the air. She felt the lighter hit her in the chest. She looked down and saw the flames spread in a flash, and then that was all she could see.

Her scream died. A deep breath sucked in flames and the heat poured into her, drowning out sound. Her arms flailed as she stumbled around, her thoughts being slashed away by the tear of pain as the fuel burnt out. Then the world went black as the gunpowder caught hold.

The last sound Sarah heard was the noise of her body falling to the floor as her hips exploded and her legs left her body.

# Fifteen

When we arrived back at the apartment, I flicked on the television. I found a local news channel and sat in front of it, munching on a sandwich. Katie was in the bathroom, getting ready for bed. I was waiting to be asked where I wanted to sleep. I knew my answer already.

I was nearly done with the food when the news turned to a well-lit scene somewhere, a reporter sheltering under an umbrella, police cars visible in the background, crime-scene tape fluttering.

I didn't take much notice at first, but I felt my skin crawl when I heard the reporter talk about the body of a young woman being found in mysterious circumstances in Wakefield.

I shouted out to Katie, "where's Wakefield?" I had an uneasy feeling.

"Oh, up away from here," she shouted. "Out by the I-95."

And then as soon as she said that, the bathroom door flew open.

In my head, everything slammed shut. Katie came and sat down, staring at the television. She drew her knees up to her chest, wrapped her arms around them, a look of shock on her face.

I felt disbelief, but something inside me told me what I knew was the truth. It was Sarah.

Katie looked at me. I nodded slowly. She ran her hands over her face, tired-looking.

I grabbed the phone and rang the lieutenant's home. It rang out a long time before anyone answered. When I told him what was on the television, he went quiet. I then told him that if he was going up there, I was going with him.

He didn't argue. He told me to be ready in fifteen minutes. I told him I was ready now.

I put the phone down and looked over at Katie. She had her head buried in her knees. I could hear the soft sobs, could see the slight shaking. I pulled her to me and felt her nestle into me.

"I'll be back soon."

She nodded, and we held each other until I heard John Cornwell's car arrive outside.

It was raining in Wakefield.

We'd raced through driving rain, the roads quiet, and the cars that were out were slowed to a safe crawl. John's car hurtled along, sending rain too fast for the wipers. I felt like we were travelling blind, relying only on John's police training and the occasional glimmer of a white line to keep the car pointing in the right direction. We flew over bridges, speeding through a blinding swish of water and darkness.

John didn't speak until we'd passed Stoneham, half way to Wakefield. Then the pace lessened, and I watched the urban sprawl thin out. Patches of darkness broke up the glow of Greater Boston and clusters of trees replaced fast food and gas stations. Robert was there as well, collected en route to Katie's apartment.

I had my head back on the headrest, starting to stew, thinking of home, when John spoke.

"If anyone asks, you're a writer, shadowing me for research purposes. Okay?"

He hadn't looked at me when he said it. And he said it mean. The mood in the car went from tense to hostile. I heard Robert shuffle in his seat and give a small cough. I think it meant 'lay off him'.

"What am I writing," I asked, "for research purposes?" I was trying to be friendly, speaking softly above the strong silence and the rub of the wipers on the windscreen.

He looked at me now. He didn't say anything. His face said it all. It said, 'you can say what the hell you like, just as long as you keep out of the way.'

We arrived in Wakefield without a fanfare. I was expecting the Hollywood crime scene, metal barriers keeping the crowds back, cops flying around, lights glaring over a flurry of ambulances and blue flashes. Instead, we came off the I-95 at exit 39 and made straight to an old cemetery and a fluttering ribbon of police tape. A young policeman stood in the rain and tried to shrink under the peak of his cap.

A large searchlight rescued the scene from darkness. I could see the lights of passing cars just a few hundred yards away, but they were just distant glimpses and didn't seem to affect the lighting.

Just inside the ribbon was a tarpaulin hut, all grey and wet, standing head-height like an emergency latrine. I could see two people stood inside through the flap, hunched over something black. Two men and a woman stood outside in the rain, smoking, two large umbrellas held by the two men keeping all three dry. As I looked over I saw a bright flash from inside the tent, and I realised someone was taking photographs. The two figures in the tent stood up, and what I thought were white shirts turned out to be paper forensic boiler suits.

John flashed a badge at the uniformed officer who glanced his way and clambered under the tape. He headed straight for the small huddle under the umbrellas, Robert and me following.

I tagged behind John as we got to the huddle. John still had his badge out.

"John Cornwell," flashing his badge, "Boston Police. I called before. Sorry to intrude on this, but that corpse there might interest us." He sounded firm but cheery, businesslike, cop-to-cop.

A fat guy smiled but didn't introduce himself or any of his colleagues. He had a short crop of ginger hair on top of a round pale face, his bright features shining out in the murkiness. His neck bulged out of his shirt, but I could tell it wasn't muscle. His cheeks flushed even in the cold rain and the grin fought hard to get to the surface.

"Yeah, we got your call," he said icily. He nodded towards the tent. "Looks like you didn't get to her in time."

John didn't laugh, and I guessed that he wasn't supposed to find it funny.

"What do you know?" John asked, ignoring whatever agenda was going down.

The fat cop just shrugged. "I might wonder what business it is of yours," he said smugly. "I see some jurisdictional difficulties."

John dropped his shoulders, hands outwards in a submissive gesture. "C'mon, you guys, we aren't seriously going to be arguing about jurisdiction, are we? Can't we just share information?"

The fat cop gave a cold smile. "What about? All we have is a dead woman by a lake. Would you give me some information the next time someone gets mugged making a night-time crossing of the Common?" He flapped his hand towards John in a dismissive gesture. "Would you hell." He shrugged nonchalantly. "Anyway, it

195

looks like all that hoil, toil and trouble eventually caught up with her."

I saw John stiffen. I felt myself sink. I heard nothing from Robert. It was obvious I hadn't made a unique discovery after all.

"What are you talking about?" John asked quietly.

The fat cop tilted his head to one side and smirked. "C'mon, you know what I mean. You make a call, telling us it might be a murder suspect of yours, Sarah Goode." He laughed a mean laugh and I could feel the heat coming off John. I was expecting his wet coat to start steaming, and I saw his hands jam back into his pockets. "Yesterday, you're flying around asking for information on old murders." His eyes gave a wicked twinkle. "I have friends, lieutenant, and people talk. And I grew up in Salem. I recognised the names. There's something going on here."

I looked at his two co-cops. The other man smiled nervously, as if not enjoying the conversation but feeling obliged to pretend that he did. The woman was stony-faced.

The fat cop turned to the woman. "You deal with this jackass. I'm going to see how our guys are getting on." And with that he handed the umbrella to her and headed over to the tent.

The two Wakefield cops turned back to John and I was once more stood apart from the group, with water trickling down the back of my neck. Rain ran into my left eye and it stung as I blinked it away. I looked at Robert and grimaced, looking skyward into the rain. He was in a nonchalant slouch, taking in the scene. He nodded. It wasn't a good night to be skulking around.

The female officer held out her hand. "Sergeant Tauris," she said. "Amanda Tauris."

John took it and shook. "John Cornwell. Lieutenant Cornwell."

She looked towards the tent. "What is it all about anyway?"

John stayed silent for a while, then shrugged and exhaled loudly. "This limey here has got some idea that a local crazy is bumping off people who share their name with a Salem witch." John shook his head slowly. "I thought he was wrong, but now I'm not so sure."

His conversation drifted into silence.

"What do you want to know?" Amanda asked, looking shocked.

I saw John's mind jerk back to the conversation. He sighed and then shrugged. "For tonight, nothing I suppose. I was hoping you guys would cut me some slack, but it looks like your guy isn't so keen."

She smiled. "I'll see what I can do," she said. "This is a Wakefield case, but if this is part of something wider, we might have to step aside."

John looked at her. "Won't you mind?"

She gave him a shrewd look. "Don't worry, it won't come free. I have a long career, and it isn't all going to be spent in Wakefield. It's good to have a few friends spread around."

John laughed for the first time in quite a while.

"What can you tell me?" he asked.

Amanda glanced back over to the forensic tent. "Not much. We received a call from the fire service. They'd attended what they thought was a minor arson, you know, kids setting trash alight. The residents from over there reported it, said they could see a glow in the trees. When they got here, they found her naked and burning. It looks like somebody stripped her, poured something on her, and set her alight. She was dead when they arrived; there was never any doubt." She paused. "Also, strangest thing."

"What?"

"She was burnt out, for sure, but she had half her abdomen exploded. It looked like someone stuck a giant firecracker up her ass and lit it."

"Shit!" John exclaimed.

I felt my stomach lurch.

John looked around. "Why did your guy let me come up here?" he asked eventually.

Amanda smiled. "He may be an asshole, but he's a good cop, and he knows how to avoid fuck-ups. He'll move aside, he'll do his bit. He's just pissed that he might lose the case."

"So what do you know?" John asked.

"Not much. We're going to have a look around at dawn, but otherwise, it's too early to tell."

"Witnesses?"

Amanda shook her head. "It's still early. We've got the people who saw the fire once it was going, but no-one has come forward to say they saw it start. But the trees shield it from the road, and there are plenty of ways to sneak down here."

John glanced around him, peering into the blackness.

197

"How's this area for security cameras?" John asked. He was looking away and into the trees, and towards a grouping of small stores near rail tracks. Their lit signs were visible through the trees, spoiling the rural appeal.

Amanda followed John's gaze. "Too small for decent cameras, so they'll be too far away to have caught anything. We'll check in the morning though."

"Where do you think he parked?"

"We don't know if anyone else is involved yet," Amanda said. "It could still, in theory, be a bizarre suicide. She comes up here, lonely and depressed, perhaps worried about her impending arrest, pours gasoline over herself, and puts a match to it."

John gave her a sly look. "And sticks a firecracker up her own ass?"

Amanda smiled and tilted her head. "That's a tough one." She looked over at the forensic tent. "Are you sure she came in a vehicle?"

John looked at her and smiled. "Oh yeah, I'm sure. And she came from the I-95."

Amanda looked puzzled.

Her colleague looked at her and shrugged, and then smiled at John. "Hi, I'm Jim Tressel. What information are you looking for?"

John looked over at him. "For the moment, just where he parked. There might be something there."

Amanda looked back at Jim Tressel, and then back over at John. "There are plenty of places to park. There's a motel just up the bank, and there are a few residential streets roundabout."

John paced up and down, his hand stroking his head, and then he asked, "there are traffic cameras on the I-95?"

Amanda nodded. "I think so, but they don't show down here. They are just that, traffic cameras."

"But will they show the exits?"

Amanda nodded slowly.

"And do they record?"

Amanda nodded again, and then began to smile. She reached into her pocket and pulled out a mobile phone. She dialled a few digits, and then I heard her asking someone to get onto the Highways Department to ask them to save any traffic footage that would cover the Wakefield exits for the preceding twenty-four hours.

"The motel may have security cameras," Amanda said, when she had come off the phone.

I felt the urge to smile now. I was within yards of Sarah's smouldering body, my local reputation going the same way as my quarry, but I couldn't help enjoying the excitement of seeing dead-ends becoming unravelled.

"Good," said John. "Get the tapes, don't let them be destroyed."

John tugged at his lip. I looked at Robert, who looked back at me and smiled. John's mind was trying to stay awake, racing through possibilities, whilst mine was just numb with failure and fatigue. Robert, however, looked as calm as the beginnings of the dawn I could see appearing over Wakefield, a cool blue shining off the wet white rooftops of the town at the other end of the lake.

I looked back to where Sarah's body had been found. That way lay my failure. I'd found Sarah, but under the wrong circumstances. When I'd set off from Morsby, I'd naively imagined either a summer in the sun or a clandestine meeting, handing over credit cards and reassuring her mother that all was well. I hadn't imagined this: rain running down the back of my coat, Sarah charred and twisted in death a few yards away, and the unmasking of a dangerous killer acting out a fantasy unknown.

All of a sudden, the lack of sleep hit me. I wanted to return to Boston, just to return to Katie's apartment, climb under the covers with her, and lose myself in the forgetfulness of dream sleep. I rubbed my eyes.

John must have been reading my thoughts. "Go home," he said softly. "Go see that Katie's okay. She shouldn't be alone. There's nothing you can do here."

"What about you?"

"Oh, I'll be here awhile yet."

"How do I get back?"

John pointed towards Wakefield. "There's a rail system in Wakefield. It'll take you right into North Station in thirty minutes." He looked towards Amanda. "When's the first train?"

"About 6am." She checked her watch. "By the time you walk down there, you shouldn't have too long to wait around."

I knew what she really meant. This is police business, there's a train, and you should be on it.

Robert looked at me. "It's okay, Joe, I'll ride along."

We turned to walk away, but I turned back when I sensed John looking at me. I turned around and caught him watching my departure. I nodded and smiled. He shook his head, and then he returned the smile. It knew it was as near to a thank you as I was going to get. I turned away and walked away from the grisly scene, Robert keeping pace with me.

And so we walked down the side of the lake, seeing the morning lights of Wakefield grow brighter. I looked back to the cemetery, and I thought to myself that it seemed a nice place to end up, in a collection of crosses overlooking a lake.

But then I looked back to the crime scene lights, they were still visible through the trees, and I realised I was wrong. However idyllic the setting, it isn't home, and to be so far from home, from loved ones, when that final moment comes must be as lonely as it is possible to be.

We were silent on the train. We rumbled through Boston's commuter belt, Greenwood, Melrose, picking up workers on the way, while I looked out of the window. My chin kept hitting my chest as the slow rock of the carriage reminded me of how tired I was, sat on wide comfortable seats. I looked across and saw Robert asleep, dozing contentedly.

By the time we arrived in Boston, the morning was well underway. Robert and I grabbed a coffee from Dunking Donuts in North Station and made our way through Boston. We could have caught the subway, but it was growing into a nice morning and I think we both wanted to walk off the crime scene. We ambled slowly, two dishevelled and quiet figures amidst the bedlam of a growing rush hour, saying little, just looking into our coffees and remaining deep in thought.

We were just getting near Quincy Market, on our way through the close quarters of Union Street, when I asked Robert what he thought of what he'd seen at Wakefield.

He didn't answer for a while, and I wondered whether he'd heard me, but then he looked at me with interest and asked, "do you need to know? I'd figured you'd be packing your bags today."

I let out a resigned sigh. "I'm going to have to explain all this when I get home. I just want to understand it all."

"So you can tell yourself that it wasn't your fault?"

I gave a half-smile. "Yeah, something like that."

Robert tried to look consoling. "It wasn't your fault. You did what you set out to do. You came to Boston and found Sarah, and found a whole lot more besides. You found the link. The only thing you didn't have was time. That was our fault."

"Did you see anything in Wakefield that helped you?" I asked. "What sort of person are we looking for?"

Robert looked at me with something approaching amusement when I said the word 'we'.

"*We* have seen nothing to change my opinion from what we talked about earlier. The body was found by the I-95. The method of killing was hands-off. There was an element of display about it." He took a sip of coffee. "There is still one thing puzzling me."

"What's that?"

"What the hell is the connection with Salem witches? What is it about the witches of Salem that makes him want to kill?"

I drained my coffee and tossed it into a litterbin. "That, my friend," I said, with a flourish I didn't feel, "is the million dollar question."

Robert patted me on the shoulder in a way that told me that I would probably never find out.

We walked on, past the Old State House and along the line of the Heritage Trail. We were heading towards the Common when I said, really just thinking out loud, "what makes someone start to kill? Why does a person cross the threshold from being a man with murderous thoughts to being a man with a murderous past?"

Robert made a face and exhaled. "Many reasons," he said. "Sometimes it's just the logical next step. If a man has spent his live tormented by twisted images, sometimes the only way to cope is to make them reality. Many killers have always been cruel, sometimes to animals, sometimes to other children. Multiple murders just become the next step. You and I deal with stressful events in a normal way, but somebody pre-disposed to murder would deal with them by becoming murderous." He looked at me.

"Identify the catalyst, the stressor, and you identify the point at which the murders begin."

"Or," I suggested, "look at when the murders begin, and then identify the stressor. Identify the stressor and you find the stressee, and that is the murderer."

Robert drained his coffee. "You are wasted. Go back to college, do something different, but don't waste away serving court papers."

I smiled. We were getting to the other side of the Common, near the Public Gardens, when I sensed a parting.

"You going to the station?" I asked.

Robert nodded wearily. "I've work to do now."

"Okay," I said, feeling fatigue take over again. The thought of sleep overpowered me, and I felt my energy drain from me as the adrenaline subsided. "Thanks Robert."

"What for?"

"Oh, you know, your time. I can tell Sarah's parents that people gave Sarah their time. It will be small comfort, but any comfort will be some comfort."

Robert just nodded.

We shook hands and I watched him walk away until he was lost in the bobbing heads.

I walked on to Katie's apartment. Despite the sun, the morning was still cold, the result of a wet night, and my extreme tiredness made me vulnerable to dark thoughts. Despite my failure to find Sarah before it was too late, I had still felt the rush and excitement of being at the centre of something big. I hadn't felt that in a long time. As I walked back to Katie's, I knew I was going to face different things. Katie would be emotional, and I'd have to ring Sarah's parents to tell them the bad news. The day was about to focus on the bad things, leaving the excitement and intrigue behind in Wakefield.

I blew out noisily. It was going to be a tough day.

Katie's apartment came eventually. I let myself in and went to her bedroom. As I looked in, Katie looked at peace. Tiredness must have taken her over late. The sheets were tangled, the signs of a restless few hours, but she slept now, her arms hugging a pillow. I was worried I might wake her so I went instead to the living room.

I went first to the telephone. I rang Lucy back in Morsby and told her the news. She said she would go and break it to Sarah's parents. I thanked her for that. Once I'd hung up I leant back in the chair. Sleep enveloped me like a shroud. I was lost.

# Sixteen

Katie was watching me as I woke.

I ached from a few hours in the chair. I tried to sit up but my back groaned and my shoulders went taut. I was getting too old for this.

I looked at Katie. I was looking for signs of breakdown, of grief. I saw neither. I thought she seemed calmer, less uncertain. She was smiling to herself, although her eyes were distant, her mind elsewhere.

"Are you okay?" I asked softly.

Katie nodded. "Yeah, I'm fine."

I smiled and wondered what to say next. At moments like this, when words of comfort are expected, I was at my worst.

Katie saved my blushes.

"It's over, isn't it," she said, matter-of-factly.

"Sarah?"

She nodded.

I smiled. "Yes, it's over."

Katie smiled back, a relieved smile. I thought I knew what she meant. That it was over for Sarah, so it was over for her. A watershed

"I don't know how to feel?" she said, her hand rummaging through her hair. "You know, do I cry because I miss her, or should I be glad because it's over?"

"Perhaps you should just go with your emotions. If you feel it, show it. You've done nothing wrong. I would expect grief, but who knows what Sarah has gone through in the last couple of weeks. Death may have been a blessing in the end."

Katie agreed with me but looked sad.

Then came her next question.

"What are we?"

I said nothing. I couldn't think how to answer. I'd been overwhelmed by thoughts of tenderness when I'd returned from Wakefield, but now, creaking like a geriatric, I wasn't sure. I knew one thing: I wanted to stay with her.

"If it's over for Sarah," she continued, "then you'll be going home, won't you?" Her eyes were focused now, sharp and keen, although her body belied them, relaxed in a chair, her legs tucked up.

I stayed silent. I wanted to be truthful, wanted to say how Katie had begun to dominate my thoughts, how I dreamt of her warm body, her rising laugh, her sing-song voice whispering desire through the still moments of night time.

But I held back. Something English in me told me to keep quiet.

Katie could see me struggling. "I won't give myself up for just anybody, you know," she said. "I've never been just somebody's conquest." Her eyes misted. "I would for you, Joe, if you want that."

I smiled at that and felt warm. I recalled our softer moments, and I remembered how close we had come last time to her doing just that, giving herself up for me. "I thought maybe that you wanted me because you needed somebody, and I was just there," I said softly.

"It was you I wanted, Joe Kinsella, just you."

At that, Katie came over to me. She sat in my chair with me and put her arms around me, so that her face nuzzled into my neck. I held her, rocked her gently, until I felt her go calm, her breathing settled. I ran my hands through her hair, stroked her head gently, felt my breath go hot against her. She smelled of sleep and new clothes and shampoo and warmth. At that point I knew that I wouldn't be going back to England in a hurry. If you'd asked me then, I wouldn't have been sure if I was ever going back to England.

I think we would have stayed like that for most of the day, but the doorbell broke the moment. Katie climbed off me, kissed me on the lips, hot and hinting, and went to the door.

I was stretching myself awake when Jimmy Walsh walked in.

Katie followed him into the room. Her softness had become hard and I could tell that she wasn't pleased to see him. I didn't know what to say. The last time I'd seen him, I'd been tailing him around the streets of Boston.

I put my hands behind my head and tried to look nonplussed. "What can we do for you, Mr Walsh?"

"I came to say how sorry I am." He made his remark to Katie, ignoring me. "I saw it on the breakfast news."

"What are they saying?" Katie asked.

Jimmy sat down. I eyed him with suspicion. Lieutenant John Cornwell might put him in the clear, but there was something about Jimmy Walsh that I didn't like. He was putting himself with people who didn't want him there, but yet he persisted. And if it was only Sarah who kept him around, why was he still here?

But he seemed sad. I could see grief in his eyes, and for a moment I relented.

"They are saying she killed herself," he said, looking at the floor. "They are saying she set herself on fire, grief and guilt over Brad's murder." Jimmy paused and looked up at me, dewy-eyed. "Is that right? Did she kill herself?"

I was confused. I was at the scene and I remembered suicide wasn't high on the list. I thought of Lieutenant Cornwell and feelings of anger and betrayal began to simmer just below the surface. Was this the big cover up, save the face of Boston Police and write everything else off as just another coincidence? And what about the young man languishing in jail? What about him? Is he the proof that Boston police need to show that they missed nothing, because there was nothing to miss?

I looked over at Katie, who looked confused. I tried to stay calm, but it was difficult. I thought about all we had talked about and I realised now that John hadn't been listening. He wanted self-justification. And then I thought of Sarah's parents and I became angrier. All their faith, all their trust. All gone. Taken away by the political decision of a police officer who put his self-interest before truth and justice. The lack of sleep and aches and pains began to mix with the anger and betrayal and I could feel fury. I felt like punching the wall, or the window, or anything.

Then I remembered Jimmy Walsh.

"Could you leave us, Jimmy?" I snapped.

He paused. "Are you sure? I mean, Katie, is that what you want?"

Katie looked at me, then at Jimmy, and nodded sadly. "Please Jimmy. I'll speak to you later." She gave a small nod in my direction. "There's something we need to sort out."

I saw his eyes fill with water. He mumbled and stood up. "Okay, okay," he said quietly, "I'll go." He looked at me and I could see a tear making its way down his cheek. It made me feel like shit.

Jimmy made for the door.

"Hey, Jimmy," I shouted, trying to stop him before he left. "I'm sorry, okay. We'll talk later." He stopped but didn't look round. "It's just a difficult time for us, you know. I'm sorry."

"Yeah, difficult. But you didn't know Sarah. I did, so that must make it more difficult for me. Just remember that."

And at that he went to the door and left me sat there, shocked. The door slammed as he shut it.

I slumped back in the chair and rubbed my face with my hands. I was full of thoughts but I didn't know what they were. I was part anger, part bewilderment, part disbelief. I told myself that I was in a different country and perhaps they do things differently. I turned on the television. I found New England Cable News, realised that I had a few minutes to wait for the next news bulletin.

I could feel Katie looking at me.

"What did they say last night? It can't be suicide, not after all we talked about. Can it?"

I shook my head. "No. It was murder. I was there, and I know what I saw in their eyes." I sneered. "Can you believe it?" I punched a cushion. "Why does everything come down to self-interest? We've got to do something."

"Like what?"

"Do what I told John Cornwell I would do: go to the Globe with the story."

Katie made a time out signal. "Just hold on. Have you seen the report yet?" I shook my head. "Well let's see it first before we go charging into anything."

I held up my hands in surrender, my face still burning with suppressed anger.

The story was about the fourth item in. A slick, smooth-talking anchorman said that the mystery of Brad's death had finally been resolved. It started with some of the footage from around the time of his murder and flashed up a picture of Sarah. The picture changed to footage of the lake and woods I'd been in earlier that day. I could see the remnants of the crime ribbon fluttering, and just behind that, the spot where Sarah died. A woman with a microphone spoke at the camera:

*"I'm here at Wakefield, on the edge of the Boston and by the side of Lake Quannapowitt. And it's here that one of the mysteries dogging Boston Police came to rest.*

*Just behind me is a charred piece of woodland where Sarah Goode, an English history student, died. Sarah Goode had been wanted by Boston Police for questioning in relation to the brutal stabbing of her lover, Back Bay fireman Bradley Howarth. It seems that guilt caught up with her at last, because in the early hours of this morning Sarah Goode came here, poured gasoline over herself, and lit a match. Her fuel-drenched clothes burst into flames and Miss Goode died in seconds."*

The picture then flashed to an interview with John. He was stood in front of the crime scene and I could tell it was still early morning. I listened astounded as Lieutenant John Cornwell lied to the watching public.

*"It is a moment of extreme sadness for me that Sarah Goode chose this route, but I am pleased for the family of Bradley Howarth, and everyone should remember that he was the first victim in this, that his killer has now made this dramatic confession."*

*"How do you know this was suicide?"* an off-screen voice asked.

*"Because we have a witness. This witness saw Sarah Goode kneeling down in the woods, sobbing. Then Miss Goode poured gasoline over herself and lit a match. This passer-by ran the fire service and ambulance, but they couldn't arrive in time."*

*"How do you feel about this, lieutenant?"*

*"It's a sad case, and I would have preferred to see the due process of law carried out to a conclusion, but I think the family of that brave fireman will believe their nightmare is starting to end."*

I snapped the television off. I was aghast. "It's like a different story," I said, shocked.

"Did John mention a witness when you were there? Did anybody mention a witness?"

"No, no." I was stood up now, pacing again. "It was murder, they said it was."

I walked around the room, grinding my teeth and thinking of the injustice, when something occurred to me. I felt something lift from me, and I almost felt like I could smile. I'd heard the tumblers click into place, and when my mind opened the door, it all seemed so obvious.

"It's lies," I said, my smile spreading, "all damn lies."

Katie looked at me wearily. I wasn't sure she was ready for a fight. Katie wanted an end to it all, not a new beginning.

"It's a media stunt." I was excited now, my mind racing ahead, my thoughts tumbling into my head like a rock fall. "Lieutenant John Cornwell is misleading the people of Boston deliberately. It's a calculated lie, and he has told it to the camera."

"Whoa, Joe, take it steady. You have to be careful what you say. You can't know everything about the case. Something might have come out after you left."

I was smiling. "No, no, John was lying, and I bet he will admit it later, if his plan works."

Katie sat up straight now. Her fatigue was replaced by curiosity.

"The clothes," I continued. "The report said she poured fuel over her clothes and set fire to herself." Katie was staring at me. "That can't be right, because she was naked. Photographs were being taken. Whoever killed her, fried her. There will be photographs of a dead Sarah Goode, and in those shots, she will be naked."

"So what does it mean?"

I went to the window but didn't look out. My eyes couldn't focus on anything. My mind was shooting through possibilities and explanations, each one being touched on for a moment before it rested on the obvious one: it was a smokescreen.

I whirled back round to Katie.

"John Cornwell is an intelligent man, and he's a family man. He isn't going to throw his career, his family's income, on one case. If he is lying, it's for a reason, and he will have approval. There were no Wakefield Police in that report. No, I think there is a reason why it was best to tell lies, and I want to know."

"So what are you going to do? Ring John?"

"Yeah, and I'm going to shadow him. He owes me, and I want in on it."

I reached for the telephone and called Boston Police. I couldn't get through to John at first, but within a couple of minutes, and after some threats to contact the Globe, Lieutenant John Cornwell came free.

"You better make this good."

I could tell I'd rattled him. "Hi, John, how are you doing down there?"

"Cut the bullshit. What do you want?"

"I want in, that's what. I want to shadow you, as we agreed."

"What makes you think there's anything to shadow?"

"I saw the news. Suicide? C'mon, John, I know that wasn't true. If you're covering up, I'm going to the press."

There was silence at the other end. I knew I had him. I knew now that it wasn't a cover-up, but I knew John would have to tell me that, and if he does that, he will have to tell me everything else. I didn't say anything. I let the silence do the talking.

"Okay," he said. "Do you know the Old South Meeting House?"

"Yeah."

"Bookshop across the road. Meet me outside in about a half-hour."

And then the phone went dead. I looked at Katie and gave a thumbs-up. Game on.

I waited for an hour, reading a newspaper.

I was just thinking about reading the business section when I felt someone sit down close to me. I looked up from the page and saw it was John.

He smiled, which surprised me, and nodded a greeting. I didn't say anything at first. I just put my newspaper down and folded my arms in a "well?" kind of way.

He shrugged and his grin broadened. I tilted my head and gave a disapproving look.

"I know why you rang," he said eventually. I said nothing. "The suicide," he continued, "you know it's bullshit."

I laughed. "Even I could spot that one. What the hell is going on?"

"Ah," he said, his eyes widening, "don't you worry, it's all under control."

"I thought at first you were covering up."

He patted me on the shoulder and looked around, his eyes partly shielded by sunglasses. "You can say many things about me, but I don't cover up."

"So what is going on?"

John looked back at me. He raised his sunglasses and his eyes twinkled. "I'm never going to get rid of you, am I?"

I shook my head slowly. "No, not yet."

John turned back to the street scene. He gazed around the little part of Boston we could see, and then pointed at a young white male pacing up and down by the kerb.

"See that guy?" he asked.

I nodded.

"Keiron Kennedy. Bad to the core. Taking enough drugs to wipe out a family of four. He's looking to snatch bags, or pick a pocket. He loves the Japanese. They always have expensive equipment, don't worry about hiding it, and they aren't that big."

"Very interesting, but what's your point?"

John smiled. "Just watch." And with that he took his sunglasses off and shouted over, "Kennedy! Hey, Kennedy, I've spotted you, man."

The young man whirled round, saw John waving at him from the bench, flicked John a 'fuck you', and walked off.

"You see, Joe Kinsella," John said, turning back to me, "that's my life here. When you've gone back to England, I'll still be doing that, and next year, and the year after that. I don't fuck with my career, and so my bosses don't fuck with me."

"Okay, fair enough, but you lied. You are on camera, lying. What's it all about?"

"It was an operational decision."

"It's a trap."

He nodded and smiled. "It's an operational trap."

"What about Sarah's parents? Don't they have a right to know?"

"If it was my little girl, I would want to know. But the Goodes are coming over on a flight tonight. I'll tell them then."

I blew out a whistle. "That won't be easy."

John sighed. "When someone dies, it never is," and he looked distant for a moment before adding, "particularly when they might be able to blame me." He looked at me. "What are they like?"

I shrugged. "A decent couple. She's in charge, but they are good people. They were protective of their daughter, but then she was a suspected murderer. I don't know how they'll be now."

John nodded. He was silent for a moment, clearly not relishing the task ahead.

"Who made the operational decision?" I asked.

"I did, on advice."

"Robert?"

John nodded and smiled. "I had to give him something to do."

"What's it all about then?"

"Oh, something Robert said. We talked this morning. I had just come from Wakefield and I had a difficult team meeting ahead. I had to tell everybody about the possibility of an undiscovered serial killer running around Greater Boston, so I wanted to go in with an idea, make it seem like I was ahead of the pack. If there was a link, we had to trap him somehow. Forensics may not be enough."

"So what did he say?"

"Simple. He said adopt a low-risk strategy. By saying it was suicidal guilt over Brad's murder, it may prompt a response from the killer. And it helped me, because if the link that you suggest isn't present, then I'm right, and I've gone on record as saying it. Heads I win, tails you lose."

"But what do you hope to get out of it, telling lies I mean?"

He looked at me and his face set. "A response."

That's all he said, and I could tell that John was playing the patience game, waiting for something to come in, and until then he could do little.

I looked around. I found it hard to believe that I was talking about murder on such a beautiful day. The leaves on the trees I could see were bright green, new and fresh from the spring growth, and the bright sun made the buildings shine. I began to wonder if I'd ever really understood it all. I had been chasing a girl I'd never met in a country I'd never been in before. Everything had taken place in the abstract. I thought then of Sarah's parents, and how much I didn't want to see them.

"Do you think it will work, the trap?" I asked.

John shrugged. "Only time can answer that question. Robert thinks it will."

"Why? It doesn't seem the most complex trap."

"No, it isn't, but Robert thinks the killer is unravelling, losing the control. The letters sent to Katie are a first. None of the other murders seem to have coded clues. So why are they being sent?"

"To taunt you?"

John shook his head. "That's what Robert thought at first, but now he's not so sure. You see, the letters were sent before Sarah

Goode died. I would go with the taunting thing if they arrived now, the day after her death, but not then, when Sarah was still alive. So they can only mean one thing."

I raised my eyebrows in query.

"We were supposed to stop him," John said ruefully. "He warned us in those letters what he was going to do, and why he was doing it. As we didn't stop him, he may have unravelled a little bit more. If he thinks his deed has gone completely unnoticed, he may get back in touch. If we told the press the truth, he may be satisfied with that, so that his genius can be appreciated by all."

"Do you think he will get in touch?"

"Robert thinks he'll do something. Organised killers do that, as a generalisation. It's part of the control thing. They seek to play some part in the investigation. They might ring in with a lead that throws everyone off the scent, or else be some figure in the background. He will do something to reveal himself. We just have to wait and see what he does."

I pondered on that. I watched people going about their daily business and realised one thing: I could rejoin them. My job was done. I had no reason to feel guilty about finding Sarah, because she was beyond discovery. I felt sure John would tell Sarah's parents how much I'd helped, and eventually they might appreciate that, and I knew, deep down, that I had done all I could. I had no reason to feel guilty. I should file it all away in that drawer marked 'bad day' and forget about it. I could go shopping, perhaps hire a car and leave Boston. New York sounded exciting, or I could just head out west and see where I ended up. I could ask Katie to show me around Kansas.

So why did I feel bad, incomplete?

I knew one thing. John wasn't going to let me take any further part. It had become his investigation. He knew my threat to go to the press was an empty threat. He knew I wouldn't do anything to derail the investigation. He had told me just enough to let me know that I shouldn't go to the press, and that there was a reason behind what he was doing.

I held out my hand to him.

"It's been good to meet you, Lieutenant Cornwell," I said, shaking his hand and smiling.

John smiled back. "Take a trip to New Hampshire. Or get out to the Cape."

I nodded. "I might just do that."

I stood up and went to move off.

"Hey, Joe."

I turned around.

"You did good, Joe. You would have been a good cop."

"Is that a compliment?"

John smiled. "Some might say that it's better to be a good cop than a good lawyer. More good will come of it."

And with that, I gave a mock salute and headed off into the city, making like a tourist.

# Seventeen

I was sat in my seat at Fenway Park nice and early. I'd watched both teams at batting practice, and then I walked around the ground, buying hot dogs, beers, a couple of t-shirts.

I had a seat at the back of the stands, up behind third base and with a good view of the ballpark. The sun was still shining, but it was getting a little lower in the sky. The ground was only half-full, and the Crackerjack vendors still had full boxes as they patrolled the aisles.

I was getting a little restless now.

I'd had a good day, all things considered. I'd gone to Charlestown, done the tourist thing. Walked up the Bunker Hill Monument, strolled around the streets, curved and twisted, before heading back into Boston and then catching a train to Harvard. I spent more time there, not worried about Sarah or money or about having something more important to do. I tagged onto a guided tour of the university grounds, and then wandered up to Longfellow's House, a yellow clapboard treasure amongst the charming old houses of Brattle Street.

I'd spent a couple of hours in Harvard before I thought of the best way of relaxing, of trying to put this whole Sarah thing behind me, behind us. I caught a cab to Fenway Park, bought a couple of tickets for the evening game, and then took them to Katie's. She wasn't in, so I made do with a quick shower and left her ticket by the answer machine.

But that was a couple of hours ago and Katie was nowhere to be seen. I was charitable about it: she might not have been in the mood, taking into account all that had happened that day, but it would have been nice to see her bounding up the steps towards me.

I watched the game for a while, but it was a slow starter. People were drifting in and not much of interest was happening on the field. Then the big hitter for the Red Sox strode to the plate, a colossal black guy, stood straight like a girder. I smiled when the crowd cheered and I saw the pitcher limber up his right arm for a contest.

I thought back to my last visit here, with Katie next to me, all vivid and excited. That was when I realised that she was something special: those excited eyes, that warm spell, her enthusiasm for life. I looked again towards the entrance ramp. No sign of her.

The pitcher pulled his knee up sharply and let loose with a fast one that I wasn't sure I saw. I whistled. Strike one.

I looked around the ballpark. Katie had been right about something she had said, that it was creaky and cranky and old and bent. It would be a shame if they tore it down to build a new one.

The pitcher was a bit slower with the next one, trying to get the hitter to swing early, but the ball was dipping, and as it dropped to the dirt in front of the umpire a 'ball' was called. One strike, one ball.

I smiled to myself. This ballpark was full of history. I could see it in the jagged corners, the dents in the Green Monster, the huge left field wall. It makes the ballpark. I thought about what I would be going back to, that little house by the sea. Maybe my own history made me the man I was then, sat in Fenway Park, an aimless private detective, meandering from case to case without any thought for the long term.

The next pitch was another fast one, high and inside. The hitter rocked back on his heels to get his chin out of the way, and the crowd 'oohed' their disapproval, but he judged it well. The pitcher snarled towards home plate and took the ball for another go. One strike, two balls.

The importance of history. I started to feel a prickle, some kind of a niggle, a thought I shouldn't really pursue. I tried to make like the hitter and swipe the niggle over the Green Monster and into Lansdowne Street, but instead I swung and missed. The niggle lay spinning at my feet, willing me to pick it up and dust it down. The lure became stronger, so I tried to find the thought so I could send it away as worthless.

The pitcher stared the hitter down, leant back until his back arched, wrestled the ball between his middle two fingers, pulled his knee to his chin, and let loose with another one. Neat, fast, a split-finger, and over the plate. The bat hurled itself at the speeding ball, re-adjusting downwards to account for the late dip of the ball. The re-adjustment wasn't far enough, and the ball crashed off the bottom of the bat, thudding into the dust at his feet. Strike two.

I took a long pull on my beer and thought hard. The niggle bit. The importance of history. But whose history? Sarah's? I shook my head. No, that can't be right. Then I thought of whoever must be behind of these killings. What made him follow the path he has chosen? Did he choose it, or was it pre-ordained, fixed by the coincidence of events, and the sum of those events making the man everyone was seeking? What is that man's history? Why is he doing what he is doing? Or is it men? I remembered that there must be two, as the young man in jail for murder had an alibi, a decoy to get him away from the scene. What is their history? Everything has a reason, at least to the person that is doing it. History. It lies behind everything, like a shadow slowly crowding out the light.

The pitcher didn't pull back as far on this one. He'd shaken off the first signal by the catcher. This time it looked more measured. As the pitcher pulled his knee up, I saw the outfield take a couple of steps to their left, anticipating the flight of the ball along the first baseline. It was high and outside. The hitter saw it early, the ball curling harmlessly away from the plate, and the catcher had to move some to stop it careering towards the low green wall towards first base. Two strikes, three balls. A full house.

The crowd were on their feet now, clapping and cheering. The pitcher flung his arms about, stretching and flexing, getting ready for the decisive throw. I looked down to my left and saw a young boy on his feet, cheering. And then he started to blur as the niggle bit harder. The sound of the crowd began to retreat into the background, the clapping, roaring on the hitter.

The pitcher stared down the hitter. The hitter was flexing the bat over his right shoulder, the wood twitching and moving like a metronome. He was leant back onto his right foot, glaring, chewing, snarling. The pitcher stood up, hid the ball with his glove, and tensed.

The niggle became real. History, it all starts with history. Look into the past. See how things start to see why they are. Robert said it, about people. Look for the trigger. Go back to the beginning and work forward.

The pitcher brought his knee up and pulled his arm back.

I knew what I had to do. I didn't know why I hadn't done it before.

The ball left the pitcher's hand in a blur. It made for the hitter's chest, high and inside. The hitter leant back defensively, watching the curve and dip of the ball.

I had to get out. There was still something I hadn't done. The police might find it, but what if I can find it first. I could do it for Sarah.

The ball started to come back over home plate, dipping towards the ground, the hitter off-balance, his weight going away from the ball, not into it.

I stood up with the rest of the crowd. They were willing the bat onto the ball. I was looking away from the field.

The hitter started to swing. The bat was swung fast, and with the swing the hitter's momentum was regained. He began to shift his weight onto the front foot, the bat streaking towards the plate.

I was turning for the exit.

The bat hit the ball as sweet as could be. The ball began to climb. The hitter dropped the bat and started his run to first base. But it was a slow run, his eyes following the flight of the ball, his mind urging the ball over that green wall.

The crowd roared as the ball cleared the nets and made its way to Lansdowne Street, the same place I was headed.

As I got outside the ground, I began to run.

I ran most of the way to the police station. My chest was aching, fighting for air, and I leant towards the floor, my legs losing the will to stand. It wasn't that far, but I don't run much. I crashed the doors, panting.

"Joe? Are you okay?"

I looked up. It was Robert. He had joined a bemused desk sergeant.

I caught up with my lungs eventually and got them under control.

"It must be important," he said, a wry smile crinkling his eyes.

I shook my head, gasping.

He stayed quiet as I spoke.

"This morning you said, as we were walking into Boston, that if you identify the stressor, the event that makes person cross the line from murderous thinking to straight murder, you can identify when the murders begin."

"Yeah, I remember," he replied, "and you said that if the stressor is discovered, then the person who has lived that event, who is crossing that line, can be identified. I remember it. Why?"

"Well, it was something Katie said, back when I first came here. She said that history is behind everything, as history is created every minute, every hour, every day, moulding the next day, which itself will become a history all of its own. She was trying to say how important history is, because we can't understand the present until we understand the past. Katie was only talking about a cranky old ballpark, but I was back there, tonight, and I remembered what she said. And then I remembered what you said, about the stressor, and I realised the importance of this person's past." I stopped to scratch my head and gather my thoughts for a while. "We need to go back to the beginning."

"Which beginning?"

"The beginning of all this. Look at the first murder, look around it, and we might find something that points to whoever did all this."

"Hold fire, Joe. What is all this 'we'? You've done your bit. Take my advice: Lieutenant Cornwell will go wild if you go poking around. And I'll join him. He's going through all the murders, trying to find that something. He doesn't need you."

I gave a small scornful laugh. "I hadn't realised my contribution had been so well received."

Robert shook his head and then held his hand up in apology. "I'm sorry, okay. But you have done your bit. Let the police take over."

"I have. I'm just trying to help. I have to face Sarah's parents back in Morsby, remember that."

Robert nodded that he understood that, but continued, "Joe, go home, or go see America. If you want to see history, go to Virginia. Or get a car and head west. Before you know it, you'll be heading through mountains so beautiful you'll think your roof is going touch the sky, or else you'll wander through farmlands so green and simple that you'll forget cities like this exist." He gave me a hard stare. "But don't stay in Boston."

I said nothing, disappointed with my ending. I didn't think Robert would be so dismissive.

"If you stay in Boston," he continued, "and do anything that might upset the inquiry, John will haul you to the County Jail." He tried to look sympathetic. "You wouldn't last in there. Not even a weekend."

"I don't want to upset the inquiry. I just want to complete the job I started."

Robert nodded. "Okay, if that's what you want to do, but why come here to tell me?"

I shrugged and smiled. "I was hoping you'd help me."

Robert stared at me for a while, weighing me up.

"I'm a police officer, Joe."

"But don't you fancy stepping out of the box for a while?"

"No, absolutely not. This is my career, Joe, and I still want to be doing it when you're gone." He sighed. "I'm sorry, Joe, but if you want to chase old stories, you are going to have to do it on your own. And hope we don't catch you doing it."

I nodded. I understood. Perhaps I should forget about it. But then I thought about Sarah, and I had this image from the photographs I had, of a smiling young woman, as carefree as the spring, but she was in fear, waiting for her rescuer to arrive. I was that rescuer, and I didn't get there in time.

"I'm going to Saugus tomorrow."

Robert looked at me with resignation.

"What the hell for?" he asked.

I raised my eyebrows, feigned innocence. "You said I should see a bit more of America. That's what I'm doing. I'm going to say hello to America, and I'm starting with Saugus."

"You asshole."

I smiled.

Robert tugged on his lip, his mind working fast.

"I suppose I had better go with you then."

I smiled again. "Lovely. See you in the morning, here at eight."

I walked away, and as I closed the door, I heard Robert lift the phone and dial out. I knew he was calling John. It didn't seem to matter.

The walk back to Katie's was refreshing. A light wind had picked up, cool without the sun, and I was glad to get back to the apartment.

I went in and shouted for Katie. No response. The lights were off and the apartment was silent.

I went into her bedroom but it was empty.

I was about to get worried when I saw the red light flashing on the answer machine. I should have noticed it before, but it was light then. Now the red light was flashing bright in the darkness.

I hit 'play'. It was Katie. She was with Danny. He was taking her to Wakefield, to see where Sarah died. She thought it might be therapeutic. Closure.

I smiled to myself, despite the twinge of jealousy. She wasn't back yet, but she'll be okay with Danny. I remembered him, the guy from my first time at the Pour House, from my first day with Katie. Nice guy. Katie will be fine.

# Eighteen

The morning came round quickly, but there was no sign of Katie. I jumped into my clothes, left a message scrawled on some paper by the answer machine. I told her where I was going and why.

I was about to close the door when I thought of something else.

I went to Katie's bedroom and rooted through her drawers. I wasn't sure if I would find what I was looking for, but at the back of the bottom of drawer I found them. Katie would understand. I put them in my pocket and left for Robert's room at the university.

I couldn't help feeling jealous about Katie's absence. She was with Danny, an old friend. Katie might have needed someone, and I hadn't been there. Danny had.

I tried to forget about my feelings and concentrated on the job in hand. I didn't think I would be in Boston for much longer, so worrying about Katie might be unproductive. Instead, I tried to think of the warm sun on my face, the buzz of early morning city life.

As I reached the station, I saw Robert and John waiting outside.

"Good morning. Glad you could make it."

John gave me a curt look and then said, "you didn't think I would just let you wander all over my investigation, did you?"

"I'm not," I replied. "I'm doing the tourist thing. Saugus sounded a nice place."

"Don't be a smartass."

He was firm and I knew it spoke of silent threat. I stared him down, knowing that my presence scared him as much as he might try to scare me.

"I'm just trying to find some answers, that's all. I think Sarah's parents are entitled to that."

He smiled, but it was thin and mean. "I know you won't, because I'm coming with you, and I either come with you with your consent, or else I have two men assigned to you to watch every step you take. One step out of line and I'll lock you up."

I shrugged. "Whatever."

John looked like he was about to say something, but Robert intervened, pointing at a purple Buick parked by the sidewalk. "Why don't we just go?"

John said nothing. I nodded and smiled, before climbing into the car.

We were on our way.

We arrived in Saugus in no time at all, just a short ride up Route One.

Saugus was like a sanctuary. We came into town along Main Street, a tree-lined route that led to not much more than a traffic island, with a liquor store, gas station, and a few general stores.

Saugus sits around a meandering river, its twists and turns creating fertile banks and a town that seemed slow and easy. It seemed like sanity on the edge of suburban Greater Boston, sheltered from the harsh winds that howl off the Berkshires but within touching distance of the sprawl.

We stopped outside the Eastern Bank on Main Street, marked by a swinging wooden sign by the sidewalk. As we got out of the car, John looked at me and asked what I wanted to see.

I looked around and couldn't see much. We were stood on a deserted sidewalk, staring at a small wooden church and the occasional conifer. A gas station was next door, and that was the only real sign of life. The shops were low-level block affairs, and behind those I could see houses set in their own little piece of neighbourhood.

I knew where I would normally start: the local newspaper. But I didn't know where the offices were. If we were looking at the first murder on the list, the young teenage girl found bound and gagged and sexually assaulted at Prankers Pond, then the local newspaper archives should have some articles.

Then I caught sight of a turret on a large building near the traffic island. I looked at John, and he smiled at me, forgetting his frustration at me still being around, and made a playful tugging gesture on his neck to show that I was looking at the Town Hall. I remembered the first death in the series, the woman who hadn't been murdered, had instead been fond of group sex and attaching sharp wire to her neck. John had said that she was well known in Saugus, trawling the bars for excitement, perhaps never quite finding what she hoped she would find.

"So that's where she jumped from?"

John nodded. "Yup. She picked a good stage. Right in the middle of town."

It certainly was that. It stood next to the traffic island, the focal point it seemed for the whole town, and it provided a grand opening for those arriving into town from Route One.

We walked over until we were stood right beneath the town hall. It was an impressive building, gothic in appearance, with two gables joined by the large trunk of the building. A little tower sat on the front, and I imagined that from the top a person would appear to be over everything else. It seemed a good place to give the town the finger from, if a person was so inclined. Mary Bradbury had been so inclined, when she gave a last display of her nudity, with sharp wire wrapped around her neck.

I looked at John and then back at the tower. It would have been quite a sight, the young woman hurtling towards death on the sidewalk. Instead, she was yanked into eternity by the combination of gravity and a length of wire too short for the fall.

I looked back at John, but then I looked beyond him. I could see a sign outside a building: "*The Public Library*."

"That place might help."

John raised his eyebrows.

"They will have newspapers," I explained, "and newspapers will describe how the girl was found at Prankers Pond. That's why we are here, to find about her."

"No, that's why you're here. I'm here to keep an eye on you."

I didn't respond, but John's tone softened and he went on to ask, "what do you hope to find?"

I shrugged. "I don't know. I hope I will know when I see it, or rather, you will."

"Well, c'mon then, Sherlock, let's go unlock the mystery."

We ended up on the second floor, heading for piles of yellowing newspaper print bulging out of shelves.

Saugus Library is a modern, open building. A counter by the stairs keeps watch on a couple of computer screens, and leaflets on Saugus adorn the desk. The books themselves are kept neatly spaced on metal shelves that clank when you go to them. I could see the Town Hall out of the window, and if I didn't know better, I would think I was in some busy town somewhere.

I heard John join me, and then Robert, as I scoured the shelves and eventually found the local newspapers for the year of the discovery of the girl's body. The news came out weekly in Saugus so they were easy to find. I grabbed an armful and we made our way to a table and spread them out. The newspapers had been well looked after and were all neatly in order. In no time at all I was leafing through a yellowing account of the discovery of the girl's body.

A large picture showed police tape across a muddy path through an avenue of trees. A solitary grey rock sat by the path, and a white cross on the photograph showed the people of Saugus where the body had been found.

I read:

*"Saugonians woke to a grim find this morning: the discovery of the body of a murdered young teenager by a path at Prankers Pond.*

*Police say a local man walking his dog made the find.*

*"His dog was sniffing around a bundle of rags, and he thought at first that it was discarded trash," said Saugus patrolman Bob Harrington. "He went to investigate and found the body of a young girl. She was naked from the waist down, with bindings tying her limbs together. It was a disturbing sight."*

*Saugus police are asking anyone who saw anything in the Prankers Pond area on Wednesday night to come forward.*

*"The proximity to Route One means that the person responsible could be from outside the Saugus area, so if anyone saw anybody new to town acting suspiciously, please give Saugus Police a call."*

*Police confirmed later that the dead girl was Abigail Hobbs, the Arlington teenager who went missing from home on Sunday night.*

*The family of the dead girl are said to be devastated.*

*"She was such a sweet young thing," said Emily Hobbs, Abigail's aunt. "She was so full of life and with so much ahead of her. Why would anybody do anything like this?"*

*Sandra Matheson of Saugus said, "why choose Saugus? We are a peace-loving community. Who would want to come here and do this to us?"*

I put the newspaper down. The story carried on for another page and a half, but it was the usual thing. A body found, witnesses sought, horror expressed.

I went through all the newspapers I had. The story stayed on the front page for a few weeks, but then it dwindled into the occasional mention when it was clear that nothing was happening on the case.

What was noticeable in the reports was the lack of any progress. No suspects, no arrests, no leads reported. The case tumbled to the ground with the certainty of a falling leaf.

I looked at John and Robert, who had been reading the reports as I passed them over.

They must have seen the appeal in my eyes.

"It was good to see the local perspective, but there's nothing new," John said.

I had to agree with him, and I felt frustration drain me as I put the papers to one side and sat back in my chair. Why was I still here? I had finished my job, Sarah had turned up, kind of, so why hadn't I just packed my bags and headed for the airport? Or taken a ride to Avis and hired a convertible Mustang, taken to the hills? I could just relax instead with Katie. I could stay in Boston, get to know the place, and help her through her end of year exams. We could make love until summer and then head out west, go see daddy in Wichita, or get her to show me around awhile.

What I didn't need to do was sit in a library in a quiet little town, trying to do a job that was no longer mine to do.

I looked back at the counter and noticed a sign that said "*Local History*". I sauntered over and found an old guy with a pointed grey beard and a checked suit, like Custer in plaid.

I coughed and he looked up at me. He had half-moon glasses perched on the end of his nose, and as he looked towards me his eyes crinkled with a smile and he ambled over.

"Good morning, sir, how can I help?"

I told him that I was a crime writer, researching unsolved murders. He looked surprised, wondering why the hell I'd landed in Saugus, so I told him that I was aiming to deal with lesser-known murders in an attempt to solve them. I was trying to do to old murders what Truman Capote did to the Clutter slaying in Holcomb in the 1950's: bring them alive. I told him I was interested in the murder of young Abigail Hobbs. I gave him the basic details, tried to jog his memory.

226

He nodded and looked serious.

"Nasty business," he said, tutting. "Did Saugus no good at all, that one. Saugus is a nice place to live. Kids grow up safe and clean, full of kindness and fresh air. That little girl took that away for a while." He shook his head. "We'd had some trouble once before, with the motels nearby. Some family had tried to check into one, told that trade was done by the hour. The family went to the police and the town made the papers for being a sleazepit. This murder didn't help. Not only was it a sleazepit for affairs and ten-a-dime whores, it was a dumping ground for dead little girls. Everybody said she must have come from one of the motels, you know, a good night gone bad."

"Was anyone suspected? I've looked through the newspapers, but they don't say much."

He shook his head. "No-one suspected, no-one arrested, no-one charged. The only one thing you'll do is stir up bad feeling." He shook his head again. "No, leave it."

"You can't help?"

"Can't? Won't? I won't 'cos I can't, but if I could, I wouldn't."

I thanked him and returned to the table. I slumped onto the seat, but when I looked around I saw John's wary eye.

"Hey, don't worry, I didn't say anything. I just asked him about it generally. Told him I was a writer."

"What did you think he would say? 'Hey, now you came to mention it, they never did speak to that guy who was seen dragging a corpse down Prankers Pond.' C'mon Joe, get real."

"C'mon John, it won't be the name. It will be some detail. You know, you're a cop. Some detail that might be viewed differently now that there is a bigger picture."

John sat back in his chair.

"Why don't we go to see Saugus Police then?" I asked. "They might have had suspects that weren't leaked to the press. They might speak to you. Any lead is better than no lead."

John shook his head firmly.

"The local guys will wonder why some cop from Boston has started sniffing around an old unsolved murder. It will create more rumours than leads, and will alert the press to everything that is on standby over in Boston." He shook his head again. "No police, not yet." And then he must have heard my thoughts, because he added, "and if you go there, I'll have your ass."

I saw a look in his eyes that said that maybe he would.

I stood up and walked out of the library. The weather was warm outside now, and the surrounding greenery made a colourful backdrop. As John and Robert joined me, I heard John's cell-phone ring. John answered it, made a few nods and grunts, and then hung up.

"I've got to go back to Boston. We're having a tactics meeting and update. I have to be there. C'mon you guys, we're done here."

I was about to go when I thought once more about that murder all those years ago. It just didn't feel right to go then, as if some tiny voice was whispering at me to stay.

I shook my head at John. "I'm having a look around."

John looked angry, and I thought he was about to launch a tirade when Robert stepped in to say that he would stay and show me around. John looked at his phone as if someone was about to call with the answer, but when he realised that it was going to stay quiet, he turned to stomp off down Main Street.

"I'm watching you," he snarled before he went.

As I watched him walk quickly away, I smiled to myself and said quietly, "I don't think you are now."

Robert and I made small talk as we walked around Prankers Pond. I found out a few more things about him. He was born on Christmas Day, liked to watch the sun come up, and painted watercolours of the sea.

It didn't take us long to reach the scene. John's car had been parked at the bottom of the street leading up to Prankers Pond, so once John had accelerated away, we ambled up the road and soon found ourselves strolling through a tunnel of spreading green. It had been a peaceful suburban scene, with spacious white properties and generous gardens, but then a path by the houses led to a small diamond-shaped lake. Trees crept right up to the edge, making the place seem secretive and hidden.

But the trees also made it shadowy, and I could imagine how it must have appealed to the killer of Abigail Hobbs. Once the killer was tucked amongst the trees, he would be invisible from anything around the lake.

We'd done one circuit of the lake when Robert pulled out of his pocket a photocopy of the front page of the old local paper. He pointed at a rock.

"I think that's where she was found," he said.

I looked at the photograph and agreed with him. We'd come across a scene exactly like that in a forgotten old newspaper in a building half a mile away. The trees were bushing out a bit more, but nothing had really changed.

I walked over to the rock, the site of the cross in the old photograph, and touched it.

I don't know why I touched it. I suppose it might have been a desire to make it real, to touch something as solid as a rock, so that it would become more than a collection of old murder stories bundled together by some crackpot theory.

The rock just felt like what it was: a rock. An ugly block of weather-moulded stone set by a winding path on the banks of a placid lake. I felt no great connection. Instead, I felt just deflation. All the wild imaginings I'd had over the last few days had gone as cold as that stone. That rock may have been the dumping ground for someone's daughter, but it was still just a lump of weather-worn crystals bonded together by the accumulation of time.

I sat on the rock. I looked about and saw through the trees the glimmer of sunlight playing on water. I could just hear the traffic from Route One making its way somewhere. I turned that way and saw a collection of signs peeking through the trees. Gas stations, motels, restaurants. I could see paths worn into the countryside in-between and realised again why it would have appealed so much to someone involved in murder. So many paths in, so many paths out, hidden from view, but near to everything. Mainly, near to that busy road that would lead to the I-95, and from there, the rest of Massachusetts. An anonymous goal in a vast sprawl of people.

"It's over for you now, I guess," Robert said, more by way of a comment than a question.

I turned around to him. "What do you mean?"

"What I say, that it's over."

He walked to the rock and touched it.

"It's nothing special, is it. I can see it in your eyes. When we were walking up here, I could sense an expectation, as if something

229

ghost-like would emerge from the waters, handing you the answers like Arthur being handed Excalibur. I look at you now and I see reality biting. You're in a quiet New England town, looking at the scene of a forgotten discovery and seeing why it was forgotten. It was just another one of life's tragedies, and its effect on the landscape is as undramatic as the murder was brutal."

I stayed looking at the rock.

"There are other places," I said, "other towns that might reveal something more than Saugus has done. The list of deaths was a long one. There's no reason why it should all end at the first one."

"It ends because this is all there is. One rock, one lake, one forgotten news clipping. Let it go, Joe. Don't try and make up for blowing your legal career. You don't have to prove yourself."

I looked at Robert. The lawyer jibe didn't hurt. I'd said it to myself enough times. And I realised why he had stayed after John had gone. He knew I would carry on in the face of John's objections. He feared that it might have been John's objections that were driving me. But he knew that I would find nothing before the end of the day, and when that happened, he wanted to be there to drive home the advantage.

I held my hands out in a helpless gesture, as if to say that I'd tried. Robert's smiling nod showed agreement.

"It was my second chance, I suppose," I said sadly. "I don't see thirty more years of what I've been doing. I was hoping I would crack this case and then doors would open. Or perhaps I would get better work, could buy better equipment. Listening devices, car-tracking gadgets, hidden cameras." I shrugged. "It just didn't work out."

"Don't knock yourself, Joe. You've done okay."

I smiled and turned away. "If it's over, it's over, so let's got for a last drink."

The bar looked like all the others from the outside. It was on Main Street, just by the turn-off for Route One. A squat, square, bland brick building with darkened windows and darker doors. A painted logo of some wild looking cowboy adorned the old black wooden door, oddly out of place in the suburban setting. A Coors sign marked the entrance, and inside I could see a barman wiping a wooden bar and passing comments to a couple of guys sat on stools.

We went in. No-one stopped to gawp at the two strangers.

We perched ourselves on two rickety stools at the end of the bar nearest the door. I thought it would give us the best opportunity of escape, but we didn't need it. The barman gave a wave, a 'hi, you guys,' and shouted at us for our order. We shouted it back; he gave us another wave, and then brought two cold-looking beers over.

The bar didn't seem so bad once we settled in. It was dark, most American bars seemed to be dark, but it was clean. The other customers weren't old drunks, but a couple of old timers passing a couple of hours and a young couple eating burgers. A dartboard stood at one end of the bar, next to a jukebox and a cigarette machine. All the doors were painted black, but the bar was clean hardwood, and the floor looked polished, black and white tiles leading to the jukebox.

The barman wandered over again, when he must have heard me speaking. Robert had been asking me about my plans.

"Hey, you guys Australian?"

I laughed. "No, English, although that's only me."

His eyes widened. "England? What the merry hell are you doing in Saugus?"

I gave a quick glance towards Robert, and after a discreet shake of the head, Robert interrupted, "we just pulled off for some gas. Thought it seemed like a nice place so we came in for a drink."

The barman chuckled. "I've never heard of my bar pulling in tourists before." He chuckled again and shook his head. "If you fellas want anything, just give me a shout."

I waved him off and took a pull on my beer.

"What do we do when he sees us getting onto a bus? Tell him we've had our car stolen?"

Robert smiled. "It will give him something to talk about. Not much else will go on around here."

We sat and drank our beers and talked for a while. Robert asked me about England, about my career changes. I asked him about his career prospects.

He didn't reveal much about himself at all, whereas I felt myself give in to a desire to unburden my woes. It must have been something to do with it being the end of the investigation. I wanted to unburden myself of all the bad feeling before I boarded a flight back to England. I may have spent a couple of weeks in Boston, an international private eye, but pretty soon I would be returning to my life as a small town process server.

Robert seemed interested and sympathetic, but I realised pretty quickly that he was supportive of my plans to go home and critical of any hint that I might stay. John and Robert made a good double act, but I didn't want to leave Saugus until I had found out all I could. If I were leaving Boston anyway, what harm would it do? And I suspected there were two knowledgeable oracles in Saugus. The newspaper and the local innkeepers. Some things are done and said when in drink that are never intended for the public domain.

I called the barman over and asked him for two more beers. He sauntered off, whistling, and returned with two more cold ones.

When he dumped the drinks in front of us, I asked him, "hey, wasn't there a girl from Arlington once killed in Saugus? Young girl, found up on Prankers Pond?"

The barman scratched his chin while Robert looked at me sternly. He didn't have John's firepower, but I could tell he was angry.

The barman shook his head, and then asked me when this was. I told him. A distant memory returned to the barman and he shook his head, this time disapprovingly. "That was bad news for the town. It was good trade for a week, those journalists like a drink, but it gave the town a bad name. You don't want your hometown to become known as a baby's graveyard."

"What happened to it all? Did they get anyone for it?"

The barman looked grim and then said, "no. Some guilty sonofabitch will take that one to the grave, and I hope there is someone there to greet him when he gets there."

"The police must have had someone in the frame for it, surely?"

The barman shook his head. "That little girl came to Saugus under the cover of darkness, and that's where the killer stayed. The police believed it was someone passing through." He gave me a curious look. "What's your interest in this?"

"My uncle lives in Arlington. I think he knew the girl. I'd heard him talking about it. Being sat here just reminded me, that's all."

The barman seemed satisfied with that. He cleaned glasses and kept an eye on the other customers' drinks.

"It was a bad business," he carried on. "As if Tom Bradbury hadn't had it hard enough already." He looked sorrowful then. "You get over one shock, and then something like that comes along and it puts you right back at base camp."

I heard Robert gasp. I looked at him and he looked like he'd been slapped.

My eyes tried to ask him what was wrong, but he wasn't looking at me. He was scratching his head, looking like he was elsewhere. I was surprised when I heard him join in the conversation.

"Tom Bradbury. Was he Mary's husband? Or her son?"

The barman nodded eagerly. "That's right. Mary's husband. Man, he'd had a bad run of luck." Then a thought struck him. "How do you know about that? You said you'd only pulled off for gas."

"It was Tom Bradbury who found her, wasn't it? He found the young girl, up there at Prankers Pond."

The barman nodded slowly, cautiously, but his attraction was drawn to a drinks order from the two old guys further down the bar. He asked us to hang on and then he went off and served his other customers.

I felt like I'd been hit too. Like a re-awakening. A link, a coincidence. Tom Bradbury, husband of the woman who'd jumped from the roof of Saugus Town Hall, had found the dead girl up at Prankers Pond. Mary Bradbury had been the first girl on the list, but that had been suicide. A leap, a yank, and a pea-pod decapitation. Abigail Hobbs found bound and dead, raped and mutilated before she'd even approached womanhood, discovered by the man left behind by the jump from the Town Hall.

I looked at Robert, and for the first time I saw him nervous. He was staring at the small area of bar in front of him, his teeth chewing his bottom lip to blood.

"What are you thinking?"

He ignored me.

"Robert? What the hell is going on? What's wrong with you?"

He looked up from the bar, his eyes wide. "Murder is what is going on. We are about to find ourselves in the middle of murder."

I must have looked shocked, because he went on, "it proves the link, because now there is more than one. The letters, the names, now this. Tom Bradbury. He's the man. He is the fucking man."

"Why? What's going on?"

233

"They always put themselves forward, they can't help themselves. Organised killers like to stick around, try to inject themselves into the investigation. They become witnesses, they speak to the press, they make sure they are somewhere where they believe they can control what is seen. Remember what I said, that it's all about control. Control of the victim, control of the scene, control of the investigation. Oh yeah, a lot of them just like to get their kicks from the morning papers, some kind of notoriety. But it's also a kind of damage assessment, so they can see what's going on, see whether the police are closing in."

Robert thumped the bar.

"They should have thought of it," he said, sounding angry. "They should have checked for key names in each case."

I raised my hands. "Hey, don't get angry at yourself. This is fucking amazing. John can go get Bradbury, and we can wrap this whole thing up.

I took a gulp of beer and felt sad and elated all that the same time.

Then I thought of something else.

"We'd decided there had to be two, because of the false alibi in the case of that young man John sent to prison."

Robert looked at me quizzically, and then he blinked a couple of times and nodded vigorously. "The son," he said. "The newspapers said that when Mary Bradbury jumped off the Town Hall, she had left behind a young son. A little blonde kid approaching his teens. Mary jumped about thirteen years ago, so he will be in his mid-twenties. Shit, you're right." He slapped the bar and pointed at me. "He's the accomplice."

Robert jumped off his stool.

"I'm going to give John a call," he said, voice raised. "This is the breakthrough."

Robert left the bar to use his phone. I leant on the bar in triumph, a victorious smile starting to eat up my face. I glanced out of the window and I could see Robert's eyes and mouth dancing in animated conversation towards his telephone.

Then another thought occurred to me. That thought sent me cold. A blonde boy, mid to late twenties, injecting himself into the investigation? I found myself clapping in excitement. Jimmy Walsh. I'd known all along. Went out of his way to get to know

Sarah, and has hung about since, calling round to work out the state of the investigation, mistrust of me.

I was about to rush out to Robert when I remembered what I'd grabbed from Katie's apartment. I'd thought about Jimmy as I left the apartment. Somehow, his presence niggled me, always had done. I'd grabbed some of Sarah's photographs, snapshots of Sarah and her friends, and put them in my pocket.

I looked over at the barman, who was still eyeing me with suspicion. I was going to show him a picture of Jimmy Walsh to see if he was Tom Bradbury's son.

I beckoned for him to come over, and he did. I pulled the photographs out of my pocket, a bundle of around twenty pictures. They were the usual college type of picture: groups of young people hugging and laughing, or standing around in bars raising glasses at the camera. I passed them over to the barman and asked him to take a look and see if he recognised anyone. In there was a picture of Jimmy Walsh, stood by the bar in the Pour House, gazing towards a face I recognised as Sarah's. Katie was on it too, grinning behind the bar.

At first he looked suspicious, but I saw him glance down at the bar and he clocked that no tip had been put down yet. Not a time to start insulting your customers.

He went through them patiently, taking in each face on each picture, breathing out, breathing in. He took his time, giving slight shakes of the head as he moved through them. He got to the end, and then went back through them. He stopped at one picture in particular. He looked at the picture, then back at me, then back at the picture, before looking sternly at me and saying, "what kind of game are you playing here?"

"This is no game."

"It looks like one from where I'm standing. What are you doing here?"

"Why? Who have you seen? In the pictures, who have you seen?"

He was getting angry now. "You know who I've seen, so quit the 'we've pulled off for gas' horseshit and tell me what's going on."

I shook my head firmly. "I can't, but if you don't tell me, you'll be telling Boston Police in about thirty minutes. It's your choice.

You either tell me and I leave the bar, or get yourself a lawyer, because you might need one."

The barman slammed the photographs on the bar. He looked angry, the photographs almost screwed up. But he'd left one on top, and after grabbing our drinks he pointed at the photograph, jabbing at the image.

"That's who you want, isn't it?" he snarled. "You came looking for him. So now you know, get out of my bar."

I looked at the photograph, and then back at the barman. I was confused. I heard myself ask, "who is he?"

The barman replied that the face in the picture was Tom Bradbury's son. He'd had a hard time, with his mother killing herself at an early age. I should leave the hell alone.

I felt my knees sway, my tongue hit the roof of my mouth, and the sound of the jukebox retreated into nothing. A million thoughts tried to rush into my brain, all jamming at the door, clamouring, screaming. A million possibilities, none good, all bad.

"Where are they now, the Bradbury's?"

The barman shook his head. "Ask someone else."

I glared at him. I glared so that my eyes reached right into his and melted any resolve. "Tell me."

"They've got a car repair shop, north on Route One, about a half mile along."

I grabbed the photographs and ran out of the bar. I almost knocked Robert over. I kept running towards Route One. I heard him shout. I didn't shout back. My mind was moving too fast to shout, or speak, or even think. I could just think of one word: Katie.

The face he'd pointed to, the person who was in the photograph, identified as the son of the woman who'd thrown herself from the roof of the Town Hall, was Danny. He hadn't been the main person in the shot, and he didn't look happy at being photographed, but it was Danny. Undisputedly and unmistakably Danny. From the Pour House. Katie's friend.

Katie had been with him for twenty-four hours, and I didn't know where she was.

I picked up my speed.

# Nineteen

I stopped when I got to Route One. I looked along the road and I could see a stream of cars and trucks. I couldn't see much of a walkway.

Once I'd stopped, my exertions caught up with me. My heart was beating out of my chest and I could feel my lungs screaming for air. I was bent double, wheezing and panting, when I heard Robert arrive. He had been running but didn't sound tired.

"What the hell is going on?" he asked, sounding angry. I'd never heard it before.

"Tom Bradbury," I said, spitting out the words. "I know his son."

Robert looked shocked, uncertain, like he had a thousand thoughts racing around. "How? Who is he?"

"He's a friend of Katie's, from the bar where she works."

"What? She works with him?"

I shook my head. I was just able to stand upright again. "No. He's just a customer. Katie dated him a couple of times."

"When was the last time Katie saw him?"

I looked at Robert, not wanting to say the answer. I ran my fingers through my hair, pulling at it.

Robert raised his eyebrows in query.

"She was with him yesterday," I said quietly. "He called round to the apartment. I was out, but Katie left a message on the answerphone to say where she was."

Robert shrugged. "Yeah, but you've seen her since?"

I shook my head slowly and glumly.

Robert put his hands on his hips. "Shit!" He started to pace, muttering, "shit, shit, shit."

Robert did that for a while, wandering in small circles, oblivious to my mounting panic, and then he pointed at me.

"The stressor," he shouted. "Do you remember what we said, that if you identify the stressor, the event that takes a person from murderous thoughts to murder itself, then you can identify the stressee? The stressee is the person who is doing all this." He carried on pacing. "The stressor was Mary Bradbury jumping off

237

the Town Hall roof. It made Tom Bradbury crazy, and now he's doing all of this."

"Yeah, but it's a quick turnaround, just one year as a widow and then a young girl dies."

Robert stopped pacing and shook his head violently. "No, no, not when it was eating away at him. Day after day, month after month, the pain of what happened on that roof eating away, taking away his reason, his capacity to think straight. Every day of looking into his growing son's eyes, knowing that he'd never know a mother's love, the injustice of it all, the damn, deep injustice. That would have been one long year."

I was getting calmer now, trying to see the logic of it all. I could feel Robert racing ahead, his mind screeching through theories and possibilities. One question, though, underlined everything.

"Why kill people with the same name as Salem witches?"

Robert slowed down and looked at me. The crucial question. The one thing that makes the whole thing seem ridiculous.

"That's why she jumped," he said eventually, his voice now quiet, his body returning to the calm Robert I'd known from the last few days.

He looked at me. "Did you read what she was shouting just before she jumped? It was in the reports John brought round."

I nodded. I remembered reading it. Her farewell speech. "The last thing she shouted before she leapt was, 'I am evil, I am death, but now I am at peace. I am alive.' And then she jumped."

Robert nodded. "She was obsessed with the idea that she was evil, that she was somehow cursed, perhaps paying the price for the sins of a previous life."

"How can you know that?"

"An educated guess. If she believed there was a link with her name, it can only come through some belief in reincarnation. Mary was ending her journey. She was stopping the evil so it couldn't recreate itself in the next life? She saw it as a cleansing."

I let out a heavy breath. This was heavy, way too far gone for me. "So what about the husband and son left behind?"

"Perhaps she saw it as their fault? Remember, she married into the name, wasn't born with it. If she had always been a little crazy, maybe in her mind the marriage just completed the circle?"

"And that might have sent him along the same path, except this time, he just wants revenge?"

Robert nodded. "Think about it, Joe. He is left bitter and grief-stricken. Remember her past. She was a wild one. People like that tear lives up and leave a big hole when they're gone. Think about why she killed herself. Some obsession with herself as evil, always had been, even in her previous incarnations as Mary Bradbury. She will have shared that thought with her husband. Probably talked about it, dwelt on it. And think how he will have dwelt on it after she'd gone. The injustice, the robbery of a life so precious to him. Why did she have to be the one with the obsession? Was she telling the truth? Has the evil been passed through the generations? Was he acting to stop evil? Or did he just let his bitterness, his growing hatred of that coincidence of name get him down? Did he start looking for other people with the names of Salem witches? He might have thought they were evil too and wanted to cleanse the world." Robert shook his head at that. "I don't buy that. More likely, he saw people who shared the same coincidence with resentment. Why couldn't it have been them with that obsession? Why his Mary? Why does it have to be his child who has to grow up without ever knowing his mother? Why does it have to be him who puts up with all the finger-pointing, the hushed whispers? Why him? Why not someone else?"

"So do you think he sought out young Abigail, the young girl found at Prankers Pond?"

"No, I don't. I suspect he came across her by accident. He gave in to his private thoughts and killed her, but those thoughts didn't go away, so he went looking, trying to find that elusive kill to take away all his pain." He shrugged. "Maybe he did find her, just a coincidence, but it was that coincidence that convinced him something had to be done." He paused. "And so someone else dies, then another. And each one fails to answer his question, so he carries on, until he thinks he's found the answer."

"And has he?"

Robert shook his head. "It will just get worse and worse. And he knows that. I'm sure that's why he sent those letters. He wanted to be stopped. He wasn't, and Sarah died."

"Is Katie in danger?"

He paused, went quiet. "Very much so, I'm afraid. He's unravelling like a thread caught on a nail. If he has Katie, he wants us to go looking for her. He knows we were getting close for the first time, so he takes Katie, trying to make us get even closer."

"So he'll give her up when we find her?"

Robert shook his head slowly, averting his eyes.

"No," he said quietly, "he won't let her go. If he wants to go down, he'll go down by destroying himself. And he'll take everyone else down with him."

At that I headed back for Route One. I was going to find Katie.

We arrived at an automobile workshop, 'Bradbury Autos.' Dated fuel pumps sat on a front forecourt, like a monument to the 1970's, all black and red and spinning white numbers. There was a small car sales yard next to it, used cars covered in cheap vinyl numbers. It was there that I got an image of Tom Bradbury in a suit, full of patter, and I wondered whether that was how he was able to mix in, to win people over. Behind the cars there was a rectangular building, red brick and flat black roof. A windowed kiosk was on one side, the other side dominated by large aluminium doors, the sliding type, with a step-through door on the part nearest the kiosk. All the doors were shut.

We'd run most of the way, but we slowed down near the workshop. We didn't want to be seen, to spark off any destruction. Robert was on his phone again, giving John details. I could hear John's strained tones.

When he turned off his phone, he looked at me and said, "John says that we should stay put. Don't interfere."

"I can bet he said it more colourfully than that."

Robert raised his eyebrows in mock astonishment.

We were about twenty yards away, on the other side of Route One. We stood and watched the garage for about ten minutes, half-expecting to hear the local police sirens. We didn't. It was silent, apart from the rush of the occasional car and the cries of jays in nearby trees.

After around ten minutes I looked at Robert in frustration and said, "I'm going for a look."

Robert shook his head violently and grabbed my arm. "You had better stay put. If you fuck things up, you will be in the deepest shit of your life."

240

"Yeah, you are probably right, but Katie is in even deeper shit."

Robert looked at me seriously. "Joe, don't do it. Yeah, you could go across there and be the superhero; you know, go there and flash your dick. But what if it goes wrong? What if you get her killed?" He paused to let that sink in, and then said, "remember, they'll be expecting you."

I stopped at that, feeling suddenly foolish.

"But shouldn't we do something? Check the place out?"

Robert gave me a sympathetic smile. "Take a step back, Joe. Think like a lawyer. What would you do if somebody got a relative of yours killed because they failed to follow recognised procedures?"

I looked at Robert with disappointment. Not at what he was saying, but the fact that he thought he ought to say it. I knew the answer: I'd sue his ass. But I still wanted to go across. Fuck recognised procedures.

I looked across at the building. I could see the town of Saugus behind it, framed against a background of springtime and trees. Tall ones licked the corners, and I guessed they were ancient elms, dark and majestic.

I thought about what Robert had said. It all made perfect sense. Stay put until the cavalry arrives. But then I thought of Katie in danger and I felt consumed by guilt. I could have just walked away. Danny and his father, Tom Bradbury, would have moved on to someone else. It wouldn't be Katie with them, frightened, knowing what had happened to Sarah when the cavalry hadn't arrived in time. I thought of Katie and I felt more than guilt. I felt an overwhelming desire to be with her, completely and absolutely.

"Couldn't we just go across and pretend to buy something? You could go. Danny has never met you."

Robert smiled at this, trying to soothe. "What if they are there? They'll shoot at me, and I am not prepared to be shot at."

This annoyed me. I would have risked it, the way I felt about Katie at that moment.

It was almost as if Robert could read my mind. "Have you ever seen a gun?" he asked. "Or do you still all use bow and arrow in England?"

I shook my head. Until I'd arrived in the States, I'd never seen a gun, never heard a gun, never fired a gun.

"There is no steel that will make you feel as cold as a gun," Robert continued. "We spend most of our life seeing guns. Your dad has one, your friend's dad has one, your mom keeps one by the bed. Guns everywhere. On the newsracks, on the TV, and it feels like in the homelife of every person in this damn country. But until you have looked down one pointed straight at your face, knowing that you are one squeeze from the end of your life, you haven't really seen a gun."

"Have you seen this?" I asked.

Robert nodded. "I'm a cop, remember. And you know what? It freezes you up. All that training, and it still freezes you, as cold as the metal on the gun."

"And so what do we do? Sit tight, do nothing, and wait for the police?"

Robert shrugged.

"And at the same time, Katie is feeling that same cold feeling, that same feeling of terror?"

Robert said nothing.

I looked across the road, then at the traffic, and then back at Robert. I had made up my mind.

I checked for a gap in the traffic, ignored Robert's protest, and ran across as fast as I could.

Once on the forecourt, I looked around. I couldn't see anyone. Not a sign, not a sight, not a sound. I looked towards the kiosk. It was dark, and I could see a closed sign in the door.

I wandered over, kicking dust as I walked, and put my face to the glass. Nothing. I could see a counter and a Coca-Cola drinks machine, but other than that, it didn't look as if it had done decent trade for some time. I suspected only a desperate motorist pulled in here for fuel, and the drinks machine was probably for customers getting their tyres changed. The cars for sale looked dusty.

I went over to the large aluminium door. I noticed it was padlocked on one side. I looked at the padlock. It was rusty and old and weak-looking. I put my ear to the door and strained to hear sounds. I thought I could hear small noises, the odd rustle. I pulled my ear away and I wondered if I'd imagined it.

I looked again at the padlock. It looked breakable.

I scoured the ground for something firm to use as leverage. There was nothing, but then I remembered that I was only trying to see if there was anyone there. Don't break in, don't get caught, don't go to jail. I looked over at Robert, and I could see him barking into his phone.

I looked to the side of the building. The building disappeared into bushes and scrubland, with open land over to Saugus. I decided it was worth taking a look. I was only looking.

I crept to the side and went round to the rear, shuffling along a windowless wall and ending up in a small patch of grassland. My nerves were starting to tear, my concern over Katie matched by my own concern for myself. I didn't know what I would find when I got round the building. Sweat prickled my upper lip and my heart took over from the sounds of nature, the thump-thump-thump beating a scary drum.

When I got round the back, I found a blacked-out window, staring blindly over Saugus, and a battered blue door. It looked solid, like a fire door.

I took a deep breath, felt the warm glow of safety, and I looked around me. As I looked, I caught a shimmer of the sun on a patch of water. I shielded the sun from my eyes and looked over. I recognised the shape. I could work out what it was from its position in the town. It was Prankers Pond.

I walked away from the building for a moment, trying to keep out of sight of the window. As I got to the start of the trees and bushes, I saw that I was looking down a slight incline, and as I looked down the incline, I could see a natural path, a route through the bushes. Tom Bradbury had his own hidden path down to the site of Abigail Hobbs' body. He could have moved it down there under the cover of night, no-one to see or hear him, and then returned in the morning to play the role of the concerned citizen.

I heard a snap, the sound of a footstep. It could be Robert, but it could be Tom Bradbury, or Danny.

I whirled round and saw nothing. Only a flutter of bird's wings broke the scene.

It was too quiet. I didn't like it.

I crept back to the safety of the building's shadow, out of sight of the blackened window. I listened for movement, but heard nothing.

I knelt down for a moment and thought about Katie.

I hadn't known her long. I'd hardly been in Boston as long as most holidays, but she'd got under my skin. It was childish, juvenile, but it was the curl of her hair, the glisten of a laughing eye, the softest touch. It was everything, from her giggling laugh and girlish skip when she was happy, to her soft-centred toughness when she wasn't. I wanted Katie to be with me, now, this minute, somewhere else than in the clutches of a pair of sickos obsessed with their own tragedy.

I thought of Danny and I began to feel my rage spring up like a newly-tapped well. He'd brought himself into Sarah's life, wrecked it like an unwanted toy, just because something bad had happened to him a long time ago. And then he'd put himself in Katie's life. Would he ruin that one too? What was he doing to her right now, while I dithered at the side of a deserted workshop by a busy highway?

I thought about Katie and my resolve strengthened. She wasn't going to be hurt, I would make sure of that.

I knelt down and crawled along under the window, trying to stay silent, listening out for any whimper, any shout, any threat. I could hear nothing.

I soon found myself in front of the door. I had a quick look round but could see nothing. I wondered briefly what Robert was doing, but then I realised that he would just be doing what he thought was procedure. Fuck procedure. Fuck everything. Fuck Robert. Fuck John. Fuck Boston Police. Fuck prevarication and public relations.

I reached up and slowly pulled on the door handle, the lever inching downward slowly, fraction by fraction, the slow creeping movement quieting any squeaks and creaks.

The door didn't move. It was locked.

I went back to the window and knelt down. I was right underneath it, not moving. I couldn't hear anything, apart from the cars rushing by on Route One and the warning rustles of the leaves on the nearby trees.

I scratched my nose with nerves, like a scared rabbit. I could feel my breath shortening, could sense the slow prickle of fear crawling through my gut. Fear had returned, trying to blank out resolve, but I held firm.

I inched my way upward towards the window. The window was only chest height, but I was crouched beneath it, my ears keen. My face arrived in front of the pane, and all I saw was myself, reflected back from the black paint painted over the pane. I didn't know if my shadow could be seen by anyone inside the building, but I heard nothing.

I put my hands under the top half of the window-frame. It was a sash window, and the window's security was governed by a clasp over the bottom section. As I tried to lift the window up, I could feel movement for about a quarter of an inch, and then movement stopped. I tried again, but the same thing happened.

I cursed to myself. What the hell was I doing? What were the penalties for breaking and entering? But then I heard a slight noise, like a metallic click. Was it from the inside? Was it the building equivalent to mirror shades, where I could see only my enquiring eyes but the view from the other side was unhindered? I faltered. I was in a stalemate with myself. If I dropped down, it would be obvious I was no innocent passer-by, but the longer I stood there, the longer I was a target. And don't Americans shoot burglars?

I took a deep breath and tried the window once more.

It didn't give way the first time. The clasp caught hold again, but it didn't stop the window-frame dead. There was movement, like a straining, as if the clasp was struggling to stay on, held into an old window-frame by rusty screws. I heaved and strained and gave it one bug push, until I heard a snap and a crinkle as the clasp fell to the concrete floor and the window shot upwards.

I dropped to my knees like a stone. I tried to listen again for movement inside, but I couldn't hear anything. I gave it a couple of minutes, but I heard no shouting, no shots.

I put my hands on the sill and slowly pulled myself upwards. My fringe peeked into sight and I took my first look in the garage.

It looked ordinary. Tools lined the walls on hooks. Wrench sets, tyre bars, jacks. A pit was dug into the middle of the floor, and in there I could see a caged light bulb on a flex and some oily rags. A coffee machine sat dusty in the corner, underneath a glossy calendar with naked girls and some business cards. Probably taxi firms, I thought, so customers could leave their car there for repair and get a ride home.

I looked back into the pit, and then was surprised by what I saw.

Most garage pits I've seen are just that: pits. A concrete hole in a concrete floor, whose only purpose is to enable the mechanic to get under the vehicle.

So why did this one have a little door at one end? A little red wooden door, about three feet high, with a solid-looking bolt and padlock? It might be for tools, but why the lock? And why not just a cupboard, so the tools can be reached when the car isn't over the pit?

I was curious? My mind began to race with the explanations. Only one way to find out.

I hauled myself onto the windowsill and prepared to drop down and into the building.

I didn't hear them arrive. I just felt the cold metal press in a perfect circle in the back of my head, felt that 'one squeeze from death feeling', and heard someone say, "come out of there real slow, or I'll blow your fucking head off."

# Twenty

I felt my internal organs hit the floor. There was menace in the voice and there was menace in the feel of cold steel embedded in my head.

I was hurled to the floor, face down.

I tried lifting my hands. "It's alright, it's alright, cool it." I was thrown again to the floor and I felt a heavy body land on my leg. A million bad thoughts whirled about as I felt handcuffs go around my wrists, and then I was lifted by the arms, turned around, and thrown onto the floor on my back.

The guy with the gun gave me a strange look as I let out a huge sigh of relief. All I saw when I looked up were dark blue uniforms and a silver shield that said, 'Saugus Police.'

"What's so funny?" My captor didn't share my relief.

I shook my head, still smiling, but then noticed the gun whirl to the side of the building as footsteps approached.

I gave out another sigh as John rounded the corner, badge displayed.

John looked at me and shook his head. "You stupid fucker," he said, before turning to the Saugus officers and telling them that I belonged to him.

Twenty minutes later, I was sat in the back of the Saugus black and white. Robert had filled John in on what we had discovered after he'd left. John was trying to explain the story to the Saugus Police. I saw astounded faces, heard gasps, saw the scratching of heads, the dusting of caps. They knew Tom Bradbury and his son. They had heard the tales of Mrs Bradbury and her swallow dive from the Town Hall. One of them remembered the girl found at Prankers Pond.

John walked over with the two officers. He leant into the car.

"You are on the edge of hero or villain. I've told these guys the score, but we've got problems."

I stayed silent, wanting to hear him out.

"We've got no warrant, so we can't just go in there and turn it over. But these guys caught you about to stick your fat limey ass through that window. That's a felony, and they got an arrest. It's

247

getting warm out here and these guys are thirsty. Some time back at the station processing clowns like you is what gets them the breaks."

"So what do you suggest?"

John smiled, a cruel smile. He knew he would win either way.

"You go back to that window, and you finish the job. You got five minutes. You're lucky that these guys haven't called it in yet. They're gonna call in five minutes and say that there's nothing doing. Then, during their call, they are gonna say that they hear a crash, so they are going to investigate. When that call is made, they are gonna climb through that window and arrest you."

I looked puzzled. I couldn't see the benefit to me.

John smiled coldly.

"If you find something, you'll be a hero. It might take us closer to Katie and give us just cause to get a warrant to search his house."

"And if I don't find anything?"

John laughed. "They arrest you and you go to court."

"And if I don't co-operate?"

John laughed again. "They arrest you and you go to court."

I stepped out of the car. "I suppose I better be a burglar again."

John clapped me on the shoulder, laughing. He had me.



I was struck by the silence as I dropped to the floor.

The furnishings were all around the edges, the tools, the spare parts, so the workshop had a cavernous feel. The clump of my feet echoed as I landed from my clamber through the window, so that initially it sounded like I wasn't alone, but once the dust had settled and that echo had reverberated away into cold silence, I felt very much alone.

I felt sick inside. I'd been given something of a pep-talk before I'd recommenced my burglary, but it mostly involved John telling me how it was my hunch, and so if I was wrong, then it must be me who pays for it. I thought I'd detected the slightest smile, as if he was hoping for some kind of revenge for turning up and turning everything over on its head. I knew he wanted to find Katie, he was too good a policeman for that, but to bag me in the process would make it into a good day.

Robert had been the greatest help. Look for trophies, he'd said. As clichéd as it is, serial killers collect trophies. Sometimes it's the smallest thing. A lock of hair, a piece of clothing, press cuttings, maybe even a piece of skin, a limb, a body part. The more the killer has played a part in the investigation, the more likely it is that souvenirs were kept. This killer has put himself at the heart of the investigations. He's made the discovery of one body, the girl at Prankers Pond, and sent his son to befriend his future victim. Fraught with risks, with thrills, so there are bound to be souvenirs.

Great.

I had a look around me. The workshop was just that, a workshop, as spacious and uninspiring as these things are, with tools and spare parts marking out the fringes of a grey floor. I wasn't confident.

I started first at a rack of tools by the left-hand wall. I thought I could hear John and the two Saugus cops muttering amongst themselves. I wanted to press my ear to the wall to try and hear, but I could hear that mental clock ticking, counting down to the time when two Saugus police officers will burst onto the scene and make a dramatic arrest. Around four and a half minutes left.

The rack of tools was just that, a rack of tools. There were all neat and clean, but they revealed no further information. Wrenches, hammers, saws, ratchets. The usual collection of essential tools for a modern, non-murderous mechanic.

I looked at a cupboard of tiny drawers. It seemed to contain every conceivable size and type of nut, bolt and screw ever made. But there was nothing there that could fasten together the hotch-botch collection of theories and half-trails that had led me to being on the verge of arrest and incarceration.

About four minutes now. Time was ticking as certain as time does.

When I'd done one wall, I edged along another towards the large aluminium shutters. I peeked behind compressors and a small pile of worn tyres. I could hear my shuffles echo around the room, every clang and knock making me jump and start. Nothing yet, and I was down to around three and a half minutes.

I started to get breathless. It was the nervous wait for the twitchy policemen. It was the sickening wait for that realisation that

I was wrong. But most of all, it was that anxious, gut-turning yearning to find something that would take me to where those bastards had Katie.

My breathlessness came now from anger. They'd killed Sarah for a reason that was founded only in a moment of madness many years ago. I didn't know Sarah, but I felt some affinity. She was from my town in my country. She shouldn't be dead in this one. I could recognise injustice and tragedy, and it made me angry.

And I was angry with myself. Two thousand miles and someone else's life savings. I had one death on my hands, and now I found myself scrabbling around in semi-darkness and old dirt for just something, like a prospector with no prospects.

And I was down to three minutes.

I looked over to a door. It was closed but probably went into an office. I looked down into the pit and saw the little red wooden door, its lock looking shiny and new and secure.

I went to the office. If the police want a reason to look into each room without a warrant, I might as well open a few doors for them.

There was a table by the door. A box of blank receipts sat on one corner, but otherwise it was unremarkable. I looked at the door. It looked solid. It looked locked.

I looked around on that side of the room. A sledgehammer was propped against the wall. I looked around the desk for a key, but I couldn't see one. It would have to be the sledgehammer.

I took it and hit the door hard. It didn't budge. The hammer was heavy, but the door was heavier. It threw the hammer back at me.

I felt the anger resurface. I puffed and panted and tried to imagine Katie's scared face as I looked at the hammer, and then at the door, and then at the hammer again. I re-routed that anger. It stopped sapping me and fortified me instead. I felt strength course through me like a drink in a desert, and I grinned. I was going to have that door.

I took the strain for another hit.

Two and a half minutes.

I got it right under the lock and the door splintered. I felt a slight cheer, but tempered by the knowledge that I'd caused damage as a trespasser. If I found nothing, I wouldn't see a summer in Morsby for a couple of years. I wiped my brow, wet with nerves. I took another swing. This time the lock broke, and the door swung open, the lock clanging to the floor. Got the bastard.

I looked in and sagged. A toilet.

Down to two minutes.

My short breaths felt tight in my chest. Only one thing left now: the red door in the pit.

I jumped down, shouting, angry, scared. I didn't stop to assess the situation. I had become clouded by anger and by frustration. Everything that had ever gone wrong in my life flashed through my mind like a film on fast forward, and I could feel myself beginning to lose control. It was either that red door in the pit, or the first person to come through that window, or the whole place.

Time was still on my side. I was alone in the garage.

As I swung the hammer, I thought I heard activity outside. I could hear footsteps running, more than one set, clambering over shrubs and plants, could hear the noise of branches being pushed to one side. They were coming in for me.

I ran at the door and hit it once. The padlock held firm.

I screamed in frustration, my body finding strengths it hadn't used for years. I swung again, yelling like an advancing rebel, howling, screeching, and brought the hammer down against the door with every ounce of frustration I could feel. I hit it again, and once more.

The door exploded. It was about three feet high, two feet wide, and now it was on its back, in the hole.

I could hear scrabbling at the back of the building as heavy feet trampled undergrowth and headed for the point of entry. There was shouting and I could hear the sound of metal being pulled out of holsters.

It was dark in there.

I looked around and saw the lamp on a wire. I reached down and plugged it in, the light coming on straight away.

Voices at the window. Shouts of 'what you got?' and 'don't touch anything', followed by heavy boots landing on the concrete floor.

I shone the lamp into the hole and went to my knees. My anger gave way to surprise.

"Shit?" I said, partly in awe, "take a fucking look at this."

John jumped into the pit behind me, and as I looked up I saw the two Saugus officers stood above me, looking down. Their guns were drawn, but pointing to the floor.

I was pushed to one side as John grabbed the lamp and swung it inside the hole.

I looked in over John's shoulder and saw that the hole was about six-feet long and about three-feet high. It as big enough for someone to lie in, although movement would be limited, kind of confined, or imprisoned.

But it wasn't the dimensions of the hole that had drawn the gasp. It was its contents. I'd never seen guns like those before.

The floor of the hole was covered in weapons. Big weapons. There were at least five big guns, although these weren't simple shotguns. They were military rifles, with the straps and the sights and the menace. There was a big black one, a mean looking thing with the curved magazine and army colours. A couple of aggressive little things lay next to it. They looked the same, but they had no butt, as if they just went against your chest, ready to spray into a crowd. They looked light enough to wave around with just an outstretched arm, but with the nastiness of a snarling dog, ready to bark and spit with venom. Next to those were two black rifles with sights on them, more like hunting rifles.

John gasped as well. He reached in and pulled each weapon out in turn, holding them by wrapping his hand in his coat. He laid each one out on the garage floor.

I looked up as one of the Saugus cops whistled. "That's some metal he's got there."

"Do you know about guns?" John asked.

He smiled and cocked his head. "I shoot and I buy the magazines."

"Good," John said, hauling himself out of the pit. "What have we got?"

The cop knelt down and cast his eyes over the weapons, scratching his chin. He pointed to the big black one and the two little mean ones. "Those are the same," he said, "just different styles. AK-47's, the best there is." He examined the black one, although now it was out of the hole, it seemed more like dark khaki.

These were definitely military weapons, not civilian ones.

"It's an SS-99, a semi-automatic with a range of around six hundred metres. A serious firearm. That ain't no burglar deterrent. As for these," pointing at the two little mean ones, "these aren't even legal. Hungarian AK-47's, but they haven't been modified.

These are fully automatic and will throw out some serious shit. And the barrel is too short. These should not be here. These are serious weapons. What the hell are they doing in a workshop like this?"

John ignored the question and pointed at the two remaining rifles, the hunting style ones.

"To shoot deer?" John asked.

The cop frowned and then smiled. "Yes, you could, but you wouldn't need to be so well-equipped. Those are sniper rifles. Stoners. About two and a half thousand bucks worth of deer shot. Another semi-automatic."

John shook his head, and then disappeared back into the hole. There was the sound of movement, and then he reappeared with two tool belts. But as I looked closer, I saw that tools weren't causing the bulges. I could see the handgrip of small handguns in the belt. And the square bulk of cartridge boxes made their shape known. He threw them onto the floor by the rifles and gave a sigh.

"We had better get scenes of crimes down here," he said, sounding gloomy. "This is no protection thing going on." He pointed at the rifles and tool belts. "These are for a shoot out. If their world caved in while they were here, their escape arsenal was handy and impressive. Get in a car, drive out firing one of these, and they would be heading for the interstate before anyone had the chance to stop them. They'd blast out of this place with a tool belt full of handguns, ready for a few hold-ups to fund their life on the run, and spraying all those in the way."

John looked at the faces of the two Saugus cops. "You had better get some of your guys down here. This isn't going to be quick."

The two Saugus cops disappeared out the back. John turned to me and said, "do you know what really worries me about this?"

I looked blank.

"This is just the escape arsenal. What the hell have they got at home?"

I tried to offer a supportive smile, but I was still shocked by what we had discovered. Robert said the killer would be in control, because the method of capture and killing was so organised. But this was organisation beyond anything I expected. I was expecting a drawer full of souvenirs, maybe the odd photograph. I was not expecting John Rambo's back-up stash.

Then I wondered what would have happened if they had been in when I clambered through the window.

I shuddered. I wouldn't be stood in a pit, like some kind of semi-hero. I looked up at Robert, who was surveying the scene with a dispassionate eye. He gave me a knowing smile. He'd just guessed my last thought. His eyes told me, 'I tried to warn you.'

I looked away from him, tried to gather my thoughts, when something small and black glinted at the back of the hole. I knelt down and peered in. It was a small plastic box. I went to reach in, when I felt John's big hand on my shoulder.

"No, you don't, you might contaminate the scene."

I looked up at him and pointed. "There's something else in there."

John squinted and tried to make out the contents of the hole. He mumbled to himself and picked up a screwdriver. He reached in and managed to nudge the box into the light of the garage, for what it was, and gave a loud, "fuck!"

"What is it?" I was trying to see over his shoulder.

"It's fucking trouble, that's what it is."

"Why?"

He showed me a box the size of a walkie-talkie, with buttons and lights. An aerial was ready to extend itself on the top. I guessed what it was, but I couldn't believe it. I felt the need to ask John.

He looked at me and he looked worried.

"It looks like some kind of detonator, for explosives."

"Why would they want that?"

John gave me a look that made me wish I hadn't asked. 'To blow something up,' was the obvious answer, as obvious to me as to anyone.

"Shouldn't we get out of here?" I asked instead.

"Why?"

"Explosives. If they have a detonator, there must be something to detonate, right?"

John shook his head. "Why would they blow up this place?" he said. "There's nothing here. By the time they needed it, they would be high-tailing it towards the interstate. They are not going to blow the place up while they are in it, as why would they want the escape weaponry? No, this is to blow something else up, something away from here."

I felt my stomach drop.

"You mean, wherever their victim is?"

John nodded slowly. "If they still have a prisoner when they get raided, that prisoner becomes instant ashes, along with the evidence. This is bad news, not your usual screwy maniac. This is thought out, and thought well."

"So what do we do?"

John shook his head. "We do nothing, remember. You are under arrest. I'll worry about the Bradbury's. You worry about your ass down at the lock-up downtown."

My heart sank. "What am I under arrest for?"

John shrugged. "I'll think of something. Breaking and entering, for starters. Look at the door on that john. I betcha I can find your prints on that hammer."

"You bastard."

John winked. "You bet."

# Twenty One

They didn't put me in a cell. I was glad. They walked me past them and already a couple of drunks were sleeping off the effects of a bad afternoon. There was an old smell of stale urine and cleaning fluids. It was a smell I remembered from my lawyer days, one that takes a while to shake off your clothes when you get home. It's a smell of no sunlight and contempt, locked up and unwashed for longer than it ought to be. It was the smell that was in my head when I flew for that client, and it was the smell that surrounded me when I sat in a cell of my own, watching my career slip through the bars and into the night.

This time I was sat in a chair in a room full of detectives, watching the huddle expand and excite.

John had told me that I was arrested to cover their story. The police would have to go in there to arrest an intruder. If they found him rifling through the contents of a cupboard in a mechanics pit, stacked full with illegal weaponry and detonators, the police would need to investigate it.

And so I was taken into police custody, where I would give my version of events to a detective who would know the background. The expected outcome was that I was investigating a bona fide concern over a young woman from Boston who may have been kidnapped by the owners of the garage. A stern ticking off and a promise to pay for any damage caused would earn me a reprieve and a lift to the airport.

I wondered about Katie. If she was with the Bradburys, I prayed that she was unharmed.

And then I realised that even if she were unharmed, I wouldn't see her again. I would be back in England pretty quick, whereas she would spend some time in therapy of some sort, trying to come to terms with what had happened.

I ruffled my hair. Another end to a brief romance.

A uniformed police officer stuck his head round the door to tell someone to turn on the television news.

There was a brief hunt for the remote control, and then a television on one of the desks came on. A flick through the channels brought on New England Cable News, and soon I saw a reporter, microphone in hand, standing in front of a group of police vehicles, and then the camera focused in on a tumble-down house hidden away in the trees. There was some muttering as the guy with the remote worked out how to turn up the volume, and then I heard the commentary.

Reporter: *"I'm in Lynfield, on the edge of Greater Boston, in the middle of a police stand-off, with a lot of local firepower concentrated on a little house amongst the trees. I've been here about a half hour and nothing much has happened so far, but the police presence is building, along with a contingent of fire-fighting equipment."*

Studio: *"So what's going on, Greg? Have you been able to speak to any of the police there?"*

Reporter: *"The police are being pretty cagey, Bob. Although we are out here in Lynfield, many of the police officers are from the Boston City Police. The different police divisions have been co-operating, each making sure that if anything happens here, they don't take the blame alone. The buzz word here is Waco."*

Studio: *"So is this a cult thing?"*

Reporter: *"I don't think so. I don't know how well you can see behind me, but the building at the centre is just an average-sized house. If there are people in there, they're not big in number. No, Bob, the rumours flying around point somehow to Sarah Goode. You may remember her, the young English student who was wanted by the Boston Police for the slaying of her boyfriend, Bradley Howarth, a fireman from the Back Bay area of the city. Sarah Goode herself was found dead just the other day, down the road in Wakefield, apparently a bizarre suicide. She was found naked and burning by the side of Lake Quannapowitt. The police aren't saying much right now, although there is a strange rumour doing the rounds in police circles in Boston."*

Studio: *"What rumour is that?"*

Reporter: *"Well, Bob, it's hard to know where to start, as rumours have been flying around the bars around the downtown division that some officers have been investigating witchcraft activities. It's all been denied, officially, so not enough detail has been available to let us broadcast it, but there is a belief that the witchcraft investigation has led us here."*

Studio (laughing): *"Well, you make sure you avoid any black cats, Greg. And keep us posted."*

Reporter (laughing): *"Sure will, Bob. This is Greg ......., whoa!"*

The signing off was punctuated by the crack of a rifle, and the reporter ducked for cover. The picture became shaky as the cameraman found himself a safe place to film.

The picture on the screen went straight back to the studio, and the anchorman looked flustered. He muttered a few words and then went straight to a commercial break.

In the room I was in, it seemed like everyone in it dived for their coat and ran to the door. One guy, a senior-looking detective, grabbed the phone and barked at someone to let him know what's going on.

I sat back.

I felt strangely calm. I had been right. I hadn't found any right answers, saw no chances for a clean-cut victory, but it was mainly my work that had led to a major police operation and hopefully the capture of a pair of serial killers.

The only drawback was Katie. If she was in that house, I wanted her out of it. Let her go back to Wichita, let me go back to England, and hopefully she will recover enough not to resent me for what has happened to her.

I closed my eyes and prayed for a peaceful end.

The scene at the shack calmed down.

A bullet had hit the side of a police van. Had it been one foot to the left, it would have taken away the face of a newly-wed young officer named Hannah. It hadn't. It had given young Hannah the fright of her life and sent everyone scampering for cover.

And it had made the mood at the scene deadly serious. This was a potential hostage situation and someone was taking pot-shots. Every firearm in that clearing was now trained on the house hidden in a forest of elms and chestnuts.

The house was just a dark, wooden single-storey shack, with a simple veranda and screened windows. An early scout around had shown only two windows at the back, with one at each side, and two at either side of a dusty screened front door. Including the door at the back, there were eight points of entry, with no snipers from above to worry about.

Lieutenant John Cornwell was at the centre of it all. He wasn't in charge, but he was the one most people were looking to as the man who knew most about the background. He was in the middle of a huddle of senior police officers, which comprised of captains from Boston, Saugus and Wakefield. Robert Lehane was in the background, but as the top brass talked, it was from Robert that John sought advice.

"So what do we know about these guys?" It was Captain Flynn from Wakefield Police.

"Not much," John replied. "Just a couple of mechanics from Saugus. Father and son team. We believe they've been involved in a number of abductions and murders spreading back some years. The boy's mother killed herself when he was just a little boy. We think that might have been some sort of catalyst."

"Before we go bustin' in there," Flynn said, looking through the trees at the shack, "how sure are we that these two are guilty? I mean, there's a lot of TV here, so we can't afford any fuck-ups."

John shrugged. "Nothing to convince a jury yet, but the build up of coincidences makes the hunch pretty strong. And the guy is taking pot-shots at us."

Captain Jones from Saugus Police joined in. "These two are regular guys. They've been working in Saugus for twenty years, or at least the daddy has, and we haven't heard from them. The guy's wife was well known at the time she jumped, I remember that story, but he was a quiet guy."

"So," Flynn surmised, "we can't go steaming in there, guns a-going, because we might just find him watching TV with a couple of beers?"

"Well, if he is," John replied, "looking at all the cameras, he's probably watching this, and I just can't help thinking that he would have come out to take a look."

Captain Flynn smiled at this. "So," he said, "what are our plans? He's got a hostage, hasn't he?"

John nodded. "Yes, we think so. Katie Gray, a friend of the girl who we believe might have been their last victim."

"There's a lot of belief here, lieutenant, but not a lot of fact. Are you prepared to put your career on the line here, ready to apologise to the relatives of the people in that house when we blow them all away when they reach for the TV remote?"

John shook his head. He could do without this. He knew what Flynn meant. He had shared that same disbelief a short time ago, but it had started to fit together. The coincidences had mounted up, and there were some things beyond explanation. He knew, though, that he would have to play it very carefully. He'd already played out the scene in his head a few times. There's a rush for the door, a flurry of panic inside the house, and two quiet mechanics from Saugus are splattered all over the feature bookcase. Just when the blood stops running down the walls, Katie Gray strolls in to her apartment and wonders why everyone is so surprised to see her.

John tried to shut those doubts out. The Englishman was in police custody at Saugus, and if this turned out to be some tall story, he would make sure that he never saw English soil again.

"Don't worry," he said, "it's my ass."

Just then a loud bang made them hit the floor.

John could hear somebody screaming by a squad car nearest to the house.

"What the fuck is going on? Give me a 10-12," John barked into a radio. He could see everyone lying down, all with their guns trained on the house, but now everyone was behind something. He could hear the screaming, and as he looked over he saw two paramedics rushing over.

"We've got a 10-31, Code 1. It's Bob Simmonds, sir," a panicky voice shouted back on his radio.

"Clarify," John snapped. A bomb incident was not what he wanted. "What's the 10-45?"

"He was by his car when something hit it. Looked like a tennis ball, but it blew up. He got hit in the face by shrapnel. Man, his face looks a mess. And I can't see his eyes."

John snapped his radio off angrily. He had come across home-made bombs before. The curse of the internet. Any young punk could pick up advice on how to do any old damn thing, even making bombs. The FBI now had a unit monitoring these web sites, and the traffic going in and out of them, but it was frightening. Some angry young fool could have an argument with his teacher in the morning, and by lunchtime, the teacher could find an explosive device strapped to his car, the victim of a quick surf on the web and a trip to a hardware store.

Tennis ball bombs were the choice of juvenile hellraisers. All you needed was a tennis ball, a mix of match-heads, gunpowder and ground flint, and a hard surface to throw it at. It won't blow up any buildings, but stick in a few nail heads, make sure it hits something close by someone, and you could blind someone. One good fastball from the window, and Bob Simmonds lay screaming with pain on the ground.

John got back on the radio.

"Despatch? This is Unit 412. We need a 10-53. Get a team down here."

There was some static, and then a calm voice replied, "10-5."

"This is Lieutenant Cornwell. You know my location. Get a 10-53 down here, now. We've had a Code 1, 10-31, with possible 10-63. It's 10-20, but we're taking no chances."

"10-4."

And at that, the dispatcher set about despatching.

10-53 is radio code for a STOP team. John knew this was getting out of hand. If those crazy bastards were throwing explosives about, home-made explosives, any attempt to storm the house was going to have to be quick and effective. He'd told the dispatcher that the incident was under control, and it was, but there was a danger it might not be for much longer. He had an officer injured, perhaps badly, with a couple of crackpots sitting on a house full of fireworks, ready to blow, and he didn't want frayed tempers making a bad situation worse.

John got back on the radio.

"All units. From now on, 10-90 with the radio. If anything goes on, I want a 10-18." Essential radio traffic only, with activity updates.

John scanned the area around the house. He could see police cars dotted around all the angles, but it bothered him that he could see more television vans than police cars.

There was an agreement with Boston's media that in the case of barricaded hostage situations, only one ground level camera would be used, with another one being allowed from a helicopter. Coverage would be limited to bulletin updates until the situation was resolved. This agreement wasn't popular, because it limited the blanket coverage these situations normally encouraged, but it was essential. The media agreed to it on the basis that they were promised greater access to the key players once the incident had ended.

This was not quite one of those situations yet, but it was getting close.

John was trying to decide what to do next when something small and black came flying through the air from the house. Everyone ducked

It was a video tape.

John passed the binoculars back to the young reporter who'd passed them over.

Captain Flynn asked him if he wanted to send someone over to get it.

John shook his head. He was wearing a bulletproof vest. If a risk had to be taken, he would take it. "Just let me know if anyone appears at a window."

John strode through the line of cars with his arms in the air. He walked slowly and deliberately, trying not to cause anyone watching to get twitchy on the triggers. He looked towards the shack, but couldn't see anything. It looked dark inside the house, and all John could see were shadows.

He reached the videotape, picked it up, and backed away and into the line of police vehicles.

Once safely among the line of parked cars, John ran towards the New England Cable News van, with Captain Flynn ambling after him.

"Hey, you guys got a VHS machine in here?"

"Yeah, sure. What you got?"

"Don't bullshit me. It's what you saw me go and fetch."

The technician smiled. He pointed towards a silver machine by the side of some TV screens. "Put it in there. Let's see what you got."

John put in the video and leant towards the screen.

The first image to come up was a room, a regular living room, with a chair by a TV, and replica Rockwells on the wall. It looked ordinary, suburban.

Then the picture started to pan. It took in the fireplace, then a bookcase, shelves full of popular fiction, and then a chair came into view.

The chair was plain and light-coloured, straight-backed in the Quaker style. The camera was panning slowly, and John saw the tins first. They were the size of paint tins, a circle of them around the chair. And attached to the chair were pipes, one on either side of the seat. As the camera pulled out, John saw the legs attached to the chair, and then the arms, and then the body.

John's heart sank when he recognised Katie, strapped to the chair, her face streaked with dirt and tears, a bruise welling up under her eye. Her head was upright, a show of defiance, but she looked taught, fearful.

John turned to the news crew.

"We got a hostage situation. You fellas know the drill."

The technician groaned. "Oh come on. We turn this off, everyone goes to the Disney Channel."

John raised his eyebrows and gave a look that said that he meant business. He carried on watching the video as the technician muttered expletives and got on the phone to his producer. They would need to sort out the pool camera rota. John didn't give a rats ass, as long as it kept them out of his hair and his decisions off national TV.

The picture carried on moving around the room. It went up to the windows at the back of the room. More of those paint pots lined the floor underneath the window. The picture swept around the room, and by the door, more paint pots.

"What the fuck are those," he muttered to himself.

The picture then clicked off, but then switched to a close-up of a telephone dial, with the number clearly visible.

Then the image turned off, and John was left looking at the silver swirls of an empty videotape.

John muttered to himself again. He knew what it meant. They've got Katie, she is surrounded by some nasty stuff, and they want someone to give them a call.

John knew the call had to be made, but he wasn't an expert in hostage negotiation. He knew one thing: those that take hostages need the hostage alive. For as long as the hostage is alive, the kidnapper has a bargaining position. If the hostage is lost, the kidnapper is lost. John could wait for a hostage expert to arrive. Time was on his side.

John called over to the technician, "hey, can you get me a close up of a shot?"

The technician shrugged a 'yes', and slid over to the screen.

John showed him which bit needed zooming in on, and pretty soon John was looking at one of the paint cans, filled with liquid, and then at the metal pipes strapped to the chair.

"What the fuck is that?"

John didn't look at the technician when he replied, "that is bad shit, that's what."

John knew the luxury of time had become impoverished.

He went back outside and spoke to Captain Flynn.

"Do you think you could get plans of this place? You know, get the layout?"

Captain Flynn scratched his head. "There should be a way somehow."

"Try the power company, or the water company. Someone must have been in that house for repairs or maintenance. Or an architect or structural engineer. They might be able to work out the internal layout from the exterior. You know, from the position of the joists and supports."

Captain Flynn nodded and then walked over to where his force was situated. Although this was all taking place on their beat, they were glad to hand the reins over to Boston. This was going to be an expensive operation, and Flynn didn't think the Wakefield community would thank him for incurring the bill because of some jurisdictional point-scoring. If Boston Police wanted the inhabitants of that cabin, they could pay for it.

Just then, the STOP team arrived. It came in three buses, all serious looks and armoury. Just behind that, a Bomb Squad vehicle arrived.

John walked over to the Bomb Squad, sticking his head through the cab window. "How you doing fellas?"

The guy in the truck gave a lazy wave. "I heard you got someone in there throwing home-made shit around."

John nodded. "And he's got a hostage surrounded by cans of gasoline. That's what it looks like anyway. There are pipe bombs attached to the chair, and we know he has detonators, because we found one at his workshop. If those pipe bombs go off and ignite that fuel, we're in for one hell of a big kaboom."

The Bomb Squad guy shook his head wearily. "These home-grown fuckers are crazy. They don't know what they are sitting on;

one stray spark and they wonder why their ass is in New Hampshire. What have they used so far?"

"Tennis ball bombs."

"Great. Sophisticated shit may be beyond these guys, provided we can get to them before they try."

John nodded towards the shack. "I want to know what will happen if we go shooting around in there, whether we will trigger anything. If that is gasoline in there, I'm worried about the air quality. A room full of gas won't smell nice, and it's getting to be a warm day. Katie looks okay now, but what about when things hot up in there? They've put us on a time switch, and they may not even realise it."

The Bomb Squad guy shook his head. "It will be volatile. You go in there triggers pumping, and you might set off a spark, which will get hold of the fuel, and everyone in there will be pan-fried."

John shook his head. That wasn't good news. He knew he had to get on the phone to Bradbury. That final shot of the phone dial could only mean one thing, and so he looked over at the shack, took a deep breath, and then headed over to the STOP team.

The room I was in was getting warm.

I'd been a captive of Wakefield Police for a couple of hours. The television played constantly in the corner, and the news from the house was getting serious. Shots had been fired and there was talk of a minor explosion.

I leant back and took another swig of coffee. The caffeine threatened to give me a headache, but it could have been the stress, or the heat.

I worried about Katie. I didn't worry for her safety, I'd seen the determination on the faces of those officers coming in and out of the room, and I trusted John Cornwell. No, I worried about her for a different reason. I worried about what would happen afterwards, what would happen when the Bradburys were conviction statistics and Katie was left to cope alone in that apartment in the South Side, or left to wander the flat wilderness of Kansas. Would she return to normal, a happy jewel at the start of life's upward curve? Or would she retreat into post-trauma distress, shunning stability or security? Would daddy be there to catch her if she falls, or would he be impotent, hundreds of miles away in Wichita?

And I worried for selfish reasons. Will she shudder when she hears my name, some reminder of a nightmare that left scars that cannot heal? Or will she remember me as a glimpse of happiness in the middle of misery, a diversion from the worry for her dead friend from England? Will she forget that it was my interference that led her into her current mess?

Or worse, will she just forget me?

I took a stroll around the room and ended up at the window. The surroundings didn't match my mood. I was gazing over a town of clapboard suburbia, framed by hexagon church towers and the weeping leafwork of spring. But I felt dark and angry, too many jagged edges.

I moved away from the window when I heard someone come into the room. I looked over and recognised one of the officers who had been in the room earlier. He seemed the quiet type, spending his time looking industrious rather than goofing around near the coffee machine. He was shuffling through a collection of paperwork, muttering to himself.

As I looked over, he gave a wry smile and shook his head in mock disapproval. "You've uncovered a quagmire," he shouted out across the room. "Our very own Butch Cassidy and the Sundance Kid."

"I can't see them making it through the mountains somehow, and they certainly aren't Redford and Newman."

He laughed. "Redford and Newman, they ain't, although maybe they'll get wasted in the same way."

I smiled with him. "Ah, the wonders of the criminal justice system. How long do you think I'll be here for?"

He shrugged. "Who knows? Whatever way it blows, it seems you were right, so I wouldn't lose any sleep. Enjoy the view, enjoy the coffee, and look forward to your place in the morning headlines."

"Gee, I can't wait," I replied.

He wagged his finger, picked up a large sheet of paper that looked like some kind of map and then left the room.

It occurred to me that no one was in the room with me, so I wondered how feasible, or wise, it would be to just stroll out onto the streets and come back later, when the activity up at the house had died down.

I quickly put it out of my mind. I didn't want to go into a cell. Instead, I wandered around the desks until I came across a newspaper. I settled down in a nearby chair and began to read.

The STOP team, the Massachusetts State Police Special Tactics and Operations unit, was just what John expected: all hard glances and testosterone, roaming the state, answering requests for help. Specialists in hostage negotiation and high-risk situations, the unit works well in the smaller towns, where the local police force couldn't hope to assemble a team with the expertise and the firepower.

The unit's team leader, a Lieutenant Gerard Marconi, was a cool customer. Six feet six in his socks, steel in a vest, with a look of ease in his eyes. He'd seen it all before, done it all before, and John was sure that their mission, if they had one at all, would be a stroll in the sun for them.

The ring of police had been pulled back now, well back, John fearing some kind of unintended explosion. The house sat in a clearing in the trees. There was about twenty yards of rough grass in a circle around the house. It seemed somehow peaceful, friendly, disturbed only by the swinging of a fly screen with a broken latch. Trees started just where the grass petered out. The police line had originally started just outside the clearing, crouched behind trees, cars and bushes, but now they were pulled back fifty yards from the house. There were a large number of trees between each officer and the house, so they would be hard to shoot at, but each officer had at least one direct line of fire at the house, picking its way through the trees to the much bigger target.

John feared a blast most. Although a sprinting police officer could clear the clearing and be on the ramshackle porch in about three seconds, the blast would be much quicker than that, so John wanted the woodland to take its brunt if it went up. He'd called the local fire brigade at the start, remembering that detonator, and their trucks were now by the highway, kept on permanent standby.

John went back to his car and picked up his phone. He'd understood the message on the video: this is my number, so ring it or the broad gets it, or some other B-movie cliché like that. He was joined at the car by Lieutenant Marconi from the STOP team.

"I think this is your call," John said, holding out the phone to him.

Marconi shrugged. "If you're okay with that."

"Sure, sure."

Just before Marconi made the call, something occurred to him.

John called over to the Saugus contingent and asked if there was anyone there who was involved in the suicide of Tom Bradbury's wife. He was met with shaking heads, but then one of the younger officers there, a ratty-faced young officer still bearing the reddish residue of rampant acne, said that the cop who knew Tom Bradbury best was now working in despatch. He'd taken a desk job after his hip became a slave to arthritis. Good, John was pleased. He asked the young officer if he could get the old guy down there. You never know it might help at some stage, a familiar and friendly voice.

John turned back to Marconi, who nodded and made the call to the house.

The phone rang seven times before anyone answered it.

Marconi was expecting nervousness or fear, some hint at desperation. The important thing is to keep calm, make his voice on the line the one area of calm in the kidnapper's world at that time. What he wasn't expecting was the quiet serenity he heard when the phone was answered.

"Hi, Tom Bradbury here."

For a moment Marconi thought he'd got the wrong number, or maybe Tom Bradbury didn't know what it was all about, but then he remembered the shots from the window and the tennis ball bomb.

"Mr Bradbury, this is Lieutenant Marconi from the Massachusetts State Police here."

He could almost hear the polite smile crack at the other end of the line.

"How ya doing, lieutenant? You got the message then."

John set his jaw. He was listening to the call over headphones, the loudspeakers turned off in case the echo made him twitchy. But he was calm, as if he thought the call was about a parking ticket.

268

"Yes, I got the message," Marconi said coolly. "I saw Miss Gray. Is she still okay?"

There was silence for a while, John straining to hear anything going on in the background. Tom Bradbury's voice returned eventually. "Yes, she's still alive."

That sent a chill down John's back. 'She's still alive.' It covered too many possibilities.

"Is she unharmed?" Marconi ventured.

"As I said, lieutenant, she's still alive."

Again there was silence as John tried to evaluate the position. There was so little being said, even though it was clear that Tom Bradbury wanted the call.

Robert had approached John by now. John had told him he was going to make the call, so Robert wandered over to see if he could be of any help. Robert picked up some headphones and gave a thumbs-up sign.

Robert scribbled a note a passed it to John. It said, 'remember what I said about killers like Tom Bradbury, that control is the key. Let him believe he is in control. Go at his pace; let him make the decisions.'

John nodded. He understood. He passed the note onto Marconi, who glanced at it and nodded.

There was silence still, so Marconi broke it.

"What do you want us to do?"

There was further silence.

Marconi was about to further prompt him when Robert made a hush sign to his lips. He stayed quiet.

After an age, Tom Bradbury spoke. "We just want out."

"Okay, okay, out where, and who is 'we'?"

"My boy and me, we just want out. Anywhere, just away from here." The voice sounded sad, pleading.

"What, you want a new start?" Marconi tried to sound comforting.

A small laugh, a sad note to himself that things weren't as he would like them. "Yeah, lieutenant, something like that."

"What is it you want a new start from?"

There was a pause, although John though he could hear deep nasal breathing. Eventually, Tom Bradbury replied, "I'm not about to enter the confessional, so don't expect it."

John took a deep breath. Tom Bradbury sounded calm, but John was starting to detect an underlying instability, like bad news waiting to happen.

"Okay, okay, I apologise. What can I do for you? Where do you want to go?"

John couldn't help admiring Marconi's style. The dialogue had turned away from him for a moment, but he'd kept his head, swallowed his pride, apologised and let Bradbury get back in control.

"I'm not going to tell you where I'm going. It wouldn't be much of a new start if you were knocking at my door before I'd opened my first beer."

John glanced over at Robert, who held his palm outwards and then lowered it, as if to tell Marconi to take it slow. John gave a helpless shrug as if to say that it was all out of his control.

"So you just want to be able to leave, is that right, without us on your tail?"

"That's pretty much it."

There was silence again. John thought about Katie, and he wondered if she could hear the call. He was relieved not to be in charge of the call, but then felt guilty about that. There are experts at this kind of thing, and Marconi was one of them, and John was just relieved that the buck wouldn't stop with him. There was probably enough fuel in that shack to blow everyone in it into bird food.

His relief wasn't to last long.

John's ears pricked up as he heard a murmuring in the background, and he could tell it was becoming heated. It sounded like an argument was taking place, with Bradbury's hand over the mouthpiece. John wondered who was in charge, Bradbury or his son.

"Put Cornwell on." The calm had become terse.

John's mouth dropped open. Marconi shot him a look and raised his eyebrows in query. While he waited for John's answer, Marconi kept the dialogue going.

"I'm not sure if he'll be allowed, Mr Bradbury. He hasn't got the power to authorise anything, so he won't be able to agree to anything that you want us to do."

"Bullshit!" Tom Bradbury's voice had risen quickly, the instability raging to the surface, now clipped and angry. "He's got the authority, I've just given it to him. It's Cornwell I want to talk to, and you should remember that little Katie Gray has got my boy's gun pointing at her head, and you saw the tins around her chair. Any messing about, I set those fuckers off, and you'll have to explain to her family why she has been pureed. I'm not doing deals, I'm going to decide what I want, and I'm not going to be side-tracked by you bastards. I want someone I can talk to, or wish Katie Gray goodbye."

Marconi looked over at John, who still wore a look of shock. Where had the resigned geniality gone?

"Can I get him to ring you back?"

Bradbury considered this, and eventually agreed. "One minute, and I want you smartasses away from the phone. I want Cornwell on his own, at least for now. And on his own means that, on his own."

And at that the line went dead.

Marconi looked at John, who looked at Robert, who said, "good luck."

John gave a smile rich in sarcasm and slipped off his headphones.

John thought about Robert's one word of advice: control. Let Bradbury believe he is in control. Don't bullshit him or underestimate him.

John picked up the phone. His hand was sweating. This is it. It was his turn to pirouette on a pin with those two sickos.

The phone rang seven times again. Bradbury's voice was cool again. "Lieutenant Cornwell?"

"Yeah, I'm here."

"Good. This won't take long. It's not you I want. I want the English guy. I want you to get him down here. I want to speak to him. Until then, nothing."

"English guy?"

"Cut the crap, Cornwell. The English guy who has been hanging around Boston the last few days, playing at being a royal pain in the ass. You've got one hour. If he isn't on that phone in an hour, just him, then I'll kill this bitch. You get him here and we talk."

John started to protest, but then the line went dead. The order had been made and it had to be carried out.

# Twenty Two

I'd dozed off three times reading a magazine, gravity pulling my head to my chest, my eyelids slipping down without me noticing. One minute I'm reading, the next I'm not.

It was John Cornwell who came into the room. He looked stern. I was about to wave a 'hi', but his glower made me decide otherwise.

"I guess I'm in trouble?" I said in resignation. I'd seen that look on John before. It usually preceded a threat to lock me up.

"You're coming with me."

"Where?"

"To where I tell you, that's where," and he started to walk out of the room.

I jumped up and followed him out. He just kept heading out of the station, down corridors and past rooms, and then skipped down the stone grey steps onto the sidewalk. His car was parked in front of the police station, and he opened the door for me. It slammed shut hard once I'd got in.

John jumped in the driver's seat and pulled away fast, his warm tyres screeching on the hot tarmac.

"What's going on?" I asked, gripping the door handle as he hurtled down Main Street and then onto Chestnut Street, a tree-lined shop parade.

"It's Katie," he said simply. He said it as if that was all he had to say to get my attention. He was right.

"What's wrong?" I asked, worried now, my heart starting to match the speed of the car. "Is she alright?"

"No, she isn't. She is anything but alright." He shook his head. "The Bradburys have her. They've got her tied to a chair, surrounded by unstable explosives and fuel, home-made shit, and they want to get away."

I looked out of the window, feeling sick. It was what I feared, but worse.

"Where do I fit into all of this?" I asked quietly.

"If it was my call, you wouldn't, but he wants to speak with you. He won't talk unless he's talking to you. He doesn't want some highly-trained guy leading him into dead-ends. He wants the English shit who has stirred up all of this."

"Whoa, whoa, slow down. What if this all goes wrong? I'm no negotiator. I'm just some shit-kicking process server from England. What will I know? How will I get on if somebody's life depends on it?"

I folded my arms and simmered. This was way too heavy.

"What if I say no?"

At this John whirled to look at me.

"Look, you moaning fucker, I've helped you out while you've been here. I could have run you out of town a long time ago, so you owe me. I've got one hour to get you to the scene and on a phone. We've lost twenty minutes already, so stop being difficult and get your talking head on."

"And what if I say no? Don't you listen?"

"Then I'll make sure that you're the one who tells Katie's parents what happened to her, because if you are not on that phone soon, they're going to kill her. And then I'll arrest you for practising as a private investigator without a state licence. I'll hold you just long enough for her parents to get here from Wichita, and they might be on their way right now, and then I'll make sure they're by the door when I let you go."

I said nothing. John was clearly angry, and I guessed it wasn't really with me. It was the situation, the loss of control, the burden of responsibility. Tom Bradbury was calling the shots and John didn't like it.

"Will you tell me what to say?"

At that, John calmed down. He looked almost sorry for me, for a moment he looked apologetic, a drop of the mask.

He sighed. "Yeah, don't worry, we'll tell you. That's why I'm rushing. We need to spend some time with you, give you advice. And we need to fit an earphone to you. We will be able to hear everything he says, and everything you say. If you take it nice and slow, we'll tell you how to approach it, how to answer. Just don't let on that we're involved."

"And if I do, inadvertently?"

John looked impassively out of his windscreen.

"She'll die."

273

I looked into my lap and felt my breakfast take a lurch. I thought of England. It felt safe, distant. Massachusetts suddenly felt like it might break me.

When I'd been to where Sarah's body had been found, I'd been disappointed that the scene hadn't resembled the Hollywood version of crime scenes. There'd been no parade of blue lights, no fences to keep the onlookers back. But when I arrived near the clearing it did resemble a film set, and now I wished it didn't. I wanted to stay in John's car and dream about my return to Morsby. Unfortunately, life owes no-one any favours, especially me.

As we arrived, a couple of state troopers were keeping guard on the approach road. A gaggle of journalists, some with pads, some with news cameras, hovered nearby, waiting to give their impressions from the scene. It was clear that they'd got wind of my role, as when the car swung past them, cameras whirred and panned and I was aware of my impending infamy.

John parked behind a crowd of police vehicles. I was surprised at their variety. A couple of vehicles near to John's had the Wakefield Police Department logo on, some kind of shield within a shield. Beside that were two Boston Police vans, or at least that's what I first thought when I saw the light blue stencilled writing. However, as the vehicles came in closer view, I saw the words "Bomb Squad Special Operations" on the side.

I looked at John. "This is serious, isn't it."

He nodded gravely. "As serious as it gets."

John stepped out of the car. I stayed in there for a while, hoping to put off the moment when I took my brave step forward, but as I looked at the array of manpower employed and waiting my arrival, I knew it was no time to balk.

We walked over to a Boston Police truck. It looked like a small camper van, but inside it there were no beds. There were video screens, radios, and maps of the area strewn around. There was an air of steady calm that I didn't share.

As I stepped in, everyone's face turned to me. It was an all-male affair, and it would have been all-white if John hadn't been with me. I was introduced to Lieutenant Marconi from the STOP team, to Captain Flynn from Wakefield Police, and then to three technical guys, each wearing shabby grey suits. The technical guys were all standing, leaning on fancy black electronic boxes like they would a lover, whereas Flynn and Marconi were seated, relaxing on swivel seats. A seat sat vacant, and I presumed this was for John. The seating arrangements said more about seniority than any badge could. Behind all of them sat Robert, and when he looked at me, he just nodded and smiled.

"I wish I felt more like a hero should," I quipped, trying to break the ice, but no-one laughed.

"We don't have much time," Marconi said, businesslike. When he spoke to me, I became aware of his size, his chest and shoulders like a bag of cannonballs. He looked like he lifted weights with his neck. "Has Lieutenant Cornwell explained to you why you are here?"

I nodded grimly. "Yes. Katie is being held by the people who killed Sarah Goode, and they have asked to speak to me."

Marconi nodded. "That's pretty much it. You need to be on that phone soon, so let's cut the bullshit. Firstly, do you agree to doing this? It could go bad, really bad."

"Do you think it will?"

Marconi shrugged. "If you are right, and I'm told that it's your nose that has led us all to this, then those guys in that house are killers. We already know they have weapons, good weapons, and they have home-made explosives."

"What will they want?"

Marconi sighed wearily. "What these assholes always want: a route out of here without being caught."

"And will they get it?"

Marconi smiled a hard, no-nonsense smile. "No. Only they don't know it yet."

I doubted that. I reckoned the Bradburys knew exactly what would happen. That was why I was worried about what they wanted with me.

"Is it wise to let a civilian get involved in negotiations with hostage-takers?" I asked. "I mean, what if I fuck it up and Katie gets killed?"

"We're not asking you to negotiate her release," Marconi replied. "We just want you to speak to him, find out what he wants, and then we'll make the decisions. You'll be wearing a transmitter, and there's a microphone on the phone, so we'll hear everything that's said. You'll be wearing an earpiece so we can tell you what to do. We've attached a party line to the phone, so if it gets out of control we can step in. Don't worry about getting blamed. We'll be with you every step of the way. You are just the spokesman."

"I wasn't worried about getting blamed," I said sharply. "I was worried about Katie getting killed."

Marconi faltered for a moment so John stepped in quickly. "Don't worry Joe. Our aim is to get Katie out. And we'll do that. We just need you to speak to Bradbury to find out what he wants. Remember this, if he is going to kill her, he'll do it anyway, but you speaking to him may stall that and will hopefully give us enough room to get her out."

I nodded. I didn't want to be there, but if it helped, I would do it. I turned to Robert, who until then had been silent.

"What do you think Robert? How should I play it?"

Robert stepped forward. "Do you remember what I said about control? That's the key. Let him have the control. He will have a reason why he wants to speak to you and he will have an outcome from this that he wants to achieve. Let him lead you there. Don't try and outwit him or take control. That's what he wants, so let him have it."

"That's right," Marconi interjected. "You get on that phone and do exactly as we say. Don't go off on a whim on your own. Take your time, listen to what he's saying, but more importantly, listen to what we're saying." He flicked a look to one of the technical guys, an older guy, looked in his late fifties, sagging fat face with a grey tangled mess wrapped around it. His suit looked like it had never been washed, and his shoes had broken laces in each one.

He shuffled towards me, holding something in his hands.

"You need to put this in your ear," and he handed me what looked like an earpiece from a personal stereo, with a flesh-coloured clip to fasten it into my ear. "We can speak to you using this. Hold the phone to the other ear. We'll tell you what to say."

"How much do I speak to you?"

Marconi shook his head. "Try not to. We can't afford any unexpected pauses while you speak to us. To Bradbury, he has to believe he is dealing with a scared Englishman, and him alone. If we sense you are in difficulty, we'll tell you how to get out of it.

276

Just keep it calm, keep it natural, and listen. Don't try and be a hero and we may get Katie back. If you fuck up and they panic, we might lose all three."

I nodded as if I understood, but really I couldn't make sense of anything. I could feel my nerves trying to stage a mass breakout and my mouth had become as dry as Death Valley. I was jerked awake when something heavy and fabric landed in my lap.

"Put that on, and this," and I felt something hard and round land alongside the other item. I looked down and the truck seemed to tilt. A bulletproof vest and a crash helmet with visor. I looked at John, who raised his eyebrows. You'll be okay.

I put them on slowly, trying to put off the moment when I would have to test their efficiency. Eventually I was kitted out in the rudimentary protection and I emerged into the filtered light of the woodland.

The woodlands of Eastern Massachusetts might otherwise be described as beautiful. Black-capped chickadees can be heard creaking like an old wheel, while horned larks tinkle their way through the early part of the morning. The leaves hang wide and heavy, creating shelters out of elms and chestnuts oaks and silver elms, and the blotted-out sky keeps the soil moist and gives the light a cobwebbed feel.

But here, in the clearing by the Bradbury house, that beauty was disturbed.

John walked me over to the line of cars, and when I reached them he told me to crouch down. Once down behind a Wakefield PD car, he pointed the house out to me, sitting quietly amongst a pleasant stretch of trees. The house seemed to be holding itself up by some sort of mutual support, as if to take away one plank would cause the rest to tumble into driftwood. It had a ramshackle charm that seemed typically old America, all verandas and fly-screens. Light blue paint peeled itself off in places and the dust that comes with rainfall dulled everything else.

I looked to my left and to my right, along the line of police cars. I could see a line of men, two behind each car, each with a weapon cocked and ready to go. They seemed tense, alert, not affected by the rural charm of the surroundings. Birds sang in nearby trees as the moving leaves flicked old rain onto the faces of those below, but they were ready to kill.

John pointed to a phone on the dashboard. "That's yours for the duration. Pick it up and press redial. It will go straight to the house."

I looked over at the house and then down at the phone. It all looked so innocuous, so ordinary, I still expected to be told it was a joke.

John reached into his jacket and pulled out a piece of paper. He slid it across on the door of the car and asked me to read it and sign it.

I looked down and read, and then looked at John with disappointment.

"Is that all you think I'll care about?"

"England won't have lawyers like ours. One sniff of stress after this and you'll be swimming in business cards. I'm no lawyer, so I don't know if it will do any good, but someone may thank me for it one day."

I looked down and read again:

*"I, Joseph Kinsella, do confirm that I agree to take part in negotiations with Thomas and Daniel Bradbury, this agreement being made of my own free will. At the time of this agreement I am aware of the following:*

> *1.  that Katie Gray is being held captive under threat of death.*
>
> *2.  That I have been requested to attend as the chief negotiator by those holding Katie Gray captive.*
>
> *3.  That as a result of things said either by me or to me, the death of Katie Gray may ensue.*
>
> *4.  That the events of this day, as of the date of my signature, may cause post-traumatic stress or other personal injury to myself.*

*As a result of the above, I confirm that I am fully aware of the risks involved, that I willingly accept those risks, and thus consent to their infliction should that event occur, and I will not instigate proceedings against Boston Police for any of the consequences of the events of this day.*

*Signed:*
*Dated:*
*Witnessed:"*

It sounded even worse on a second reading. I was going to tear it up, but then I wondered what would happen to Katie if I didn't sign it. Would John let me make the call? Would Katie remain at risk in that house?

I didn't sign it. Instead, I grabbed John's pen and quickly scribbled underneath:

*"I, Lieutenant John Cornwell, acting on behalf of and with the authority of Boston Police, confirm that in asking Mr Joseph Kinsella to assist in the hostage negotiations relating to Katie Gray, Boston Police undertake to underwrite any civil judgements obtained against Joseph Kinsella in respect of any of his actions on the date below.*

*Signed:*
*Dated:*
*Witnessed:"*

John read it, looked at me, smiled, and then screwed the piece of paper up. "Fuck the lawyers."

I smiled back. We agreed on one thing at least.

John held out his hand to shake mine. "Go to it, Joe."

I took his hand, shook it, and said thanks.

"Remember what I told you," he said. "And keep your head down."

I nodded and swallowed. As if I could ever forget. I had a lot of things to remember and most of those I had the feeling I would never forget.

# Twenty Three

I picked up the phone and pressed redial. John retreated back from the line of police vehicles and left me on my own, crouching behind a police car. As the numbers stopped going through, I heard someone whisper, *"good luck"* into my earpiece.

The phone rang seven times.

I sensed the birds go quiet and the whispers of the leaves brushed the best wishes of the watching police officers over me. I felt completely alone and isolated.

"Kinsella?"

My throat tightened when I heard the voice. It wasn't Danny. It was an older voice. It was cautious, nervous, tentative.

I found my voice eventually.

"Hello, good afternoon." I cursed myself for making a crass start. "What do you want me to call you?"

I heard a whisper in my ear, *"good. Let him take the helm,"* before the person on the phone replied, "Tom, call me Tom."

"Good, Tom. Why did you want to speak to me?"

"Well it wasn't for a weather forecast, was it," came the sarcastic response, followed by a low chuckle.

*"Don't worry about appearing foolish,"* someone whispered in my ear. It sounded like Marconi. *"It will give him control. Just let him lead the conversation."*

The silence widened on the telephone, like two naïve young fighters, each waiting for the other to start but hoping that no-one does.

"I wish you could see her now."

It broke the silence like smashed crystal at a séance.

"How is she?" It was a lame question, but I had to know.

I heard a grunt, some kind of exertion, and then a yelp, a female yelp. I guessed at a kick at Katie, although it could have been a punch or anything.

"She's alive."

It didn't seem like much, but at least I hadn't become involved too late. The voice in the earpiece whispered for me to be calm, but the thought entered my head that if Katie was alive when I started speaking and then she died, it might be my fault. I pushed it to one side, although not completely away.

"It looks busy out there. How about losing a few?"

"What do you mean?"

"Get them to retreat. I want to see every police car outside of my house back to the road."

"I don't know if I can do that."

"You can do whatever you want, Kinsella. You are in charge now."

*"Don't worry, we'll get them to move back. Tell him it's okay, you'll give it a try, and then shout at the officers to move their cars, get back to the road,"* Marconi whispered.

I nodded in agreement, although to anyone watching it was a nod to nothing in particular.

I dropped the receiver to my chest and shouted for everyone to move back, waving my arms at them, shouting at them to move back to the road. I heard the crackle of static as they received confirmation over their radios, and then the movement started. The cars moved slowly back through the woods, a line of police cars along the track, moving back to the highway.

Pretty soon, I was behind the only car left, the others wending their way through the woods, with men backing away, rifles still trained on the house. I was surprised at the agreement to the request, but then a voice started up in my ear, *"it's alright, Joe. There are men behind trees to your right and left. Don't look at them. There are men behind the house, well-hidden, and those backing away now will crawl back through the undergrowth to get a good view. You are not alone now, and you never will be. Just don't let him know that. He thinks he has flexed his muscle. Let him retain that delusion."*

I went back to the phone, bolstered.

"See, Kinsella, do you see the power you have? I know they will be crawling back through the undergrowth, trying to get a good line of fire on the house, but you got them to move. They will do what you say, and you can do what you want."

I stayed silent. Perhaps Marconi had underestimated him. Perhaps the request had been made for my benefit, not for his, although I couldn't work out why. Marconi's truck had moved back as well, so I didn't know if I was still within range to receive instructions.

"Do you want Katie back?"

Before I had chance to answer, I heard Robert's voice. *"Don't say yes. Don't play into his hands too soon. Just say you want her back unharmed."*

"I just want her to be alright, that's all."

"Well, she can be. It's in your hands, Joe Kinsella. Fuck up, and there is blood on them."

I felt a flash of anger. It wasn't my fault, it never had been. I wasn't the one spilling the blood. I was just trying to find out who had spilled it. In my earpiece a voice said, *"stay calm and stay silent. Let him start up again."* I was still angry, because I knew he was just playing with my feelings, but I did as I was told.

There was silence for a while, although I thought I could hear harsh words spoken over the whisper of stifled sobs. They went through me like a skewer.

"Why don't you join us, Kinsella?"

*"Don't agree,"* a static-filled bark commanded me.

"Why would I want to join you?" I asked.

"Because you care about Katie."

*"Don't do it, Joe. Let him control the conversation, but don't let him control you."*

I ignored the voices in my ear.

"Yes, but I care about me. Can't we just talk like this?"

A throttled yelp came down the line at me like an advancing express train. I knew what it was, that it was coming, but I knew I couldn't get out of its way in time. I heard the sound of feet kicking on a floor, and then sobbing. I knew Katie had been grabbed around the neck and had been hurt.

*"Don't get involved in this,"* Marconi hissed. *"Remember, it's his surrender you are negotiating, not yours".*

"But why do you want me?"

"I've heard you're good company. It gets lonely in the woods," and then a laugh, a screaming guffaw. It rattled around me and blew the cobwebs from the trees.

When the laugh subsided, he started again. "Come to me, Joe, make it alright for Katie. She wants to go home. You can help her."

"What, you'll let her go?"

*"Don't do it, Kinsella. He's mocking you."*

"I like to think of myself as a man of my word. Come on Joe, come see how she is, before it's too late."

"Joe!"

"Why don't you just leave her?" I hissed, frustrated now. "All you've done is abduction. I don't know what that carries here, but it must be less than murder, especially multiple murder."

Bradbury laughed. "Not in Texas. I hear murderers down there spend a lot less time in jail than kidnappers."

*"Don't get into an argument with him. Stay focused and agree with what he's saying."*

The laughing stopped. "Anyhow, who said I killed anybody?"

"Just something I heard. Look, just let her go and take your chances in court. It might work out okay."

"You like Katie, don't you."

I nodded, knowing my unseen silence for Bradbury would be enough.

"Don't you want to be with her again?"

"If I didn't care about Katie, I wouldn't be here, on the phone to you. I'd be in a bar, or on a beach."

"She's important to you. How would you feel if she was taken away from you?"

"Who, Katie?"

*"Joe! Take it steady. Don't let Katie become a pawn."*

"Yes, Katie. How would you feel if she were taken away from you? Bereaved? Heartbroken?"

"No," I said quietly. "I would feel responsible, like it was all my fault."

The phone went dead.

I looked over to where Marconi and John were, out by the technical van. I was expecting a blasting, but it didn't come.

*"You're doing okay, Joe,"* Marconi said into the earpiece. *"Give it two minutes and ring back. Just don't agree to go with them. There is one hostage at the moment. Let's not double it. And don't give any hint that you can hear me. Just get back on the phone. Remember, don't agree to anything we can't deliver and don't give yourself up. Let him agree his own surrender. Start to explain the positives in letting Katie go."*

I looked back towards the house, relieved.

It was easy for Marconi, and for John. They were trained to deal with these situations. I wasn't. I'd been trained in negotiating as part of my training as a lawyer, but that training was based on the premise that the other party involved would be a respectable person in a business suit. Gun-toting kidnappers and serial murderers were not scenarios involved in the role-playing games.

I remembered the formula though. Concede some to win some. I realised that I would have to delve deeply into my memory to get the most out of this.

I looked at the phone in my hand, said a silent prayer, and pressed redial.

The phone rang out seven times before it was answered. It still wasn't Danny. It was Tom Bradbury again.

"Is that you again, Kinsella?"

"Yeah, it's me."

There was a moment's silence, so I decided to press on.

"Look Tom, this is difficult for me, and I suppose it will be for you too, but I think we can work this out."

A barked laugh, bitter in taste, came down the line at me. "There is no 'we' involved. I tell you what we want, and you do it. If you don't, my son kills Katie."

"Okay, I hear what you say," I said, trying to stay calm while my mouth turned to dust. "But I don't think our agendas are in conflict. I just want Katie back, unharmed, and you just want to get away. That's fine by me. You can retire to a sun-bleached villa in Florida for all I care. I just want to be able to return Katie unharmed. What happens to you is out of my hands, and, to be honest with you, the least of my concerns."

"That's very gracious of you," came the sarcastic response.

"What do you want out of this?" I pleaded.

A low chuckle and then the phone went dead.


*"You did okay,"* said Marconi in soothing tones. *"Let him ring back, not you. He knows now that he has to decide what he wants. When he has decided, he will call back."*

Marconi's words of encouragement did not dispel my feelings of unease. I'd heard Katie's pain, sensed her discomfort, and now Marconi wanted patience. I was left alone in the woods, visible and vulnerable. I could sense my heart beating a fast rhythm and my chest rose and fell with deep, nervous breaths.

"What about Katie while we're waiting?" I was sounding, desperate.

*"He won't harm her at the moment. What will he gain? He doesn't know whether we can give him what he wants."*

I thought about that and I agreed that it seemed logical. But still my disquiet began to make itself heard in my mind. I wondered what she was going through and how much more we could do to help.

But I knew one thing: this wasn't my field of expertise. I knew I should leave it to those who know.

The ringing of the telephone quietened the noise of my misgivings. I looked at it as if it had just burst into flames.

*"Pick it up, Joe. You'll be okay."*

I picked it up cautiously, putting it carefully against my ear. It was Tom Bradbury.

"She's not very well, Kinsella."

My stomach dipped like a yo-yo.

"What do you mean?" I was starting to panic again, images of Katie, injured and dying filling my head.

"It's the blood that concerns me," he continued smugly. "The pain has passed now she's unconscious, out of it, but she won't stop bleeding. Christ, she's a mess. I'm no medical man, you see. I'm just some bum of a mechanic trying to hold his life together. So, Kinsella, what were you saying before I hung up?"

*"Don't join in this, Joe. Just play it easy, don't get drawn into mind games. Katie is probably okay, but he is trying to freak you out. Think about it: what has he got to bargain with if anything bad happens to Katie? We'd just sit here and starve them out. Just ask him to tell you what he wants."*

"I thought you were the one talking?" I said, nervously trying to play the game. "You were going to tell me what you wanted."

I paused, waiting for a response, but all I heard was a short snorted laugh. I was about to blurt out more, panic and nerves taking over my decisions, when I remembered Robert's instructions to let him direct the conversation. Stay calm and be driven. If I become the driver, I might get lost.

Ten seconds felt like ten minutes, and then he spoke again.

"I want Katie to be alright," he said, in a mocking tone, "we both do, but we're getting bored in here. My boy gets impatient, and when he gets impatient he loses his temper, and when he does that, he ain't rational. He starts cuttin' an' a slashin'. Man, if you could see her now. I'm surprised you didn't hear the screams. She was wriggling and squealing and sobbing. I'm not sure she didn't just soil herself right here in front of me. Man, she is making a mess. I don't want her to bleed to death in front of me."

"Where is she cut?" I shouted, my mind darting between panic and helplessness, rage and contempt.

A laugh came down the line. "A lot of places."

I shut my eyes and tried to shut out the imagery. But I couldn't. The Katie I saw had that dewy smile when she was soft, or that coyness when she laughed, but each time it flashed in, something slashed out, and I could just see a silent scream, a wide-eyed terror.

*"Hold tight, Joe. He's bullshitting."* Marconi again. *"If you want to bale out, you can do, but you are doing okay. If I was doing this, I wouldn't be worried. Kidnappers do one thing very well, and that's make threats. What they don't do very well is carry them out. And remember that he needs Katie alive. And remember something else: we don't have much evidence of his involvement in the other killings. We can prove Danny Bradbury knew the guy who is in jail for some murder he may not have done, and was with him on the night of the murder, getting him out of the way and giving him an alibi he couldn't prove. We can prove he went out of his way to get to know Sarah and Katie, but over and above all that, we can't prove much more without forensics. You used to be a lawyer, I'm told, so you know how strong evidence has to be before someone is convicted. So hang loose and stay calm."*

It didn't calm me down, but it made me feel confident enough to carry on.

Bradbury's laughing died down and fell into the silence between us. He spoke again.

"You can do one thing, Kinsella."

"What's that?"

"Join me over here."

*"I've already told you, ignore it,"* Marconi barked. *"Increase his hostages, you increase his bargaining strength. He could kill Katie and just keep you. Think about it: there has to be a reason why he wants you there, one that only benefits him. Why help him out?"*

"Why would I want to do that?" I asked Bradbury. "There's nothing in it for me."

"To get Katie back. I'll do a straight swap. The way I see it is that Katie is hurt bad and going to die. She dies and them cops are gonna fuck me and my boy up bad. I need another body to play with. I do a swap now, and Katie gets thrown out of the door alive. She gets saved. But," and now his voiced turned cruel, "if you don't, Katie dies, we die, and you will have achieved nothing. You'll go back to England with Katie's death on your conscience, as well as Sarah's."

*"Joe!"*

My mind pricked up. "What do you mean, Sarah's?"

"Oh, she was a sweet girl. I was so sorry to hear about her death. I understand you came to America to find her, but failed. What do her parents say about that? They paid you good money, their life savings, but I hear she ended up being barbecued somewhere near Wakefield. If only you had been quicker. Well, here's your chance. Come on, skip over that lawn and join me in here. As soon as I see you run through that door, I'll throw Katie out and I'll talk with the police about your release."

"And if I don't?"

"It's easy. Time marches on, Katie dies a slow death, the police burst in and kill us, endgame. You live of course, if you can call it living. No-one will criticise you. I'm sure the police are telling you not to come across, but you'll always know. You'll know it could have been different. It will seep back into your dreams, come back at you in your quieter moments. Think of Katie's family back in Kansas, grieving and hating you. They'll want to know why you didn't get her out when you had the chance. Come on, Kinsella, run now, run like the wind."

*"Joe, stay where you are! Tell him that there must be another way. If this carries on, we're cutting the phone link."*

"Why don't you just let her go anyway," I pleaded to Bradbury. "What will they have? Assault. Think of your son. He'll say he did it under your influence, that you were the main one. He'll get a short sentence. If you let Katie go, you'll be giving more than just her a life, you'll be giving your son a life too."

Bradbury laughed. "I can tell you don't really know my son. He enjoys this. He likes the pain, the pursuit, the end."

"I bet he does," I said, my voice turning hard, determined. I remembered the way he was in the bar that time, and round at

287

Katie's apartment. The friend, cool, calm and supportive. I lost my temper, and I started to say things I shouldn't.

"It would have fucked me up if I'd lost my mother in the way that he did," I shouted. I could hear Marconi warning me to stop or he'd cut me off, but I started, so I was going to finish. "Is that what it's all about, some kind of revenge for his mother's suicide? She convinced herself that she was evil, so she did the only thing she could. She killed herself rather than live with that belief? Is that what this is all about, Mr Bradbury? So you and your son convince yourselves that maybe she was evil, and try to carry on her work, the work that she started and finished on herself? Is that it? Or is it just the injustice, wondering why those dark thoughts had to come to your wife, his mother? Why not someone else? Why not all those who share the same coincidence? Why are their lives untouched and your destroyed? Is that it, Bradbury?"

I was breathless when I finished, fuelled by anger and helplessness.

I didn't know what I expected. Perhaps confessions, or tears, or fury. I didn't expect laughter, loud guffawing laughter.

"I love it," he said, between the laughs. "The arrogance, as if you could see straight through me, my life distilled down to one angry outburst. Is that how highly you regard yourself? Come on, I thought better of you. Come here, come to me, and Katie goes. You've got two minutes. If you don't come through that door, I won't ring back and Katie will die. If anyone other than you comes through that door, I shoot their head off just after I shoot Katie's. It's your call."

And with that, the phone went dead.

I ripped the earphone out and threw the phone down. I didn't need the tirade from Marconi. I could do it myself.

"Fuck!" I shouted, and I kicked the car.

I stood by the car and looked over at the house.

I was calmer now. When he'd first put the phone down, I was angry. I was angry at the situation, I was angry at Bradbury, I was angry at Marconi for putting me in that situation in the first place, but most of all, I was angry at me. I was furious for once again letting my temper get the better of me. I was back in that police station in England, once again facing that grimy criminal, and once again I'd seen the red mist ruin everything.

I'd had a minute or so to calm down. I knew I wouldn't have much longer. Marconi and John Cornwell will be trying to speak to me, not knowing yet why I wasn't listening. My earpiece lay discarded on the floor, a yellow glint in the long grass. I could see an arm waving at me to come back, a police officer lying down in the grass, and I could hear a hissed command to get down and get out of there.

I didn't know what to do now. If Bradbury was to be believed, Katie was dying a slow death. Slow, but certain. Leaving the Bradburys to the police would achieve nothing except prolong the rescue period, and Katie would die. If Bradbury was lying, it wouldn't matter, Katie would still be alive and the police would sort it out, but what if he was telling the truth?

My motives were selfish. I was worried about me at first. What would I do if I my actions led to her death? How would I face her parents? I already had Sarah's parents to face, and I didn't want another pair to avoid.

But then I worried about Katie. What was she going through? Was she in pain? What had they done to her while I had shouted at her captor? I remembered her happy face, the smile in her eyes, and I wondered if they were gone forever.

I felt sick. I felt angry. I felt contempt. I felt worry. But most of all, I felt responsible.

At that moment, I knew there was one thing I wanted to do it, and in a flush of madness, I decided to do it.

I looked down at the police officer hissing at me and shook my head slowly at him. He barked at me to do as I was told. I shook my head again.

I looked over at the house. I couldn't see any weapons, but I couldn't really see anything. Just a tumbledown shack and dark windows.

I looked back to the control van and saw John Cornwell coming out, his arm waving at me to get down and go to him.

I looked back to the house. I could do it. I could be across that grass and in that house in a few seconds, and then Katie would be passed out to be looked after and kept alive.

I thought about Katie and my resolve strengthened. There was only one thing I could think of doing.

I ran at the house.

I ran hard, I ran fast. I ran as hard and as fast as I thought I would be able to, and soon my head echoed with the thump of my feet pounding the grass. My breaths came quick and eager, my chest aching with effort. My helmet flew off as I put my head back, trying to hit the house at speed

As I approached the veranda, my mind flicked across the notion that there may be some kind of tripwire or booby trap, there had already been one home-made bomb, but by the time the thought was flicked away, I was leaping over the two steps onto the porch and throwing myself at the door.

The door was ajar. I hit the door and fell through into a large living room. It looked normal. A sofa was facing me as I sprawled on the floor, and to my right a television sat blankly. Ornamental items were sparse, but it contained the usual signs of life, like newspapers, used cups and plates. A kitchen was at the back of the room, separated from the living quarters by a breakfast bar. But most of all, it smelled of fuel. It smelled like a loose cough might send it all to heaven, and now with me in it.

I panted, coughing from the sprint, gagging on the thick air. I brought myself to my knees, spluttering, and looked at the breakfast bar. I gasped. Katie was sat against it. She was sat up, bound, with her hands behind her back, an old cloth stuffed into her mouth. It was unimaginative but effective. She looked at me wide-eyed and scared, but otherwise she seemed unharmed. No blood, no unconsciousness. I'd been cheated.

I felt a dry panic, knowing now that I shouldn't be there. There was to be no exchange. He had me.

I stood up slowly, flicking my head around, looking to Katie for help, not knowing where Bradbury was. Katie's eyes looked wide at me, a shout losing itself in her gag. Then I heard a snigger and my stomach dropped like a weight. From behind me I heard Tom Bradbury say, "my name is Tom Bradbury, and you're gonna die."

# Twenty Four

All hell broke loose in the police control van. It was John Cornwell who shouted first, running back into the van.

"What the fuck is he doing now?"

Marconi was at the window, his jaw dropped, shaking his head. "He has fucked up." He was angry. His fist banged the worktop, scattered pens and pieces of paper, the product of a few minutes working out routes to the house. "I hope for his sake she comes out of this okay." He kicked a small desk by one of the smoked glass windows. "Because if he she doesn't, I'll have his ass."

He banged the desk again and turned round to John, eyes glaring. "Why did you say he'd be okay? The guy is a fucking liability. You said let him do it, and now, boy, has he done it. If this goes wrong, it will be Boston Police at the news conference apologising, not us, and fuck to co-operation."

John did nothing at first. He knew Marconi was right. He had trusted me, and he'd been let down. He'd watched the sprint for the door in disbelief, watched his trust evaporate like a quick shower in June. He knew this would mean trouble for him. Questions would be asked about his judgement, and John knew that this would lead to questions about the secrets he had held back from his superiors.

John started to bellow into the microphone. "Joe! Joe! Get the fuck out of there."

A crackle of radio static. It was one of the members of the STOP team, one of the ones who had crawled through the undergrowth to get nearer to the house. "He can't hear you lieutenant, his earset is in the grass here. I saw him rip it off."

John clicked the microphone off angrily. He didn't look at Marconi.

It was Marconi who spoke next, calmer now.

"We need to go in."

John looked round at him, and he saw the determined look in his eyes. He was going to do it.

"Shouldn't we see what happens next?"

Marconi didn't say anything. He just returned his gaze to the view out of the vehicle windows.

John knew what the silence meant. He had fucked up once so cut down on the advice. He wasn't happy about it, but John knew Marconi had good reason to feel like he did. It had been his call, and he'd blown it on a moment of poor judgement.

But John worried about what would happen if they charged in, about a burst of manpower and firepower in an old wooden shack, stacked high with home-made explosives and fraught with tensions. That house could scatter itself among the trees, along with all its contents, and then they would find out nothing of what has gone on in the past. John wanted to know what the truth was, needed to know whether he had once been badly wrong.

John thought about the tennis ball bomb. It wasn't impressive, but it spoke of volatility and a willingness to maim. This wasn't the usual hostage situation, where the hostage-taker is usually too scared to do anything meaningful and usually just wants a route out, one that will allow them to pretend it had never happened. There is no such route, and that's why most sieges end up with the hostage-taker blowing his own brains out.

John remembered the Bomb Squad van arriving and John thought that if they said it was too volatile in there, it might stall Marconi. John knew Marconi would listen to them. It was time for a walk.

He nodded to the technicians in the van, who looked scared, as if in the middle of something in which they held no expertise. They were fine with technical wizardry, flicked through computer programs the way some people flick through magazines in a waiting room. This was different. It had become operational and they knew they would play no part.

John hopped out of the van and walked over to the Bomb Squad van. He was met by a small guy wearing black t-shirt and pants and a bored smile.

"Hi. You guys wondering when something is going to happen?"

He smiled at John and shrugged. "You know, it's a nice setting but we're getting kinda restless."

"Isn't that a good thing?"

He didn't say anything. He kicked at the ground and rubbed his left eye, as if John had just woken him up.

"You remember the cans of gasoline in there, and the pipe bombs?" John asked. "Did you mean it when you said what would happen if we open fire in there?"

The Bomb Squad guy blew out. "I don't fuck about in these situations. You get a stray spark in there, some bullet flying off a can, or hitting the TV, and that lot will blow. No-one will get out, and no-one will get in. Most home-made bombs are made out of fertiliser, ammonium nitrate, because it's easy to get hold of. If those pipe bombs are ammonium nitrate and they go off, you have got bad shit. Ammonium nitrate is damn good fertiliser, and a damn good explosive. React with gasoline and it will blow those fuckers into atoms. If they can get on the internet, they will find all the instructions they want. Blaster caps; home-made timing devices; different types of pipe bomb. It's all there."

John looked over his shoulder and nodded back towards the control van. "The STOP boys are thinking of going in. They've got a second civilian hostage, so they wanna go in there quick to get them out. One of them may already be injured. If there is ammonium nitrate lying around, should they go in there heavy-handed?"

The bomb squad guy whistled and shook his head. "I would play it careful. If the guy in there is making pipe bombs, he might have them around the windows or doors. If made well enough, they will take away anyone stood near them." He looked serious. "Keep away, no heroics," he urged. "Ammonium nitrate explodes at fourteen thousand feet per second, and has similar nitrogen contents as dynamite. If it goes up, it can go up big. Pack it with nails, and you have big, bad shit. Mix it with motor oil and ignite it with gelatine dynamite, and round here you'll have a deciduous Hiroshima."

"So what should we do?"

He looked at John and smiled. "Hose it down. Get a chopper and hose the whole house down. Get the whole place wet. Get water down the chimney, through the windows, anywhere that will soak the pipe bombs and hopefully get to the powder. Ammonium nitrate gets off on gasoline, but it don't like water. That may do enough. And it will disperse the fuel, break it up into smaller pools."

"Anything you boys can do?"

He shook his head. "We can dismantle them once we get in there, but if the STOP boys are going in, we'll wait over here. Way, way over here."

John nodded. He understood.

"Just one more thing," John said.

"Shoot."

"Could that lot blow just on the build up of gases? You know, what would happen if we just sat it out?"

He shrugged. "It depends on a lot of things, like concentration, ventilation, proximity. But if nobody's eyes are stinging, it might be bullshit."

John saluted a thank you and headed back to the control van. An idea was forming.

I turned around slowly, the sound of my knees shuffling on the ground screaming at me.

As I turned, I became aware of a dark shape sitting against the wall, and from that dark shape, I could see a metallic glint pointing out at me. I was looking straight down the barrel of a gun. It looked like a shotgun.

My heart grew taut like a drum and I swallowed to try and get some air. I shut my eyes for a moment, as if to shut it out would take it away. But when I opened them again, the gun was still there, and he was still there, exuding menace and contempt like he had it to spare.

I forced myself to peer past the gun. I squinted into the darkness until I could see him against the wall. His legs were crossed, almost nonchalant, and I could see a grin spread across his face. He was enjoying himself.

He wasn't like I imagined. I suppose they never are. When I saw him, I felt less threatened. He was skinny, his cheekbones casting shadows in the half-light. He looked sinewy, lean, and his sandy hair was disappearing to the back of his head. But I could see his eyes, and they looked cold. He was looking straight down the gun, the glint in his eyes bouncing off the metal.

"Kinsella, at last," he said. "My son has told me all about you." He looked me up and down. "He said you looked like a loser. I think he was right."

"I don't see you winning much," I said, sounding braver than I felt.

He jumped forward and rammed the butt of the gun into my knee. I felt a shot of pain and dropped to the floor. I was seething through gritted teeth, the pain fuelling hatred to replace the fear.

"You bastard!" I yelled. "You cowardly fucking bastard!" I was squirming around, trying to see him properly, trying to be somewhere so he would never come at me from behind. The pain in my knee made my breath draw, and I took deep breaths to drive it away.

He stood up and walked over to me. I shuffled away, my leg dragging and throbbing in pain and protest. I moved round in an arc, trying to get against the wall.

He stood over me and looked down, smiling coldly. He watched me look up, tried to see the fear, but he wasn't going to get it. I was panting, seething, spluttering contempt.

He snarled and stamped on my hand. I pulled my fingers away, shouting in pain. I could feel my fingers swell, and from the shots of pain I knew he had broken at least a couple.

My head hung to the floor, black spots flashing in front of my eyes, the pain in my hand making me cough. Was this it, I thought? Was this to be the way? Was this how I was going to finish my days, with my limbs broken one by one until I slipped out of consciousness through pain? My mind was already losing focus as I tried to keep away the messages being sent by the cracked bones. The pain in my kneecap was making me catch my breath and almost vomit, and the pain in my fingers made me want to claw at the floor.

I stopped crawling and lay down on the floor. I was out of breath but had done nothing. I looked over at Katie, who had her eyes clamped shut. I thought I could see tears squeezing out.

Bradbury pulled a wooden chair towards him and sat down. He shuffled the chair up to me, so he was looking down at me as I lay on the floor, panting. He pointed his gun at me and slowly brought it towards my head. It crept closer, the chasm of the barrel getting darker and more hypnotic as it came closer, opening and drawing me in. It blocked him out, his leering look of triumph replaced by a steel ring and the darkness of death.

The gun only stopped when it reached the tender spot between my eyebrows. He pushed against it slightly, so I could feel it there, could sense the menace. It was cold.

He looked down the barrel at me and smiled.

"Danny?" he shouted, never taking his eyes of me.

Within a couple of seconds, Danny Bradbury appeared.

My eyes flashed to him when he came into the room, and I felt stronger. Here was the biggest bastard of them all. He looked different now. He had lost that genial look he had when I saw him in the bar that time. Now he had a mean look that went much deeper than just his eyes. It was a look that seemed to take over his whole body, his whole sense of himself.

Tom Bradbury pointed at Katie. "Get the support."

Danny smiled at me and went out of the room. I looked at Tom Bradbury, who never took his eyes off me. Danny returned with what looked like a small gallows, five foot high, and put it in the middle of the floor. He shuffled it and moved it so that it was facing the door.

Bradbury flicked his head towards Katie. "You know what to do."

I watched in horror as Danny went over to Katie and began to untie her bonds. Katie flashed a look at me, fear and dread, and I felt myself go dry. I looked at Bradbury, who must have sensed my thoughts, as he pressed the gun into my head a bit more and whispered, "don't."

Katie was dragged towards the gallows, the gag still in place, hands bound together, her feet shuffling on the floor as she tried to resist, screams and strangled pleas forcing their way out.

I looked at Bradbury and pleaded with him. "Don't, please."

Katie was thrown against the structure, her head banging on the wood, and I saw blood trickle onto her forehead, saw her wince through tears. Then I was surprised to see Katie strapped to the structure, but not in a hanging position, but instead with her body behind the upright wood, with arms bound along the top. Her hands were clasped tightly against the end, so that she appeared to be tied around the gallows, not hanging from it.

I looked at Bradbury, confused, but then it dawned on me, a slow, creeping realisation. I felt contempt. Another one of his games. Katie was strapped around the structure, but from a quick glance, it would look like someone stood with their arms together and outstretched. Like someone holding and aiming a pistol. And it would be the first thing the police would see when they burst in, rushing, adrenaline pumping, looking for a target to shoot at. They would see straight away someone stood towards them, arms outstretched and forward, and they would shoot. They would mistake Katie for the enemy and shoot her, riddle her so full of bullets it would take a public inquiry to work out who fired the fatal shot. Bradbury's last joke.

"You bastard," I whispered.

He waved me away. "This is no time for compliments." He turned to Danny. "Put your gun against her head."

Danny did so. I saw Katie's legs stiffen as she struggled against the cold steel, but she was fastened tight.

Tom Bradbury then looked back at me and gave me a warm, friendly smile.

"Two gunmen, two guns," he said. "One shot from in here, and those guys out there are gonna come hurtling through that door, ready or not. We're ready to go, so it's your call. Who is going to live to tell the tale? You or Katie? One of you is going to die; the other one might get out. Make your choice.

I looked across at Katie, saw the fear in her eyes. I closed mine.

John ran over to where the fire fighters were standing. They knew a fire was likely, and a big one, so they had their hoses at the ready, hooked up to the hydrants and coiled neatly on the floor.

Wakefield Fire Department isn't the biggest in Massachusetts, nowhere near, but they are an enthusiastic bunch. Split between two stations and divided into four groups, each shift of ten kept Wakefield intact. This situation, however, had made the department whole again, and all the vehicles were present. John looked around, and he saw eager faces and ready eyes.

The engines from headquarters were there, Engines 1 and 4, along with Ladder 1, a 100ft aerial truck designed for fires in high places. Engine 2 from the Greenwood station had also come down, along with the maintenance truck complete with 34ft bucket, and all the engines together looked like a field full of strawberries topped with cream. The fire chief, a friendly old man making his way towards retirement, had wondered why they were all needed, but if the bomb squad asked for all the trucks, it was wise to bring all the trucks. If it all went wrong, the fire chief had the common sense to make sure he was blameless.

John gave a smile he didn't feel as he approached the chief. The fire engines were gathered by the entrance road, sat on the edge of a large field and overlooking the highway. The fire-fighters were fully uniformed, but the heat was creeping up, the humidity making their suits stick to their backs.

"Captain," John said, as casually as he was able, "I appreciate you being so patient. We appreciate it," John qualified it, gesturing towards the policemen in the adjoining field.

The fire chief nodded and gave a wary smile. Gracious police officers usually mean trouble.

"I was hoping your men might be able to help us out," John continued, and when he was met only with a raised eyebrow, he continued, "could your hoses break glass?"

"What the hell are you talking about, lieutenant?"

"Can the pressure from the hoses break a small pane of glass?"

He looked at John quizzically, weighing up whether it was wise to answer truthfully or not, before cracking a smile. "If it isn't too big, I reckon they could make a mess. Depends how strong it is, I suppose."

"What about if we break it first? Could you get a good stream going, enough to knock a man over inside?"

The fire chief smiled. "Those hoses can blow some. If you got in their way, you'd know about it."

John smiled. He had what he wanted.

"Chief, we need to talk."


I opened my eyes again.

I still had the terror, but something joined it alongside, some kind of serenity I didn't expect. I could see Katie strapped to the plinth. She wasn't looking at me. Her head rested against her wooden support and seemed to be taking most of her weight. Her legs didn't look strong anymore, as if they would buckle with a push, and her wrists hung loose against her rope restraints.

I took my eyes away from the gun and looked at Tom Bradbury. The pain in my hand and knee had subsided to a loud throb, and my head had become clearer by necessity.

"What if I say nothing?" I sounded defiant, confrontational.

Bradbury smirked and shrugged.

"I get to kill the one I choose. I choose you, she says you died a coward for not nominating yourself," and he leant forward into my face, spittle peppering my face, "and from here you don't look so fucking brave." He leant back again, his smirk returned. "I shoot her, everyone says you're a bastard. Looking after number one."

His smirk broadened to a smile. "Your choice. Make it. You've got ten seconds." He raised his eyebrows. "Tick-tock, tick-tock, tick-tock."

I did my best to smile back at him. "You kill us, it all ends up as one big fuck up, just because your wife popped her own head off."

I tensed as I waited to see his reaction.

I expected anger, fury, expected that gun to come lashing across my face, tearing at my skin, taking away my nose, my cheek, my eye. I expected a shot, the last I would ever hear, but I wanted to delay, to make him angry, less rational. I needed to knock him off his beat, try and change the pattern.

His smile simply broadened. He started to chuckle.

I looked over at Danny. He wasn't chuckling. Whatever happened in the past, it had happened to his mother, and that wasn't something to laugh about.

My mind flashed briefly to my own mother back in Morsby. As far as she was concerned, I was on a short break to the States. She had simply assumed that business was good and that I was grabbing a few luxurious days before my next job.

I looked once more at Danny. That was the weak link. I knew it then, as I looked first at Katie, and then back at Danny. It suddenly struck me that he wasn't enjoying any of this, he never had. It had been through Danny that the road had led to here, to a crippling standoff with a local madman. He had hung around even after Sarah had gone. It meant I knew him, could identify him as Danny, Katie's friend, Tom Bradbury's son. He had got too involved with Katie, and I wondered then whether he enjoyed seeing her like this, trussed up and target practise for the local police. How had he coped with seeing Sarah die, after knowing her as a friend, a person? Whichever part he plays, he does it for his father, not for himself. And I could see that any joking about his mother's death would not make him happy.

I looked back at Tom Bradbury. He was still chuckling to himself. But his gun never wavered once. It kept its one-barrelled stare at me, unwinking, unmoving.

"Why did she do it?" I asked. "Why did your wife kill herself?"

The chuckling dwindled until Tom Bradbury returned to a smile, and before he answered even that disappeared.

"It's too late for therapy," he replied contemptuously.

I flicked my head towards the window, towards the police waiting outside. "I think it's a little too late for anything. Is it therapy you want?"

He pushed the end of the gun deep into my forehead, so I could feel it pressing into the bone of my skull. It was making a deep red ring and made me want to jerk my head away. But its threat kept me still.

His eyes took on a darkness stronger than the dim lights of the room, like a cloak passing in front of daylight, a reflection of the inner shadows.

"There is no therapy," he hissed, "only the cold, hard truth, and you wouldn't like that."

"Don't prejudge me. I might be stronger than you think."

He smiled at that. It wasn't a smile that relaxed me. He stood up and walked over to Katie. He tilted her chin up tenderly and smiled into her eyes. He leant forward and kissed her softly on her lips, and then on her forehead. He lowered her head gently onto the support and looked over at me.

I did nothing. I tried to shuffle forward, some vain attempt at rescue, to get up and put him through the wall, but my knees screamed pain at me again and his gun was still hanging loose in one hand.

He looked again at Katie. He lifted her head up again, her hair in his hands, but this time he didn't kiss her. He lifted the gun to her face and stuck the muzzle between her lips. They parted almost tenderly, and he just pushed it gently into her mouth, fear and fatigue making her teeth give way.

I wanted to shout out, wanted to rush over. I looked at Katie and saw a solo tear tumble down her cheek and rest on the muzzle of the gun. I was paralysed. He was in control.

"Make your choice, Kinsella. Tick-tock, tick-tock."

I took a deep breath to calm my nerves and make my voice strong.

"It's your choice, not mine," I said, with unnatural calm. "If you want to kill her, kill her. If you want to kill me, then kill me. Do what the fuck you want. But as soon as you do, it's over. Premeditated murder. You'll either die here or in prison, and I don't think you want to do that."

I sat back against the wall, eyes shut, waiting for either a response or a shot.

For some long minutes I heard nothing, then I heard movement, and as I looked up, I saw Tom Bradbury come back over. He knelt down opposite me and pointed the gun back in my direction.

"You are going to die today, Kinsella, I've already decided that."

"If I believe you, why don't I just rush you now, end it one way or the other?"

He tilted his head in query. "Because you don't want it to end. You want to be the rescuer, reap the rewards, be the hero. You rush me, you die, and you are still hoping to find a way out of your fuck up."

"So why aren't I scared?"

He smiled. "Death Row is one of the calmest places in jail."

I sat back against the wall and tipped my head back towards the ceiling.

"You could get help, you know. Your wife's death might buy you a defence, or at least a plea bargain. No sane person goes around killing people because of the reason behind your wife jumping."

Bradbury leant forward and tapped me on my injured knee with the gun, two taps. He whispered. "You have such insight. You are so very, very clever."

And then he leant back and laughed. It was a loud laugh, brimful of contempt, and I felt my nerves spring shut when I saw tears appear in his eyes.

\*　　　　　　\*　　　　　　\*　　　　　　\*

John was tense. It was now or never. His radio fizzed in his hand. He hesitated for a moment, and then lifted the radio to his mouth.

He dropped his hand and sat down on the bonnet of his car.

He had a position by the gate. He was sheltered from shots by a large gatepost and the black bars of the main gate. Its high arch and tight lats provided vision and afforded a slight protection.

This was the part of the operation that he was dreading most. He could handle the thought of Joe and Katie getting killed. There would be an inquiry, but John knew that the finger of blame would point towards Bradbury. But now he was putting other people at risk, other professionals whose risk-taking didn't normally extend to being shot at.

He'd engaged the help of the fire brigade. John had thought hard about what the Bomb Squad had told him. Get it wet, get it very wet, but don't go in there with sparks flying.

John looked ahead, at the assembled men.

There were four units of police officers, eight men in each unit. In each unit, four were holding riot shields to the floor, another four holding theirs overlapping the others but higher, so that each unit consisted of a four-by-two bulletproof shield, protecting the men behind them. Each eight-man riot shield allowed a small gap in the middle. Behind that gap stood a line of three firemen, one behind the other, the front one holding the high-pressure water hose, the two behind helping, with the nozzle of the hose protruding through the gap, the shields clamped like vices around it to limit any way through for bullets.

Four man-made moving bulletproof shelters, each with the nozzle of a high-pressure fire hose protruding from the middle. One set at each side of the house.

Behind each unit of shields, just behind the firemen, were three STOP team officers. They were carrying automatic rifles across their chests, the settings set to rapid fire.

"Move forward, as instructed. Go slowly and carefully. Stay low."

John gave the command and watched nervously as the woods filled to the sound of shields banging together and heavy feet shuffling through long grass.

The lines advanced slowly, the officers with the shields moving carefully, making sure they stayed together as a solid wall.

One unit shuffled towards the window of the main room in the house, the room from which a shot had been fired. Another unit was heading towards the house from the side, but sneaking along the front of the house towards the front door. The unit at the other side of the house was aiming for the side window of the main room, while the unit at the back of the house had the kitchen as its target.

John lifted binoculars to his eyes and looked at the house. There were no signs of movement. A curtain flapped around the swinging front door, but everywhere else was as peaceful as Sunday morning. John didn't like it. He could feel nerves making his stomach crawl, and his shirt stuck to his back. He put the binoculars down and looked at the control van. All eyes were trained on the house.

The units crept forward at a pace almost too slow to see. Each unit was waiting for the signal to pull back if there was sign of adverse movement from inside the house. The STOP officers had instructions not to put the fire officers' lives at risk under any circumstances.

After a lifetime of shuffling, each line came to within ten feet of its intended target. There was nothing from the house. The woods were quiet, except for the buzzing of radios, clipped to jumpsuits and waiting for the signal from Marconi, the STOP commander.

Bradbury's laugh died when Danny shouted, "they're coming!"

Tom Bradbury looked out of the window, a quick dart above the sill. I saw a flash of panic and his gun wavered. I tried to jump up from the floor and go at him, but my knee gave way, and I fell to the floor, screeching with pain.

He punched me in the jaw, and as I lay stunned for a moment, he jammed the butt of the shotgun into the other side of my face. I heard it crunch as it connected and my face screamed in pain. It felt like fire as I felt the cheekbone split and one half of it come loose. My face had collapsed.

I almost passed out, but as everything went distant, I heard Katie straining on her bindings. I fought the image to vomit, but before my vision cleared he had me pinned to the floor, the gun pressed against my shattered cheekbone, making my nerves shear and shriek.

I took deep breaths, tried to clear my head, tried to see through the panic and the nausea. I could feel my cheekbone swimming around under my skin, every breath making it click and grate, and I felt a jab as sharp as a sword run through me.

"Getting brave, Kinsella?" he snarled. "We die together."

At that moment I knew he was probably right.

I summonsed up all my anger, all my venom, tried to get past the pain, and spat at him. It landed on his face, bloody and angry, and he swiped me across the face with his free fist. I felt my face cave in, and for a moment I sensed a door closing. I shrieked, trying to shut out the pain. Consciousness was a battle I was determined to win.

I tried to stand but fell down again, my head spinning out of control.

"All of this because your wife killed herself," I shrieked at him, blood spewing forth, every word agony. "Too fucking weak to deal with it yourself, so you make everyone else deal with it for you. Years of misery, looking for revenge for someone else's hang-ups. You make me sick."

I collapsed back onto the floor, panting, my outburst draining me. His gun followed me, its metallic presence constant.

He laughed. It was an evil, bitter laugh, one that chilled as if it carried all of his sickness with it. It was low and rumbling, hollow and deep, dark and terrifying.

"She wasn't unstable," he said, snarling through his laughter, mocking. "I made her unstable. You don't have all the answers, Kinsella."

"But what about all those people you killed, the Salem connection?"

His laugh started again.

"I made that link because it was fun." He was snarling now. "It was a theme, a hobby. Picking victims is easy. You go for the frail, the old, the young, the adventurous. But what about choices based on chance, based on a freak coincidence? That's the real joy. There's no mutual vulnerability, no usual route to the end. Pick people based on a common theme rather than a common trait and you get a real mixed bag. And if you have a collection of different

304

strengths and weaknesses, you have a sterner test. Who is the strongest of them all?"

I felt the gun pull away from my face, as if his attention was becoming distracted. I had to keep him distracted.

I spat blood onto the floor, panting, struggling for breath. "So this witchcraft thing was just some link you pulled from a hat, like you might have picked a common birth date, or hair colour?"

He nodded with satisfaction, then gave a dismissive wave. "I've done the natural victim thing. It's not the same. What fun can there be in controlling someone who is already under control?" He shook his head. "None, that's how much. Children co-operate too early because they are scared, old ladies co-operate early because wisdom tell them it's best to," and then he leant forward as if sharing a confidence, "and let's be honest with each other, fucking babies and old ladies is no way to spend an afternoon."

He laughed too loudly.

I was shocked, taking away the pain for a moment. He had no fixation, no curse. It was all a game, the Salem witches just a test for the police, to see if they could spot him.

"So why witchcraft?"

He shrugged. "Why not? It had to be something."

"But your wife, she killed herself. That can't be just coincidence. You can't claim that one."

He looked smug. "No, I killed her, as sure as I'm going to kill you." He sneaked a quick look out of the window. "Tell a person enough times that they're evil, that they are the devil reincarnated, tell them enough, and they'll believe it. Get them drunk and tell the fruitcake how to shock the town and free the evil, man, they'll do the job properly." He got in my face. "It took some time, but she cracked. They always do."

I became aware of movement behind Bradbury, like an unsettled shuffling. I glanced up and saw the horror in Danny's eyes as he listened to his father talk about his mother. He had the same dark look as his father, but it wasn't aimed at me. I remembered Robert saying that Bradbury might be showing off, the letters a display of intelligence. If that was true, then Tom Bradbury would keep talking, and Danny would become more unsettled.

"So you moulded your wife into a suicide?" I asked, trying to keep the dialogue going, my damaged hand trying to hold my busted cheek, keeping my good hand free.

"Ah, why not? It was less messy than killing her."

Danny's body had tensed up into a mass of fury.

"So all of this is built on that?" I was incredulous. "You liked the theme, so you decided only to kill people with a link to the Salem witches?"

He smirked. "No, no. There's been a few that were unconnected, but everyone needs a drink during a drought."

"Was your wife the best?"

He tilted his head as if thinking hard, going through fond memories.

Danny raised his gun.

Tom Bradbury started to nod in satisfaction. "It was the toughest."

Danny's gun was pointed in our direction, and I saw his bared teeth as he began to squeeze on the trigger.

John looked over at Marconi, who looked pensive for a moment. John then glanced at the fire chief, who looked worried but proud. Marconi looked at John, then back at the shack. He turned to John and smiled. He unclipped his radio, spent a second or two surveying the scene, and then shouted into his radio, "GO! GO! GO!"

Fire officers manning the hydrants twisted the yellow wheels like maniacs. Water coursed down the four hoses, making them stretch and writhe and buck like sidewinders. As the fire-fighters braced themselves behind the shields, the STOP officers burst out and sprinted towards their targets, one set for the door, three sets had a window each.

The door went in with two swings of a hammer; the windows only took one each. The officers dived to one side just as the water rocketed out of the hoses and into the house.

\*   \*   \*   \*

The window smashed behind me.

I whirled around in panic. I saw a flash of light reflect off police shields, and then I saw movement in the grass behind them. I threw myself against the wall, driven by instinct.

Tom Bradbury was jerked back from his memories. He looked up at the window, then at me, a look of surprise.

I looked past him at his son. Bradbury looked round at Danny, his gun still pointing at me. He whirled back round at me, raised his gun at me and began to scream. He began to pull at the trigger.

And then the water came through.

A torrent shot across the room, catching Tom Bradbury in the chest like a liquid battering ram. The gun flew out of his hand. Bradbury went to the floor hard, the gun skittering away from him. He tried to get at the gun, but slipped in the water gathering on the slippery wooden floor.

Danny looked around quickly, his eyes scared. Katie started to pull at her ropes, her eyes screaming for help.

A second burst of water came through the side window, glass scattering across the floor.

Danny turned to face it. His face became a mask of fear, the reality of the end coming to him.

Water was crashing off two walls, moving across, taking down pictures, clocks, books. Wallpaper on the walls began to look sodden, starting to wrinkle up and peel. The tins of fuel began to tumble over, the contents lying in a sheen on top of the water before soaking through the gaps in the floor and away.

Danny turned back towards me, gun raised, and then I braced myself for the shot. Tom Bradbury got to his knees, pointed at me, and screamed at his son, barely heard above the noise of water crashing around the house, "kill him!"

I shut my eyes and waited for the end.

But then the water must have moved across. Danny had been near its path as the jet roared across the room, soaking everything in its way. The roar had a steady rhythm, a deafening drumming on the opposite wall, but for a moment I heard the sound change. It went for a second to a high-pitched smack, and as I flung my eyes open I saw Danny hit in the face by a spear of water coming in so fast it snapped his head back onto his shoulders and sent him tumbling to the floor.

307

It could have been the water, but I thought I saw tears in his eyes as he fell.

As he went to the floor, he shifted the gun and let off two shots, shrieking. Above the sound of the water, I heard a grunt.

I looked at Katie, panicking. She was being buffeted by the water. Strapped to the plinth, she was being thrashed against it, trying to keep her head out of it, but the power of the spray was too much for her.

I tried to get up and get to her. I was knocked back by the water, taking a hit in the back like a punch from a heavyweight. I fell into Tom Bradbury and heard a moan. It was the sound of breath being expelled from hell. I looked down and I looked into hollow eyes. I saw him gasp, his hand clasped to his chest. I glanced down and I saw his shirt billowing red. He'd been shot. Blood was soaking into his trousers, running down his arms, pushed around by the water on his body, diluted, keeping the blood flowing.

He looked at me, his eyes becoming distant. He'd been hit. Danny had shot him. Was it an act of revenge for his mother, or a stray shot meant for me? I didn't care either way.

I tried to get a good look at his chest, but didn't lose sight of his eyes for fear it was a trick. I reached down with my good hand onto his chest. His shirt felt like tarpaulin, thick and oily with blood. I pressed hard onto his abdomen and I felt him buck beneath my hand, his teeth gritting and rolling, his voice an almost silent roar.

I looked down. I could see two holes in his shirt where the blood was thickest. Two shots, two hits. I knew the answer now. He had taught his son well.

I looked back into his eyes, my hand still over the wound. I ignored the sound of glass smashing as the water jets knocked things over, took out more window panes. My mind was only on Tom Bradbury.

I glanced at Katie, still strapped to the plinth, and let my anger run wild. I thought of Sarah, the girl I'd never met. I thought of her parents, waiting for news back in Morsby, nothing left but old photographs and a head full of memories. I knew then how much I hated the person in front of me, how much I wanted him to suffer.

I gritted my teeth, summonsed up all my strength, and went looking for the wounds.

I stared into his eyes as I felt along, my hands wet and sticky, his breaths coming quicker, his eyes widening as I pressed and prodded.

I found both wounds, two neat little holes four inches apart.

I looked at him hard in the eyes. I thought I saw a pleading, a beg for mercy.

I plunged my thumb hard and deep into one of the wounds, jerking my hand upwards as I did it, my teeth bared in anger. I jerked my thumb in there, backwards and forward, his eyes wide in pain, his mouth open and screaming. I could feel him tight around me, could feel every second of pain with every push of my thumb. His put his hands around my neck, tearing at my hair.

I was snarling by now. I kept my thumb inside him but went searching for the other wound with my index finger. I found it and plunged my finger in deep. He dug his nails hard into my back, drawing blood, increasing my anger. I forced my middle finger in there, and I felt him push himself hard against me, his eyes rolling in their sockets.

I was gripping him like a bowling ball. I could feel him around me, the wetness, the movement of pain as he screamed and bucked against my hand, my fingers and thumb hard and straight inside him. I could feel tissues, veins, muscles between my fingers. I looked into his eyes and I could see fires burning. I hoped they were the fires of hell burning, ready for him. I felt his body between my fingers, his agony in my grasp.

Then I clenched my fist hard.

He opened his mouth to scream some more but only blood came out, a stream covering his chin, and he started to shake.

I helped him. I shook him by the tissues and muscles I gripped in my fist and I screamed for him. But my scream wasn't a cry for help or a scream of pain. It was a shout of victory, my own rebel yell. I was going to win, at any cost.

I yanked my hand out, making the two wounds one, still holding parts of him in my hand.

He slumped back, staring at me in disbelief. He fell back into the water, the splash as he landed in the growing pool of red water lost in the roar.

He tried to lift his head and I saw the end in his eyes. I knew at that moment he was dying. And I knew that he knew it. I could see it in his pleading, his silent cry for help.

His eyes looked away from me, and as I followed his eyes, I saw his gun.

I knew what he wanted. He wanted out.

The water was still crashing into the room. The floor was six inches deep now; the flow in was too fast for the flow out. The old wooden floor had become treacherous.

I scuttled over to the gun, splashing through the water, my clothes now heavy and wet, blood from Bradbury mixing with my own. I grasped it and wondered what to do. I looked back at Bradbury, who was breathing death breaths, his chest wracking itself for air, his mouth open, his pallor white and laboured.

The water kept me awake. I couldn't close my jaw and every breath in and out was like the draw of a sword. The pain twisted my thoughts, made me angry. I saw Katie being knocked by the water, and I saw her knees sagging, as if she was beginning to lose consciousness.

I turned the gun on Bradbury. I was sat on the floor, the water coming in above my head. Pictures were gone from the walls and I could hear glass smashing in the kitchen.

Then the water stopped.

The house became deathly still, silent apart from the dripping of water from the ceiling and shelves.

I realised I was cold.

Tom Bradbury looked at me pleading. I shook my head and smiled. It wasn't going to happen.

I threw the gun into the water and plunged my hands deep to soak away his blood.

Then I heard the door crash in.

I lay on my back in the water. The water cleaned the blood off my hands and cooled the pain in my cheek. I could hear the shouts of the police officers as they ran through the house. Danny Bradbury was still alive, was just coming round, and he was in handcuffs, not moving.

I lifted my head up. The pain almost sent me back down, but I had to see.

Tom Bradbury was breathing short breaths, his chest going hard like a piston, trying to draw air in. His cheeks had sunk hollow and his eyes rolled in their sockets. I could see his blood painting the floor red.

There were two police officers stood over him, each with their gun drawn. But it was me he was looking at. Someone was reading his rights. He smiled, thin and weak. He knew he wouldn't need them.

I looked over at Katie. She had been cut free from the support and was kneeling on the floor, resting her head against someone's shoulder. I could hear running footsteps, shouts and yells, and someone appeared with a blanket. I thought I saw a paramedic.

I looked back at Tom Bradbury. He groaned and his chest rose one last time, his back arched, his eyes wide and scared, one last effort for air.

I grinned at him, pain shooting through me. "Rot in hell," I hissed, before collapsing back down.

I heard footsteps around me and I looked up. It was John Cornwell.

"You stupid bastard."

I managed a smile. "Sue me."

And then it all went dark.

# Twenty Five

I stood in the cage, swinging the bat, eyeing the machine that was about to send a ball towards me. I didn't see it. I just heard it, like a rush of wind and then a thump as it hit the cushion at the back of the cage.

"Whoa, I'm out of here," I cried, laughing, stepping out of the cage.

Katie laughed, and her father clapped me hard on the shoulder, tears of laughter in his eyes.

"Maybe the fastball cage was a mistake," he said, wiping his eyes. "Get in the forty miles per hour cage, you might see that one."

I was in Wichita.

Kansas wasn't how I imagined. The people were friendly, they liked my accent, and the towns were a mix of frontier and twenty-first century.

I'd been in Kansas three weeks. It was spring again. Cows grazed on parched-looking fields and the winds blew dust across unsheltered countryside. Tom Bradbury was a distant and bad memory.

It had ended in Bradbury's house.

Danny's trial was still some time off, delay after delay as psychiatrists argued about the effect of his father's control on Danny's developing mind.

It was all bullshit. His mother had been neurotic and impressionable, his father a controlling madman. Danny was a victim of genetics and socialisation. His mother's genes made him impressionable, but the way he was able to ingratiate himself with his future victims, to help his father lure his victims to their ultimate death, was the product of his father's genetics, a hidden code that removed pity, remorse, and guilt from his mental process.

Unfortunately for Tom Bradbury, the one thing that Danny did have in abundance was respect and love for his dead mother. Until that day in their house, when everything for them came to a stop, Danny had been fuelled by the belief that he was somehow filling the gap left by his mother's suicide. What he had never considered was that the gap was made by his own father, who had cajoled and abused the young Mary Bradbury into a spectacular suicide. That had been too much for Danny.

What no-one knew was what had happened to Tom Bradbury to make him come out into the open. There hadn't been coded letters sent in any of the other murders, no clue as to some hidden motivation behind seemingly unconnected deaths. Theories abounded. The common conclusion was a desire to be caught, some deep-seated remorse that he was unable to express. He knew that no-one would understand his motivations in a way that would set him free, life imprisonment was the best he could hope for, so he wanted to go down in a blaze, make it somebody else's fault.

Another theory was that it was a display of arrogance, a test of intelligence so he could lead the police on a dance they would never win.

I didn't accept those theories.

I put it down to boredom. Bradbury just wanted to raise the stakes, put himself at greater risk, just to change the routine.

We would never know, unless Danny spoke about it, and Danny's version of the truth was still some time from being heard.

John Cornwell came out of it okay. When the real story came out, or at least the spin that Boston Police put on it, he'd been working on a hunch highlighted by the disappearance of Sarah Goode.

The young man in jail for one of Tom Bradbury's earlier crimes took it well, largely through John's humility. He'd lost six years of his life, but he respected John Cornwell for having the guts to admit his own mistake.

It had been John Cornwell who had broken the news to him. He had attended the jail, and when they both met, all John got was a spit in the eye. Once John told him the reason for his visit, however, and the news that he would be freed later that day, on bail pending the overturning of his conviction, he hugged John and sobbed, a mixture of relief and anger, joy and bewilderment.

The hapless young man had trouble adjusting to the instant celebrity. The press all wanted to speak to him, and he found the persistent requests an interruption in the rebuilding of his life. But he is recovering. A literary agent approached him and advised him of the money he could earn by telling his story. The figures were big, and would be a healthy addition to the undisclosed sum paid in settlement by Boston Police for the years he had spent in jail. Money couldn't make up for the lost years, but they would make the remaining ones good ones.

I'd had similar approaches, but my media profile was tainted by the surgery I had screwing my face back together. I couldn't be photographed punching the air outside the Suffolk County Courthouse in triumph. I was in hospital, being fed through tubes and trying to ignore the pain that was always there. By the time I left, the media attention had been overtaken by something else, and anything I had to say would be lost in the jungle of hastily-written paperbacks trying to tell the story, written by people who weren't there when it happened, and who wouldn't be there when it was old news.

But it was Katie I had wanted to see. I didn't see her for nearly a year, and I thought I would never see her again.

Thankfully, she hadn't been harmed physically. The trauma would longer to heal, but she was a strong woman and I thought she would get over it.

I returned to Morsby when I had healed enough to travel, stopping for one last game at Fenway.

I went with John Cornwell, and it was a typical man thing. Neither of us talked about what had happened. We just shared a few beers and talked about the game. At one point he asked me what I was going to do, I think worried that I was going to hang around and spoil the spin put on things by the police, but I just said I was going home.

We went our separate ways after the game. We said our goodbyes by a hot dog stand, the smell of fried meat and onions filling the air. I thought he was going to hug me, a final sharing of our mutual experience, but I patted him on the shoulders and said, 'see you around.' He smiled, as if he knew that was to be the goodbye, and we went our own ways.

The last I saw of John Cornwell, he was heading for the Kenmore Square T-stop, a dark bobbing head disappearing into the crowd. I watched him go, and then I went for a beer. I didn't want to think about Tom Bradbury. I just wanted to have a beer and listen to a crowd talk about ordinary things, like the game, the Yankees, the traffic.

I returned to Morsby the following day.

I'd been in Morsby a couple of weeks, trying to get my life back in shape, when I thought about Sarah's parents. I thought that Sarah was the one person who had been forgotten in all of this.

When the police searched Bradury's house, they found a locked cupboard. When they burst it open, they found videos. No body parts, no press cuttings, no clothing. Just videos.

But when they watched them, they realised they had stumbled into hell. Home videos of victims. Tom Bradbury had kept the footage of each one. It showed them being tortured, being raped, and they showed them being killed. They had video'd Sarah burning, even their drive away was filmed from the safety of the vehicle, Sarah's burning figure receding into the distance as they headed back to the I-95.

The victims were all eventually identified, and as they were all American, apart from Sarah, the media turned their attention to the relatives who were left, New Englanders sobbing into the camera as they described how they had lost hope long ago for their forgotten loved ones.

In the middle of all this, Sarah was somehow left behind, so when I had been back in Morsby a couple of weeks, I paid her parents a visit.

The visit didn't last long. We didn't have much to say to each other. They were polite. They didn't blame me for not finding Sarah in time, and were grateful for finding who had killed her, but I was a reminder of bad times and they didn't want me around.

They told me they were going to put a memorial bench on the cliffs at the top of the town, so somehow her memory would rest in a place of beauty. I said that sounded nice and bade my farewells.

Then summer turned to autumn, then to winter, and I struggled to find work. My phone would ring but I wouldn't answer it, not wanting to do what I had been doing before. I watched some TV, drank some beer, and just tried to get through the best I could.

Katie's parents had sent her to counselling, and she had proved as strong as they had hoped. They treated her to a European holiday, and the family spent some time exploring the European capitals, her father thinking that after so much horror, Katie should spend her time surrounded by beauty. They toured the art galleries of Paris and Milan, the ruins of Rome, the preserved beauty of Prague.

Eventually they landed in London, and after a couple of days sightseeing, Katie called me. I was glad I answered the phone that day.

We talked for an hour, and she suggested that she come up to see me. I agreed nervously. We spent three days together, not all of it in bed, and before she went, I asked if I could come to Wichita.

We were on a plane within two days. I sold my business to an ex-policeman, put all I had into storage, and headed for Kansas.

I stepped into the slower batting cage.

We were at a small amusement park on the edge of town. The heat made me yearn for the shade and my t-shirt was pinned to my body by sweat.

"How do I stand?" I shouted.

"Just get your weight on your back foot, however is most comfortable, and watch the ball. When it comes at you, hit it."

I shrugged. It sounded simple enough.

The first ball came at me, so I swung and ended up spinning round to face the side of the cage, the ball thudding into the cushion at the back of the cage.

I heard her father laugh.

Three more balls went similar ways, and I was beginning to think about walking out of the cage and leaving the rest of the balls to fly into free space, when Katie skipped into cage and whispered something into my ear.

I smiled, but I tried to shield it from her father's gaze. I didn't think he would want to know what Katie had promised to do to me later if I could hit a ball.

I hit each of the next five, the last one clearing the pitching machines and only kept out of the car park by the high netting.

I turned around in triumph. Katie had a look of innocence, while her father eyed me with amused suspicion. When he walked away to get some drinks, Katie blew me a kiss.

I smiled. I was going to like Kansas.

# Acknowledgements

I would like to express my heartfelt thanks to all those people who considered the original manuscript and offered advice and encouragement. It was always invaluable.

In particular I would like to thank Steve Cummings, Mercedah Jabbari, Sophie Lorimer, and Teresa Feely, along with Duncan McAllister for keeping the beer flowing in Massachusetts. I am, of course, eternally grateful for the patience shown by Alison.

Available in 2005


# Creek Crossing

## Neil White


Visit the TSJ website for more details
www.crimewriting.co.uk